AMERICAN CHROME

Novels by EDWIN GILBERT

AMERICAN
CHROME

A NOVEL BY *Edwin Gilbert*

G. P. PUTNAM'S SONS
New York

FOR VIRGINIA AND HOLLY

"No," said Amory, shaking his head. "Money isn't the only stimulus that brings out the best that's in a man, even in America . . . the best men would all flock for the one other reward which attracts humanity—honor."

The big man made a sound that was very like boo.

—F. SCOTT FITZGERALD
This Side of Paradise

"We in America make love in our cars, and listen to ball games, and plot our wooing of the dollar: small wonder the landscape is sacrificed to these dreaming vehicles of our ideal and onrushing manhood."

—JOHN UPDIKE
Pigeon Feathers and Other Stories

Author's Note:

This is a work of fiction. Though some actual places, institutions and persons are mentioned by name, all the characters and incidents of the narrative itself are purely imaginary; and any resemblance to any person, living or dead, is unintended and coincidental.

Warning must also be given to the aficionado of the automotive world. If he should discover some technical impropriety or impure nomenclature, it is hoped this will be heroically condoned in the name of creative fiction.

—E.G.

AMERICAN CHROME

1: Scott Quinnley

He had been away for a long time and he was coming back to where he had started. Though he didn't think of it like that. Not anymore.

The jet liner, dicing it up, streaked westward, and he stared out the spherical window, waiting for the first meaningful view. He was glad, for once, not to be driving: to fly made the transition from one kind of life to another swift and unalterable. New York an hour behind him, and his farewell image of it—giant prismatic tombstones in an over-crowded cemetery—was, he had to admit, darkly induced. He'd wanted to see it that way: like a man who must trade or sell a fine vintage car which he has loved and which he is reluctant to part from, and so chooses to spare himself at the very last by regarding not the car's uniqueness or beauty or the performance of its engine, but rather its most woeful flaw.

An hour behind him. Overlapping now were other feelings. In a few minutes the plane would land and in a little while he would be back among the streets of his boyhood. Among the population below, whom did he know? Almost no one now. Some people would know him because he was Red Quinnley's son, and many people knew Red Quinnley. But a stranger he would be, a stranger nonetheless.

So that the prospect of seeing Philip Rothe in a few minutes seemed all the brighter. Phil was an old friend—they had been kids on Calvit Street—although he was not really Scott's closest friend. They'd been at Columbia together but Phil had quit midway to enlist in the Marines. Scott saw him seldom but when he did it was always Old Home Week; except the last time, two years ago, when Scott's wife had died and Phil had come east for the funeral.

Fasten Safety Belts.

A sudden revving-up in his chest. For in the clear raw morning light, an exceptional day for late February, Scott saw much of the area, even began once more to feel some of its special essence—the sprawl of the Midwest city—The Motor City, Cartown, Chromeville. Near the river he saw the stone-shafted, steel-veined heart of Downtown and, along the river side, the architectural triumph of the Civic Center. And he could see how the city had grown, spread, spoked out (from the once primitive wooded shores where the French had landed, where in 1707 Antoine de la Mothe Cadillac established Fort Detroit) and how the expressways and freeways like great tentacles wound through it, around it, reaching out to touch all the secondary municipalities.

He saw the social bastions of automobile wealth—Kent Hills to the south, Grosse Pointe to the north, Bloomfield Hills to the west— emerald clusters in the drab urban mosaic.

And the vast tracts of Ford, General Motors, Chrysler. And that splendor of water shimmering in Warren was the front yard of the G. M. Tech Center, and that mighty kidney grooved in the earth at the edge of Greenfield Village was the Ford Proving Grounds. And there to the northwest were the lesser of the automotive colossi, the Bellgard Motor Company, the Jefferson Motor Corporation and Vanguard. And feeding all these bodies and in turn being fed by them were the myriad subcontractors of allied industries, and the plants, machine shops and offices of the auto parts suppliers.

(But not harsh industry alone, they will tell you, not cars alone; they wish to soften the image that existed when Scott was a child. Ours is a changing city, we're running on the culture circuit now; look what Saarinen has wrought, and Yamasaki, see our museums, our galleries, hear our music, witness our colleges.)

Now near Kent Hills he could make out Greenwood Park, where his father lived, and where Philip Rothe and his wife lived, a handsome community where, it was said, young management executives lived in a tense limbo of ambition until they might move upward and gain admittance to Kent Hills.

Kent Hills, the coveted paradise, not of the sovereign families but of the aristocracy of the production line—here where presidents and

[16

vice-presidents of motor companies holed in. Kent Hills was also the address of Codman Smith, president of the Bellgard Motor Company. Scott had met him once, and he had known Ann Smith, but . . .

Ladies and Gentlemen . . .

The plane changed course. Gazing down, Scott sought the intersection of West Main Boulevard and Timber Trail Road where Quinnley Corners stood: an enormous property housing the glittering showroom and offices, the long Service Wing and the Used-Car lot—this remarkable enterprise which Red Quinnley had developed from a secondhand auto shed to a mighty institution of flimflam and razzledazzle which could once boast of selling more Bellgard cars than any other dealer in that zone of the country—a record of the past which, Scott knew, his father was battling to revive.

He stiffened a little at the prospect of the encounter. It was hard to think of Red Quinnley having been struck down by anything as ordinary as a heart attack, Red Quinnley forced to retire even temporarily. Hard to imagine, even though it had happened; almost as unexpected or unreal as Scott's having to come here now, breaking off his life and work in the East, leaving Suzy for his mother to look after, turning over his car magazine to his associates. Even so he was two months too late, for at the time his father had been stricken, Scott had been flat in the pit himself, down with flu in Southern California. (He'd been invited out there to participate in a national seminar on "The Automobile and Air Pollution.")

Scott checked his watch: nine twenty-five. In an hour or so he would be at Quinnley Corners, seeing him again, *facing* him again. And once more he tried to summon all his resolve, even his guilt, so that when he saw his father he would be able to communicate something which, beneath his long hostility, he had once felt as a boy, and which, he told himself now, must still exist.

Abruptly now the sharp loss in altitude, and soon the airliner made its approach for landing: and with it, as the ground rose to meet his closer vision, he sensed a kind of vibration rising from the city itself, like a brash wand of welcome or warning.

In the morning shine of the air terminal, he filed through the gate, already seeking out Philip Rothe. He would be easy to see; Phil, bulky-big, bespectacled, rose-cheeked. But almost at once he knew in dismay that Phil was not there. Finally he halted, blocking the path of the people behind him. He frowned, puzzled, disappointed, rubbing

17]

his chin, as if seeking to gain time on the alien ground of his home-town.

He glimpsed a face then and would have recognized it, had he not still been searching for Phil. When he turned back, the face reappeared. He saw who it was, and somehow he was not surprised to see her. Ann Smith had always had a way of turning up when you least expected her.

"Ann—What're you doing here?" He said it as if there had been four days instead of more than four years between them. "Meeting someone?"

"Yes."

"Oh," he said.

"You."

"Oh," he said again.

She waited, as if needing an additional instant to study him. She said: "Phil Rothe called me at eight-fifteen this morning, of all the ignoble hours, and asked me if I wouldn't pick you up. He just couldn't make it, Scott. A last-minute order from Above to show up for a wind-tunnel test."

Scott nodded, a movement to conceal his disappointment. He shifted his briefcase to his other hand.

"You look . . ." Ann stopped, uncertain, still appraising. Then, almost at once, he saw growing in the gray-blue eyes a familiar and mischievous sparkle. She lifted the jacket of his dark suit. "Still wearing it," she said.

Scott glanced down.

"That good old red belt." Her slender face was suffused by a warmth of affection or nostalgia. "It's funny, I mean how you think of people, remember them. You think of a blink, a scar or a haircut, something like that. But you, I always think of you with that wild red firehouse belt, the way it hides under that good correct suit"—she laughed—"like a sin or something you're a little ashamed of."

"Ashamed, I'm not, Junior."

"It couldn't still be the same one." She wanted to prolong the reminiscence.

No, he said, he'd bought two others in Italy. Then: "Junior, you look nothing less than great, glorious. You've become a very chic cat, haven't you? I didn't recognize you at first."

"Oh"—she stepped back, adding in a kind of self-derogatory tone —"same old Smith body, except with a phony new grille."

[18

But despite her glibness, the change in her seemed profound. When he thought of how she'd looked during her year at the Sorbonne, at least during the months he'd known her, her appearance today was all the more marked. Almost five years ago she'd looked or tried to look like any poor student, except poorer; she'd affected the old faded blue jeans, the loose sweater, no makeup—all to imply some sort of anonymity, though she never quite succeeded in the role of Average Annie, never quite brought it off. She was a little too tall, her posture a little too graceful, too erect to go unnoticed; and her faintly Roman nose gave to her face an air of haughtiness. The lively eyes, the finely curved mouth, the long very light hair, had seemed to defeat what she'd been after.

So that now, as Scott looked at her, the contrast to the past was just short of being dramatic: the blue jeans replaced by a wool suit obviously of Paris origin; the pale amber hair no longer stringy, but neatly massed and fringed by soft slanting bangs. Gone were the dirty tennis sneakers, replaced by the lizard shoes. Now she carried a lizard handbag, probably from Hermés, which was honest enough testimony to her rank or wealth. "I don't know," Scott said, "I think I miss the sneakers."

"To hell with you," she said. "I got up at this ignoble hour, let's make the most of it. I promised Phil I'd give you the Treatment. In my rush I forgot the champagne, but I'll make it up to you, anything for my old buddy. Good God, this is the last place in the world I ever expected to see you—and if I know you, you won't be around long. Come on, Scott—"

But he had to telephone his father first. Mrs. Coombs, the housekeeper, was excited to hear his voice, but his father wasn't in, she said. Cardiography at the hospital. And he had left word for Scott to go straight to the office.

"How is he, Mrs. Coombs?"

"He'd be a lot better if he followed the doctor's orders. He's—well, he's a very sick man. But I know your being here now is going to do more for him than all the medicines in the world. He's supposed to take a golf lesson today—"

"Golf?"

"Oh yes, that's part of the cure." And Mrs. Coombs chatted on. "Your father has had to move downstairs now. I don't mind telling you, I know you'll understand, but your father is not easy to work for or look after, and I don't mind telling you that just before it happened,

19]

I told him I couldn't stay on any longer, not after almost ten years, I said, and I said there was an opening in the Executive Dining Room out at G.M., and I didn't see why I should have it so hard when out at G.M., they—oh, before I forget, Mr. Philip Rothe called early this morning about not being able to meet you—"

It was a soliloquy of marathon proportions. Finally Scott hung up and made his way to the front of the terminal, looking for Ann. No sight of her. He started along the pavement, passing the throng of taxi-bound passengers. What he saw first were his two large suitcases, except that they were in the hands of a uniformed chauffeur who was placing them in the luggage compartment of a car. It was not a taxi, nor could it have been Ann's car—not this special wire-wheeled Bellgard limousine whose ebony grandeur, whose total length and wheelbase, were proudly excessive, a remarkable product blending the honest with the meretricious, a vast and startling creature combining a false aerodynamic dash with solid, high-executive respectability.

And there was Ann trying to look impassive, but unable to keep the sly trace of a grin from her face: "Well," she said, "I know it's too big, but at least it's pretentious."

"Is this the best you can offer?"

"Listen," she said as they settled in the overcommodious seats—the interior of the car was the color of a mourning dove, there was a telephone and a dictaphone on the left, and fitted in a long panel was a vanity case and liquor cabinet: "Listen, I had to move heaven and home to convince dear old Dad to let me have this portable workbench. I thought it might give you a blast. Anyway"—her voice came a little defiantly—"anyway, I'm awful damn sick and tired of having to keep down with the Jones's. *Merde alors,* what a bore." She lit a cigarette, and when she glanced back at him, she said: "What's the matter, Scott? Aren't you impressed? Believe me, I wouldn't have done this for anyone else except my old buddy." A pause. "I think you're still miffed that Phil Rothe didn't get here."

Scott looked at her. He knew he hadn't quite come up to her expectations, hadn't quite been able to make the occasion, the gesture, as funny or dramatic as she'd hoped.

She said: "Well, where to now? It's early, but we ought to celebrate your arrival with something absolutely grand, though all I can offer is a Bloody Mary at Ye Olde Kent Hills Country Club—"

"That would be fine, great. I'd love it. I could use a drink. At least two. But I can't. I have to get to the office."

[20

She told the chauffeur to go to Quinnley Corners.

And, curiously, actually hearing the local name by which the intersection of West Main Boulevard and Timber Trail Road was known gave Scott an unexpected tremor of apprehension.

"Tell me all, Scott. I mean . . ." Ann floundered, as if she was suddenly conscious that her attempt to be gay, to bring an air of cheerfulness, might have been overhasty or misplaced. "I mean . . ."

"There's nothing very much, Junior," he said. "Except that I'm going to work."

"Yes, Phil told me about it," she said. "He told me you're going to keep your child in New York."

"She's with my mother temporarily."

"Is that good?"

"It could be better."

An unsatisfactory silence. Then Ann said: "But you really don't mind too much, being back here? I remember how you used to feel about it. You never even came here for your magazine."

"I didn't have to. They came to us more or less." True enough. But he said: "I suppose it was easy for me to sound off from New York. Being here is a different matter."

"Very. You're really staying?"

"I'll have to. At least for quite a long time. But it's time I got into it," he said.

"The good old ratty race, you mean?" She took Scott's hand, held it in a kind of protective way. "Oh balls," she declared then. "Why?"

"Well—" He looked away, out to the roaring current of freeway traffic. In less than half an hour he would be at Quinnley Corners. "Well," he said, and the force in his voice surprised him, as if what he was about to say was something he might not have wanted to admit to himself before, "I think I've been making trial runs long enough, Junior. That's why I'm glad this happened—not about my father, but that I've had to come back."

2: Ann Smith

"BUT *having* to come back and *wanting* to come back aren't quite the same, are they?" She regarded him more attentively.

"Even so," he said.

She nodded: the car captured, held, warmed the chill sunlight, and she saw more clearly, and not without some shock, the snips of gray at his temples: Scott, thirty-two, seven years older than she. Even knowing what he'd been through, the sight of him failed to lessen the impact.

She thought of this morning and how furious she'd been with Philip Rothe for awakening her—yet who else should he have called? Not that they knew each other all that well. They didn't. He and his wife, at Scott's urging, had invited her to dinner the summer she'd come back from Paris, and she'd seen them many times since, mostly at industry functions; and a year ago she'd got her sister Myra to help push that exhibition of Phil's automotive paintings. She probably wouldn't have resented his early morning call today if she'd made it to bed at a decent hour the night before. But of course the news of Scott's arrival was a total surprise, and being fond of him and knowing what he'd been through, she'd gone to the airport as one goes on a dutiful mission. No, that wasn't quite accurate, not really. She did want to see him. And she did like the drama, the idea of popping up so unexpectedly after all this time. But a damn shame he was as preoccupied or disturbed as he seemed now.

It had to be remembered that when she'd known Scott, before his marriage, he'd been younger; true, he'd always been rather serious and inward, but like the red belt he wore, the other color of his personality seemed inconsistent . . . his sporadic drinking, his period of racing. . . .

They used to talk about it, and when she'd suggested that he might only be trying to race his way out of a boyhood in which he'd been overwhelmed, squeezed by powerful parents, Scott used to say yes, he supposed that was true, but still, he implied that he preferred not to use an oppressive childhood as a convenient alibi for his own life.

She might have said the same thing about herself, but in those days she hadn't had the courage. Yet, it was those talks they'd had, bent over the countless coffees in the countless cafés, which caused her later to reexamine her own troubled life and helped her make up her mind about herself. This she owed to Scott. Though, in all honesty, she sometimes wondered how much she'd gained by it and if, in reality, she was any better off now than she had been then. But that was beside the point, it had nothing to do with her special appreciation for Scott's friendship.

"I must tell you about this morning." She turned to him now, knowing she couldn't tell him everything. "And how I got my hands on this sacred four-wheeled cow."

That morning, immediately after Philip Rothe's call, she'd dived into her clothes, not just any clothes but one of the new suits which did not come from the approved local store. She'd run along the wide hallway of the second floor, past the room where her mother was dressing in approved tweeds, down the white curve of stairway (which was more gracious and Southern than the one in Virginia from which it had been freely copied).

She'd only been able to catch up with her father because he'd been detained by business. He'd been in the dining room with its sentimental mural depicting the history of the automobile. Her unsentimental father had been talking on the private wire to his office, and when she'd opened the double doors, Codman Smith had glanced up sharply to make sure it wasn't the maid or the cook. But seeing her, he proceeded with his talk, and she'd had to wait until he finished and until the familiar issue of R-Day (Reuther Day) had been run to the ground.

Codman Smith rose from the long mahogany table, and in that deceptively cheerful, relaxed, calm way of his, had said: "What's the trouble, honey, the house on fire? What're you doing up so early? I'm just leaving—"

"So am I," Ann had said. She kissed him and she thought how her father was really at his most felicitous in the morning as he anticipated with zest and grim pleasure the daily pressure plays at the company.

"I'm late again," Codman Smith said as he always said, when they'd stepped out to the circular driveway. Codman Smith regarded any time after 8 A.M. as late, and the fact that he happened to be president of Bellgard Motors cut absolutely no ice with him. On the contrary, he felt he had more reason than anyone else to be on the job, and he expected all his subordinates to be there too. And anyway, you couldn't have kept him away. Not Cod Smith; he was often described not very originally by his associates as "cool as a cod," though it was only the eyes, sea-green and formidable as the sea itself, that entitled him to this sobriquet. For he had a rather jolly face, his once-blond hair was now pewter-hued; a big man with an easy gait and solid friendly shoulders. Codman Smith seldom raised his voice in anger; he usually smiled and when he talked, his words seemed soft and easy, though with that indisputable edge of authority.

"Would you mind," Ann had said very lightly when they reached the long black car where the chauffeur stood waiting, "would you mind letting me borrow this gorgeous hearse for about an hour or two?"

As if he hadn't heard her, or as if the request were so academic it didn't require an answer, he merely said: "Honey, I'm late, but if you want me to drop you—"

"It's like this, Father dearest . . ." she began.

And Codman Smith, hearing the familiar overture, grinned warily: "You've got your own car, honey."

"I'm asking for a very special reason."

"Darling, we can't have you driving the limousine all over the city just to satisfy another crazy whim, you know that car is limited for business only."

"Yes, I know." Having to add: "Outside good old Kent Hills, we have to look like just plain folks."

"Now see here, honey"—his eyes stern, though the voice was still soft—"let's not forget that this city has been—"

"—has been pretty darned good to me and to you," Ann finished the twenty-fourth psalm of the industry's bible. "But here's the situation," she went on, "Scott is arriving at the airport and I have to meet him."

"Scott—?" A hasty glance at his watch. "Scott who?" Turning to the car.

"Scott Quinnley."

Her father moved back: the name, like a wall, had blocked his departure.

"Yes," she said, and getting to what she knew would be of the most

[24

pertinent interest to her father, she added: "He's come to—according to Phil Rothe, he's going to take over the dealership." She saw she'd established her point. "So don't you think we can take out the family jewel?"

Codman Smith puckered his mouth, giving the matter new attention, beginning now to riffle through the cards of memory. "Scott? Oh yes. The boy we met in Paris at the automobile show— remember now. Nice kid." Then: "Been running that car magazine in New York. Right? Yes. Well, harmless enough. Some of our people get their backs up when they read those snotty pieces of his. But they never got under me. If we listened to every self-styled car critic, we'd have been out of business long ago." Then: "You say he's going to take over Red's place?"

"I think so. At least that's how I understand it."

"All right. But don't go tearing all over town, get back here as soon as you can. I'll use your job." He looked back to the five-car garage at the rear where, among the other automobiles, she kept her Bellgard convertible. "Incidentally," he said, "while I think of it, Ann, you'd better get that front bumper replaced, that nick is developing a rust stain. Looks bad."

"Our bumpers," she said and smiled, "are guaranteed rustproof."

"Not," he was quick to say, "when you chip the chrome off. Now honey, I want you to get over to the plant and have them put on a new bumper." Then: "Red Quinnley's son. Nice kid. I remember he used to race, didn't he?"

"Oh, sometimes," she admitted, prepared, ready for the sniff of disapproval. "I know that's a dirty word." For Bellgard, unlike some of the other companies, wanted no part of racing, fearful it might create an image of danger or recklessness.

But Cod Smith said: "All right, honey. But don't make a public spectacle of it, people can get the false idea we're showing favoritism to one dealer."

"Really, Father, you know that's ridiculous," she said. "In case you've forgotten, it was Scott who saved me from a fate worse than you-know-what."

"I haven't forgotten. And I don't agree with you. You could have done worse, much worse, now that I think of it."

She looked up at him. "Tell me something, do you think you'll ever be really pleased with whoever I want to marry?" Before he could reply, she went on: "The answer is no. And I won't make any refer-

25]

ence to the current situation." Yet she remembered what had happened in Paris, how Scott had been responsible for undermining her involvement with the first man she'd wanted to marry—or rather, as it turned out, who wanted to marry her for the same reasons her brothers-in-law had wanted to marry her sisters. "Anyway, thank you for Black Maria. I'll be very discreet, I'll tell Edward to drive down all the back alleys."

"Hmm?" her father said. "Yes, I recall it now. He lost his wife."

Ann nodded. "He's had a lot of perfectly foul breaks. She was about my age when she died."

"Yes. Too bad." Her father still seemed preoccupied. "You know, Ann, as a matter of fact—" He stopped, took her arm and walked her away, beyond earshot of the chauffeur, a precaution more habitual than necessary. "Between us, Red Quinnley's operation, I understand, is sliding—"

"Oh Father, drop it. If he sold a million Bellgards you'd say it should have been two million."

Codman Smith didn't seem to hear her. "Naturally, he's been sick, out of commission, but even before that, we weren't too happy out at the shop with the way—" He stopped. Then: "Like to see the boy. Ask him out for brunch. Sunday."

She wasn't quite ready for that open welcome, though she should have been. What else was Sunday for? Or any other time at *Chez Smith?* . . .

"See you tonight, honey." Her father had kissed her. And, after giving instructions to Edward, moved with vigorous pace along the side driveway to the garage.

As soon as she got into the limousine, she'd said: "Come on, Edwardo, let's see what this monster can really do."

And so they'd driven away from the plantation-style house, whose white simplicity sometimes deceived those Sunday drivers from the city whose sport was to while away an afternoon looking, ogling, snooping, envying the milieu of the auto colony's elite citizens. But Ann knew her house was a kind of artful ruse, its severe exterior offering only a hint of the splendor within, the fifteen guest bedrooms, the hotel-sized kitchen with four refrigerators, the drawing room, recreation room, the family bedrooms, each with its own color television set, the library of hundreds of magazines and not enough books—an establishment that was set in only five modest acres cultivated in tennis courts and a baseball diamond.

[26

And then they'd gone down Old Sussex Lane, past the house of her sister Myra, whose husband was chief stylist for Bellgard—this residence, mostly hidden from view by high sculptured foliage, was flat-roofed, walled in cedar and glass, of contemporary Japanese architecture, though so self-consciously Oriental that Ann could sometimes not resist taking off her shoes before crossing its threshold.

And then they'd turned into Cotswald Drive and passed the house of her oldest sister Phoebe who, like Myra, was a car widow of Kent Hills; her husband, like Myra's, was never around very much, his night and day energies dedicated to his vice-presidency at Bellgard. Their nest was steep-roofed, timbered, worm-wooded, multichim-neyed; decidedly old English, very cottagey, except that it contained over twenty-five rooms.

And then along Buckingham Gate Road, and the other lanes whose names, Ann had decided, had the function not of inspiring the nostalgic Anglophile heart, but rather of giving to the auto colony a sense of continuity or impregnability which the members associated with Olde England.

And then out past the Country Club whose property looked like a vast jade carpet amidst the hills; and then around to the new freeway near the river, moving northward past Greenwood Park, and soon passing Downtown, and northwest then, the great black hearse taking on, in its forbidden speed, a flighty youthfulness. And then reaching the airport, to find Scott Quinnley.

Being with him now, driving back, past the city, she finished re-counting part of her tale of the early morning with her father: "—and of course, as you might suspect, dear Dad made the big gesture for all the obvious reasons." She glanced at Scott, pleased to see that she had managed to divert him, pleased to hear again something of his old robust laughter. "So you see," she said, "you count now."

"I think you're exaggerating a little, Junior, aren't you?" he said.

"Am I?" she said. "Well, let's just say you don't know Cartown the way I do." She saw from the way he looked then, that she might have sounded foolishly tactless or ominous. She quickly turned her attention to other matters: His luggage, wouldn't he want his suitcases dropped off at his house? Yes. He'd forgotten about that. And so they drove to Greenwood Park and Edward took the bags into the house, and then they made their way back to the city, and she saw now that he was retreating into new silence.

27]

And then Ann remembered Sunday, and she asked him to come out to Kent Hills; she made the invitation sound very gay, certainly gayer than it warranted. "You've got to come, I'm very anxious for you to meet Ben."

"Oh?"

"Well," she said, "in case you've been wondering why it is that a girl like me, who has everything—money, smoker's breath, dishwater hands, housemaid's knee, baby's itch and V.D.—hasn't gotten married yet, I ought to tell you I've been *almost* married five times in five years. Paris, you know about. Then my last semester at Smith, then three times here. Not bad, eh? Like I mean I'm really nubile, Man."

Scott laughed; at least she'd accomplished that much.

"You will come, won't you? I'm sure you won't object to my choice this time," she said, and feared she might have sounded overdefensive. "Noonish. *D'accord?*"

"D'accord." But now, even as he spoke, you could see that his attention had left her. The car was nearing the suburban intersection of West Main Boulevard and Timber Trail Road, and even Ann's gaze was lured upward to the roof of the dealership, to the gaudy imperatives of the high neon signs: SAVE AT QUINNLEY CORNERS . . . BUY BELLGARD . . . WIN WITH QUINNLEY.

They had reached his father's headquarters. For better or worse, one of the county's most flamboyant landmarks. She said good luck and she'd see him Sunday. And Scott said yes, Sunday.

3: Scott Quinnley

SCOTT looked up: the magnitude (the reality) of Quinnley Corners, the high one-and-a-half-story whitewashed buildings spiked above by the skyward thrust of the orange and blue neon letters; the glass-sheathed showroom on whose dustless, shining floor stood eighteen shining new Bellgard cars; the mammoth service garage which held the square of showroom and offices in a vast L-shaped embrace; the Used-Car lot adjoining, a carnival, adazzle with flags, bunting, posters and neon peppermint poles—none of this should have made such an impact on him, for as he saw it now, rendered even brasher and more unsubtle by the clean sunlight, it should merely have confirmed what he already knew.

He stepped back, recalling how he'd told Ann Smith with all that conviction how his coming back was what he needed, what he wanted. He believed it, he still believed it, except that the force of his belief was thinner now.

Absurd to let the mere sight of it begin to undermine his resolve. He'd seen Quinnley Corners often; you couldn't be in this industry, not even in the peripheral way he'd been in it, and not know something about the Corners, or how it had changed, expanded, since he'd been here last. You saw it frequently in the *American Dealer's News,* in *Automotive Monthly,* in the *Bellgard Bulletin*—yes. What he hadn't known, however, was what the reality of it could make him feel.

So that now without warning everything within sight and sound became magnified, and part of him: even the couple who were peering into the high glass window-wall, a young woman and her husband gazing intently into the showroom, and you couldn't help see that they must be more than just lookers, that they must be close to decision but still hesitating, eager and yet afraid to go in, tempted yet resisting the temptation, speculating now about trade-in value and the least amount of cash outlay and what the monthly payments might be.

He lit a cigarette, inhaled too deeply, brought his view beyond the couple to the inside of the great showroom, to some of the salesmen in their blue suits, to the tall man, balding and beak-nosed, who could be no one but Marty Calhoon, his father's chief salesman. Calhoon, now a part of his life too. Marty Calhoon sauntering toward the window, his practiced eye already appraising the young pair outside.

Beyond the showroom, in a raised area at the rear, Scott could see the glassed-in offices, yes, and there would be Mr. Waterman, the accountant who would be waiting for him.

He dropped his cigarette, and prepared to enter when the big glass door opened and Marty Calhoon stepped out and, addressing the young couple, his voice friendly, paternal, said: "Whyn't you folks just come on in and look around—"

The time was perfectly chosen: not a flash too late or too soon; the young man and his wife seemed to welcome the salesman's casual hospitality.

Scott followed them inside, moving rapidly, briskly, toward the rear, conscious of the glances of the other salesmen, conscious suddenly of how he looked, the conservative suit in gloomy contrast to the sharp, jaunty blue suits, the uniforms, of the other men.

Five steps up to the anteroom of the offices. A girl sat at the desk, a cheerful, health-exuding girl whose hair was yellow as a ripe banana, and whose breasts also brought to mind images of tropical fruits. She was not bent over the electric typewriter, but sitting back, laughing, looking up at the young man in the blue suit of a Quinnley salesman.

As Scott cleared his throat and advanced toward her, he heard behind him the sound of footsteps, purposeful, hurried, heavy, and he heard his name spoken in a rasping, breathless voice.

And the girl at the desk brought her attention back to the keyboard, and the young salesman, after picking up a batch of papers, returned to his post in the showroom. When Scott turned around he found himself confronted by the unexpected presence of his father.

He was unprepared. (Cardiography. Golf lesson. Isn't that what Mrs. Coombs had said?) He couldn't even summon a few simple words. Not because his father had turned up here, but because of the way he looked. Red Quinnley: his wild russet mane seeming too massive for the now hollow-cheeked, ravaged face; the clear glinting blue eyes now glazed, pink-veined; the once splendid mustache now lackluster; the mighty restless hands weighted.

Scott felt the unwanted wrench in his heart. He tried to smile briskly, smile away his feelings. It didn't help. He recognized in the man's pale staring eyes the long recrimination, and could read into that effortful, penetrating gaze all his father must be feeling. Red Quinnley saying to himself: *This boy, my son, here he is, at last, coming at last to give me a hand, no idea of how I've had to battle to build this enterprise, no idea what it takes, Scott, who's always had it soft, Scott so goddam smart, critical, the snob who's refused to soil his hands, Scott who's never had to face the tough odds, who's been protected by his bitch of a mother, the biggest snob of them all—she let me pay all those years at school, for what? Honor grades and that goddam useless little key, even using Scott for her climb up to a new life, and all this time poisoning the boy against me, letting the boy play at racing and old-car collecting and running that goddam, highbrow car magazine, and now Scott coming back only because Red Quinnley's heart is stalled for repairs.*

They stood confronting each other, Scott trying to say something that might take them beyond the moment. He wanted to express, if not tenderness, at least some warm sentiment that might, right from the beginning, show his father that though the time was late, maybe it wasn't too late and maybe Red and he might have learned enough to make the best of what had happened.

He was about to speak, to say something like: you shouldn't be here, you're supposed to be taking care of yourself.

But before the first word left his tongue, he saw his father move, pull the cigar from his mouth (that forbidden cigar, jutting from his mouth at a pugnacious angle, a warning that Red Quinnley still had a lot of fight in him). And then he swung his arm around, glanced at his watch:

"Goddammit, Scott, do you know what time it is? How'd you get here from the airport, by way of Saginaw? We don't keep New York hours here, this shop opens at eight o'clock! We're in business to sell and service cars—and more cars than anyone else! Do you know what that means, what it takes to keep an operation like this going? Do you know what happens if I don't unload the rest of my quota for this year? Do you know who gets stuck with the tab? You look like you just dropped in for lunch. You better goddam quick peel off that coat and get to work!"

31]

The outburst left his father gasping for breath and Scott drained of all feeling except anger, but that at least was a true feeling, and he was almost thankful for it.

It catapulted him back in time, to another time of anger: that one doomed summertime when he'd worked for his father, between his freshman and sophomore years at college, when against his mother's protests, he'd come to Quinnley Corners "for the experience."

He'd been helping out in the lube pit when Red had hurried over, told him to clean up, dress, and deliver a new Bellgard to the customer who was waiting for it. He had scrubbed his hands with the ball of grease-cutting soap, changed his clothes in the men's room. And then —it was late Friday afternoon of the July Fourth weekend—he'd driven off with the new Bellgard and half an hour later he'd had the smashup.

Not his fault, nothing to do with him—he'd always been an expert driver—he'd come to a stop at the traffic light and then just before the light changed, the car behind him had jolted forward too soon and crashed into the rear of the new Bellgard sedan.

When he had telephoned his father, Red Quinnley's rage was of course understandable. What was unforgivable was that he had never allowed Scott to explain how the accident had happened. Early the next morning Scott had fled the house and hitchiked his way back to New York.

Now, in the anteroom of the offices, Red said: "I told Waterman you'd be here and he's waiting for you. I want you to know I laid this out especially for you and I want you to get everything under your belt as soon as you can, so that you'll—" But even now, his father's instinct had been aroused to another, more immediate matter; his attention had swerved to the showroom, and he kept glancing downward to the bright sales arena, he kept frowning, observing Marty Calhoon and the young couple: "He's losing 'em, he's going to let 'em slip out," Red Quinnley muttered, already detecting, despite the barrier of glass wall, the climate in the showroom. He turned back to Scott. "Where's your luggage?"

"I dropped it off at the house when—"

But his father was no longer listening, and without another word, started down the steps, and Scott saw him now moving across the gleaming black floor of the showroom, past the men at the desks, past the multihued, diamond-bright Bellgard models, to the Luxury Com-

[32

pact which Calhoon was showing to the young couple, and he saw how Red's features lost their constraint, how the famous friendly, courteous, folksy smile was already abloom on his face, and he saw how Red moved in on the sale and how he shook hands with the two young prospects.

Scott lit another cigarette. His anger was still so rampant he must have stood there a full minute before becoming aware of the secretary's presence. He noticed then that she seemed not at all embarrassed—certainly not as much as Scott—it was as if what she'd witnessed had merely been part of another working day.

"I'm Miss Mergenfreed," she announced in her Midwest voice. She went on to say that she'd been "employed" here for almost three years, and that she'd heard about him ever since she'd come to Quinnley Corners. "I hope you're not too upset," she said, and touched the bright dyed hair. "You know how your father is—even now when he should be taking it easy, isn't that true? He gets over it just as quick as it starts, doesn't he? Personally, it's my opinion that he's a wonderful man. In his own way."

To this there was nothing he could say. He glanced around the anteroom. There was a small arched opening in the wall through which he could see the cashier's office. From far beyond in the garage there came like a mechanical fugue the faint staccato hiss of the lube guns.

At the beginning of the fifth day, Ann Smith telephoned, as Red and Scott were preparing to leave the house.

"Scott—I'm calling you at this ignoble hour because I didn't want to ruin your weekend, I mean I wanted to change Sunday. Ben's had to go to Flint to finish a nuts and bolts film there, he'll be almost three weeks, so could we make it for Sunday the twentieth?"

"Certainly," he said.

"Because I do want you to meet him." A pause. "But I'll try to arrange something meanwhile."

33]

"Junior, you don't have to feel responsible for my social life," Scott said.

"Yes I do, and also I can't see an eligible male like you hang on the vine."

"There isn't time for much else," he said.

"You're sure?"

"Afraid so."

"Really?" She paused: he could tell she was trying to get around to something else. "Everything going all right?"

"Yes." He waited. He saw his father going into the hall for his coat.

"You haven't changed your mind? I mean, how are you liking it? Are you really glad you're here?" It spilled out in a rush then, her curiosity.

"Of course," he said.

"You're not just giving yourself the old jazz, are you?" She persisted.

"I don't think so, Ann," he said. Then: "I'm sure in traffic like this I can expect to get dirtied up."

"You do sound all right," she said.

What he couldn't tell her was that a certain real excitement was living in him now that he was actually here, or rather now that he was part of something which until this week had been a remote world. He could admit, finally, that as much as he'd loved his life in the East, the magazine had more or less gone as far as it could go, at least his initial appetite for it had grown blunted; he could admit in all honesty that he'd been sitting it out in the pit, enjoyably, safely watching the contest, being removed from and superior to the heart of the industry. He might have continued in this agreeable rut for God knows how long if he hadn't been forced to come here by his father's illness. He'd been a perfectly round peg in a perfectly round hole and all that perfection had been making him flabby. Now, despite many reservations, despite the cryptic warnings of buddies in New York, or of Phil Rothe or Ann Smith, he found himself conscious of a new exhilaration.

"Of course, speaking selfishly," Ann was saying, "I'm awfully pleased about your being here. Ben and I don't have all that many people we really like to talk to."

"Thank you, madame," he said.

A silence, as if, her curiosity having been at least partly appeased, she had to regain her social balance. Then: "Well, since you're one of us now I want you to remember"—and a faint and familiar air of mischief began to creep into her tone—"remember, sir, that Cartown is Our Town, I mean over seven million car sales per annum. I mean we use one-fifth of all the steel produced. Think of it, boy, over sixty million cars on the road now, and by 1970, you know what?"

"What?"

"There'll be seventy-five million of these monsters around, and by then you won't have to use a steering wheel, you won't have to lift a finger, you won't have to walk to the toilet either, there'll even be a car for that. What horizons! And I know this is what you want to help perpetuate, isn't it?"

"It is indeed, baby," he answered properly, for by now they were embarked on the kind of little vaudeville bit they'd invented in Paris.

"Oh good," she said. "But tell us, Mr. Quinnley, as I recall, weren't you once one of those exceedingly angry young men?"

"Fit to be tied."

"And didn't you used to tell your hip friends in Paris, like five years ago, how pukey the U. S. auto product was?"

"I did. I was a cat ahead of his time."

"And tell us," Ann said, "is it still pukey?"

"No."

"No? But how can we be sure?"

"Seven million car sales can't be wrong," he said.

"Correct," Ann said. "Tell us something more about yourself, Mr. Quinnley. You've done some racing, and you've edited a decidedly *In* car magazine. Now does that mean you're what they call an autophile?"

"A buff, a car buff, Man," he answered.

"And what else?"

"A nut, a car nut, Man."

"And tell us, what make car are you driving now?"

"A Bellgard."

"Ah. Would you mind telling us why?"

"All us tigers prefer the Bellgard," he said. He saw that his father was opening the front door, and he broke off the vaudeville turn.

"Good-bye, darling. That's Sunday, the twentieth. Good luck."

"Thank you, Junior." He hung up. He joined his father, and they started the drive.

Scott drove the new car his father had given him. He'd sold his Porsche in New York on Red's warning. Red didn't care what kind of car Scott had here as long as it wasn't foreign or any make except Bellgard. It was a compact, one of the models of this year's line which hadn't "moved out of the tent," as Red had said. "Why?" Scott had asked, though the answer was plain: the compact was no longer a compact, it had been "improved," its wheelbase excessive, as was its gas consumption, its design now hybrid, the former clean simplicity now embellished by brightwork. "Why?" Red had answered, defending loyally, stoutly, even admirably. "Because this machine is too goddam fine, that's why!"

Red was beside him now in the car, in his topcoat, and the tawny, wide-brimmed hat rakish over his thick titian hair, and being outstandingly paternal as he asked him about the call from Ann Smith, disappointed that the Sunday in Kent Hills had been called off.

This was the first time since that first day that Red was going to the office. Scott couldn't be sure if it was the industrious showing he'd made that had given Red enough confidence to stay away from the Corners, or if—and this was probably closer to it—it had been all the snow, wind and rain, the prelude to spring, that had kept him indoors obeying his doctor's program. Now he was seething to get to work—this was the first time they'd gone together—and his geniality was touching. Maybe it was because yesterday during lunchtime Scott had happened to make his first sale. True, he'd walked right into it; true, as salesmen went he knew more than most about engine performance; and true, his technical knowledge had been in his favor—a freak sale, yes; but a sale. It had been dimly resented by the other salesmen, but to Red, evidently, it was a signal of hope as if, no matter how removed Scott had been from the core of the business, he was, after all, his son, Red Quinnley's son who must have in him, somewhere, the Quinnley magic.

"No, no—take the right fork there," his father said now, as they reached the freeway near Greenwood Park. "This is the way I always go."

Scott turned into the torrent of traffic leading downtown. "I've been taking the short route west," he said.

"No—this is the way you have to go," Red said. "Builds good will."

Puzzled, he glanced over at his father, but Red offered no explanation.

Soon, as they neared the city's heart, Scott had to slow down to 40 mph.

[36

"Meant to tell you," Red was saying, "those suits of yours, they don't have any jump. When you're on the floor you have to look sharp, not just think sharp. Want you to go to Laird's. Joe Laird's been one of my loyalest customers, a new model every year." He squinted at the dark gray jacket.

Scott said: "You certainly don't expect me to wear one of those blue—"

"No, no. All right," Red retreated. "Nothing wrong with it, just looks so—old. *Old.* You can have Laird make you the same thing if you want, but let's have it look new."

He didn't want to dwell on it. He said yes he'd go to Laird's. His father then said: "You might pick up some ties there too. A little jumpier. You need to flash some life in a tie. Get what you want, son. But you know what I mean."

Scott nodded. Traffic had stopped, and now Red was peering ahead, studying all the cars.

As the line began to move, his father edged forward, his light blue eyes darted from one car to another to see which had been bought at other dealers, which ones carried the rear insignia of Quinnley Motors. Whenever he saw the Quinnley trademark, he told Scott to pass the car, and then he'd wave to the driver—there was scarcely one he didn't know:

"Take it easy there, Mr. Foley!"

"Hiya, Mr. Betts—mighty fine-looking car you're driving there!"

"How they treating you, Mr. Greenberg?"

Downtown, not far from Cobo Hall, Red asked him to make a stop. No parking. But he seemed to know many of the policemen around, and many of them had a word for him, and when they asked about his health, Red would always say: "In the pink, officer, in the pink now. And just remember when Red Quinnley goes, the first one he's going to sell a Bellgard to is St. Peter himself."

Red took Scott to the offices of Fellowman Finance Company and introduced him to the president. Afterward, as they returned to the car, Red explained: "You can't depend on just the profit per car—if any. Our daylight comes in the financing when the deal is tight. Now you make it your business, when you sell a car, to send the buyer to Fellowman Finance, understand? We get a nice scoop of ice cream on each piece of paper we send over. They put it to our account, and at the end of the year we get us our big dessert. That's how it is, how it has to be. You have to survive. This is a hog-eat-hog business."

Westward now on West Main Boulevard, Scott was still besieged by the same feeling that had held him all week: he felt more like a student than a man who'd come to take over his father's dealership. During the past days he'd been cramming like an undergraduate. There was, however, one tonic effect. He was at least beyond seeing all the landmarks of memory, beyond all the daily reminders of Ellen's decline and death. Though their marriage, in truth, had not been the best, he'd begun to think of it as such, out of loyalty and guilt. Hounding him all that time had been Ellen's remarkable courage, right to the end; it left him with outsized guilt for his own shortcomings. He'd asked himself so often: Would I have this kind of guts under the same despairing conditions? And the answer had always been, and still was, no.

Being in Cartown, and at Quinnley Corners, at least helped to fog the past. And as soon as he brought his child from New York, he might come closer to feeling whole again.

"Pull in there, Scott," his father instructed abruptly. "Need gas."

"We've got enough." Scott said. The needle was at the half-full mark.

"I always stop in here. Once a week. A policy." Red turned up his topcoat collar and stepped from the car.

"Morning, Mr. Quinnley." The young attendant was at the door.

"Fill 'er up, Frank." But Red did not linger at the pump. He sauntered around the Taj Mahal magnificence of the white-tiled service station, stopping to talk to one of the mechanics, waving to another, meeting with the proprietor. When the attendant had fueled the car and cleaned the windshield, Red gave him three dollars, though the price on the pump read $2.19. "Put it toward a gold-plated Bellgard, kid," Red said to the young man, and got back into the sedan. To Scott: "You want to keep this up. We have to use these Bird Dogs. Service stations, barbershops, restaurants—they'll all bird-dog for you if you treat them right, and every once in a while they put in the right word at the right time and send in a sale."

Red was quiet then, his breathing came with more effort. The trip resumed out through the congested boulevard, past the blocks of garish storefronts, the hat stores, furniture stores, supermarkets and appliance emporiums which had turned this once-sedate thoroughfare into a kind of grim bazaar. This sector, Scott thought, had once been his home ground; it was almost impossible to recognize today. Behind the merchandise marts where once elm trees shaded the plain neat houses and apartments, you could get glimpses of the blemished faces of the same houses and apartments which had been allowed, by their landlords, to fall into desrepair, to accommodate the moiling mass of colored people and poor whites who'd churned north to the city to fill the demand for labor during World War II.

After a while, Scott said: "Do you know Dean Stratler very well?"

"Dean Stratler? I only know Stratler from running into him at Bellgard conventions. But he'll know Red Quinnley."

"I was thinking," Scott said then, "if you could possibly call him. . ."

"Call him? About what?" Red said.

"About Phil Rothe. When I was over there for dinner the other night, it occurred to me you might possibly put a word to Stratler. This is my idea, not Phil's. But I know damn well he can use the account. He's never been able to make it with Bellgard."

"A guy like Phil? He's one of the busiest artists in the field, I always thought," Red said. "Always see those drawings of his, those ads in all the magazines. What does he do with his money—put it all into antique cars?"

"Phil's got a lot of people to support," Scott said. "He's also acquired a real beauty of a Duesenberg S J—he swapped it with Tony Kerwin for the old Bellgard. He doesn't know Kerwin. It was all done through a third party." After dinner the other night he and Phil had gone out to the garage and Phil had shown him the lovely vintage car: it had been the best part of the evening. Scott owned a 1928 Pierce Arrow, but he'd left it in storage in New York. "Anyway," he said, "I'd appreciate it if you'd call Stratler and kind of let it be known that Phil might bring some new life into the Bellgard scene."

"Sure thing," Red said.

The route to Dean Stratler, Scott thought now, had to be foolishly indirect. Ann Smith could easily talk to her brother-in-law. But of course you could never ask her to intercede.

"I'll call him today. Remind me," Red said. He slumped lower in the seat, his chin deep between the lapels of his blue topcoat. Once, peering outward as they passed the old neighborhood with its old memories, Red said: "She always used to scream every time you stayed over at Phil's house. Remember that?"

She.

Her.

That was how Red always referred to Scott's mother: in twenty years they had not spoken to each other.

"Yes, I remember," Scott said. "You used to cover up for me when I stayed there for dinner or for overnight."

"Listen, I loved Leonard Rothe. Used to be headquarters for our Saturday night poker game, and when I think of the food they'd spread out—" Red said in soft reverie.

Even to this day, Scott could recall Phil Rothe's father, a wholesale jeweler, a plump man of droll humor who always smoked gold-tipped cigarettes, the rich Turkish aroma pungent in all the rooms of the friendly house.

"But *she*," Red said now, "*she* used to think they weren't swanky enough for her. Nothing in this town was ever good enough for her."

"Look . . ." Scott began.

"Yes. You're sold. She sold you the whole package. Kids always buy it from the mother," Red stated bitterly.

"You know that's not true," Scott said. "I know Mother's faults as well, if not better, than you. But she—she was never geared for this kind of life."

"Do you think what she has now—that whole phony New York package—do you think she's got a life now?" Red revived the old cry.

"Well, there's no point in getting yourself worked up over it again," Scott said.

"She was a climber right from the start," Red went on. "Nothing I ever did was ever good enough for her. That family of hers, you'd have thought they built Grosse Pointe. But that house of theirs in Oakland Heights, because it had a tennis court, she thought that made her queen."

Then why, Scott could have asked him, had Red married her? And why, too, had Red been only too glad to accept that money from her family when he'd gone into business?

Scott said nothing, however. He'd heard the same sounds of the same battle too long.

Once, when he'd asked his mother why she'd married Red, she'd replied: "Because I was a complete fool. Because Father took some kind of crazy fancy to him, and I admired anything my father did. But we all learn too late. Do you know what Red did once? You were a baby then. I gave a surprise birthday party for him—we lived in that hideous brick house on Calvit Street then—I invited sixteen people, they all brought gifts. But your father never even got there. We waited.

and waited and I was never so humiliated in my entire life. It must have been past ten that night when he telephoned—from some awful beery tavern upstate—he'd had a chance to go deer hunting on the spur of the moment with one of those chums of his, and he simply took off—mind you, his own birthday. And he never got back until Monday morning."

"And I'll tell you something else," Red was saying now. "You've been getting it all from her side, but you don't know what I—"

"Do we have to talk about it?" Scott broke in. "It's senseless for you to get yourself worked up over it now. It'll only end up with—"

"With what?"

With me in the middle again, Scott wanted to say. "It's no good for you to get agitated like this."

"You think that? Why?" Abruptly Red's voice rose. "Listen to me, goddammit, just because my heart broke down, that's no reason for you to lie or act like some pussy-footed diplomat. I want you to say what you've got to say, not keep everything to yourself. The last time you did that you ran away, not a word, you ran away that summer just when I needed you."

"I ran away, as you know, because you—"

"Goddammit, listen to me! I want you to open up, say what you've got to say. I don't mean about *her*—I mean about anything and everything from here on. I mean Quinnley Corners and everything about it!" His father slammed his right first into the palm of his left hand, bringing his outburst to a resounding close. "Understand?" Then as the rasping of his breath subsided, he said softly, winningly. "Do we have a deal?"

"No." Scott held his eyes hard on the traffic.

"Hmm?"

"No," he said very quietly, "it's no deal. Because I think you're using your bad heart like a wedge, for a bargain!" He regretted having said it, it was a kind of cruelty which was new to him and unwarranted.

But then he heard, in astonishment, his father's burst of coughing laughter: "By Christ, Scott, I think you're a smart boy! I think I'm going to live to see myself proud of you!"

The wheels of the morning's business were whirring by the time they reached Quinnley Corners.

"Friday, Saturday—" Red was saying, pointing now to the car-

41]

clotted entrance of the garage, "everybody wants service for the weekend. Monday morning it's the same, that's when they all come back
crippled *after* the weekend. Bless 'em."

As soon as they reached the door, Scott said he thought he'd better
stop in at Mr. Waterman's office; it wasn't necessary to do this now,
but he knew he'd feel easier if he was alone. He'd discovered in
the course of the week that most of the people at Quinnley Corners
watched him with a kind of suspicion, their manner reserved, fearful;
or they had been overfriendly, even obsequious, which was also a sign
of their apprehension and distrust.

Son of the boss. Moving in cold from New York. Getting it all on a
platter.

What does he know? How much? What goes, what's the score?
Will there be cutbacks? Policy changes? Where will it hit me?

Seeing it in their eyes, hearing it in their voices, he had gone out of
his way not to feed their fears. He'd conducted himself, or tried to,
like a man new in the business and anxious to learn. Which he was.
Yet, except for Waterman and Marty Calhoon, most of the personnel
continued to hold back.

"Want you to stick with me, this morning, son." Red clapped him
on the shoulder. Reluctantly he agreed, though this was just the sort
of thing he had hoped to avoid, tagging along after the old man,
shadowing the boss.

They moved now through the long passage to the general anteroom
and hearing Miss Mergenfreed's chirping Good Morning, and on into
the smaller anteroom where Mrs. Bowsley, Red's secretary, sat; and
then into the large office where by the bank of windows, and standing
like an anachronism amidst the recently modernized room, was Red's
big, nicked and worn walnut desk. At the opposite end of the room
was the chrome-rodded desk installed for Scott.

Everywhere on the walls were the framed photographs: Red
Quinnley posing proudly beside early and late Bellgard models; Red
Quinnley trowling the mortar on the cornerstone dedicating the new
Junior Athletic League Clubhouse; Red Quinnley standing with Bell-
gard executives at the Dealers Convention; Red Quinnley and the
mayor of the City, wearing big bibs at the American Legion Annual
Picnic and Barbecue; and the Bellgard Certificate of Honor: RED
QUINNLEY, DEALER OF THE YEAR. 1955.

Hastily Scott sorted his own mail first: letter from his mother, and
his New York lawyer; announcements from National Raceways Asso-

[42

ciation and from the Classic Car Club of America, and the New York offices of The Sports Car Club of America.

He put the mail aside. He saw the memo from Mrs. Bowsley:

Miss Ann Smith. Kent 32444. Called at 9:55

He joined his father now, Red standing at the desk, still wearing his blue topcoat and the hat; Red swiftly riffling through the mound of mail and documents, brochures, invoices. "Won't be long before you can clear through this for me. I'll be on the golf course," Red was saying, scanning letters, now and then pausing to give him instructions, advice. When he'd finished, he removed his hat and coat and hung them carefully on the rack. "All right, let's go. Always tour the entire shop before eight-thirty. Today was different. Stick with me, son."

In the anteroom, Scott said: "Could you call Dean Stratler now?"

"Hmm?"

"About Phil."

"Oh yes." He turned to the elderly secretary. "Mrs. B., I want Dean Stratler at Bellgard. Styling Lab. I'll be out front or in service."

"Morning." From a door appeared the corpulent accountant, Mr. William Waterman; his jowled face was set, sour and saturnine. "Red, if you have a minute—"

"Bad news can wait," Red said to the man.

Waterman arched his thick gray brows and shrugged.

"Hello, Will," Scott said. "You want me now?" he added hopefully.

"This afternoon late, if you can make it."

Red said: "Come on, son."

His father led the way down the steps to the showroom for what evidently was, or had been, his daily ritual: Red moved from one new car to another, testing all the doors, opening and shutting them, peering inside to inspect the cleanliness of seats and mats. He looked up then, his blue eyes alert as he surveyed the enormous showroom, as he sought, sniffed, appraised the climate of business. Marty Calhoon and half a dozen salesmen were occupied with customers.

Now they strode across the showroom to the opposite side, where behind the glass wall ranged the rows of the salesmen's sales booths, each equipped with small desk, two chairs, telephone. Red went directly to the rear booth to study the weekly sales chart. He wrinkled his nose in a grimace of displeasure. "There'll have to be a payoff rush today and tomorrow. We're twenty-two units behind quota." He shook his head. "Don't understand it. I train these men. But today they don't grow salesmen anymore, and you can't beat it into them, they aren't built that way. Some of our boys have got it, most of them are deadheads. Until this goddam heart attack, I personally sold more units per year than the total of my entire crew." He reached out and squeezed Scott's arm: "Who knows? Maybe someday, you're going to top the old man, huh?"

Because Scott recognized the statement as being half Quinnley bull and half hope, he only smiled, saying nothing, but trying to bring to his smile an affirmative brightness, even though beneath it he suspected again that Red was attempting to turn his heart condition into a new business asset. What he couldn't deny, however, what he could only admire, was how his father kept up these spurts of zealous optimism in the face of what seemed to be a serious slump in the season's sales.

"Let's go." Red turned abruptly. They recrossed the showroom but before they reached the service garage, Red entered the Repairs Waiting Room.

"This'll be Ladies' Day," Red said. "This time of morning."

They were mostly young women, some with children, who sat in the Waiting Room. Pine-paneled walls. Bright posters featuring current models—alluring, picturesque vision of how Bellgard reflected the affluent wonders of American life. There was Mom and Dad and the Kids loading up the station wagon for the Sunday outing; there was Brother taking off in his convertible; there was Sis, legs well-exposed, yet decorous, stepping into her coupe; there was Dad again, arriving at his office building in his compact; there was sophisticated Cousin in evening dress, being ushered out of the luxury-eight in front of the theatre.

Red shook hands with some of the people, nodding to others, a word here, a joke there, and going around courteously, showing personal interest in everyone's welfare.

"Mrs. Nivok—" He stopped to greet the blond young woman with the whimpering little girl on her lap. "What's the trouble? Aren't they treating you right today?"

"They're certainly not," the young woman said, and shifted the child onto the seat beside her. She'd been here since nine that morning, she said, and she had an eleven-o'clock appointment with the pediatrician downtown.

[44

"Well now"—Red exuded paternal concern, pausing to whip from his inside pocket a cellophane-wrapped lollipop, handing it to the child—"well now, Mrs. Nivok, let's just see if we can't get you to that doctor's in plenty of time. Eleven o'clock, you say?"

"Yes. And it's already ten after ten." She crossed her legs and sighed. "The muffler is broken, or something."

"Let's see what we can do." And Red hurried from the room. To Scott he murmured: "Always the pretty ones give you the headaches. Look after them first, they're spoiled, you've got to do it."

After the Waiting Room, which was always scented by a daily aerosol bomb-spraying of pine fragrance, the odors of the vast garage came in sharp, pungent contrast—the mists of gas fumes, the smell of machine grease, oil and rubber.

He accompanied his father, who was striding too rapidly through the livid-bright Service Department, an area almost the size of a football field—Red now moving along the work bays, finding the lines all busy, going to the far wall where the machinery repair benches were, stopping at last by the brake drum lathes to interrupt one of the mechanics. "Ted—"

"Yes, sir?" The young man turned from his lathe, wiped his black-stained fingers against his coveralls.

"Get over there to that gray hardtop of Mrs. Nivok's. Check the work sheet and get her out of here quick." Then: "You know my son Scott? Scott, this is Ted Markham, one of the best brake boys in the shop." They shook hands, and then Red was off again, going straight to Mrs. Nivok's car, moving around it, peering now beneath the rear undercarriage. "Christ, that muffler is shot, won't be time for it today, those goddam units fall apart half the time before the warranty expires." Moving on then to the front, stepping back, squinting at the front wheels. "Could use some work there. Realignment. You keep your eyes open and you'll always find something not on the work sheet."

"Like what?" Scott said.

"Stick with me, son." Red led the way back to the Repairs Waiting Room. "Mrs. Nivok," he said to the woman, "afraid we're going to get you out of here in short order."

"Oh good. Thank you so much, Mr. Quinnley." Her smile was coquettish, as if Red's help had come as a special tribute to her sexual allure.

"Always a pleasure." Then Red said: "By the way, tell Mr. Nivok,

45]

will you, that I'd like to see him drop the car by one day. Those front wheels need realignment." A grave tone had stolen into Red's voice.

"Oh? Is it—is it dangerous?" young Mrs. Nivok asked.

"No, not at all. Long as you catch it in time," Red assured her. "But I'd like to see it done. It'll be on the house. No charge—not for the Nivoks."

"Well, that's certainly very nice of you, very nice. I'll tell Jim."

When they left the Waiting Room, Scott said: "Realignment is a lot of labor to give away free, isn't it?"

"It is if you confine it just to that," Red said and grinned. "But we don't. We have to keep the customer's car in top shape, and naturally when you've got the car up on the lift it gives you a legitimate chance to spot other trouble—there's usually some part needs replacing. Muffler or a rod, bearings, brake lining, not to mention tires. They never question it. They take the free service so big, they don't mind laying out for the extras. Best way to keep the Parts Department healthy," his father said, obviously enjoying this primary lesson. Then his grin thinned: "You don't have to get that look on your face. This is a hog-eat-hog business. You want to think of it this way: like the dentist cleaning your teeth. Do you think he lives on that? Hell no. But it gives him a legitimate chance to open your mouth, recommend a porcelain cap, a filling or a new bridge."

"Yes, I know. But—"

"Come on, son."

Back into the showroom then, and Scott saw Mrs. Bowsley hastening across the floor. "On that call to Mr. Stratler—"

"Yes," Red said.

"He's tied up at the testing track. I left word for him to call you, Mr. Quinnley."

Red nodded.

"Mr. Quinnley—" The woman's face, delicate and pointed as a bird's, was taut with anxiety. "They just called from Westtown Assembly. Those last thirty-five new units are en route—"

"En route? Now? Didn't you tell them I—"

"Yes, I told them you'd asked the factory for a delay and that we'd had it understood the cars would not be sent," the woman said.

Scott saw the flurry of agitation on his father's face, as now Red kept kneading his knuckled fist into the palm of his left hand. "Understood? They gave me their word! I tore the roof off when I went out there!"

[46

"They said the factory schedule had to stand," Mrs. Bowsley relayed the message in a twittering echo. "I don't know if there is still time, but if you want me to contact them now—"

Nearby, two of the salesmen lingered at the water cooler, their attention alerted though they tried to affect indifference.

Red had already perceived their interest. He swung around, his back to the men now. "No, never mind, Mrs. B., we'll handle them. Get out to Service and tell Kellogg to clear space and allocate a crew so's we can ready the new batch for show." His voice came forcefully, clearly. From his breast pocket he took a fresh cigar and lit it; as soon as the two salesmen had walked away he turned to Scott, but his tone was muted, as if he were talking more to himself. "Nobody listens at Bellgard anymore. I tore the roof off to stop those new units. I only asked for a temporary stop. But they don't listen. Midyear model changes always overlap the stock on hand, but these are coming in early. How in hell do they expect a man to unload inventory? They have the idea the more cars they pile on you, the more you'll have to push. All they go by is their quota figures, the thickheads! Pile it on the dealer and if the dealer doesn't sell them, tough titty! It used to be that a man——"

"There's no way of refusing the delivery?" Scott asked. "Or working out a—"

"Refuse delivery?" Red looked at him with incredulity, his teeth clamped down hard on the cigar. "What do you think? Certainly not. And you know why? Because I've spoiled those people. They expect miracles here. This place ought to be called Miracle Corners! Well, we goddam better unload them. I'm going to call a meeting of the crew tomorrow after closing. I'm going to read down the law, get the goddam lead out of their tails, we'll unload." He rolled the cigar to the other side of his mouth. "Maybe the new units will give us just the jump we need. I'll put them on the floor and sell them, and we'll slip in the leftover models for the pikers and pinchers looking for bargain basement deals. We'll pack 'em through!"

Scott glanced around at all the models on the floor, the leftovers from last October, and thought of the units still unsold on the back lot, and in the warehouse. Adding the thirty-five midyear models due in today to the already delivered units of the quota obviously made very little sense. . . .

Red swung his arm around Scott's shoulder. "Stick with me, we'll push this through."

"Yes." Scott was becoming a part of the mystique of his father's universe, and if he couldn't always understand Red's pugnacious determination, knowing the price he'd have to pay, he wondered how much different he himself was? During the time he'd given himself over to racing, when he knew in advance one or two drivers would never walk away from the season alive, he'd kept right on with the sport against common sense, against all statistics, not quitting until Ellen had insisted.

Yet, to him racing seemed to demand less of a man than the contest his father had to wage.

"Look at that, look at him!" Red muttered. He nudged Scott, who saw Marty Calhoon opening the glass doors, ushering three people out of the showroom. "Marty!" Red called.

The veteran salesman turned back. He rebuttoned the jacket of his blue suit as he moved across the shining floor. His lanky frame was erect, his eyes reflective. Sunlight gleamed on his balding head.

Scott could feel what was coming. He said something about having to go to the office. He didn't want to embarrass Calhoon by being present.

"Scott—" His father's voice deterred him. "I want you to take a good look at Marty. I want you to know," Red went on calmly, even cheerfully, "that Marty has been with us for over fifteen years. For my money, he's the best in the business, the prize in the Crackerjack. That's why I've been on your tail all week, because you learn from Marty in a day what it would take you years to pick up."

"I know." Scott was immensely relieved.

Red chuckled now. "Here I am, Marty, giving you all this braggadocio, even though I saw you just let those people get away. Happens to the best, doesn't it, Marty?"

"You ought to know, Red," Calhoon answered impassively.

"Yep," Red said, "it happens to the best of us. Sometimes you can turn on all the lights in the world, give them the Last Supper and the Resurrection and they still walk out, isn't that right, Marty?"

Calhoon's smile was wan; he pinched his thin beaked nose.

"Sometimes, even a crackerjack like Marty lets them walk out." Almost jokingly then, Red said: "What's the matter, Marty? Get up on the wrong side of your wife this morning?"

"Must be," Calhoon said, and matching Red's jocular tone, added: "We can't hang up a record every hour on the hour, can we?"

"True." Red touched his graying moustache, his voice slow and teasing: "And I'm glad my boy saw the courteous way you showed those people out to the street, courtesy is important. If you've lost a sale, lose it courteously."

"Look, Red—" Scott protested. "I don't see the point of going on like this. If Marty lost that sale, a postmortem like this isn't—"

"We always chew it over, don't we, Marty?" All lightness had fled from Red's voice.

Calhoon said: "It happened it wasn't my sale. It was Bernstein's. I had to move in for the T.O."

"Well, that was a nice Take Over," Red said. 'You took them right over to the street door. Even Bernstein could have done that. Ah, but what's the difference? We've only got thirty-five new units pulling in this morning and all we have to do is sell this floor clean by Monday so we can make room for the midyear models." Then: "Tell me something, Marty? You want a two-week vacation? A little rest? A man gets tired. That's how it looks to me anyway. I saw those people. I saw Bernstein too. What happened to the trade-in when you took over, Marty? I thought when you showed them out you might be going to appraise their car, but you didn't even have their keys, did you? You let them get out without getting their keys. You—a key snatcher from way back." A gradual harshness had begun to score Red's words. "Maybe it's an allergy you got, Marty. Customers' keys give you a rash on the hand? Or is it—"

"Red—" Calhoon spoke in a flat, colorless way. "I don't know. Something funny is happening. For some reason some of the people coming in here lately, they just don't seem to be as stupid as they used to be. I can't understand it."

The joke—or retaliation—Scott saw now, failed to appease his father. Scott turned. He glanced with calculated urgency toward the offices.

"But Marty," Red was saying, "you're not supposed to understand it. You're supposed to enlighten the customer. Isn't that right? Did you try to enlighten them?"

"Listen, Red"——Calhoon showed the first flare of combat—"when I came in for the T.O., I pulled out everything from the bag. I gave them the Highball, and when that didn't work, I threw them the Lowball and—"

"People like that," Red said with wildest impatience, "you have to use The Bush."

The Bush, Scott knew, was a kind of dazzling, overwhelming tactic in which you promised away the moon on the condition that the customer signed immediately a blank contract, to be filled in later in more realistic terms.

"Red," Calhoon was saying, "they laughed right in my face when I tried it. No, what it shakes down to is that they just didn't like the product. They've been shopping around. They quoted me a better deal from Max Wilkerson and—"

"We undercut Wilkerson, we have to, we always have to," Red stated. "Once you get them under the tent, goddammit, you can't let them get out."

"What it is, Red, is that they were just too stupid to appreciate the product, they just wouldn't cotton up to the Bellgard."

Scott edged back as tactfully as he could. He saw that what Calhoon had said struck Red like a slap. You could say anything to Red except this—to even hint that Bellgard was not the marque supreme was treason, sacrilege, blasphemy.

"Didn't like the product?" Red roared; he plunged his hand through the thick tangled hair. "You took that? By Christ, what's happening with you, Marty? We've got the greatest product in the industry! The greatest performers in the entire goddam field, and if you think we haven't, it's time you took off two weeks and went fishing— or to a head doctor! By Christ, I don't understand what's happening with you. Even my son, still green as a potato farmer from the old sod, even Scott here, made a sale yesterday. Don't tell me, Marty, I'm going to have to send my boy in as a T.O. for you?"

Scott turned; he felt the blood push up into his throat: the embarrassment he'd tried to spare Calhoon had instead been thrust on him. Scott was enraged with his father for having used him in this way.

Scott said: "Red—you know it's senseless for you to get this excited. You can't expect Marty or anyone else to score with everyone who walks in. And you know damn well that sale I made was a fluke. Why don't we get back to the office and—"

"What?" Red looked back at him. "Yes. You're right." But again he confronted the salesman. "Marty, stop in at the office at closing. Let's have a little talk."

Calhoon hesitated. "Can't tonight, Red. I'm tied up. I—my wife and I are going to—"

"Goddammit, your wife can wait this one time, can't she? Or isn't she interested?"

[50

The salesman held his silence for an instant. Then he said: "Certainly she's interested. You know Vera. But I promised her tonight we'd—"

"Marty, I want to have a talk with you. Vera waits. See you at closing." Red walked off, his hands thrust deep in his trouser pockets.

In the trail of silence which Red left behind, Scott said: "The trouble is, Marty, my father's been away for so many weeks, and this week he was out for another three days, so that he's overanxious to catch up. He feels he has to raise hell with me and everyone else to make up for the—"

"Naw," Calhoon interrupted him, "from his point of view Red is right.

"I'll tell you, Scott," the man continued quietly, you had the sensation he had to say it, "some days you feel, you know when you've got it. You can feel it in your fingers, your bones. You see someone coming in, you've got them under the tent, and you know right away you're going to sign them. You know they won't leave the tent without your having their keys or their signature. Today, I knew I didn't feel it. I let myself believe what they said. When you feel it that way, you're dead. Better to stay in your glass box and let one of the others move in."

Scott nodded and started back to the office. On his desk he saw Ann's message, her second call. He telephoned her at Kent Hills.

A dinner party, next Wednesday night at the Kent Hills Country Club. Could he come? The occasion, the birthday of a close friend of hers, Jennifer Thompson who lived in Ann Arbor. The club was "absolutely ignoble," but Ann said she could give parties there with the minimum of effort. (And if Scott wanted a zoo's view of all the great lions of the industry, that was the place to be.)

He couldn't make it. Wednesday was a kind of crucial night for him: two of the editors of his magazine were flying in to continue the talks they'd begun in New York; they were also planning to discuss an option arrangement with the view of acquiring ownership in the event Scott decided to give it up permanently.

"Oh balls," Ann said, "I'm *that* disappointed."

He was too, he said. But she needn't feel such a compulsion to fix him up.

"Why not? Why shouldn't you be fixed up?" she said. "Well, anyway, if not before, we'll see you the twentieth, *Chez Nous*."

4: *Scott Quinnley*

KENT HILLS, on its wooded eminence, was suffused in the pale mist of the noonday sunshine. Scott welcomed the sight, even though there was about this suburb of the auto elite a certain synthetic admixture of Beverly Hills and Greenwich. Estates nestled among the curving lanes, and the leafy landscape was broken here and there by the tapering thrust of church spires. It was soothing to see after the frantic weeks at Quinnley Corners; or maybe it was only that something, no matter how synthetic, nourished the nostalgia Scott felt for the East.

But what gave Kent Hills its particular, and to him, amusing stamp, was not that the list of families composed a kind of Burke's Peerage of the automobile industry, but that you could easily tell, by the make of the cars in the driveways, which company a man worked for: a single glance could tell you who was with General Motors or with Chrysler or Jefferson or Ford or Vanguard or any of the others.

Nearing Ann Smith's house, he accelerated the car over a rise in the road, detecting, without thinking of it or listening for it, the faint shudder of torsional vibration in the engine's innards—this in a car only a few weeks on the road.

He slowed for the turn into the Smith property.

"No," his father had said in answer to Scott's question that morning, "No, I've never been over at Cod Smith's, now that I think of it. We've gabbed a lot at conventions or at local shindigs, but hell, we always got into shoptalk and—well I've never had time for all that social stuff. It's okay for you, different. More personal." Then he had added: "If Cod asks about me, you can tell him my nose is still out of joint the way they keep pushing their goddam quotas on me and—no, hell no, don't mention it. Too late anyway. Just say, if the subject comes up, that we can hold our own, and then some."

Now, as Scott drove up to the white porticoed residence and parked in the washed gravel circle, he saw he was not the only visitor:

seven other cars were stationed in the commodious circular driveway. Just as he started toward the house, he happened to glance up the side drive and saw the sedan, the big sweep of hood angling, tilting sharply upward. Instinctively or foolishly, never able to resist peering beneath an open hood, he changed course and turned into the drive. The hood, he thought, must have accidentally sprung open.

When he got to the car, a standard Bellgard passenger sedan, he reached for the hood, preparing to close it while automatically gazing at the familiar engine. Except that he saw at once that it wasn't standard at all, that hidden beneath the car's conventional shell was a motor he'd never seen in any current Bellgard model. He looked closer, like an archaeologist startled to come upon an unexpected disclosure. The V-8 powerplant was new and shining; a surprise package. The block and head were not cast iron, but more like sand-cast aluminum; and he saw the four-barrel carburation. Yes, he mused, the bore and stroke would obviously be greater to beef up horsepower. He moved to the door, peeped inside—stub of stick shift, cluster of instruments, then back to the engine. Designed for high sports car performance, obviously this secret package was to be a cousin to the Corvette or, more distantly perhaps, the E Jag or G. T. Ferrari.

Clearly he'd come upon something that was none of his business; clearly (but belatedly?) Bellgard was planning to enter the horse-power race with Ford, Chrysler and G.M.

Scott was about to crouch down to have a look underneath, when from the garage at the rear, the chauffeur approached, carrying a tool kit and a wad of rags.

"Oh, Mr. Quinnley—say, I thought you were Mr. Stratler." At once he clamped down the hood. "Funny, must've clicked up on me—" The chauffeur's square, Slavic face was aflush, uneasy.

Scott said he'd seen the open hood and had merely "come back to close it." He paused in his improvisation.

"Oh." The chauffeur seemed to accept it.

Scott said good-bye and returned to the front of the house, feeling as if he had participated in an act of crime.

"Hey—!" Ann Smith stood by the white doorway. "Where have you been, Scott? You're late. I nearly gave you up. Did you lose your way?"

"No," Scott said. "I just kept looking for the house with the most Bellgards parked outside."

"I apologize, I thought I'd warned you." She kissed him with unabashed affection. "Come on in. Even my father is anxious to see you."

As he accompanied her inside, Scott realized why he was glad to be with her: for Ann, having known him only in Europe, still saw him within the context of the past. This was important to him. Since he'd come to the city he'd sensed the shape of his identity changing, and the idea disturbed him.

More than that, he thought as they moved through the white hallway, beyond the curving staircase, more than that, being here now, he knew how he would appear to the others: not as Scott Quinnley, but as the son of Red Quinnley. He couldn't help feel that since Red was a rough maverick whose business practices were decidedly on the notorious side, a certain stigma was bound to fall upon him also. He saw his identity merged with that of his father's; and, morally, snobbishly, or on any other grounds, he felt an unshakable resentment of Red, whose character or reputation could reach out to distort that identity.

"There's a whole batch of Bloody Marys." Ann opened the glass doors to the terrace. "Please pour yourself a quart. I'll be right back." She stepped away from him. "How do I look?" She assumed a satirical pose, one hand on her hip, the other languidly behind her head, pelvis drawn in, bosom thrust forward. "It's our new hardtop, with optional overdrive."

"Words fail me," Scott said.

"Is that the best you can do?" She dropped the pose, smoothed down the blond fringe of bangs. She was wearing stretch pants and a thin black turtleneck sweater.

"We'll be right back," she said then. "I've been telling Ben all about you. And if you don't absolutely adore him, I'll never speak to you again!"

"Ben?" he asked, but remembering then what he'd heard night before last when he'd gone out to dinner with Lorie and Phil Rothe.

"I'll go get him," she said. "He's downstairs in the—forgive the expression—recreation room. There's never been any recreation there yet—not until Ben Nodina sailed into my life. Oh, it's wonderful seeing you, Scott. We'll be right up."

Scott moved out to the rear terrace which spanned the central part of the house. A white iron garden table circled by white iron chairs stood nearby. He reached into the silver ice bucket to fix a drink. But he turned then, hearing the voices from beyond the terrace, seeing, to the right of the tennis courts, on the green expanse of property, that a baseball game, or baseball practice, was going on. The diamond was well marked, and there was a wire backstop behind home plate; along one side was what looked like a stone garden house.

Someone was waving to him. The man had left the diamond and was crossing the lawn to the terrace. It was Codman Smith.

"Ann said you were coming. We've been expecting you. How are you, Scott?" Codman Smith shook Scott's hand with cordiality. "Been a long time, hasn't it?" Smith, a big, sinewy man, was wearing faded old pants and a gray sweatshirt. He was holding a bat; his seamed face glowed with perspiration.

There was certainly nothing of the Command Performance here, Scott thought, still rather surprised by this homey spectacle of the backyard ball game.

"How's your father, Scott? Getting back on his feet again?"

"Yes, very much on his feet these days. Maybe too much."

"Well—fine. Best news I've heard. I'm delighted," Codman Smith said.

Like this sight of the Bellgard president in sweatshirt and swinging a baseball bat, the man's quick interest in Red somehow unsettled Scott.

Codman Smith said: "Could you give us a hand out there, Scott? We're shy some men today. I'm sure Ann won't mind if I draft you."

Scott hesitated.

"Come on, young fella," Codman Smith said. "With you on hand we've got even teams. Just a friendly game, we're not trying to outplay the Detroit Tigers—" He turned as another player came up to the terrace: "Oh Tony, this is Red Quinnley's son Scott. Tony Kerwin."

They shook hands. Anthony James Kerwin was Executive Vice-President of Bellgard, and one of Smith's sons-in-law. He was a lively supple man and even the mole on his roseate cheek seemed to contribute to his handsomeness; his gray sweater and chino pants were the worse for wear, though he carried them with a kind of easy elegance.

"I've been telling Scott we need new blood in this game," Smith said.

"We can certainly use it, can't we?" Tony Kerwin focused his winning smile on his father-in-law. Then, belatedly, but with courtesy turned to Scott. "You're enlisted, and don't think we're going to let you get away, Scott."

55]

"Come on, young man," Codman Smith said, adding: "After all, you're part of a big family now."

He could have declined, of course. But he decided not to, and already Codman Smith, grasping his elbow, led him to the lawn. "We'll give you some duds to wear, Scott. And we've got plenty of equipment." He showed Scott to the garden house. Inside there were lockers and a rack of baseball bats, mitts, catcher's masks, caps, even sunglasses. Smith opened one of the lockers and handed him a pair of army pants and a sweatshirt. "I think these will fit you decently enough." Codman Smith and Tony Kerwin stepped outside.

Later, as Scott rejoined the two men and walked to the diamond, Kerwin said: "Ann was telling me this morning that you're going to be taking over Quinnley Corners."

Scott nodded. "Red Quinnley is a hard man to take over from," he said.

"Your father," Codman Smith stated, "was a great institution in this town."

"Yes," Kerwin said, "Red Quinnley was one of the biggest block-busters of all of them."

Codman Smith was met by another player, Dean Stratler, vice-president of styling. Stratler was his second son-in-law, a thin, nervous man whose blond-gray hair was the hue of driftwood. He had light hazel eyes, sparking with alertness. Unlike Tony Kerwin, his playing clothes were neat and well-pressed, though he did not seem to have the sporty *élan* of his brother-in-law. As a designer, Dean Stratler was considered first-rate, though in recent years his work seemed too derivative of what other stylists had done and what the Italians had done long before them; if you looked back to the inspired concepts of Pinin Farina you would often discover years later embarrassing sim-ilarities in the Bellgard product.

"We've just been telling Scott," Codman Smith said, "how much we think of his father."

Dean Stratler nodded. "Red Quinnley. Yes, he's been a remarkable man. Part of the history of this town."

Scott looked at the three men in puzzled reappraisal, struck not only by their admiration for his father, but that they spoke of him almost wistfully in the past tense, the way people talked about dead film idols or about old Henry Ford or P. T. Barnum.

(He also recalled that though Red had telephoned Dean Stratler's

[56

office several times on behalf of Phil Rothe, the man had never returned the call.)

"Scott—" Codman Smith said when they reached the diamond where the other players were clustered, waiting, "I want you to meet the saddest bunch of potbellied ballplayers who ever set foot on first base. Gentlemen, this is Red Quinnley's son, Scott."

Scott found himself uneasily scanning their faces, seeking that hint of curiosity, suspicion, disapproval, seeking in the mirrors of their eyes the true reflection of their opinion of his father's character; for Red, after all, had long used sales tactics which were not only embarrassing to Scott, but surely to the Chamber of Commerce, the Better Business Bureau, and the National Automobile Dealers Association.

But once again he saw nothing; on the contrary, the men were quick to express their admiration for Red; in fact his sales records of the past seemed to have placed him on some high plateau of accomplishment.

Now Codman Smith took Scott around for the handshaking, and he met Ralph Alsop, the Bellgard Public Relations Chief, and Chester Ormond, another high official, and five other vice-presidents. There were only two men from outside the immediate Bellgard group: one was a perspiring man who was Chairman of Vanguard Motors Corporation; "Sunday," Codman Smith said, "is the one day we let competitors in here, and he's the toughest competitor we have." Then: "This is Vincent Eames," and Smith's voice betrayed an almost candid contempt as he introduced the man who manufactured mufflers: "Vince is no ballplayer, but he's one of the hottest peddlers in the industry. He'd try to sell you mufflers even if you were making goat carts in the Swiss Alps." Eames, a pudgy and dapper figure, proudly smiled, accepting Smith's introduction as if he had just received a knighthood.

Sides were chosen then, just a friendly game, Codman Smith said, just an excuse to give everyone a chance to work off the fat. "No coronaries around here, Scott."

It began. Six men on each team: the battery, two infielders who also covered the bases, and two outfielders.

At first Scott enjoyed himself, doing something he hadn't expected. But by the beginning of the third inning, by which time Ann had come to watch, accompanied by Ben Nodina, he found himself tensing up, conscious quite suddenly that the friendly little game was taking on a different dimension. Subtly the need to enjoy friendly play had become secondary to the need to win, to excel, to star.

As Scott's turn at bat came, his teammates, led by Codman Smith, gathered around him: earnest jabs of advice, instructions; warnings of what to expect from the pitcher, Tony Kerwin.

So that he braced himself by the plate, waiting. He saw Kerwin eying him, his ruddy face tight with concentration; he saw the infielders and the outfielders shifting, preparing almost grimly for what might happen.

Tighter silence held the diamond, as if the bases were loaded, the score tied, in the last game of the World Series, Scott's team depending on him to bring home the big money—just as their opponents were now grimly set on winning it for themselves.

Tony Kerwin massaged the ball; he only took his eyes off Scott once, to glance over at Codman Smith, as if to see if his father-in-law was appraising his performance.

Kerwin wound up and pitched. Scott swung and lined the ball toward left field. Dean Stratler started for the catch as Scott ran toward first base. But the ball landed foul, and he returned to home plate.

Immediately, Tony Kerwin called in his team; there was a brief huddle of strategy.

Scott gripped the bat; seeing, with some surprise, that Codman Smith and the others were bent forward stiffly, watching him, waiting.

Now Kerwin's eyes slitted, his mouth drawn in tight resolution. He wound up, and the pitch came in fast but too low. Scott let it pass. Kerwin's frown deepened.

Again Scott shifted his position slightly, as rigid and nerve-tight as if squeezing out a rival driver in contention around a hairpin. He swung and missed.

"Hey, Tony," Ann called out, "that's no way to be hospitable! Scott's my guest. I want him to come back again."

Kerwin turned, his acknowledging smile brief, gracious.

But Ann's interruption, coming when it did, eased Scott's tension. He connected with the next pitch, a single to left center.

"Good boy!" Codman Smith cried out.

Now Smith was up, and now Kerwin seemed even grimmer as he faced his father-in-law, as if he feared the older man's esteem of him might rise or fall by his performance in this crucial instant. Codman Smith waited calmly, the blue-green eyes narrowing as he measured Kerwin's windup. He let three balls pass, and then there was that sharp, clean connection as he slugged out a two-base hit, and Scott made it all the way around, skidding into home plate, bringing in the extra run, the score now two to one.

Clearly a new crisis was born: Tony Kerwin summoned his team for another conference. Then he faced another Bellgard vice-president, and the chill climate of the game grew perceptibly colder. The man hit a fly ball but Dean Stratler out in left field muffed the catch, and Kerwin shook his head like a martyr.

The final score gave it to Scott's team, five to four.

When everyone had showered and changed clothes, the air became easy again, or comparatively easy. Tony Kerwin made some joke about wooing Scott to the other team for next Sunday's match.

"No," Codman Smith said as he, Kerwin and Stratler moved across the lawn with Scott, "this fella is my find, and I expect him next time, best infielder we've had around, and he can slug."

Next Sunday, Scott thought, he would make some pretense to arrive too late. Or, most likely, not at all.

But Codman Smith, as if perceiving his thoughts, tapped him on the shoulder: "I'm counting on you, Scott. Eleven o'clock, a week from today."

Tony Kerwin, who had taken on the face of an enemy during the game, spoke up, warmly and with infinite cordiality: "Maybe you'd better stay home, Scott. You gave me some rough moments there—but then it's the rough ones I thrive on." He had already turned from Scott, so that the last half of the statement was addressed directly to Codman Smith.

They reached the terrace, there was a parting of the ways now: the other men went into the big house. Only Codman Smith remained, walking with Scott to the white garden table where Ann was sitting with Ben Nodina. "Thank you for your support, Scott," the man said. "Expect you next Sunday. Give my best to your father, will you?" But Smith did not leave. "Sorry, Ann—" he said to his daughter. "Forgive me for snatching your guest like that."

"I certainly won't." Ann put down her glass. "That was a foul trick."

Codman Smith blotted his high forehead with a large white

59]

handkerchief. "Well, I've returned him intact, and you can make up for my rudeness." For the first time he acknowledged the presence of Ben Nodina. "Morning, Ben."

"Morning, Mr. Smith," Ben Nodina said.

But Smith had already turned back to Scott. With a charm that was not cloying, he said: "I want you to feel you're welcome here any time, Scott. You're sticking around for a while, I trust. After the girls are back from church, we'll all have a bite."

"You see," Ann said when her father had gone, "I forgot to tell you we're still on the old image. Mr. and Mrs. Everyone." A faint belligerence attended her outburst, as if she had to compensate for her father's frosty manner toward Ben. "I mean the Smith family is supposed to be your neighbor next door, just plain folks, that's us."

"I don't know," Scott said. "I saw those pictures in *Life*, and I said to myself, now there's a girl who has both feet on the ground and knows the value of a dollar."

"Oh it's simply wonderful having you here, Scott, it really is," Ann said. "You will come again, won't you? Next Sunday." She paused. "Of course, now that you're back, we'll be leaving."

"Oh?" Scott said.

"Ben and I are going to Greece," Ann said.

"You never told me," Scott said. "When?"

"Soon as his divorce is—" But Ann looked across the terrace and waved to someone, calling out: "Hey, Jemmy—!" When the house guest reached the table, Ann said: "Scott, this is Jennifer Thompson." A tall, drowsy-eyed girl with straight black hair. She was holding a cup of coffee. Nature with a generous and compensatory balance had given her a body which made the beholder unaware of her unpretty face. "I used to spend half my vacations from Smith at Jemmy's place," Ann was saying. "Not a single male in her house was in the automobile industry."

"They are now." Jennifer Thompson said her father, a former professor at the University of Michigan, was working for a Chicago market survey company. "He analyzes public opinion polls to find out what people want or don't want in a car."

"Didn't someone do that for the Edsel once?" Ann said.

Jennifer Thompson put down her now empty cup. She palmed back her dark hair. To Scott then: "Could I interest you in convoying me back to the dining room for some more coffee?"

But then the other women appeared, and Scott was introduced to

Ann's mother, and the two sisters, Myra and Phoebe, and to another guest, a pink-cheeked young clergyman, Reverend Cass.

"We insisted on bringing Mr. Cass along for dinner," Ann's mother said.

Ann said. "Let me pour you a Bloody Mary, Mr. Cass. You must be bushed after your sermon. Tell me," Ann went on cheerfully to the clergyman as soon as Mrs. Smith had gone, "how was attendance today? I'll bet you count the house, don't you?"

"Indeed I do," he said. "And it wasn't too bad. But you know how busy the men of this community can be—even on Sunday."

"You know what," Ann said, "I'll bet you'd draw bigger crowds if you put a shining new car up there beside the altar."

The clergyman accepted this amiably enough, but then a silence was born.

Scott turned to Jennifer Thompson. "Why don't we get you some coffee?"

"Why don't we?" She picked up her cup, and Scott accompanied her into the house.

5: Ann Smith

MOST of the young wives and daughters of Kent Hills, and many of the older ones too, convened once a week at Kent Lanes, a bowling alley built at a cost of one and a half million dollars to accommodate what Ann called the W.W.'s—Widows of Wheelville.

It was here that she drove on this Monday morning because she knew her mother and her two sisters would be together, and what she had to say, had to be said to all of them.

She hurried into the building to which the general public was not admitted: members paid a yearly fee to keep this oasis of exercise as their own preserve. To elevate the tone of the popular indoor sport, the management had resorted to many measures: the alleys were known as "lanes"; the gutters were called "channels"; the beauty shop had a French name; the large snack-room was named "The Ten-Pin Coffeehouse"; and there was the "Terrace Restaurant" and the "Rub-a-Dub Massage Parlor." As for the bowling area itself—"The Futurama Bowl"—it had thirty-six lanes. It was electronically operated, neon-lighted, and air-conditioned. To add a flourish of chic, the building committee had imported a decorator from New York.

"Why, Ann—" Mrs. Codman Smith looked up from the table in the coffee shop, "what on earth are you doing here?" Her mother's still-youthful face was wreathed in surprise, even pleasure. "Sit down, Ann. What would you like?"

"Nothing, thank you." Ann settled herself in the semicircle of the red-leathered booth. The entire wall across the room was decorated with a black and white photomural showing all the automobiles existing at the turn of the century.

"Do have some coffee, darling," her sister Myra said.

Ann shook her head; she took out her pack of cigarettes. She'd arrived precisely at the right time, midmorning, when the women after their first round of bowling took their coffee-break. Her mother and her other sister Phoebe were wearing slacks; Myra wore a skirt. All three women had cardigans draped across their shoulders.

She lit her cigarette. This would be a battle, another one, and she dreaded it.

"Well, have *something,* Ann." Phoebe Smith Kerwin dipped her spoon into the mound of Dr. Hover's Vita-Health Yogurt. "Or try this. They have it here now. I got them to order it. Not an ounce of butter fat and it's so good too, does wonders for your intestines and your complexion." Her eldest sister, having been very plump during her teens, had become obsessive about her weight. Now, at thirty-nine, Phoebe had dieted enough, fretted enough, exercised enough and been massaged enough to achieve her goal. "Why don't you try some, Ann?"

"No thanks, Phoebe." She said: "I'm in no mood for yogurt."

"Oh, you've always been so lucky," Phoebe said. "You and that husband of mine. Tony could eat whipped cream all day and still—"

"Look—" Ann was so intent on speaking up that even Phoebe's soliloquy about health and yogurt, which at times had the lyrical passion of a TV testimonial, failed to amuse or divert her. "I came by because there's something I want to get off my chest—"

"Darling." Her other sister, Myra, smiled at her. "Then why not get on with it?" she said, evoking another of those cliché British expressions for which she'd developed a fondness, finding in their familiar music something which she believed set her apart from the easy, unpretentious Midwest informality of her friends. "We have another lane reserved for half-past eleven." Myra Smith Stratler, unlike Phoebe, needed no exercise to remain slender because her nervous system was in a constant state of conflict; the thrusts and tensions of her emotions kept her body supple and attractive. It was her oval face which betrayed her age, for it was beginning to grow gaunt. She was thirty-seven.

"Do you have to get Downtown now?" Myra was saying. "Why don't you bowl with us for a bit, Ann? Then we can have a nice old-fashioned chat afterward. We're going to the club for lunch—"

Ann saw the smile, friendly, determined. Not natural. For Myra and Ann had more or less stopped communicating with each other years ago. Once Ann had absolutely worshiped her; that had been when she'd been thirteen, and Myra twenty-five; that had been when Ann had tried to imitate her in dress and manner, when she'd confided in her and when Myra had now and then returned the confidence.

63]

Myra had been at the zenith then: popular and admired. Curiously, what broke the bond between them was that Myra, whose scholastic record had been inadequate, failed to get into Smith College; whereas, later, Ann made it without any difficulty, and also took her third year at the Sorbonne.

After that the line became drawn between them. If Ann was the only member of the Smith family to go to Smith, Myra set out to dominate in another area. She became a forceful leader in the society of the community; she took on the ambitions of her father, seeing in his rise in the industry a path for her to parallel. Since, unlike Ann, she had to remain in the strictest sense "a local girl," she'd turned her unwanted status into a kind of virtue or asset; her desire became to create a superior race within the Motor City, to show that she, like the city, had emerged from its drab, gauche past; that she and the city could rise to heights of social and cultural levels that had to be recognized. One of the main reasons she'd married Dean Stratler had been because he held the same beliefs, and because he seemed to complement her image of herself: Dean Stratler was "artistic." She would say: "After all, Dean is a designer, he's not just another third-floor executive." Though she soon discovered this to be less than true, she still did not regret the marriage, for Dean did have a way, a façade, which Myra admired.

As Ann knew, however, Myra's marriage was in fact held together only by certain of these external elements. The truth was that Dean's obsession with work, which Myra so approved, had left her emotionally bare and stranded, and she'd begun to look elsewhere. Yet, consistent with her nature, she confined her interests to men whose social position in the community seemed impeccable. She might have preferred men of another type, but as Ann often thought (and once told her), she had to be "a snob even in bed."

"What's the matter, Ann?" Myra was saying now, "you haven't got a hangover, have you? If you have it doesn't show. You're blessed with one of those divine faces that thrive no matter what." Myra paused, turned to regard herself in the wall mirror. She was wearing a wide violet band across her light hair, but it had the effect of making her appear more coy than youthful; it reflected, accented, the shadowed hues beneath her wide eyes. She looked across at Ann: "Ann, you're not on the warpath again?"

"Yes," Ann said.

[64

"Well," Myra smiled, though faint apprehension scored her voice, "I can face up to it, if you can."

"Can't it wait, Ann?" Mrs. Codman Smith said.

"I came here to bowl, not to have another row," Phoebe said, and glancing anxiously to the adjacent booth: "We're not alone, you know."

"Fortunately," Mrs. Smith observed, "they're leaving now."

"Oh—hello, there!" Myra called to the two women (Chrysler, Plymouth).

"It's nothing new—" Ann inhaled deeply on her cigarette, "but after yesterday, it was just too much. The way all of you behaved toward Ben was unforgivable, absolutely unforgivable, and if you were trying to crush Ben you damn near succeeded."

"Why Ann," her mother said, "how can you say that? Ben sat next to me at dinner, between me and Myra, and we—"

"You both might have been sitting next to a leper!" Ann said. "You talked the whole time to Scott Quinnley."

"Aren't you being unfair? Mother and I only chatted with Scott now and then," Myra said.

"Yes," Mrs. Smith said. "He's new here and we only wanted to make him feel at home." Waving then: "Hello, Betty." (Wife of Pontiac Public Relations.)

"That's true," Myra said affably. "He seemed quiet or shy, and I felt—"

"You felt what?" Ann broke in. "How can you look me in the face and tell me you weren't deliberately cutting Ben? He happens not to care, at least he says he doesn't. But I do. When he's at the house, I expect my family to show the commonest kind of garden variety politeness even if it kills them. You're always saying: 'Ann, why don't you stay at home, why do you have to run a mile out of your way to stay away from us?' But all that's forgotten when I have Ben there!" She saw the exchange flashing between the three women.

"Ann darling," Myra said, "I can understand your being sensitive, I was like that when I used to have Dean at the house. But really, it's all in your imagination."

"It surely is, Ann," Phoebe agreed at once. "Purely in your mind."

"Oh nuts," Ann said. "All of you didn't have to make it so obvious how you felt. I know how you feel, this stupid prejudice you have against Ben just because he happens not to fit in with your picture of what you'd like to see in the family album! As if we had anything special to be so proud of!"

"Now Ann," her mother said.

"I think"—Myra smiled, her voice almost purring with sympathy— "I think Ann has some foolish idea that we care about Ben's background. Of course, you know, Ann, we don't care a whit. After all, if one objected to people merely because they happened to come from Italian honkytonk or because their father had been a bootlegger or associated with gangsters—well, a lot of us in this town would be hard put to select their friends. Don't you agree, Mother? Don't you, Phoebe?"

"Well . . ." Phoebe pursed her thin lips, hesitating, not quite ready to join the game.

"I can't say I'm a great admirer of Ben Nodina," her mother said. "I only say, since the subject has come up, that your father and I think you deserve something better."

"That's nonsense," Myra made the gesture in Ann's defense, "parents always think their children deserve something better. Actually, you have to admire Ben. He's not ashamed of what he is, he even goes out of his way to tell stories about it—colorful stories, I'll admit, but you can't help admiring a man like that."

Ann refused to let that pass: "I don't remember, Myra, ever hearing you tell colorful stories about how your grandfather ran that junky, dubious Used-Tire store on Bush Street."

"All this is beside the point," Mrs. Smith asserted.

"The point is," Ann had to say then, "that God created Bellgard and Bellgard created us, and I'm fouling it up because I'm marrying a man who won't look True Blue on the Board."

"Ann!" Her mother protested.

"Well," Phoebe put aside her bowl of Dr. Hover's yogurt, "to be perfectly practical about matters, Ann—Tony told me—"

"What did Tony tell you?" Ann said, again chafing with impatience at Phoebe's echoing refrain; Phoebe, whose only authority on all world issues, was her husband.

"Tony did say that Ben's wife is being very vindictive about a divorce. It *is* going to be messy, Tony says."

"You can tell Tony for me—" Ann began, thwarted, regretting having come here, feeling again closed in, squeamish and ugly, as the old in-fighting rose hatefully to the surface.

[66

"No, I doubt if she's going to be vindictive," Myra offered. "She's merely being sensible, as I understand it. She has some idea that we'll set Ben up lavishly, and naturally you can't blame her for holding out for a whopping big settlement."

"That happens to be absolutely untrue!" Ann said. "They haven't even been living together for a year. She has an income of her own and as for Ben, he's doing awfully well. My God, he makes industrial films, not only for us but for two of the biggest—he's never mentioned the subject of money. In fact, if you'd like to know the one thing I don't like about him, it's his reluctance to discuss money with me at all!"

"Well," Myra spoke lightly, glancing again into the mirror, "no man, certainly not a paragon like Ben Nodina, would be tactless enough to discuss finances before he was part of the family—"

"You mean like Dean?" Ann had to say.

"Dean, in case you've forgotten," Myra raised her voice for the first time, "Dean was making fifty thousand a year before we got married."

Yes, Ann thought, and she could have said, among other things, that as soon as Dean's engagement to Myra had become official, he'd shut down his offices, left all his employees suddenly jobless, doing it in this manner not only because he was taking on the vice-presidency of Bellgard's styling department, but because he hoped to eliminate all further competition from those employees who might get together to form a new firm. The abrupt sweep of his maneuver had succeeded.

"And also"—Myra stepped quickly into the silence—"let's not forget that Dean's reputation was impeccable, you never heard any of those rumors around town—not that you can believe everything that you hear here—I mean, if one believed everything about Ben—"

"Like what?" Ann was almost trembling with anger.

"Oh, it's too absurd to even repeat," Myra said. "It's probably sheer nonsense."

"Not according to Tony." Phoebe's frown was troubled, her mouth in a prim pucker. "Tony says that Ben's become—well, positively indifferent to the way he guards material that's supposed to be confidential. Tony says Ben is so anxious to make a pile before quitting, he doesn't even—well, he says when they were shooting that film for us—they were photographing our new rear suspension system, I think it was, and Tony says that Ben's studio was like open-house week, I mean, anyone from Ford or G.M. or anywhere, could just walk in—"

"Really? You mean that, Phoebe?" Myra seemed startled, dismayed. "Are you sure?"

"Of course she's sure," Ann burst in, "she got it from On High, didn't she?"

"I can't believe it." Myra now spoke soothingly, she touched the violet hair band, addressing not Ann but her own reflection in the mirror. "I'm sure Ben Nodina knows better than to let out any information among competitors, even though he's planning to take off for Greece—no, it's simply that everyone in this business is too touchy. Ben wouldn't be that stupid. Let's at least give the poor man his due."

Ann knew she was losing hold of her resolve, and she didn't care. "Okay," she said, "we won't hold up Ben to my two honorable brothers-in-law. Dean is one hundred percent True Blue. And so is Tony. Tony is even *two* hundred percent True Blue."

Phoebe blinked. "What is that supposed to mean, Ann?"

"Yes, exactly what? I'd like to know, too." Myra said.

"That'll be enough." Mrs. Smith insisted.

But Phoebe, leaning forward from the lofty ramparts of her indignation, demanded: "No, let her say it, I dare her to say anything about Tony!" She blinked again, facing Ann: "Well, why don't you say it?"

"Do I have to?" Ann said. "Am I the only one who saw Tony and Vince Eames in that dogfight last night? The Reck Room was shaking, the way they were going at it, it started right after the ball game and never let up, except during dinner."

"Vince Eames was drinking too much—" Phoebe said at once.

"All I know," Ann said, "is that Bellgard is giving Vince Eames another muffler contract and a lot of people around town seem to think it ain't cricket."

"I beg your pardon!" Phoebe's thin voice cracked with indignation. "People only talk because Tony and Vince happened to be partners once, but everyone knows Tony has no more connection with him, he sold out his interests years ago when he went with Father. Anyway, Eames has been making those units for Bellgard for years, it's practically a tradition, like Champion Spark Plugs, and if Tony approved the contract you can be sure it's because—"

"That'll be enough, enough!" Mrs. Smith cried out.

"I should think so." Myra leaned back regarding Ann and Phoebe with a censorious eye, for Myra finding herself free and above the sordid battle, finding the wave of recriminations receding from her,

[68

looked very pleased, sitting there now, a quiet and demure ally of her mother.

"Ann began this," Phoebe went on, "and I'm not going to let it end without—"

"I said this was enough!" Mrs. Smith said, and gazed around her. "If your father heard the way you—we've been talking—" She paused. Soberly, quietly, changing her course, she said: "Ann, I want you to listen to this, I want all of you to listen." Mrs. Smith brought an agitated finger to the strand of pearls around her throat. "We can have no more of this, but no more. There *are* certain problems—your father would never let it be seen, you know how he is—but problems *have* come up, serious ones. And by the time of the next stockholders' meeting—"

"Oh, really, Mother," Ann protested. "I've been hearing that ever since I first wet my panties. Annual stockholders' meeting. Every year the same stupid jitters and no one can open his mouth."

"This year it's different," Mrs. Smith said.

"All right. So be it," Ann said. "I came here to ask everyone to please keep their hands off my life from now on. I assure you my marrying Ben will in no way affect the high destiny of the Bellgard Motor Company—or the proxy fight that's probably starting up in a lot of dirty little corners."

"Ann," her mother said.

"I've never understood you, Ann," Myra said. Abandoning her earlier pretense of friendliness, forsaking even her oblique attempts to undermine her, she added: "There's no excuse for this attitude of yours. Exactly who do you think you are that you can afford to stand aside and flaunt any idea that comes into your head? You don't care who you hurt or what you—"

"This town has been very good to us, Ann," Phoebe reprised the sturdy family slogan. "And the least you can do—"

"I'm sorry." Ann's voice was unsteady. "I can't help it. I can't stand any of it, not anymore!"

"I know how you feel, dear." Her mother reached out for her hand, pressed it in feeble reassurance. "I know how you are. You've always taken too much to heart." She released her hand. "But Ann, for your father's sake—"

"Yes," Phoebe stated, "but she doesn't think of anyone except herself. She holds up a yardstick to everyone else, but her own reputation—that's different!"

"My reputation!" Ann answered. "What is that supposed to be exactly? All I've ever done is try to correct some of my stupid mistakes. And"—she turned to her two sisters—"that's better than marrying them!" Before they could retaliate, she went on: "So please keep your hands off my life. It was absolutely disgusting yesterday, the way all of you—not only you, but Dean and Tony and even Father—fussed over Scott Quinnley just to cut Ben. I happen to be very fond of Scott. Very. But that doesn't blind me to why everyone was suddenly making such a fuss over him. Even Scott was bugged by it. He as much as told me so. He's very sensitive about his father, but even Red Quinnley's reputation didn't seem to bother anyone, did it? No. All that counted was that Scott is new, new blood. He happens to be honest, so everyone was trying to snatch on to him, graft on to themselves what they haven't got. It wasn't only because of Ben—it's deeper than that. It's because everyone is so damn shaky and scared, that when they meet someone like Scott Quinnley who still has no fish to fry and who for some crazy reason still thinks the automobile can be a decent product—everyone clutches on to him. It was incredible the way they took him on, even listened to him, they weren't afraid to ask him what was wrong with this year's line or what he feels about the—oh, it was absolutely sickening, and all I could think of was Faust and the Devil—I think I'll have a drink." She signaled for the waitress. She slumped back against the red leather banquette. "Oh, I feel utterly hateful, why does it always have to be so ugly and hateful?"

Her weary final question sealed a silence among them.

She stared at them: she saw the melancholy way her mother looked at her; she saw in Phoebe's eyes that the pale smug light of innocence had dimmed; but it was Myra who, in that hovering instant, looked the most changed, as if suddenly her darkest, inward thoughts had seeped through the pores of her face, bringing to it, curiously, an ineffable beauty which Ann hadn't seen in a long time.

And Ann, floundering now between her regret at having come here and her relief at having tried to cleanse herself of her grievances, remained rigidly slumped in the seat, like an old woman who has lived too long to expect human beings to alter their ways. . . . Yet, that was absurd, she told herself, absurd and futile; she wasn't that old or that readily resigned, and couldn't she see that what she'd said had some kind of impact on her mother and her sisters?

At least she had the consolation of knowing there was Ben, and that maybe before next Christmas she'd be in Athens, and even if Ben couldn't be free, she'd still go with him to Athens, she'd go anywhere . . .

Yes.

She stirred, and there was a moment in which she felt that her spirit had been recharged, and then she saw that the self-questing silence of the others was over, and that their faces were abruptly taking on the familiar hues again: for now at the adjacent table two young women with their two little children had just arrived.

Immediately there was waving and greeting to the group.

"Hi, Eva—how are you?" Phoebe called to the first woman (wife of a Ford engineer).

"Hello, Helen," Myra greeted the second woman (husband also with Ford).

"Just about ready to drop," the woman answered. "Wait till you see that score we ran up. That'll give you something to shoot for. I think you've got our lane next, haven't you?"

"Yes—" Myra rose at once, paused before the mirror and retied the violet band around her hair. "So we have."

"Won't you stay, Ann?" Mrs. Smith and Myra and Phoebe rose.

Ann crushed out her cigarette. No, she said to her mother's gesture of truce, she couldn't stay, she was on her way to have lunch with Ben Nodina.

She was alone then, and when the waitress came over, she said, absently, she'd like a brandy. But it was too early, the waitress reminded her, the bar wasn't open yet. "Is there something else you'd like, Miss Smith?"

"What?"

From the next booth: "Wouldn't you just know it? Ted called and said he wouldn't get home for dinner—another late session with the U.A.W."

"Coffee or Coke—" the waitress was saying.

"No. Never mind. Thank you." Ann picked up her bag and gloves, and rose to leave.

"Hi, Ann," called a woman passing (husband a vice-president at Chevrolet).

6: Scott Quinnley

THAT spring the poets of the auto companies piped their lyrics, and the word went out to the nation.

Everywhere in America the roads ringing the cities, suburbs and countryside grew even thicker with traffic, the sweet blue air was deliciously choked by the fumes from the single and dual exhaust stacks, the now less discreet lines of chrome captured the sun's rays, the great wraparound windshields were aglitter with golden light and the optional wire wheels were like spinning galaxies.

The seasonal uptrend had begun, and optimism was rampant and justified. Except for certain companies. Like Bellgard. And hence for certain dealerships. Like Quinnley Corners.

By now Scott Quinnley was no longer a novitiate, nor was he a veteran, but he had a better grasp on the framework of his father's enterprise. Living with the ways of the dealership from early morning to late evening, every day, he'd only been absent from business a short time in April when he'd flown to New York and brought Suzy back with him. The last lap. And the move lifted from him the protective mantle of the newcomer and left him exposed to the harsh weather of the permanent resident. For a while, with Suzy at the house in Greenwood Park, his father took off more time; a three-year-old granddaughter gave him much pleasure; he took her for walks and rides and he bought her extravagant gifts, mostly toys and dolls, as well as a whole line of miniature plastic models of Bellgard cars. But this kind of domestic harmony was alien to Red, and to work off his restlessness, he began to play more golf, reestablish bonds with old friends who were in better condition than he was and whose capacity for liquor he tried to match.

Yet, like the spring season, Red's best intentions were not enduring.

One May day Scott undertook to make two major changes in Quinnley Corners' operation: the first, to reorganize the Service Department; the second—and the more serious—to try to reduce the suffocating monthly quota of new cars from the factory. In the middle of the morning he was summoned to Red's office.

Red was bent over his great walnut desk, his mane of russet hair even more wild than usual; his head was tilted, he concentrated on his specially installed sound system. He kept muttering in small bursts of agony as he listened in on a transaction transpiring in one of the salesmen's booths.

He looked up, motioned for Scott to come over. "You'll see what I mean, I want you to get this. Sit down."

"Red—right now, I have to talk to you about—"

"Right now I want you to sit down, I want you to get this, I don't give a goddam that you think it's unnecessary, it's the only way you're ever going to get the real feel of how a sale can—"

"It's something I happen not to—" Scott began.

"I know," his father said. "You've told me. But get those ideas out of your head. This isn't 'spying' or 'demoralizing.' " Red threw back his son's earlier words. "Every man on the crew knows we listen in; it's the only way you can keep track of what's going on."

"I have to talk to you about the Service—"

"Service? For good almighty Christ, son, we're going to get the entire June quota pushed in on us. Don't talk to me about service now. Something else you don't know, is that I just heard McGregor is coming by at three o'clock." Halister McGregor was the Bellgard Regional Sales Manager.

"Yes, I know," Scott said.

"You know?"

"I called him," Scott said.

"You *what?*" Red switched off the sound box. "Did I hear you right?"

"Yes, I called him. I want to see him. I want to get a cutback on the quota now, not in June."

Red's eyes widened, bulged. He opened his mouth as if to emit another roar. Scott stepped closer to the desk, stood facing him, knowing that sometimes a calm, resolute silence could cool his wrath.

"All right—" Red reconsidered. "Let's see how far you get with him. You don't know McGregor. He's a two-fisted, cast-iron sonofabitch who doesn't admit the dealer is alive, he thinks the dealer is a goddam number. He'll goose you with his gab and his charts and graphs, and if that doesn't work, he pulls muscle!"

73]

But having delivered himself of these sentiments, Red turned away; he even looked relieved. "All right, son." He pressed a lever of the sound box, listened in for an instant, switched it off, tuned in then on another sales booth. Slowly a smile began to blossom on his flushed face. "Ah. Listen to Dave Toff. He's capping it. He'd better!"

"—to tell the truth, sir," Salesman Toff's voice was honeyed with conspiracy, "this is confidential, between us. It's my wife's birthday today, and I don't mind telling you—man to man—I'm out for my commission. Very frankly, I'm going to have to see the boss, I'm going to try to get this price for you. I don't have to tell you, Mr. Arken, that we're going to have to absorb the excise tax, state tax and transport costs to let the car go at a rock-bottom figure like that. But let me try." Dave Toff's voice came urgently through the sound box. "Let me try. If the boss is in a glad mood, well—here, have a cigarette, Mr. Arken. And keep your fingers crossed. I'll go tackle the boss now."

Salesman Toff, as Red pointed out now, would only go to the Men's Room.

After a tantalizing silence, Toff's voice burst afresh from the sound box: "Mr. Arken—this must be your day, you must have a little of the Irish in you. The boss, he said go ahead. If I quoted you that price, which I shouldn't have done, he said we are honor-bound to stick to it—"

"Well . . ." Arken's words came slowly, thoughtfully. "I was thinking . . ."

Red slapped his palm down against the desk top: "I knew it! Toff stayed out too long!"

"I was thinking," Mr. Arken was saying in a dry, deceptively backwoods way, "before I rush into this, I'd better talk it over with my brother, we're going in on this together. He's sick, in bed with a bad leg—he'll like the price I think, but—well, as I said out there in the showroom, my brother likes a car sporty, and I remember now he said something about he wants bucket seats—"

"Bucket seats?" Toff's voice was heavy with dismay. "But Mr. Arken, they're optional extras on that particular model. Do you know what they cost? And at the price I quoted you, sir—"

"Seems to me," Arken went on, "that it's supposed to be a kind of sports car anyway, isn't it? I mean it's called The Santa Barbara isn't it? I meant to ask you, is that because this model was tested on the Santa Barbara speedway?"

"Say, can't be said you don't know your sports world, can it, Mr. Arken?" Toff replied, nimbly blurring the truth which was that the car was given its name merely to create in the public's mind an image of sporting danger, a hint of hot racetrack performance, a flavor of Ferrari, a whiff of scorched rubber.

"Well, not me so much. It's my brother," Mr. Arken answered with a gnawing persistency. "That's why I don't know for sure if I ought to rush into this without bucket—"

Immediately Red swung around, snatched up the interoffice telephone, pressed a button. You could hear over the sound box the steady buzz in the sales booth.

"Yes?" Toff answered the call.

"Mr. Toff—" Red spoke in a brisk, impersonal way, "you're wanted in Service." Red hung up, and at once called another booth. "Fogarty, get into number sixteen for the T.O. The Santa Barbara, quote is $2,810.00. But it's no sale without the buckets. Have to do it."

Red frowned, muttered to Scott: "Have to do it. No out, cuts the daylight down to under one percent! But what are you going to do?" He flicked his finger toward the large metal reference file. "I know about Arken. He's a pincher, he plays it dumb like a hick. But he's sharp as a pickle, runs a chain of Hamburger-Drive-Ins, and he'll bird-dog for us. It's worth the loss." Red now pressed the lever, tuning in again on booth sixteen.

And now Al Fogarty's gravelly voice came over for the Face-Saving, Bargain-Boosting gambit: "I'm Al Fogarty, sir. Mr. Toff asked me to apologize, he's been called out, but he explained the situation and I think I know how it stands." Then: "Mr. Arken, can I say something? Dave Toff is one of our best men—and a good friend of mine. But all's fair in love and war, as they say. If I can give you an edge on a deal, I'm certainly going to try. I know you'll drive off in that Santa Barbara if it has bucket seats. And, well, I'm willing to take my own personal loss and close the deal at the quoted price—mind you, *including* the bucket seats. I'm willing to take the consequences from the boss. And I also know you won't go back to Toff and tell him. This will have to be strictly between you and me. Now would you say I'm trying to give you a package you couldn't buy anywhere else? That's the policy of Quinnley Corners. Could you ask for anything fairer, sir?"

"No, fair enough, I guess," admitted Mr. Arken.

"Good!" Fogarty cried. "You've got a deal. Naturally, we'd better get those papers signed pronto, because what's a deal today, isn't always a deal tomorrow. And while the boss is—"

"I was thinking—" Mr. Arken said, "what about backup lights? I have to have those."

From Red a sibilant breath of exasperation: "And they say *I'm* a bandit! Some of these bastards, these customers, make me look like Santa Claus! Backup lights!"

Something Marty Calhoon had told Scott two weeks ago, came back to him now: "You can see what's happening," Calhoon had said, "it used to be that we had to be bandits because the factory was a bandit. Now, it's filtered down to the customers, they're getting so larcenous I don't know how to beat it anymore, they're getting so's they're sharper than we are. Where's it going to end?"

"Backup lights?" Fogarty groaned. "That's an extra."

"Well," Arken said, "if this is the kind of model they used on the Santa Barbara track, seems to me it ought to have—"

"Mr. Arken," Fogarty said, "you're giving us a hard time today, aren't you?"

"Me?" Arken retorted with masterly innocence. "No, I just sort of assumed with this kind of car, those lights would be standard. Otherwise I wouldn't—"

"Mr. Arken, can you bear with me for a moment?" Al Fogarty's patience seemed raw. "I'm afraid I'll have to confer with Mr. Quinnley himself—"

But before the salesman had finished speaking, Red had left the desk, stepped out into the showroom and darted into the narrow glass-walled corridor along which the booths were lined; he paused at number sixteen just long enough to give Fogarty the nod.

"We got him," Red announced when he returned to the office. "And I'll tell you something: if I could get that Arken on our sales force, I'd have the hottest man in town, the sonofabitch'll walk off with the furniture and fixtures before he leaves here!"

To his surprise Scott had become so absorbed in the series of sales ploys, so hopeful of a victory against customer Arken, that he scarcely gave thought to the real nature of the transaction or the sacrifice made in order to gain the sale.

Red looked at him. "Our profit on that Santa Barbara? Any idea what it is?"

Scott shook his head.

"About twenty-two dollars. Net," Red stated. "But it's a question of moving the backlog or letting the inventory swamp us." From his breast pocket he brought forth a fresh cigar.

Scott said: "That's why I've got McGregor coming here."

"You've got him, he'll be your baby." Red lit his cigar, rose.

"Red—" Scott detained him. He laid out the plan for the reorganization of the Service Department. And afterward, approving the plan, Red went into the garage and within less than half an hour returned with the Service Manager's cooperation and goodwill in his pocket, where Scott himself had failed that morning.

At three o'clock, when Bellgard's Regional Sales Manager appeared, Red had still not gone; it was as if he had to stay to witness the truth of his prophecy.

"Mr. M.," he said to McGregor, "I'm a sick man. My son here is the boss. He's the one you're going to have to do business with today."

Halister McGregor, a burly figure in white (suit, shirt and tie), featured a big, shining, indefatigable smile enclosed by deep grooves that curved down into his hearty jowls; his face had become suntanned and wind-whipped, for he drove his Bellgard convertible with the top down, speeding across the open plains of his Midwest territory, making the rounds from dealer to dealer: his very manhood seemed to be potently directed at the wombs of his vast harem of dealerships.

"Mr. Quinnley"—he was shaking Scott's hand, gripping the fingers with fierce friendliness—"I've been looking forward to meeting you, looking forward. Been hearing excellent things about you, and let me say how happy I am to welcome you to the team, I want to welcome you. I want to tell you that your father was, is, a dealer the entire company is proud of—"

"Come on, Mr. M., you don't have to give out all that horseshit here," Red said. "We know each other too well, don't we?"

"Red, I see you're back in form." To Scott then: "Whenever I'm up against some dealer who thinks he's having troubles, I always hold up Red Quinnley as an example. All ginger and firecrackers. Sit down, boys, let's talk."

Red relit the soggy stub of cigar as McGregor settled himself into a chair which flanked Red's desk.

"I wasn't planning to hit Quinnley Corners until day after tomorrow," McGregor was saying. "But your son here sent out such a hot S.O.S. I made the detour." He tilted his gray-haired head toward Scott. "My office passed on the word, radio-telephoned me the word while I was on the road, beelining for Kalamazoo."

Scott cleared his throat. "What I wanted to discuss with you, Mr. McGregor, was—"

"Let me guess," the man said. "You want the factory to increase your monthly quota, you're going to try to get the factory to ship you more cars. Right?"

"No." But Scott was foolishly unsettled by the maneuver.

"Tell you a secret." McGregor had already pursued his momentary advantage. "You haven't got a chance, my boy, we can't ship you more units, everything at the factory and all the assembly plants is quota-set. We can't stop the body-pressings, not now. From Detroit to Duluth, the dealerships are socking the competition, and the spring upturn is proving Bellgard's got the edge, the edge."

From McGregor's sunny pronouncement, uttered with such dynamic conviction, it was hard to believe the darker truths: that since 1960, dealer failures were up 43 percent; or that during the past winter one of the biggest dealers of Denver, Colorado, had closed his doors; or that in Cicero, Illinois, bankruptcy proceedings were underway against Bellgard's principal dealership. "I'm not as optimistic as you are, Mr. McGregor," Scott said then. "And I know we're not the only dealership feeling the pinch."

"My friend," McGregor said, "from where you sit it's understandable you might get the blues once in a while, and sure here and there we know there are men chickening out. But let me say that from my wheel, I see the entire picture and let me say it looks mighty good. Mighty. Bellgard's earnings for the first quarter this year was over five million dollars. Now I'd say that doesn't sound like the public isn't endorsing the product. What would you say, my boy?"

Scott found himself stiffening against the man's barrage: "I can only talk about our operation here."

The Regional Sales Manager closed his eyes while his smile lingered in a bemused kind of way: "For example?"

"For one thing, the balance between the units on hand, plus the monthly factory quota, is out of all reasonable proportion to the demand. It's insane to think that by—"

"Now wait a minute, son—" It was Red who, to Scott's astonishment, was speaking up. "Let's not forget that, tough as it was, Quinnley Corners sold nearly two hundred units this past month."

[78

"But not new units," Scott said. "That included Used-Car sales. And it's a month and a half."

"Still," McGregor opened his eyes, "I'd say that was a mighty respectable figure considering."

"What I want, what I'm asking for, is for the factory to cut the quota down. By thirty-five percent. If you can't see your way to get this through, Mr. McGregor, then I'll put it up to the factory directly," Scott stated.

Red leaned forward in his swivel chair: "Hell, Scott, ease off—"

"Red—" Scott looked at him in utter bewilderment, as if to ask him whose side he was on.

"Boys," McGregor stood up for the first time, his smile still undiminished in brilliance, "your schedule for June calls for two hundred units, and two hundred units is what I know you'll sell. Before the month is out you'll be calling in begging us for more. Why? Because the season never spelled better. Would you like me to show you how we are increasing the national TV and newspaper coverage? Not to mention how this will double results from local advertising—"

"Which we pay for, of course," Scott said.

"No—not all of it. It's co-op. Let us not forget that," McGregor said. "You'll be riding in for this, you'll clean out. Clean out. And when you see the next Ward's Report, you'll——"

"Mr. McGregor," Scott said, "why can't we have a working arrangement that makes sense? A quota based on a rate of sales rise. I looked at the figures for last February and March and I—"

"My son," Red said, as if to placate McGregor, "my son belongs to another generation. He likes to go by a slide rule, I go by the seat of my pants."

"Red—" Scott tried to contain his impatience, "can't we just go by plain common sense, plain intelligence? I mean, you don't have to be a Harvard economist to see how one-sided this operation is getting. I don't give a damn what the factory schedule is, I refuse to keep carrying it. What are we going to do with all the cars? I don't know who's going to buy them all—unless they start teaching dogs and babies to drive!" He faced McGregor again: "We've got to work out a system that'll allow us to reduce the number of units, based on a—"

"My boy—" McGregor's gaze was incredulous, "that's like asking the President of the United States if he'd mind cutting down his term to two years."

"I'm going to the factory then."

"My boy," McGregor said, and a new fiber of toughness threaded through his tone, "as far as the factory is concerned, I'm it."

"I'm sorry. I'm going to the factory myself."

"With what?" McGregor stood, his legs splayed in a stance of confidence. "Let's assume you get up to the third floor. What's your weapon, my boy? Do you think you can walk in and organize a new system when the system we have produces a first quarter of over five million dollars? What's your weapon, my boy? But before you try to figure that one out, let me just give you a few hints as to how the future stacks up. I've been privileged to peek in on the top-secret future and I can tell you that what's going to come out of the mill is going to kick the competition in the balls. What's on the drawing boards for 1965 and '66 is staggering! And the word is going out to one and all. We've had over one hundred applications for franchises for next year. Why? Because in this business you can smell a good thing, and everyone wants to get in on it, in on it, which means the company is going to be very choosy about its dealerships, which means that by 1965 they might be scratching off the gripers from their back, which means they only play ball with the happy teams. Now, if I know anything about Quinnley Corners—and I personally have been doing business with Red for only nineteen years—I'd say you'll want to get in for the big blast-off, I doubt if you'll want to bow out just when it carries the biggest payload, the payload that's the biggest yet."

"I wasn't talking about bowing out," Scott said.

"You might not have known it," McGregor said softly, "but you were."

"I see." He matched the man's soft, but even tone, as if undismayed by the implied threat.

"Now, let's have a quick rundown to see if I know what I'm talking about." McGregor had opened his fat briefcase. He unfolded a large multicolored chart. "This is the latest stack-up on what the public feels, this is a certified picture we have from our Research and Marketing System."

"I've seen it," Scott said, and passed the chart to his father.

Red looked up. "You've seen it?"

"Yes." He did not amplify the statement. He had spent most of an evening out at Jennifer Thompson's house last week—having been out with her often during the past month—and he'd come to know her father. The sociology professor had shown him much of the work on the newest public survey. According to this study "in depth" people were keener than ever to buy new cars, people wanted "second cars" and even "third cars"; people were tired of the plain small economy car, they seemed to want more space, more power; people were admitting their romantic love affairs with foreign cars had tapered off; people were saying . . .

Except that Scott didn't really believe in what people said in surveys. What a man said on the telephone when he knew his opinion was being scientifically tested was not what he really thought. The expression on a man's face when he was alone was different from the face he put on for the photographer.

"Well"—McGregor seemed to take on a churlish, boyish disappointment—"if you saw all this you must have got up earlier than I did. We just received these figures, and no one has seen them until—"

"The point is," Scott interceded, "this is completely meaningless, as far as I'm concerned. I don't think car producers should go around asking everyone's opinion. Making cars is a special science, and the job is to *lead* the public, not follow it. You don't go around hospitals asking patients how they think a brain surgeon should operate." He paused, seeing his father's woeful look. "To get back to prime point," he said then, "we've got to get a new and more reasonable working arrangement with the factory—not only less units, but I also want to discuss the warranty problem here—"

"Not so fast, son." Red put down the chart. "I don't know how you can ignore this. And, even if Mr. M. lets the shit fly, it looks to me from this survey and the way the whole advertising schedule is being stepped up, that June's going to be big, has to be, summer's on the way, and I think Quinnley Corners is going to surprise a lot of people!"

"Sounds to me like Red here is bouncing right back!" McGregor announced heartily and packed his briefcase.

Scott said: "If you don't want to pass this on, Mr. McGregor, then I'm going to try the third floor myself."

"Boys," McGregor lifted his briefcase, "count on two hundred new units for next month!"

The man grasped Scott's hand, the wall of his smile impenetrable.

"What I said—" Scott began again.

"I'm counting on you, my boy," McGregor said, "I like your spirit." He strode to the door, turned back: "For June, boys, two hundred beautiful new sweet-smelling American beauty roses!"

81]

The office, in the wake of the man's boom and roar, now seemed desolate and still as a wilderness.

"Well," Red ventured then, "now you can see what I've been up against. Try to deal with a walking bastard like McGregor—"

"I don't hold anything against McGregor," Scott retorted. "He's doing the job he's paid for, and if his tactics are shameless or stupidly shortsighted, it was up to us to fight him. But I wasn't fighting him—it was *you* I had to fight!"

"You shut up, do you hear?" Red stooped forward, his jaw in wild, stubborn thrust. "You're not talking to me like that, not another goddam word!"

"Look, Red, either I'm here to help or I'm—"

"You're what? *What?*" Red Quinnley's eyes sparked with wrath. "You're helping how? Almighty Christ, who do you think you are, telling people you'll go to the factory? You want to go crawling up to the third floor like some goddam baby, you want them to think Quinnley Corners is a—"

"Quinnley Corners," Scott broke in, "isn't the United States Treasury. How long do you think you can operate like this?"

"As long as Red Quinnley is alive. We're still enough in the black, and—"

"Not in sales," Scott said. "Not on this end. If it wasn't for Fellowman Finance, and the insurance and Used-Car lot, you—"

"You looked at the books?" Red's armor seemed to draw protective strength from the power of his rage. "Have you? Do you know what I put back into this business in the past five years? Do you know what it cost me to build all that space on to the garage? A hundred and ninety thousand dollars! Do you know what I spent on my own radio and TV time?"

"Yes," Scott said, "and I can't understand it."

"It's my money! I know how to use it!"

"Red, I just don't know if I'd put all my money back into it, I'm just not sure if you can win anymore, simply by expanding, when the—"

"Then you'd better get yourself straight back to New York on the first plane," Red cried out bitterly.

Only now, at the sight of his father, did Scott remember his earlier resolve. He clenched his hands behind him, as if in that way he could hold his tongue, lock his temper, but the spectacle of Red's face told him it was too late.

[82

But then Red, as if recalling his own demands, spoke with sudden calmness: "All right. I told you to always level with me, didn't I? I told you that when you got here. I'm glad I know where you stand. Maybe it's healthier that way." A pause. "Now tell me why you say we can't win anymore?"

"I only said that," Scott groped for the most moderate way to sustain his position, "on the basis of how the operation seems to be running now and on the basis of my feeling about the product."

"Ah—the product! That's what it is, huh?"

"What I meant—"

"The product. What the hell is wrong with the product?"

"There's no point going into that, it's something we can't do anything about. What I was getting at—"

"Goddammit!" Red's spell of reasonableness had once more given way. "I'm selling the finest product in its class! And I've always sold it. I'm not selling pushcarts, I'm selling *Bellgards!*"

His voice rang, thundered like an evangelist's. Scott held his silence once more.

"Now you listen to me! I don't want you going to the factory, I don't want you to open your mouth, you understand? Don't think because Cod Smith or any of the rest of them are handing out free booze or taking you on like a pal, that you can tell them how to run the company! You think we're not getting enough cooperation from them now. But you open your mouth up there on the third floor and you'll see how it is if they really want to play rough! Didn't you get that even from McGregor? You listen to me now. Save your ammunition for when it counts."

"When will that be?" Scott asked quietly.

"Wait until after July," Red stated. "Remember, even an ape like McGregor has to have something to go on. Do you think the company is budgeting all this money if they don't expect a gold rush to come out of it? You're a smart boy, Scott, and I want you to keep leveling with me, but goddammit, you're still crawling in this business. Wait until you learn to walk!" More softly then: "I want you to stick with this. You've never seen Red Quinnley when the chips are down. That's when I play it best."

Red suddenly caught his breath, paused and sighed, and his hand touched his chest in a movement that seemed spontaneous, though it might have been to gain sympathy or consideration. "Scott, you stick here with it. You've made a hell of a lot of progress, you've got it in your head, but you haven't got it in the seat of your pants yet. From now on, right through the summer, right through to the new fall line, I want you to get out there on the floor, I want you to forget everything else, everything, you understand, except selling those cars! Talk to me after that. Can you try it, will you promise me this? Will you?"

When Scott said yes, almost without hesitation, he saw Red peer up at him, as if his quick acquiescence might have had some hidden purpose.

But with immense relief he saw that his father had been calmed, soothed, he seemed steady again, and the scarlet hue of his sagging cheeks had subsided.

"One thing, Scott, before I leave—about Marty Calhoon. I'm getting nowhere with him. He's been clamming up on me, and whatever it is, I don't like it. Last month he took home less commission than any time since 1958. He likes you, I want you to see what the hell's pulling him down. Tell you what you might do"—Red moved across the office, and put on his wide-brimmed, cream-colored hat—"you might just drop in at his home, away from here, where it's quiet and relaxed, see what you can do. I'd appreciate that."

"All right," Scott said. "I'm busy tonight, but tomorrow."

It was almost nine o'clock by the time he met Jennifer Thompson at the hotel bar in Midtown. And it was well past midnight when the evening with the Rothes and Ann and Ben was over, and he drove Jemmy out to the small cottage of her cousin on the shore of Lake Erie.

7: Scott Quinnley

UNTIL tonight the lovemaking of Scott and Jemmy had suffered. A dud, a bomb. He had to admit to himself that their first two weekends they'd never really got off the starting grid.

She'd even undressed methodically; she'd reclined on the pink-sheeted, canopied bed (in this coy little house, the bedroom all pine-boarded and chintzy, hand-painted hearts on the chest of drawers, a cuckoo clock and a beige carpet figured in a pattern of edelweiss) and there was all the passion of puppets. Claustrophobic, self-conscious, inhibited, lacking humor and spontaneity, they'd never made out.

In addition, the contrived nature of that first time acted to revive in him the old sensations he'd had after Ellen died, when he'd felt peculiar, uncomfortable, even disloyal sleeping with a woman.

But tonight they'd been able to talk about it, and then he'd wondered, aloud, if maybe part of the trouble wasn't the fact that their affair had too easily been put into motion by Ann Smith, setting it up for Scott on that virgin visit to Kent Hills, having Jemmy on hand, free and available, and Ann, however well-meaning, virtually pushing them into bed.

Yes. Though it hadn't occurred to either of them until Scott drew it out of the artificial air. And now suddenly in this mildewed cottage the climate became natural and right. And almost from the beginning they smoked off the line: not even a shower; they were undressing, and Jemmy's zipper got stuck. By the time she'd worked it free, Scott had his clothes off. He waited for her, watching her as she sat on the side of the bed, peeling down her hose, her leg outstretched. She said: "Why don't you have your shower?"

"Waiting for you," he said. "I'll take it with you."

"Oh lovely." And Jemmy, inspired as perhaps she never would be again, took on a playful mood and suddenly thrust her leg outward and with her stockinged foot began to wriggle her toes against his groin.

85]

He stood before her for a few moments letting her do it, almost as if indulging a whim. Until the whim assumed more tactile sensations, her foot growing ever more personal and prehensile, until his response became painfully taut. He reached down and lifted her leg and moved it to one side, almost like a doll's leg, and then stepping in close he reciprocated, gesture for gesture, except that he did not use his foot. Playfully, or almost playfully, he grazed her, letting it tease into the small triangular darkness, probing now, half standing, half leaning, letting it play inside her for a long time, his control cool and superb, until he caught her looking down watching it. That undid him and he fell upon her and her legs rose at once to enclose him in their now fierce stockinged grip, and at last they had it together.

When they were having coffee and cigarettes afterward, around three in the morning, sitting up in bed, they got back to talking about Ann Smith, and she said: "As a matter of fact Ann told me quite a lot about you before we ever met. She said while you were in Paris you were a very busy boy with the local females, she said you were a real gasser before you were married."

"Untrue."

"I'll buy it," Jemmy answered graciously, then: "Ann said you practically saved her life there and that she practically fell in love with you for ten minutes, except that you kept trying to reform her, and that was what killed it."

"Ann likes to make a good story better," he said.

"Yes. She does. But—"

"All I did was open her eyes to a bad situation."

"What about Ben Nodina?" Jemmy put out her cigarette. "What do you think of him? Honestly."

"Ben is perfect for her," he said. "And also, all she wants is to get to hell out of this town, and he's the perfect passport. But I like him very much."

"Well—" Jemmy leaned back on the quilted headboard, "he is charming and attractive. Maybe even too much so. But he doesn't make *me* flip."

"Whereas *I*—?"

"You?" She laughed. "Oh, you—well, how *do* I feel about you? I never researched it in depth. But I think, after tonight, I'd better."

Which, though it was glib, was a fairly honest answer: for Jemmy had not tried to build their relationship into an indestructible monument of love; she was contented, as was he, to keep it on its present level. If anything ruffled him, it was that she seemed to be one of the most unneurotic girls he'd ever known. He had decided that she adored her father and mother who in turn lavished so much affection on her that she wasn't desperate to escape them; she wanted love, of course, but she did not need to make a hurried or desperate commitment.

After a while no more talking, and Jemmy lowered herself drowsily against him. He still savored what had happened earlier, and he found himself turning to her wanting to celebrate it. They did.

One night, a week afterward, Scott invited Jemmy and Ann to the house for dinner. He did it not only because the life at home was often lonely, bereft of gaiety, but also because Ann had been anxious to see Suzy.

As it turned out, the evening hadn't been successful. Red had come home late; he'd been playing golf all afternoon, and he'd been drinking.

"Playing Sniff and Snort," he announced as soon as he walked into the living room.

"Sniff and Snort?" Ann had asked.

"Only way golf is any good," Red had said, going on to explain with unconcealed enjoyment: "My partner and I versus the other two. We carry a good bottle of Jamesons, and for each hole, the low-score team gets the snort, the losers get the sniff. Quickest way I know to improve your game."

Scott had laughed with the others, though he'd been less amused. For Red was carrying the doctor's friendly concession (one drink a day won't hurt you) far beyond its reasonable borders. More than that, more than Red's natural affinity for booze, was his underlining but unadmitted concern for the state of Quinnley Corners.

For a short interval that evening his father had dominated as host, taking over the duty from him in such an exuberant but competitive way—as if Scott had been his rival—that he soon drained all his energy, having in the end to retreat to his armchair where he dozed off into a fitful slumber.

Fortunately the housekeeper, Mrs. Coombs, brought Susan downstairs then, Suzy very excited and looking clean and pretty in the new dress Scott had bought for her, Suzy going to him but suddenly shy of the others, clinging to him, and showing little of the charm she possessed.

Jemmy wisely kept her distance, but Ann, who'd been so curious about the child, and who'd been taking an almost proprietory interest in Scott's life, went directly to the little girl only to overwhelm her with her effusions—Ann having to make yet another conquest or having to prove herself dazzling in the art of hearth and home. When she failed to win her over at once, she tried all the harder to enchant the child, with the result that Susan drew back, resisting, sullen and obviously betraying her jealousy at this intrusion which was usurping the precious time she customarily had with Scott.

An awkward, uncomfortable time it was. He lifted her up, hugged her to him and then carried her back upstairs. He undressed her and put her to bed and read to her.

"Well—" Ann said when he returned to the living room, "the next time I'll come here laden with bribes. She's really such a darling, Scott —but God, wasn't I an absolute bust?"

The following day there arrived at the house a large package containing a doll and an extravagant wardrobe of doll clothes. It was from Ann, of course.

When Scott called her that evening to thank her, she said: "Well, I had to do something." Then: "I tried to reach you all afternoon, but no luck. Are you free tomorrow night? You've got to be."

"Yes."

"Oh good," Ann said. "Tell me, how did Suzy like the doll?"

"Need I say? But you didn't have to do it."

"Oh yes I did."

"Why?"

"Making a conquest," Ann replied. "Someone once said you can win over any child if you play with him long enough. Well, this was the next best thing." A pause. Then: "Jemmy and I were talking about you—or rather, about your problem—"

"Oh? Do I have a problem?"

"I mean, if you're going to remarry. Isn't it going to be a problem about Suzy?"

[88

"Without doubt," he said too airily: for though he was well aware of the situation, he still could not project himself far enough into the future to contemplate second marriage.

"Listen, I'm definitely trying to marry you off, Scott. I just wanted you to know where I stand."

"Thank you, Junior," he said. "What's tomorrow night?"

"You and Jemmy have to be my guests at the club. Phil and Lorie are coming also."

"Phil?" He was surprised, for though Ann, as a member of the Kent Hills Country Club, could invite any guest she chose, the actual membership was restricted—just as in Kent Hills itself the Community Committee had discreetly managed to discourage Jews from buying or building in the area.

"Oh don't worry," she was saying, "Phil knows all about that stinking, ignoble joint, and he knows why I want him to be there, he's very good about it. It's a policy of mine, and it's working, slowly, but definitely. The house rules are going to be changed someday, and Phil's the kind of guy who can hurry the change along. But he did say he wouldn't go unless you did, and I promised him you would."

"Why make such a big—"

"Big deal?" she said. "Mainly because my father wants me there. I really have to. There's a whole pack of newspapermen in town for that A.A.M.A. meeting, and some of them are being feasted at the club."

"All right. I dig."

"And misery wants company," she said. Then: "How's it going for you?"

"It could go better."

"None of that now," she said. "Good Company Man like you has to keep his tail pipe up, *n'est ce pas?*"

"May I suggest, Junior, what you can do to yourself?"

"Yes. But it's more fun with Ben," she said. Then: "You *do* sound grim. Is it getting that bad?"

"No."

"You can tell me, Scott. It's just possible I'll understand," she said.

He said he'd see her tomorrow night. And once more, on the next evening he was late getting underway after a long and decidedly dismal day. He drove home to dress and then out to Kent Hills to meet the others.

The expressway at that hour was fairly cleared, but he cut over to the seldom-used, abandoned road parallel to the highway, for he wanted to move.

Move he did, far and fast away from the larcenous voices of Quinnley Corners, from his father's intolerable pride, from the despair of Marty Calhoon, from the bull-snorting threats of Halister Mc-Gregor and the unnerving prospect of uncut quotas.

The needle touched ninety, a hundred, a hundred-and-ten. But feeling it. He'd had the standard engine of his Bellgard replaced by the beefed-up optional 359-cubic-inch powerplant and she performed well enough, though of course you didn't get what you wanted now, what you needed—that real tensed exhilaration, that adrenalin-on-the-rise sensation you had in the cockpit of a race-built machine.

What he got now, perhaps, was more controllability (he couldn't help recall driving the Alfa in the Oceanside time-trials and the grief when the scavenger pump kept packing up on her).

Going flat out now for no more than five seconds, easing off then, as a rough bend in the road loomed ahead. It was no G.T. ride, and the Bellgard steering wheel was certainly not positioned for straight-arm driving, but by the time he reached the country club, windows down, hair on the wild side, he felt a little less fiendish: He could, he hoped, leave Quinnley Corners behind him.

8: Scott Quinnley

THIS being his first time at the Kent Hills Country Club, Scott was to be diverted (at least for a while) by the tribal customs of the members.

He hesitated now, at the end of the Gothic vaulted foyer which was massive enough to have supported the tower of St. Thomas' in New York; on either side were the lofty lounge rooms, ceilings ribbed with oak beams, the breastplates of the fireplaces encrusted with heraldic shields. Yet in startling contrast, the wall at the rear, facing on to the grassy sweep of the links, was all glass, framed outside by a cantilevered canopy of concrete: obviously a recent and necessary alteration, though the architecture gave the impression of a hasty marriage between second-rate Christopher Wren and third-rate Eero Saarinen.

Scott started in the direction of the sounds: the tintinnabulation of crystal and china, over which in counterpoint came the brassy pulsings of dance music. He was halfway across the lounge when he saw Ann hurrying into the room. "Scott—we're in there. We couldn't wait any longer." Her dark green dress was sleeveless and short.

"I'm sorry."

"Just remember I warned you about this joint," she said as they entered the dining hall. "Everybody and his wicked stepmother is here tonight." She led the way to the large round table; Jemmy, the Rothes and Ben Nodina were there. "We had our drinks transported here," Ann said as Scott sat down beside Jemmy. "This Martini has your name on it, Scott. If it's not too warm by now."

"Do you want a program, or can you tell all the players?" Ann continued, and proceeded to enlighten, pulling few punches, on her subject: the major personalities of the automobile industry, the high-echelon officers of General Motors, Ford, Chrysler, American Motors, Studebaker, Vanguard, Jefferson and Bellgard who were here with their wives or guests, along with many men in allied fields. "Could you ask for a better show?" she said when she finished.

"It's enough to make a man fall to his knees and face toward Dearborn," Scott said. "Junior, I'm awed."

But in truth he was interested, if not fascinated, by this spectacle, this collection of men who guided an industry which still had such a powerful grip on the economic fate of the country. Though the rituals at this club could not have varied much from those at other clubs, there was for him the notable difference that here the society was so conspicuously homogeneous.

After dinner, as he held Jemmy's chair back for her, Scott became conscious of someone watching him: it was Ann's sister, Myra Stratler. He nodded politely. Mrs. Stratler remained motionless, the cigarette between her fingers unsmoked, her wide, lavender-shadowed eyes acknowledging him with a speculative yet somehow indifferent interest.

He thought this exchange was completely covert, but as they left to go to the bar, Ann said: "Well, that's interesting."

"What is?"

"Must be you're definitely on your way. When my sister Myra gets that look on her, it's a pretty good sign that she's taking your measure, I mean she can spot people—I'll hand her that. And I'm sure she's already spotted you as a hot candidate for the third floor."

"I don't think I've even spoken to her more than twice," he said. Then: "What've you got against her?"

"Oh God, Scott, that would take twenty years," Ann answered after a moment. "Of course, I could easily say she's very neurotic, but who isn't? And I could just as easily say she dislikes me because I'm the so-called baby of the clan, but it's more than that, too. Let's just say she gives me a royal pain in the *derrière*. Anyhow, she has you marked."

"She must be getting her signals mixed," he said. "Because a hot candidate for the third floor I am not."

"I hope you're not," Ann said.

"Why would you hope that? I'm eager and earnest, as you keep telling me," Scott had to remind her, going on then less kindly: "Look, I can't help it, I'm just a swinging firebrand, a hero of no small proportions, and what I'm bucking for is to be middleweight champ in the great middle-class ring. How's that?"

She looked at him, shaking her head. "I think maybe everyone could use some brandy."

The party seated itself at a bank of pushed-together tables in the main barroom, a huge recess or alcove shaped like a watermelon slice, the small tables black and numerous as pits. Behind curved the long bar, and to the far side was the dance floor and orchestra.

Scott saw nearby the circle of tables being set up to accommodate a brace of newspapermen; adjacent to them Codman Smith and the others were settling themselves. And soon, as if on invisible conveyer belts, booze in prodigious supply began to flow into the room.

Jemmy and Scott danced for a while, as did the others, and then went back for more brandy and soda, and talk.

The proper interval of sociability had come to a close. More and more women sat alone at tables, for there had begun what might be called a form of ballet—a series of steps or movements leading to and from the bar, a choreography performed, with certain exceptions, to a single theme: the automobile industry.

The music of this ballet, Scott discovered, comprised a series of subtle strains beneath a deceptive melody of jollity and man-to-man-ness.

The first solo movement had begun: Dean Stratler, Vice-President of Styling for Bellgard, came by Scott's group and before passing on to the bar, paused for a brief murmur of small talk with Phil Rothe. From his manner you would never have known he'd taken Phil out for a two-hour lunch last week, and had given him his first Bellgard assignment.

Another dancer, this one Anthony James Kerwin, Executive Vice-President of Bellgard, performed a casual arabesque around the table of newspapermen to tell a joke and to move on to the bar where now many other men had assumed positions. Then, one of the stars of the troupe, Codman Smith, was poised by Scott's side. "I hope no one minds if I borrow my best rookie." He favored Scott with his familiar, cheery but agate-eyed gaze. "Want to lay out some strategy for next Sunday's game."

And then Scott too became part of the ballet, knowing or suspecting that the strategy of the Sunday ball game might be nothing more than a flimsy prelude to something else. Possibly Cod had had a report from Halister McGregor, and possibly he wanted to set Scott straight. For Cod it was a minor matter and normally he would never have concerned himself with it. But perhaps he temporarily enjoyed this paternal role.

But as soon as Codman Smith and Scott started on their brandies, Tony Kerwin took his place beside them, and then another figure appeared out of nowhere to spring up at Cod Smith's elbow: "Gentlemen"—a hearty and oleaginous air—"you're not going to let this expense account of mine go without a workout for the Internal Revenue Department, are you? Let's see if we can't get some more brandy to wash down that brandy—"

"Very nice of you, sir. But no thank you." Codman Smith's polite but frosty dismissal of the man diminished his ardor for an instant, and then he turned to Kerwin.

"Tony, what's your choice?" The man, a parts manufacturer, said.

Kerwin's smile was nothing less than charming. He had the grace of a sportsman—an elegant sportsman in English-tailored gray suit and dark foulard tie. The mole on his right cheek and the prominent aquiline nose gave to his face a distinction of sorts. He was a hard-drinking man, as his florid complexion testified, yet he looked extremely fit. He was, Scott knew, an avid golfer, yachtsman, hunter and a collector of classic cars. And, from a woman's viewpoint, obviously a swordsman.

Before Kerwin spoke, Codman Smith intervened. "We'll have to take a raincheck, I'm afraid." The cool finality catapulted the man away. As if he had to apologize, he turned to Scott. "Sorry. This is one of the occupational hazards we have to put up with. You let a peddler like that buy you half a drink and he'll be out to the plant the next day, orderbook in hand, pushing his wheel disks, door hardware, shocks, or whatever.

"I think we'll have a couple of extra fellows for next Sunday's game," he continued, though Scott knew this was only his way of cornering around into the straight. And presently he said: "By the way, that discussion we had one of those Sundays back in April, I've been meaning to ask you, Scott, if you still feel the same, that is, now that you've had more direct experience. Or have you forgotten?"

"No." Scott could not very well have forgotten. The subject—the wisdom of expanding the number and variety of models—was one, among others, that he could sound off about without encouragement, and Smith had encouraged him. "No, I remember it," he said. "And I still think it's bad business. The whole policy of trying to give people ten cars in one—basic transportation, elegant motor carriage, sports car gimmickry and all the rest—is bound to create a kind of phony product. And when you multiply it, keep extending the spectrum, it's going to be like a box of mixed chocolates, a piece for every taste, but nothing of a piece."

[94

"In other words," Kerwin spoke up then, "you think the sales success the industry is having with wide spectrum selection is a temporary success?"

"What I meant was less model variety and a lot more quality," Scott said.

"Well, there we are," Codman Smith said cryptically, and directed a swift glance at Kerwin.

"I'd say a five-year warranty suggested quality, wouldn't you?" Kerwin said. "And that's what we're pushing for, but we're up against bugs and problems, and it'll take some doing yet."

"That's what I hear," Scott said.

"You mustn't get discouraged," Codman Smith said. A chuckle then: "You know, Scott, despite what you might think, we happen to be quite interested in the dealer's viewpoint, just as we try to keep tab on his problems." A wry smile: "Not that you people ever have problems."

"None at all." Scott matched his tone.

"We couldn't squeeze a single complaint out of you, could we?" Tony Kerwin went along with the joke.

Scott grinned. "Nary a one."

But even as he resisted the chance to unfurl his long scroll of grievances, Vincent Eames, the supplier who sold Bellgard its inferior muffler and exhaust system, which was one of Quinnley Corners' major service woes, came into view.

"To get back to the spectrum," Tony Kerwin said in a way that suggested that it was his office rather than Cod Smith's who was pressing the policy, "the thing you have to see is that today's public has to be wooed in a new way. Like a romance, a courtship. What does a man look for in the woman he wants to marry? One quality? One type? Seldom. He wants the package that has the most, doesn't he? He wants a mother, a cook, a hostess, a mistress, and what have you." He touched a perfectly manicured fingernail to the dark mole on his cheek, turning now to favor his father-in-law with a beguiling smile, then addressing Scott again: "What a man wants in a woman is the most. What he wants in a car is no different. Am I persuading you?"

"I don't know, I don't always persuade easy—" And suddenly Scott could resist no longer, deciding now to launch his protest about the factory's outrageous quota system. "After all," he began, "I've had some experience with one Halister McGregor. In fact I—"

"Oh, you saw McGregor?" Codman Smith laughed. "And did he blow you down with his hard sell? Bet he did. An amazing institution, McGregor."

"I asked him to come by for a reason," Scott began again.

"Tony"—Cod Smith stirred, murmured to his son-in-law—"here comes that peddler from Yarmin's Headlamps, get rid of him." Then: "Excuse me, Scott. You were saying?"

But Smith's sudden irritability, the frigid stare, the hostile set of the bulky shoulders, struck Scott as being more than his impatience or allergy to parts suppliers, it gave him the feeling that he might well turn the same frosty face to Scott if he stepped beyond the safe zone of generalizations into the more treacherous realm of specific protest against sacred company policy.

Yet, Scott thought, two hundred new units for June.

To be paid for how? Quinnley Corners floor-planned its cars; that is, the bank paid the factory immediately, and was in turn reimbursed as the inventory was unloaded, except that the dealer also had to pay the interest charge on each car, and continue paying it as long as that car remained unsold.

Scott said: "I'm afraid I had a row with McGregor. That is, I—"

"Nothing Mac likes better than a battle," Smith said. "He's indefatigable. Nearly breaks the company with those bonuses we have to hand him. But like us, you'll just have to bear with it."

Kerwin, freed now of his last dirty chore, having dispatched the peddler from Yarmin's Headlamps, said: "A friendly suggestion, Scott. You don't want to get yourself too exercised over Hal McGregor."

"But I am. And if it isn't out of place, I'd like—"

But now the president of Vanguard Motors appeared from the left end of the bar: "What do you hear, Cod? That talk about G.M."

"What talk?" Smith said carefully.

"Ed Cole moving up if and when Gordon retires."

"Still talk, isn't it?"

Tony Kerwin edged off graciously; he ordered more brandy and while they drank, told Scott, in a tone of teacher to pupil, that the talk between Smith and the president of Vanguard was one of the most popular indoor sports of the club: the evaluation of rumor, the guessing game that always reached high rpm whenever some company was about to vote in a new chief executive or division head or raid the styling staff of a rival firm. Yet, even as he spoke, it became evident he was also listening attentively to what the two men were saying.

Suddenly Scott saw a frown, light and swift as a cloud, pass across his features, and then Vincent Eames, the muffler manufacturer, who'd been moving toward Kerwin, abruptly changed direction and with terpsichorean agility drifted off to another group. Kerwin looked out toward the dance floor. The talk was over.

And Scott realized he had been maneuvered into a diversionary corner: his own participation in this curious ballet was being graciously cut short.

"I'd like to make an appointment to see you if I could," he said to Kerwin. "This week. I got nowhere with McGregor. Our situation at Quinnley Corners makes it impossible to go along with the present quota, and what I would like is to—"

"Certainly, Scott." Kerwin buttoned the jacket of his gray suit and tugged at his splendid white shirt cuffs. "Buzz my office and let's see if we can't get you down on the agenda. I see my wife is giving me that look. You'll excuse me, won't you? Some of us have to remember we're still husbands, you know."

Yet, Scott noticed, he did not dwell long at his wife's table, and instead sauntered beyond the dance floor toward the high glass doors opening on to the terrace; while almost at the same time Vincent Eames left the bar and approached the glass doors from the opposite end of the room.

Kerwin and Eames met as if by accident and, executing a casual *pas de deux,* ambled out to the terrace.

When Scott returned to his table, Jemmy was alone. Ann and Ben were dancing, the Rothes had left, and Scott watched as Ann, in her stocking feet, and Ben executed one of the many new hybrid forms of the Twist. A number of couples had stopped to watch the performance, or rather Ann's performance. Her smile was all joy and defiance, the strands of her light amber hair falling in disarray, her gray-blue eyes never wavering from Nodina's.

When the music stopped, she picked up her shoes, holding them like two sprigs of violets, moving now in her stocking feet with indifferent grace, the pleats of the dark green Paris dress undulating as she walked. Unescapable was the ring of interest from the women in the room; even the members of the press at the tables nearby seemed aware of her.

"Well," she said to Scott, seating herself beside Ben now, "when did you return among the living?"

"Just now," he said. Then: "I think you'd make more of a hit around here, Junior—with the ladies, I mean—if you went back to those cheap Army and Navy store duds you used to wear."

"Why?" She frowned, rearranging her hair. "Do you think I look too piss-elegant? What's money for? Why pretend to be one of the mob? That's for politicians." She glanced around the room: "Whenever I see this gang here, I think there, but for the Grace of God, go I."

"Grace of Cod," Scott suggested.

And Ben Nodina laughed, and Ann said: "What are we drinking? Still brandy? Why don't we switch to champagne?" She signaled the waiter.

They had a round of champagne, and as the second round began, Ann abruptly lifted her glass, and her smile gave way to a sudden grin as she looked over at Scott. "Here's to it."

"To what?"

"The Champagne V-6," she enunciated carefully. "It's the new car with the bubbly effervescent ride."

They drank to that.

"The Champagne V-6"—Scott picked up his vaudeville cue— "takes off like the pop of a cork. And notice that swizzle-stick gear shift."

"The true economy engine. Runs on caviar, the true economy fuel," Ann said.

"I'll buy it," Ben Nodina said.

"But we're sorry to announce," Scott said, "we can only offer you a choice of six hundred models and only nine thousand, three hundred and sixty-nine different decorator colors."

Loud approval, swelled now by the rise of hilarity from the press at the adjoining table.

"A real power-punching sports car, winner of the Bloomfield Hills Rally, the Cobo Hall Drag, the Fisher Building *Grand Prix,*" Ann said.

"And only the Champagne offers you America's true compact for true economy in a modest range of true compact styles," Scott went on. "There is the tiny basic economy compact, the medium basic compact, the super-basic compact. And there is the two-seater econ-omy sports compact, the medium-size economy sports compact and the luxury-size sports compact. There is the two-bucket, two-door *Gran Turismo* compact, the medium *Gran Turismo* compact and the four-door super-luxury *Gran Turismo* hardtop compact, and the

[98

super-luxury *Gran Turismo* convertible compact, and of course the famous economy-oriented, three ton, nineteen-foot-long, gull-winged, air-conditioned, race-tested, manual and automatic four-speed, fast-back town limousine compact."

Ann clapped her hands vociferously; several of the newsmen also applauded. Jemmy said: "Don't stop."

Ann said: "For the family who already has a second car, a third car and a fourth—why not try a fifth of Champagne?"

"At a price anyone can afford." Scott finished his third glass and poured another. "Anyone, that is, who can find out what the price is. And remember the big warranty with the small print. And if anything goes wrong, see your nearest hysterical dealer or go directly to the factory and see for yourself how willing the company is to give you that world-famous finger of cooperation! Yes, the secret of the Champagne is that it is all things to all men. Why? Because, ladies and gentlemen, it's a great big magnificent nothing!"

But even before he'd finished, before the last cry was out, Scott saw the restless-eyed Dean Stratler and his wife Myra approaching, along with the other brother-in-law, the resolutely elegant Tony Kerwin.

And Dean Stratler then bending over Ann: "I thought you ought to know, Ann, that right behind you at that table—"

"The press, yes I know." Ann smiled up at Stratler.

"Right," Dean said. Then: "Do you think you could spare a dance for your favorite brother-in-law?"

Ann hesitated, glanced over at Ben Nodina. Then she rose. "Always spare a dance for the chairman of the Vigilante Committee."

Simultaneously Tony Kerwin stepped to the adjoining table; he drew from his gray suit a gold cigarette case and in that hearty yet debonair way of his, addressed the group of men: "Well, it can't be said that we can't have a few laughs at ourselves, once in a while, can it?"

The gesture, Scott saw, found genial acceptance from the newspapermen. And when Kerwin came back, Myra Stratler turned to him and said: "My husband's left me stranded, Tony." she touched her blond hair, turned briefly to Scott, her wide, mauve-shadowed eyes dwelling on him in a kind of languid appraisal. "I was hoping Mr. Quinnley might unstrand me, but no luck."

"Well . . ." A frown deepened Kerwin's face; but with the necessary social grace, he said: "In that case, Myra, I'll do the honors." With an air of dutifulness, he led Dean Stratler's wife out to the floor.

9: Tony Kerwin

THE sensation of having Myra Stratler's coolly fleshed and slender arm around him, of feeling the discreet communication of her legs, was so satisfying that, for a few moments at least, as they danced, he could almost blur out the disagreeable sensation of knowing that this affair, so custom-built to his taste and hers, would have to be broken. *Temporarily.* He refused to think it might have to be given up altogether: though after the portent of events this week and of tonight, it took the full swagger of his sunny and athletic nature to preserve a hopeful perspective.

"I thought we'd never get out here. I thought tonight would never end," Myra was saying, but sustaining the manner of a woman dancing dutifully with her brother-in-law.

"Yes." Tony answered. He'd come to a bad turn. It had to be dealt with. Quickly. Delay spawned disaster. You had to be quick and ready to avert it. It was like sailing, you couldn't go on always depending on a good wind, and if it started blowing wrong, you had to tack around and get it working for you. The same in hunting: when the birds were flushed out and you missed, you had to correct your lead in a flash before the entire flock got beyond range, leaving you with an empty bag, a groundful of spent shells. But the bad turn that was upon him now, like a hidden curve, was more crucial, required keener manipulation, more daring and more caution.

He and Myra were too intelligent not to know the risk they were taking. They'd known it since the affair had begun almost two years ago, a July weekend on his boat when Dean Stratler had had to go to New York on short notice and when Phoebe had stayed at the Yacht Club to play out the bridge tournament.

He and Myra had always been extremely careful, their furtive meetings artfully planned, and when sometimes they met at his farm, they would go out on Thursday afternoons, a time when no one in the family or any of their friends ever went hunting. But their chief accomplishment was in making people think they disliked each other. In front of others they would invariably drift into arguments, keeping up the kind of skirmishes which made the legend of their hostility grow into one of the accepted social folkways of Kent Hills.

Now, dancing with her, he swung her around as he noticed that Scott Quinnley seemed to have been watching them. He said: "Myra, there won't be much time to talk now. Phoebe wants to go home, and —" He paused before uttering the unwanted statement: "We're going to have to put off next Thursday."

"Oh?"

"As a matter of fact, Myra—I think we'd better stay away from the farm, from any place. For a few weeks or so."

"Why? Why, Tony? You couldn't mean that, not seriously?" But her muted question, despite the impassive expression of her face, held a distinctly unpleasant undertone.

"I'm serious." He drew back, away from her closeness, seeing her more clearly now, dancing with that faintly formal posture, her dark blond hair glittering as the prisms of the chandelier above the bandstand cast its crystal brightness upon her, dappling her rather gaunt face, the darkly ringed eyes.

"Is it Phoebe?" she asked then.

"No. It's not Phoebe." He dismissed it curtly. "It's Vince Eames."

"Vince?"

"Fortunately," Tony said.

"What's so fortunate about that?"

"Vince thinks he is a chum of mine," Tony reassured her firmly, perhaps too firmly, for Tony Kerwin was unaccustomed to seeing the dark underside of life, he'd always been too lucky, he'd always been beyond the reach of grief, at least the kind of grief that had fallen into his lap this week, this evening.

He had to accept the only edge of luck there was, accepting the fact that it had only been Vince Eames instead of someone else, who'd discovered what existed between himself and Myra. But even this was incidental to the larger issue, for Vince had no interest in the affair, he wasn't concerned. No. What made the grief formidable was that Vince could, if he chose, use the discovery as a possible weapon, a subtle threat, to gain something much more crucial.

Nevertheless it had to be first things first. And that, unhappily, meant Myra.

"I know he's your chum, Tony," she was saying now, "but if you're so sure, then why are you—"

"Myra, I know what I'm doing, and I think . . ." He paused again, his resolve weakened as he contemplated her, as he saw fading from his life the particular and delicious luxury of having Myra. Having any first-rate luxury was something he could not resist, and now as he looked at her, as the memory of their past meetings touched him, he felt a bitter ache of longing, of loss.

"You think what, Tony?"

Rigidly he said: "I think we'll have to stop." He smiled down at her then. "Just temporarily, just for a while. For the time being."

"What does he know? How could he possibly have found out?"

"Just one of those things, purely accidental, a freak," Tony said. "But it's stupid to push your luck too far. Luck is something you have to respect. Nothing to worry about, darling. Leave it to me."

"Tony, will you please tell me what happened out there on the terrace? I can't see how even *you* can keep smiling like that. What is there to smile about?" she said.

He'd scarcely been aware of it. That smile of his was built in, just as his eyes radiated confidence. It was his nature, his policy, in fact, to soothe, placate, to present a situation more brightly or hopefully than it warranted—this buoyant, smiling and positive outlook had been tested in field and office and home, it had always been contagious, inspiring his friends and his business associates. And always, himself.

"I said just leave it to me," he repeated. He drew her closer. "Nothing to worry about." And even as he said it, even as the weight of crisis was upon him, he held, or tried out of habit to hold, the hope of luck: for it was true he'd walked with luck always, he'd been one of those men who seem to grow the flowers of fortune no matter where he steps; it seemed he had always been at the right place at the right time. Who else but he could have opened a foreign car agency in 1948 in a fashionable resort where he'd been totally unknown but where within two winter seasons he'd sold sixteen Rolls Royces? He'd always looked back to that time as the infallible illustration of the Kerwin luck, though the money he'd made then was insignificant compared to what he'd earned later as partner in Eames Mufflers, or subsequently at Bellgard.

But Myra said: "Really, Tony, what did he say exactly? And please don't make it sound as though you're giving me a lovely birthday gift.

[102

Tell me." There was the sudden pressure of her palm against his back. "When did it happen? Oh, it's unbearable, hideous to think we'll have to stop—I've never cared for Vince, I've never trusted him and I don't see how you can. What was it?"

"He knows. But it won't go any further, I can assure you of that. That's why I said we were lucky it was Vince. He won't open his mouth."

"Not as long as Bellgard feeds it," Myra stated tartly.

"He wouldn't because of me," he answered at once.

"Then why bother at all? Why do we have to stop seeing each other?"

"In the first place," Tony said, "I didn't let him get away with it. I told him he was way off base. I covered thoroughly. But I want to keep it that way until I'm sure we have a clear field."

Myra was silent, thoughtful. He guided her beyond hearing range of a couple close by, a Chrysler executive and his wife. Then he said: "It was last Thursday."

"Oh."

"A pure freak of a thing," Tony said. "Vince never goes hunting on Thursdays, but he was out with a new account, and he stopped by to pick up some extra ammunition from my man. He drove up just after you'd left. I'm not sure if he recognized you but he recognized your car—"

"Oh." The veneer of Myra's face cracked, the first faint crevices of anxiety veined her cheeks.

"I covered it," he said firmly.

"How?" she asked.

"I know you and Dean have been looking for a country property around there, and I said you were out with a real estate agent and—"

Myra nodded in approval. Then: "It's curious though— Why did he wait until tonight to tell you?"

"That's Vince. He'd forgotten about it, he isn't the slightest bit interested, he just happened to mention it."

"I don't know . . ." Myra hesitated, her voice tentative at first, but gaining strength as she spoke. "I don't know, Tony. If you're not worried about Vince, why worry about us? Unless it's more complicated than that—"

"Complicated? In what way?" He measured out the words with smiling, innocent interest.

"Business-wise," she said.

"Vince and I stopped talking business years ago. Where'd you get a notion like that? Don't tell me Dean has—" He did not finish, regretting at once the unwitting mention of her husband—not because he was sensitive or guilty about Dean (on the contrary: for they'd never liked each other, and despite the pretense of good fellowship in family and factory, each was acutely conscious of the accomplishments or failures of the other, and each held the same passionate drive for self-aggrandizement; no, there was no tortuous guilt; but the affair with Myra, aside from its implicit pleasures, gave Tony the kind of gratification that comes from knowing you've scored on your opponent without his knowledge).

"It's not Dean," Myra said. "Dean hasn't the remotest idea. He lives on another plane. I was thinking of something else, some chatter—"

"From Ann?" He anticipated it; he hoped his benign smile was working for him.

"I didn't mention Ann."

"What'd she say?" Tony asked, forgetting in the haste, the need of his question, that he might have betrayed anxiety. "Not that it matters, we all know how Ann is."

"Yes, rather," Myra said.

"Well"—Tony produced the kind of grin common among a family whenever they discuss the antics of one of its troublesome members— "you know I'm always very tolerant of Ann, she gets such a charge out of trying to get a rise out of us. What was it this time?"

"Oh, rather the same old thing, I suppose."

"Such as?" He waited behind the hastily erected fence of kindly and cheerful interest.

"You know as well as I do. Eames Mufflers."

"Oh, that?" But Tony's features failed somehow to take on the jolly indifference required. Even though it was only Ann's familiar voice reaching out to him now, he felt its sting. He said: "I'm sure I can quote Ann verbatim, but I won't bother. Naturally, we all know Vince has become a sore spot with some of the other suppliers—" He could not, of course, tell her of the specific case; he had to keep it free, general. "They're always gunning for our business and when they don't get it, you can hear the wails from here to the New Jersey Assembly plant." Then: "I'd say offhand, the trouble with Ann is she's still your father's precious little baby, and Cod lets her get away with this nonsense because it's good for us to hear, it's his way of needling the rest of us."

"Tony, you can be very bright when you want to, can't you?" Myra's admiration came candidly. "That's why I'm worried. I know you wouldn't be worried about us unless something more serious wasn't involved."

Tony's most beguiling smile flourished now, born not only out of grim respect for Myra's never lethargic mind, but out of his need to counter the threat that had come to him less than an hour ago. "Myra darling," he said, "are you going to leave this to me or not?"

Less than an hour ago, Vince had sauntered along the bar. Tony had seen him advancing, the thickly lashed, omnivorous eyes seeking him out, and there'd been the familiar exchange of glances between them. Vince had nodded and moved off past the tables and around the dance floor, and Tony had broken away from Scott Quinnley to join Eames and they'd gone out to the terrace.

A smoke. Fresh air. A friendly talk. The two men had done it often, though this time Tony knew it would not be the same. They moved to the far end of the terrace where, through the great hemlock rising beyond the balustrade, the moon's rays came diffused, falling in jagged brilliance on the flagged floor. Here they could speak in seclusion. The long terrace stretched away from them, looming like a mighty throne above the rolling green of the golf links.

Since Tony knew the ways of his former partner, since he knew what was on his mind, he said at once: "Sorry about the delay, Vince, but—"

"But what? I left the shop at seven tonight and the papers hadn't come in." Vincent Eames confronted him, Vince plump and too chunky for the svelte Italian silk suit, his prematurely bald head tilted downward in that faintly pugilistic angle he assumed whenever he was seriously exercised about a business problem. "What happened? You know the shop can't move until the contract and specs are in."

"They'll be there, you'll have them." Tony was quick to placate him, slow him down, just as he'd often done during the years of their partnership when Vince would go stampeding nervously around office or plant, not content until every last piece of business, every project or committment, was underway. "The contract's been awarded. You'll have it."

"When? In 1969?" Vince demanded. "When my lawyer called

Bellgard, they said the papers were over at Engineering. You know what that means, it means delays, and I have to look at my Union steward's overfed face and pay the—"

"I had to put it back through Engineering again, I had no choice this time, Vince. But relax. Leave it all to me."

"Always leave it to you."

"Vince, are you watching your blood pressure?" Tony said to divert him.

"Ever since 1953 when you left, it's been going up. Today, I wouldn't want to check it," Vince answered.

Resuming then, Tony said: "This year I have to let Engineering play with the new order, I have to do it to keep them happy."

"Doesn't keep me happy." Vince dropped his cigarette, stepped on it with a belligerent twist of his foot, addressing the flagstone floor, muttering: "Over two packs today, and I'm supposed to cut down to half a pack. Arteries." Looking up again: "I want the story, Tony. Straight. None of those Kerwin tranquilizers to make it go down good."

"I didn't say it was good, I merely said leave it to me. It'll take a bit of time. No point in getting yourself too exercised about it, Vince." But he saw that the man could not be put off; he also suspected that Vince was well informed about the many inter-Bellgard storms, one of which centered at the moment on the Eames mufflers. Since, however, it was to Tony's personal interest to preserve the calm sea of the status quo, he said: "What I'm doing is simply trying to keep everyone reasonably happy."

"Who is everyone? You're not keeping me happy."

"Relax, Vincent."

"Who is it? Kyssin Parts?" Vince waited, his hands thrust into the pocket of his jacket so that the black silk of the Italian suit stretched taut against his middle.

"Oh—not really." Tony felt a tug of dismay, but he kept his voice buoyant as the spring night. "It's just one of those intramural binds."

"I don't like it," Vince said. "If you let Sam Kyssin get his muffler in the door—"

"Vincent, you've been awarded the contract. Now it's just a matter of my pampering the engineers. I'm letting them sit on it. Leave the infighting to me."

"I don't like it," Vince said once more. "I've seen bigger suppliers

[106

than me go out of business overnight because one engineer or one accountant was allowed to frig around with a deal too long."

"Nobody," Tony agreed, not without a certain grimness, "is more aware of that than I am."

"Then what's the play?" Vince demanded. "All specifications have been met, I'm ready to retool. But how long do you think I can wait? Every minute costs me. What is it? If it's not Kyssin Parts, then it's that creep of an engineer, Kamber."

"Of course it's Kamber. It's always been. He's pushing for more quality now," Tony had to say.

"He'll get it. What the hell am I modifying the machines for?"

Tony said: "Mr. Kamber, as you know, is something of a sacred cow at Bellgard."

"He's a sacred creep." Vince thrust his head forward. "I thought I took care of him."

"You did."

"But?"

"If you'll remember, Vince, I was very opposed to it."

"The fact remains," Vince persisted in his harsh and pragmatic way, "that last August at the convention, it cost me six hundred dollars, plus the finest call girls in New York. He never had a weekend like that in all his life."

Tony nodded. "But you went too far, and you know it. He's basically a puritan, and I think now he's bending over backward to show himself he's still pure. He was the wrong man, Vince."

"No man is the wrong man," Vince stated with that bluntness which had always offended Tony. "He's a man, isn't he?" Vince went on: "He's no different from any of us."

"I'd scarcely say that," Tony ventured lightly, though as he watched him now, as he saw the turgid gleam in his eyes, he felt a sudden spasm of discomfort.

"Look," Vince said. "Why should he be any different? Put some delectable pussy in front of him and he'll take it. Just as I would—" Adding then, "Or even you."

"Those days, alas, are over for me," Tony was careful to say.

"Since when? Come on, Tony, don't spray on the rustproof. You know I couldn't care less. And," he went on more pertinently, "if you can keep it cozy within the family, all the more power to you."

Tony rocked as the first force of the implication struck him. He moistened his lips. "Vincent," he began, "you're losing me with this kind of—"

"Now don't get your back up," Vince broke in. "Just because you and Myra happen to put in a little time together, don't turn choirboy on me, I have no interest in your private life. What interests me is only one thing, and that is—"

But Tony wasn't listening: dismay and resentment had seized him and had risen, spiraled up within him. He summoned all control against the sharp churning in the core of his stomach; but already his initial discomfort was giving way to a more profound apprehension. It was not Vince's knowledge that unsettled him, but the fact that he'd waited until now to reveal it.

As if perceiving this, or as if he anticipated exactly how Tony might respond, Vince stepped forward and tapped his stubby-fingered fist against Tony's arm: "Come on, chum, forget it." But then: "I like to see you get 'exercised' once in a while too."

"Now wait a minute, Vince—" Tony had no alternative. "I'm not going to stand here and let you throw me curves. Let's get that right. Here and now."

"What's there to get right?" The hungry and attentive gaze was once more upon him. "As a matter of fact, when I saw Myra driving off from your farm I wasn't even surprised. I didn't even let on I'd seen her. What're you looking like that for? It was exactly ten after five, last Thursday afternoon, and—"

"Vince, as you and everyone else must know damn well, Myra Stratler is scarcely one of my favorite people—"

"Of course. I know it's your wife, Phoebe." Vince did not conceal his derision.

"What I'm trying to tell you," Tony held hard to the line, "is that I'm certainly not going to let Myra suffer for something that has nothing to do with her. She was out there that day to meet a real estate agent, she and Dean are looking for property—"

"Absolutely." Vince's heavily ironic voice hovered in the scented night. "And whatever you do, don't give up anything on my account."

"I can scarcely give up what I've never had." Yet, such was Tony's nature that even now, as he made his denials, as the new anxiety worked in him, there remained that one small recess in his mind, untouched, inviolate, which held in all its silken texture, the loss of Myra. . . .

[108

Ironic. How delicious it had been *particularly* last Thursday: the drinks, and talking about the success her committee had organizing the series of art lectures and films at the Kent Hills Community House; and then the deliciously, tacitly recognized moment when they began to undress.

Myra, naked and standing before him as he sat on the chair kicking off his shoes. Her incurable vanity appeased by the way he admired her, his way of admiration, which found in her narcissistic nature a response she hadn't experienced in her own marriage.

Myra, however, was not a discontented wife as such. She lacked little in life (except the love or admiration of her father, who hoarded what affection he was capable of for his youngest daughter). And Myra's husband, Dean Stratler, was devoted to her; though he chose to see her in the more cerebral terms of the works of celebrated painters, a Toulouse Lautrec or Modigliani, she welcomed these tributes.

Still something was missing, some compensation for long-locked desires and failures, and this became the full exploitation of her vanity—another man. Like Tony. Tony was not one to delve deeply into the complexities of something or someone he already possessed. But being the sportsman he was he'd discovered that Myra came to respond with surprising intensity to his admiration when, now and then, he had carelessly or with lustful humor compared parts of her body to some lithe or finely formed animal.

She adored this kind of adoration of her body (her clothed figure, her face—these were not sufficient for her any longer), so that now the final act of their lovemaking would be preceded by his active connoisseurship, just as on this past Thursday, she had parted her thighs, wanting him (as he himself wanted) to caress her there, this preliminary homage rousing her to inaudible cries, and then urging him, drawing him up to take her.

But afterward, when she'd left, the wheels of her Bellgard convertible had become rutted in the rain-soaked country driveway, and he'd had to go and push her free. That unhappy lag in time and habit had made it possible for Vince Eames to see her. In ugly moments like this, he asked himself if she was worth it, for though he appreciated her beauty and the discretion of the affair, there were, if he wished to examine them, many aspects of Myra he did not admire. But of course, all things considered, he knew what he had, and he wanted to keep it. As did she.

Vince was saying now: "Sure. Absolutely. I understand. Everything. And I couldn't give less of a good goddam. You know me, Tony, I've never had anything but plain green envy for the Kerwin bedmanship—but what I want to tell you, and I don't care if it sounds like an ultimatum—"

"I know what you're getting to." He reached into his coat pocket for the thin fine feel of the gold case. He lit a cigarette, he leaned against the balustrade, he shook his head. "Come off it, Vince. You're getting to be something of a dirty old man. Let's have no more of that—" He stopped, and immediately then, he moved in to attack, to tell him what earlier he had tried to defer, spare him; he had to put Vince where he belonged. "All right, Vince. To get back to reality. If you're really hungry for trouble, I can give you quite a bit to chew on. I hadn't wanted to get you exercised, but I think maybe you'll have to be enlightened."

"Meaning what?"

"Our situation with you is strictly touch and go," Tony stated. "It came to a head suddenly, though it's been festering for some time, as you know."

"I know everything." The fingers were balled tightly again, the forearms jutting to and fro, as if Eames were sparring with his own impatience. "Including the fact you let Sam Kyssin in the front door just at a time when—"

"Do you think," Tony asserted, "that Engineering would have given Sam Kyssin the time of day, if there hadn't been good reason, not to mention pressure? One look at what's happening in our Mail Center alone would give you part of the story. It's been jamming up with letters, complaints, not only from dealers, but from individuals. That muffler's been giving us more grief than any other single part— that is, as an external part that the average driver can see with his own eyes. They're falling apart under ten thousand miles. I was talking with Quinnley before, a very bright boy. He was sounding forth, telling me—and unfortunately, also Cod Smith—about the grief they've been having with your system. I wish you could have heard him, best index I know of what's going on, dealer-wise. Let me also tell you, Vince, that Sam Kyssin didn't just come to the plant like any ordinary peddler. He's a new breed, he's a scientific gent hard to ignore. He turned up with graphs, charts, mockups, and a two-reel film Ben Nodina made for him, showing the entire testing process of his exhaust system, and how it stands up under real heat, real punish-

[110

ment. It was very impressive. Engineering was very impressed, and that's another reason why they're studying the contract with a new and cautious eye."

"And you sat around on the third floor giving everybody the green light?" Vince said.

"Certainly. To have done anything else would have looked highly suspect, wouldn't it? I'm going through all the motions, I'm letting all the reports be correlated through my office, but I'm also sifting it down through Budget Control. And here is where I have my edge. I know Budget won't buck me, because of price. We can't afford Kyssin, there's too much daylight between their price and yours, makes it too expensive for us right now. So when Engineering is all through with their reappraisal, I'll get the green paper from Budget, and that'll drop it in your lap. But"—he paused—"it's probably the last time it can be managed unless you come through with valid improvement."

He felt partial relief. He knew he had expressed the truth. And though the Eames crisis was, in reality, not a big event at Bellgard, not certainly as acute, for example, as the grief they were having with the styling trend or their suspension system or vibrational pull or even faulty door locks—nevertheless, the inferior muffler seemed to have become a virtual symbol of product deterioration in meeting the superior craft of major competitors. And Tony knew, as a Front Office man, that meeting and beating the competition was the only religion there was.

"Valid improvement?" Vince echoed, and a tight grimace carved itself on his rotund face. "Why shouldn't it improve? Bellgard is my bread-and-butter account. It's been nourishing my company for many years. And," he added a little too quietly or smugly, "it nourishes my friend Tony Kerwin."

As if he hadn't heard the last words, Tony glanced out to the moon-lit turf of the golf course, gazing out now as if he could put distance between himself and the long past, as if to shut out not Vince's un-called-for reminder, but to blur out the fact that it had never been mentioned until tonight.

After how many years? Eight, nine? First it had been that agreeable chunk of Eames stock, put in his aunt's name in Baltimore and sold after her death, and after that it had been periodic gifts of cash: merely Vince's way of showing friendly and sensible appreciation. People in business, in government, always tried to look after their friends first. Why not? How many corporations could deny it? It had

111]

more or less become a way of life; some men he knew no longer even troubled to conceal a bit of side dealing. As for Tony, he didn't need the money or the stock; he could do splendidly, thank you, without them; his salary and bonuses and stock options had made a solid little anchorage, a very safe moorage for the roughest weather.

On the other hand, why deny that he did spend lavishly, often too lavishly? Necessities were of no interest to him. Luxuries he could not resist. In Baltimore he'd been born rich. A rich baby. Though by the time his parents moved to Michigan in 1931 they had lost everything. Tony, however, had never been weaned from money, not to this day. The wealth his wife Phoebe had, or would inherit, was merely what he expected any wife of Tony Kerwin to have. No: it was the marginal cash, the hidden assets that was the real fuel in the Kerwin engine; the extra belt of cartridges he liked to keep strapped beneath his hunting jacket; the portable umbrella for the rainy day they said it wouldn't rain.

And now, after all this time, Vince chose to talk about it.

And hearing Vince revive it, hearing him deliberately lift it from the past, Tony felt shocked, enraged, even betrayed. Like a man who, having made his peace with his wife after his first and only infidelity, goes on to forget it, grateful to her for forgetting it, letting time bury the incident, letting the everyday tides of conjugal life wash away the abrasive pebbles of memory until for some reason his wife is aroused to remind him of the incident to which she has never alluded in years. So that in resurrecting what he thinks is dead, she reveals to him that his crime has never been out of her heart, and that the marriage instead of being salvaged is, in fact, shattered. And the comparative innocence which time has conferred upon him is thus snatched away, leaving him at that moment with his guilt re-exposed and renewed.

When at last Tony turned to confront him again, he said: "All right, Vincent, if you want to dredge that up, you can. But I'd like to remind you," he said, his voice scorching with the contempt which had been smoldering for a long time, "that I didn't ask you for any favors, I wanted no part of it. You insisted, you went on without even consulting me again. This is typical of your myopic perspective, not to mention bad taste. But it doesn't solve anything now. After this order, I doubt if I'll be able to be of much help to you. After this order you're going to have to be on your own. Nothing but quality performance of the product is going to count from now on."

"Don't overlap me." Vince stood, thick legs splayed, like a granite

[112

sculpture of defiance. "Don't let's get sidetracked about perspective or bad taste. Just tell me how I could force all that loot on you? Tell me."

Tony said: "Let's put it this way. I don't know how it happened, since there's no evidence I ever asked for it." He spoke the truth, though it was no answer to his complicity. But before Vince could detain him, he was already on his way, needing all the swagger of his sportsman's stride to carry the unfamiliar weight of ill-luck, as he moved along the moon-bathed flagstones of the long terrace.

"I have every intention of leaving it all to you, Tony," Myra was saying as they danced. "Not that I have much choice." Then: "That talk you had with Vince seems to have done you in."

He said, "There are times when Vince can be a boor."

"Without trying, either," Myra added morosely. "Oh, it's too hideous, the idea of someone like him knowing."

"Let's forget it, shall we?" he said. "We ought to think of getting off the floor. We never dance this long."

"What's the difference now?"

He looked back to the cluster of tables in the barroom. "Your mother and father have left, I think. And Phoebe is waiting there alone."

"Oh, she loves it. Waiting for her husband. Phoebe loves waiting for you, Tony." Myra said. "Of course she's always been like that. She used to love waiting for Father the same way. Oh, Tony—I don't know, I still say, if you're not really worried, why can't we arrange to meet anyway, it's unbearable—"

"It'll have to wait," he said. "Just for a while." He felt her thighs grazing his.

"Yes," she said. Then: "Thank God at least Vince Eames never has any business to do with Dean. There's that, anyway. Otherwise, I couldn't sleep, feeling he might open his boorish mouth."

"He's only interested in Eames mufflers." Tony said. "You know, there are times I envy Dean. He has his grief, but at least he doesn't get involved with the kind of banditry you get in my division."

"That's a question of the other chap's grass being greener, isn't it? But you know as well as I that you wouldn't exchange jobs with Dean, even if you could."

"True." But for the first time it wasn't true at all; for the first time Tony's esteem of Dean Stratler's position was marred by envy; even though Dean carried the toughest load at the moment, the design of the current models having met with sluggish public response—nonetheless, at least the designer didn't have on his back the kind of personal pressure that now threatened Tony.

And there was something else: For the first time, Tony's view of the future began to lose its luster. For the first time that view which, like a far and shimmering mountain at whose summit shone the lure of the Bellgard presidency, the chair which would be vacated on Cod Smith's retirement—this view, so long-held, luck-prodded and natural, now began to loom mist-shrouded, more distant, its height less attainable, more treacherous to scale. He said: "We'd better quit. Phoebe's been there alone—"

In a manner as unceremonious as it was uncharacteristic of him, he stopped dancing, and led Myra off the floor and returned to the large round table, to the waiting devotion of his wife.

10: Myra Smith Stratler

THE ritual resumed. Myra Stratler, properly accompanied by Tony, returned to the family table, empty now except for her elder sister Phoebe. Phoebe in her beige dress, her rigidly waved blond hair, her pearl earrings; Phoebe sipping the glass of salt-free mineral water, sitting there amidst the other tables where the last few gregarious members were still holding out; Phoebe waiting in quiet, righteous isolation, and looking up at Tony now with that pale, loving gaze which brought to her lackluster features a shine that Myra found sickening.

"Where's Dean?" Myra asked.

"Oh—" Phoebe touched the pearls at her long throat in unwitting imitation of her mother. "I think he's—I think he went out with Scott Quinnley and Jemmy." Her attention back to Tony again, she said: "Don't you think we ought to go?"

"Yes," Tony said. "Unless you'd like to dance."

"Well—would you?"

"Up to you, Phoebe. I have to look after the Smith sisters, you know," Tony said.

Myra excused herself and moved off in search of her husband: Dean must not have been even aware of her absence.

Her nerves were tight; she still felt the sharp, irregular rhythm of her heartbeats. She hoped what she felt did not show, she strove to reconcile herself to the abominable turn of events, for the loss of Tony meant more to her than she had ever believed it might. It was not easy to admit that those hours with him would be deprived her.

It was over. Out of expediency, of course. There was no doubt of that. Yet, knowing Tony, she could not quite part with the fear or suspicion that he might have wanted to break it off anyway.

Even so, she told herself as she moved through the clubrooms, she had no choice except to get past the crisis; she had to agree with him that it was not a hopeless catastrophe, but a warning, a lucky warning, as he'd called it. Still, in her resentment, his always-summer smile darkened.

The seething inside her started again, and she was furious with herself, she knew that what she felt might spread, web out, mark her face. And that would be a disaster with which she knew she could never cope.

As soon as she came into the lofty foyer, she sought the mirror by the cloakroom and, with an expertness born of practice and love, reappraised her features, seeking any trace of the emotion that might have betrayed her.

Yet with that special vision common to people of excessive vanity, she was not the image of her true self, but of that person she believed she presented to the world—a slender, dark blond woman in classic evening dress; a face that to her seemed fragile rather than hollowed; eyes vivid in the oval depth of their frames, asparkle with youth, rather than shadow-ringed, fearful, overbright.

When she turned away she was satisfied, having like Narcissus acquired nourishment and reassurance from her own reflection.

She caught sight of her husband, Dean, and she was relieved to see that he was standing near the entryway talking with Scott Quinnley.

She would have gone directly to the two men, except that now, coming out from the Ladies' Room, she saw Ann and Jemmy Thompson, and Ann already focusing on her her inquisitive glance, so that rather than evade her, or risk being in any possible defensive position, she sauntered over to her sister, and before Ann could launch one of those unnecessarily bizarre remarks, she said: "I haven't the remotest idea what time it is. Is everybody leaving?"

"Just about," Ann said, and lit a cigarette.

"I'd better fetch Dean," Myra was quick to say, and turned away.

"What happened to you, Myra?" Ann's swift question detained her.

"Why? Was anything supposed to happen?"

"I meant you and Tony. Dancing all that time, don't tell me you two were burying the old hatchet?" Ann said with a cheerfulness that unsettled Myra at once.

"It's a bit late in the day for that, isn't it?" Myra said, but instead of leaving, which she could have done, she found herself lingering. And though she knew it might be disagreeable, she realized that even if she and Ann had another of those rows, it would give her a little extra time in which to ease herself into the rhythm of a normal or more natural mood before going to Dean—just as, on those afternoons when she and Tony made love, she needed the drive home alone to refurbish her state of mind, to soothe her conscience, to put behind her the excitement and prepare herself for the not unpleasant but familiar pattern of her life with Dean.

"I only asked," Ann said, "because poor Phoebe looked kind of stood up—I shouldn't really say 'poor Phoebe,' should I? She looked more like a happy martyr in a Bergdorf-Goodman hair shirt."

It was possible for Myra to laugh. "Yes." The moment had passed.

But it hadn't. Ann said, "Myra—"

"What?"

"Isn't it practically historical, you and Tony tolerating each other for more than three minutes?" Ann said quite pleasantly. "Or did Father lay down the old law?"

Myra said: "The only thing Father was upset about tonight was that silly, tactless game you started at the table. I don't know what got into you, Ann." Then, before her sister could reply, Myra shrugged in a gesture of friendly tolerance. "Oh, well, it's too late to hash that over, isn't it?" Going on then, swerving away still further from the initial concern: "Where's Ben?"

"In the bar," Ann said.

Myra, encouraged, showed a determined sisterly goodwill: "I must admit he certainly looked attractive tonight, it would have set you up to hear what some of the women were saying about him. I know you don't care, but—"

"Thanks," Ann said. "How come all this sudden *gentilesse?*"

"It's not sudden. I meant it."

"Since when? You mean Ben Nodina grows on one like the taste for snails?" Ann said.

"I only said you would have been pleased to hear some of the comments," Myra said. She'd come upon a new attack, it was foolish to go on disparaging Nodina, it would be much wiser to boost him, to encourage Ann's involvement with him—anything to hasten her departure. The sooner Ann was gone, the more agreeable life would be for Myra, the more prominence she would have. She was convinced too that Ann's marriage to Nodina would be disastrous, and she didn't want to stand in the way of catastrophe.

Ann had always swung her way through life; life had always been

117]

too much of a romp for her, she needed to know what it was like to take a real fall, to fall hard enough so that even her father's adoring hand couldn't help her up.

"Ben's alone, having another drink," Ann was saying. "If you're that interested, Myra."

Ignoring the remark, feeling she'd managed herself very well, Myra felt restored, enough time had passed for her to go on, and she turned away, moved off to join her husband. "Dean, I've been looking all over the place for you, we ought to think of leaving."

"Oh? Well, yes." Dean turned his attention from Scott Quinnley. It was obvious, she thought again, that her absence had gone unnoticed. She should have known.

She was proud of Dean. She admired him. Stocky but tall enough to carry his beefy middle, the rather jaundiced complexion of his narrow face ruddily veneered by daily sunlamp treatments, Dean, looking so remarkably young, the gray hair blending with the blond, taking on that young indeterminate color; Dean in the conservative dark suit and white shirt, but wearing like a banner proclaiming his "artistic" gifts as Bellgard's Chief Stylist, the handmade cravat of small abstract forms: *Well,* he would say when someone asked where he bought his unique ties, *to tell you the truth, I design my own, it's easier than having to shop around.* A kind of half truth, since in reality he merely adapted the patterns he found among his collection of books and magazines of modern paintings and textiles.

"We'll expect you then, Scott," Dean resumed. "Nine o'clock, Thursday next. Delighted Tony asked you." Grasping Scott's shoulder with a firm, if condescending spirit of fellowship, he said: "As a matter of fact it was my wife who suggested you come, Myra has a green thumb for growing ideas—"

Scott Quinnley turned to look at her. She said: "It wasn't my idea actually"—speaking with that demure politeness which implied she was merely being properly modest—"my father was the one who mentioned it."

To Myra there was not the shadow of a doubt that Scott was executive potential for Bellgard. Her father, whose interest in him was genuine, liked to say: "An automobile company is like a big-league ball team, they have to keep an eye out for a new muscle."

Looking at Scott now, noticing the dark eyes, the grace of his hands, she thought there was certainly very little trace of Red Quinnley in him—or perhaps just enough to spike one's interest.

[118

Though why, what could it possibly matter to her? Yet, it was rather a pity he wasn't just a bit older (or she younger)—he had an aura of contained power, and he had a sort of unstudied charm, or the brand of Eastern manners she found admirable—no, it wasn't Scott Quinnley at all, it was simply that she was transferring to him some qualities she saw in Tony Kerwin.

"Dean," she said, directing her concern as wife and hostess to her husband, "Why don't we have Scott to dinner Thursday, since you all have to get to the plant afterward."

Dean agreed at once, and Scott Quinnley, though he seemed to hesitate, said yes. And presently she saw him leaving with Jemmy Thompson.

Driving home later she was surprised to see that Dean drove with such zest, leaning forward over the wheel of his Bellgard which had concealed beneath this year's hood next year's engine. But it couldn't have been that, that accounted for his spirit. She was both puzzled and reassured; she took too much interest in business matters not to know or recognize on the barometer of her husband's features the rise or fall of Bellgard's progress, and she knew the company was beset by storms. Now Dean turned the car into the driveway of their low-roofed, exotically modern, neo-Japanese house (only Dean could have conceived such a house, this residence which had been written about and photographed in more national magazines than any other house in Kent Hills).

It was almost two o'clock in the morning by the time she and Dean prepared for bed.

Sitting in her white silk slip before the mirrored dressing table in the white-carpeted master bedroom, she stroked the hormone cream into her cheeks and throat, pressing her fingertips too firmly into the skin, as if she might press away the aftermath of being with Tony.

Fighting it, turning, tilting her head slightly, palming back the long strands of dark blond hair, viewing her reflection in the glass from the angle of softest vision, taking renewed inspiration as, now, the image of Scott Quinnley reappeared, but pushing it out again, knowing she was being absurd. And then discovering in the mirror that Dean was watching her—a look she recognized at once.

"What's taking you so long?" Dean said. Yet despite this obvious flare of desire, there he was lifting the ashtray, going into the bathroom, emptying the stubs.

"Why?" she said as he returned. "Don't tell me you have any dis-

119]

honorable ideas at this time of night. Isn't that a bit late for you?"

His answer, she saw, was that he took off his pajama top and hung it neatly over the chair.

Nastyneat. Even now.

Hastily she said: "Dean, I meant to ask you, have you heard anything special about the Eames muffler situation?"

"Hmm? Oh, Eames."

"Yes."

"That's Tony's package. He's going to have to rewrap it." But Dean's voice, which, when they were alone, often took on a merely casual, grudging tone whenever they discussed Tony Kerwin, now seemed more accelerated, sharper.

"Thank heavens," she said, "you've never had to get yourself involved in that kind of thing."

"Myra, are you going to cream your face all night?"

"Be through in no time, darling." Then: "You know, I couldn't get out of dancing with him. He seemed awfully—not at all himself." Probing, having to know more, as if that might somehow appease her longing for Tony—yet her being unfaithful to Dean was not as disturbing to her as the feeling that she might be disloyal to his interests, his position, his aspirations. She heard him laugh then, and she said: "It couldn't be that amusing, could it?"

"I just remembered that remark Sam Kyssin made at the plant today, did I tell you about it?" Dean said.

"No."

"It was all over the third floor. Kyssin said: 'That's no muffler Eames puts out, that's a soda straw.' I doubt if Tony passed that one on to you, did he?"

"No."

"What'd he have to say?" For the first time Dean's voice sparked with interest.

Slowly Myra replaced the jars and tubes of ointments. "Oh, it was more what he didn't say."

"Oh," Dean seemed disappointed. Then he said: "I approved the new specifications."

"You did? Why? Why, Dean?"

"Because Vince Eames is going to give me what I want—" And Dean went on to tell her that, in the battle for new design for the new sports model, The Bellstar, he wanted to raise the lowly muffler to the level of design asset, he wanted aluminum plating for the tip of the pipe, he wanted to flatten out the mouth so that the unit would integrate with the new fastback treatment.

She saw, as he told her about it, that he kept restacking, rearranging more tidily, the pile of Italian art and automotive magazines to which he subscribed. "That damn muffler is evidently a headache all the way down the line, and I'm not even sure if the modifications for next season are going to work out. Between us, I don't give a damn—it's a minor part. But Tony has had it coming to him, he's nursed Eames for years and now I think he's got a little monster on his hands."

Myra turned on the white tufted stool. "Dean, I think you do give a damn, I've never seen you this worked up over a—"

He reached for his pajama pants. "I'm not at all worked up. A man like Tony—and I'm not saying he hasn't been a strong asset in the company, but he's gotten to the point where he—I wish you could have seen him in your father's office yesterday—virtually dusting off the chair."

Yes, but her father adored Tony, forgave him when he might never forgive others. Tony had that way with him. However, Myra knew that Dean was something of a zealous chair-duster himself, he had never relaxed his campaign to win her father's highest esteem. She'd seen him acting with a cloying solicitude that could be embarrassing. "Well," she said, "I know you're not breaking your heart if Tony has his troubles."

"I'm holding up under it," Dean remarked coldly. "Tony has a bad rash of self-grandeur. He goes on the assumption no one else can be in the running after Cod retires."

"Oh, he knows better than that, doesn't he?" Myra said, having long witnessed the maneuvers between the two brothers-in-law. "After all, darling, you haven't exactly kept it a dark secret about how you stand."

"No. But I have to be more careful. I've got a tradition against me. A designer rarely gets a chance at the top chair."

"I know. But in your case, I'd say it was quite different." Myra spoke in a warm rush of wifely pride that came so spontaneously she was not aware of its source or reason. For though she had always been as ambitious for Dean as he was for himself, she had come to resign herself to the limitations of his position.

Dean, quick to observe her new hopefulness, said: "What makes you say it's different now? You never used to think so."

"Oh"—she addressed her reflection in the glass—"I can't help but feel that things are beginning to change a bit."

"Well, you're right," Dean said. "Of course Tony has more or less had the Board on his side, he's had a lot of potential votes in his pocket ready to ballot him in the minute Cod announces his retirement—if that day ever comes. But now there might be some realignment of sides, and if any of the other directors or stockholders decide to jettison Tony, I'm the last man who's going to stop them."

"Darling, you know, I thought you were in marvelous spirits tonight but I didn't quite know why." And though it was clearer to her now, she could still not absorb the change (for hadn't Dean's star descended, hadn't he been slipping downward, pushed by Bellgard's belated styling trends during the past two model years?).

"Now you know," Dean said, making it sound more like a pronouncement.

"Yes," she answered in the new silence.

"You look wonderful there—" Dean said.

"Hmm?" Oh yes: she saw in the glass what he meant, the way the thin strap of her white slip had dropped from her shoulder, baring one side.

"Right out of the canvas—that Soutine." He moved over to her, still carrying his pajama pants.

She was touched; except that despite his aesthetic tribute, he still remembered to fold his pajama pants tidily over the chair.

When she rose to meet his arms, the slip dropped to her hips. How he adored that; Dean always had to see her with some bit of clothing, some undergarment between him and her nudity. Up to a point. Then it would be forgotten.

He was kissing her breasts too suddenly, and then he was telling her to hurry. She went into the bathroom and when she returned she saw that he was emptying the ashtray into the low white brick fireplace.

The sight shattered what was left of passion. "Do you have to do that, darling?"

No, but he wanted to distract himself.

She was still wearing panties, and she took them off, and she saw the pained look on his face; it made her feel better, for Tony always preferred her nakedness vivid and unadorned—but how foolish this was, this foolish act of revenge. Why on earth did she do it?

It had to stop.

[122

In his arms now, and yes it was good, wasn't it? And then letting her hand come down to hold him, hearing at once his grunt of protest. He always feared these overtures; they robbed him of control. (How unlike Tony he was.)

He drew her hand away, and then he was loving her, and soon the very familiarity, the rightness of it, gave her a sensation of clean re-establishment. She hadn't known how much she needed that, at least she needed it tonight, so that she found a newly sweet and bitter satisfaction as she gave herself to her husband's tidy, ordered lust.

11: Tony Kerwin

LESS than a mile from Myra and Dean Stratler was the residence of Phoebe and Tony Kerwin. Their bedroom was one of the coziest quarters in "the cottage" as they called their vast and sprawling English-styled house. To Tony "the cottage" held peace when he wanted it, and he wanted it tonight. It was like a cove sheltered from stormy seawaters, just as Phoebe was to him a steadying and comforting woman, apart from and unlike her volatile sisters.

Here Tony might shut out images of Myra, and if it were at all possible, he might even leave behind the vision of Vincent Eames.

But tonight was not like other nights, not only because his own world had been altered, but because Phoebe seemed different. Something about her seemed different. Or was he looking at her through the eyes of his guilt—and since when could guilt unbalance him or distort his vision?

No. It was Phoebe. He watched her. Always the first to be in the twin bed, tonight she dawdled, lagged, as if she were harboring some sensation from which she did not want to be parted too soon . . . "poor Phoebe," as Myra or Ann called her, though perhaps not for the same reason. But poor Phoebe was, he knew, much happier than Myra, who either ignored her or used her. Or Ann who merely pitied her, Ann who had once said quite rightly: "At least Phoebe has something to hold on to, she believes in three verities: God, Father and Tony."

And thus far nothing had happened to cause her to question her faith, and certainly Tony had been careful never to give her reason to lose it.

Phoebe might run third in the family sweepstakes, yet in her own subdued way she had gained something none of the others had: her father's complete trust. Cod trusted her, relied on her, never doubted her. (And this in turn, Tony felt, had to reflect happily on him.)

In his own way Tony had a deep and abiding respect for her. And

[124

for all her seeming simplicity, her foolish obsession with dieting and faddist regimes, she was at heart very sensible and one of the few decent persons he knew—if anything, he thought now beneath the weight of his new burdens, she was too damn decent.

But this basic goodness did not make Phoebe more desirable to him. If once, he thought with vague regret, once nine years ago he had found her rather fresh and appealing, if once, as when they'd been on their wedding trip in Bermuda, he'd been titillated by the novelty of her pristine nature, it had to be admitted that this no longer lured him.

Now, as he put on his dark blue and initialed pajamas, he saw that Phoebe was still lingering at her dressing table; he watched her as she kept fidgeting with the clasp of her string of pearls; when she'd finished she placed them in the velvet-lined jewel box where she kept the diamonds which she seldom wore, being, like her parents, reluctant to make any kind of glittering show in public . . . though the silk nightgown she wore now was, she believed, an extravagance to please him.

He turned and flung himself down on his bed; he stretched; he knew sleep would not come easily tonight. The room with its sloping ceiling, its flowered chintz and the charming fireplace alcove, always rather comforting to him, was not soothing now. He lay there too rigidly. He roughed his hand through the dark thickness of his hair. His scalp tickled: for him an infallible, though rare, symptom of nerves. The club tonight had undone him. He touched the mole on his cheek; he thought with a nostalgia which seldom touched him, of the times of his youth, of those charming sporting Florida winters when he'd sold Rolls Royces with such aplomb to New Yorkers and Chicagoans, and of some of their young second or third wives to whom he gave pleasure during languid nights.

He'd come a long way. Too long?

He needed to talk, unburden himself, talk to Phoebe, confide in her . . . but what could you say to her, how far could you go?

"For God's sakes, Phoebe, don't fuss around there all night."

"What?" She turned around; the light hair, neatly waved, clean, shining, was too short, making her neck appear too long. "Oh, I'm not very sleepy." But her voice held something else and her pallid face was inflamed. "It's just amazing how much energy you have if you cut down your calory intake at dinner. Darling, don't wait up, you need the rest, we'll talk in the morning."

She was holding back. Yes. Exploratively, he said: "This isn't like you, you must have had too much club tonight."

"Oh hardly, I always enjoy it there."

At least, he thought, she hadn't noticed anything. No suspicion in her voice.

"The club was a damn bore," he heard his voice in uncharacteristic complaint.

"Really?" She came over to the bed. "Why, I thought you were in grand form." Then: "But you do look tired—"

"I'm not." Irritably he wondered why she seemed so eager to have him asleep. "What's happened to you, you're usually dead to the world by this time."

"Oh—" She looked away, her cheeks still flushed, the pale eyes undrowsy, almost sparkling. "I don't know. I'll read a while." She reached up to turn off the light over his bed.

He intercepted her. "What's got into you Phoebe?"

"Hmm?" she murmured, but he observed how stiffly she was holding herself. The eyes were vividly animated; possibly it could be that she might have wanted him to make love to her but was reluctant to shorten the span of his night's rest. She could be like that. He passed his eyes briefly over her bosom: Phoebe, he thought again, at thirty-eight, had somehow managed to retain a virginal look. He cast his view upward to the slope of ceiling, he turned back again. "What's eating you?" he persisted. "You're not yourself, not at all."

A sudden irrepressible laugh. "Do I always show everything? I suppose I do." Then, as though succumbing almost helplessly to an impulse too long contained, she said: "I really shouldn't discuss it, Tony. I wanted to wait until morning when—"

"Phoebe, for God's sake." If this wasn't like her, holding back what was on her mind in order not to mar his rest. Like the time when she'd delayed telling him she was pregnant, because she knew he was en route to the doctor for his annual checkup, and she feared the news might have some ill-effect on the tests he had to have. As it turned out she suffered a miscarriage.

"Well, actually, darling," she said, "I only came in at the end of the conversation when it happened—"

"When what happened?"

"About Father." Phoebe leaned forward, her breath came in rapid joyous release. "No one knows, just mother and I. About father, I mean. You weren't there at the table. You were outside, talking to Vince Eames. I thought you'd never get back, I thought Vince might even have found out about it, he's such a snooper—but he couldn't have."

Vince. The mere mention of that name, so long a familiar mono-syllable in the daily language of his life, came like a spasm of pain. "I don't know what you're talking about."

"I only said even Vince couldn't have known about Father."

"Oh." A measure of relief, however brief, though the name would return, joining those other unwanted sounds, other names like Sam Kyssin or Kamber the engineer, or the head of purchasing.

"I promised myself I wouldn't discuss it until tomorrow," Phoebe said again.

Tony edged himself up on one elbow. "Don't tell me Cod is talking about that European tie-up again? I thought he'd written that off."

It's not Europe, it's Florida!" she answered at once, in a flurry of daughterly, wifely triumph. "You know how long I've been begging him, but now he's definitely going to retire."

The announcement, as she must have known, flooded him with instant excitement; his fatigue vanished, a buoyant surge lifted him beyond the moment. How long, how damn interminably long had he been waiting to hear this! Cod Smith had always been cagey, evasive, permitting no one even a shred of knowledge. Now it had come and he almost feared to believe it.

"I wouldn't be too sure."

"Oh, you don't know Father, I mean when he's on the telephone over an hour to Palm Beach about buying that island house and the cost of a cruiser for deep-sea fishing and—"

"It could be for nothing more than a business junket." Tony still sought that final guarantee.

"Not at those dreadful prices," Phoebe answered, echoing the good sense of her New England-born father.

Nevertheless Tony, like other officers of the company, had always heard Codman Smith state he wouldn't retire until Bellgard had recovered its 11 percent of the total automobile market—and this was not in sight yet. He said: "I agree, though it doesn't necessarily commit him—"

"He specified the time," Phoebe protested. "A year from next fall."

The statement sealed off his last misgiving, and again he allowed himself the full luxury of the long-held dream. He saw that she was watching him, she radiated such a joyful tenderness, a pride, as if thereby she could make this moment even richer for him.

"Now you know," she was saying, "why I tried not to tell you until tomorrow. Neither of us will sleep a wink now."

Yes. He held on to the almost unbearable pleasure and gratification of seeing within his grasp the single honor toward which he had been striving. There was no doubt in his mind that Codman Smith's first act, after announcing his retirement to the board, would be to recommend him as his successor.

What about cries of favoritism shown to a son-in-law? No matter. He was the man. He knew that in addition to his administrative talents, there were other factors shaping his chances: he provided the ideal image which a corporation liked to see in its president; he had that extra fillip of charm, of tact, of contagious optimism—more than being the perfect man for the office, he *looked* like the perfect man. This factor in today's kind of warfare between automobile companies was much more serious than it might have been twenty or thirty years ago. The image of the president was, like the design of the car itself, part of the package to win the public's heart and pocketbook.

Look at Bellgard since Kerwin took over! He wasn't going to be content with regaining that 11 percent of the market sales, he'd jump that to 12, maybe even 15 percent. He'd bulldoze out all the dead-wood, move in more enterprising personnel; he'd raise a new breed of Bellgard family; above all he'd push his theory to broaden the spectrum of models, widening it to include a style and price for every potential buyer. Also, he'd push his plan for broad diversification, setting Bellgard into other fields, electronics, missiles, and allied industries; he'd—

"What is it, Tony?"

"What?" Without warning, his euphoric fancy collapsed, gave way to the present; again depression seized him, pressing its weight mercilessly upon him.

"Is anything wrong?" Phoebe was looking at him in puzzled solicitude.

"No, no . . ." He summoned his reliable smile.

"Now, you can imagine how I felt!" she exclaimed. "If Myra knew wouldn't she just about die! Not that Dean has a chance, but you couldn't tell *her* that."

He nodded, as if in agreement, though no one knew better than he

[128

that Dean Stratler had no intention of letting a tradition discourage him. He might appear dedicated to styling, he might know that styling chiefs seldom make the corner office, but this would never faze Dean, who would without hesitation throw his hat in the ring.

Tony said: "It's not going to be that easy. It's still going to be up to the board and to the stockholders."

"Oh, I know. But everyone knows you're the man."

But her wifely pride, instead of boosting his spirit, only served to make more oppressive his rising despondency.

Why now? he asked himself. Why now? Here he was within one stroke of the final victorious hole, and here he was sand-trapped.

Racing before the dark screen of his mind were the unanswered questions:

How to clean house? How to quell the assistant engineer's belated puritanism? How to eliminate the prodding, nosy, zealous peddler Sam Kyssin? How to muzzle Vince Eames? And how could he even make sure that Myra would remain discreet, reasonable? How . . . how . . . ?

"Tony—what is it, darling? Did I say something that—"

"No, of course not, not at all."

At once she got up from the side of the bed. "I knew I shouldn't have told you tonight. I'll get you a tranquilizer." She moved to her bathroom with its overstocked pharmaceutical inventory. He watched her, seeing her silhouette through the nightdress. Phoebe had acquired so much health she looked incomplete, like the unit frame of a car before the shell is fitted on to it. She returned and poured a glass of water from the silver carafe.

Stiffly, automatically, he swallowed the pill; it wouldn't touch him, he knew.

She stood back looking down at him. He could no longer even make the pretense of celebration or hope.

"Darling, you look done in. It is too much for one night." Then: "Tony, you are all right, aren't you? I mean you suddenly seem— well, not very happy—"

He didn't trouble to answer. He rose, swung over the side of the bed. He went to his dressing room, came back with a lighted cigarette.

Time enough to have made the decision. No alternative. Though he had always presented to her, as to the world, a façade of confident and reassuring optimism, he knew he had to somehow prepare

129]

Phoebe (and thus her father) for a voyage that might not be as smooth or easy as she assumed, and for which she was totally unprepared—for if God and Cod Smith's reputations were unassailable, the same could no longer be said of Tony Kerwin.

Confide in her. A man confides in his wife.

Tell the truth? Yes and no. The problem was more subtle. If he could somehow exaggerate the truth so that it would seem almost unbelievable, yet hold a grain of reality not yet visible . . . so that if trouble arose, at least she could not accuse him of not having told her beforehand.

Yet to bring it off, to make it all sound overmagnified, partly hypothetical, general, even grimly amusing, to make himself appear as just another normal victim of the normal game of corporate business—this was the delicate task; to drive straight, yet obliquely, to his target.

He exhaled the bitter-tasting cigarette smoke, he said: "Of course, Phoebe—like anything that looks good, there's sometimes an underside that isn't so good. It's something we've got to be ready for."

But Phoebe's clear and still-exalted gaze had not grasped this unpleasant forecast, she still lived within the bright and steady climate which he himself had for so long helped to create.

"Did you hear me, Phoebe?"

"Oh, of course I did, but I'm not in the least worried, not about you."

A smile to cancel out the frown of apprehension. "I wish," he said quietly, "I could count on other people the way I can on you. But"—he inhaled very deeply—"but the world ain't like that, and we have to anticipate the potshots."

"Potshots?" She seated herself contentedly on the chintz armchair by the fireplace; on her face the afterglow of excitement still shone.

"Well, you know how it can happen sometimes," he spoke more firmly, as you speak to a child who is not being attentive, "the moment it looks like you're the first candidate for the top chair, they start getting a bead on you and the potshots begin."

"Who is 'they'?" Phoebe asked almost as if she were indulging a mood which she knew was transitory.

"Anyone who thinks they might have something to lose if Tony Kerwin is elected." Patiently he set to work to put in place the stones of a psychological wall behind which he hoped to protect her.

[130

But she said: "If you're worried about Dean, that's foolish. Dean is too specialized, his job is styling."

"It isn't Dean—though don't let yourself rule it out. Dean is not married to the styling studio, he's ready to move out anytime he can. Dean thinks he's beyond that."

"That's Myra's idea. Not his. Myra's made him feel like that. She's always been the one."

"All right. But I can tell you this—" Tony had to speak forcefully now, yet keeping his tone reasonable. He had to be like a political candidate who, despite a splendid record and an irreproachable private life, foresees the venality of the opposition. "And don't say I didn't warn you. I know this industry, I know the infighting that can start. The minute it looks like I'm the key man for the chair, a lot of rather seedy characters will start in slugging, mud-slinging—"

"Tony, what could they say? What could they possibly say about someone like you?"

"What could they say?" Tony emitted a light laugh of indulgence. "I could enumerate all night, starting with my dear friend Vince. Let's say he could dig up—" Tony halted.

"Dig up what?"

He couldn't, of course, bring himself to tell her about the fattening of his income. He said: "Dig up any garden variety of disagreeable charges—not that he would, he wouldn't dare. But his competitors would. You take a peddler like Kyssin. Sam Kyssin has been pushing to get our muffler parts business, he's got a bee in his silly bonnet now. He's been saying we're showing favoritism to Eames. All he has to do is dig up something that sounds ugly and use it to rake in proxies from the stockholders. He can accuse us of collusion, conflict of interests, all that, anything to get a shake-up. After all, it's no secret in this business that a man always tries to take care of his friends, and it would look logical to say Vince Eames has been taking care of me to keep the orders coming in."

"Yes," Phoebe said, "but that wouldn't hold, would it? Eames was making our mufflers before you joined the company."

"Exactly. Now you're seeing it," Tony said, but going on, keying his voice to the level midway between truth and fantasy. "Even so, that isn't preventing a peddler like Sam Kyssin from prying around, scratching up something he hopes might be turned into a hornet's nest. Let's say the chips are down, as they're apt to be at a stockholders meeting, a man like Kyssin can make a lot of ugly sounds, it doesn't matter what—as long as the linen can be made to seem dirty. They can even question the incentive bonuses I've received, or why did I take the head of Purchasing to a hot-dog stand for lunch. Nothing is sacred, they can throw in all kinds of ridiculous muck, anything, they can have me keeping a dozen mistresses, have me in bed with everyone from Miss America to both your sisters!"

He had become almost infatuated with the way he'd presented his position; he even sensed some relief, spurious as it might be.

He turned to look at Phoebe: he was dismayed; she didn't seem to have rallied to his side; her eyes were fixed upon his in dilated incredulity.

"Phoebe—have you been listening to me?"

She nodded, not speaking.

"Now what's got into you? All I was trying to do was give you a deliberately black picture, that's all. I only wanted you to see what a man can be up against sometimes." Then, as he realized again her failure to respond, his patience gave out. "For God's sake, Phoebe, where's your intelligence? I was deliberately exaggerating so that you might have—"

"But Tony—"

"What?"

"That isn't the point," she said. "I'm aware that all this is perfectly possible—but not with people like us—not with you."

"Listen, you've got to get out of this childish cocoon you live in. You're looking at me as if I was Jack the Ripper. If a husband can't talk to his own wife—" He abandoned the attack. Until now, he had felt a degree of awe, mingled with pity, for her; her ingenuousness, the fabric of her morality, even her love and trust, had touched him. But now these feelings receded, and all he felt was a rampant wrath, impatience, contempt.

Worse than that, he saw that the core of his fury lay within himself: he had made his first serious tactical error, he had reduced his own stature, he had undermined the base of his own future.

Seeing how she reacted, his hope of making her an ally was sealed off. Yet every wife, he thought bitterly, had to carry some weakness or secret of her husband's, just as every husband had to support or protect the vagaries of his wife.

But Phoebe was obviously not built like that. If she was disappointed in him, he was even more disappointed in her.

[132

He thought he knew her. He thought he could read her at all times. He was certain that, despite her frailties, she had a resilience like her father, that she could confront a crisis and move with it.

But he did not know her at all; she'd become within a few minutes a stranger to him, someone as unknown to him as Scott Quinnley. For that matter, he could probably say he didn't know Vincent Eames or Codman Smith. Or even Myra. . . .

Probably for the first time in his life he felt compelled to examine, look into, himself—that Tony Kerwin who had always been held in highest regard by Tony Kerwin. But like most people, he found, as he tried to probe his own nature, that the examination was painful. He had to shirk it. (Just as Phoebe cringed now from the already cracked porcelain image of her world.)

12: Ann Smith

ANN'S error was not in sleeping with Ben, but rather oversleeping. It was six in the morning by the time she left his apartment, six-thirty when she reached her house in Kent Hills. And this on one of the rare occasions when her father's insomnia had got out of hand. She was appalled, dismayed, as she let herself in the front hall, to almost collide with Cod, downstairs early, on his way to the recreation room for his daily workout. Cod peering at her now in her emerald evening dress and pumps, seeming now to her conspicuous and downright degenerate at this hour, in contrast to her father in the tennis trousers and sweatshirt.

"Do you usually get home this time of morning?" he asked. He stood absolutely still. All control. Therefore all nerves.

"No," she said, "I usually try to get back at a respectably unrespectable hour." But oh God, that was the wrong thing to say. This was no time to be jaunty. Better to come out and say it and get it over with. That was the trouble though. Loving someone, loving Cod, the truth did not always come easily—at least not at a time like this. It was something she had tried to spare him.

"There's coffee in the dining room," he said now. "Why don't you get some and bring it downstairs."

An order. Not a suggestion. "All right," she said. She took off her shoes, left them in the central hall. In the dining room she had a hasty cup of coffee, poured herself a second cup and took it down to the rec room where her father was pedaling (too rapidly) on his Exercycle.

She put her coffee cup down on the edge of the billiard table and lit a cigarette. She felt a little less unnerved now. At least the worst was over. Cod had always known she slept with Ben, but it was simply something he never let himself recognize and she, until today, had never given him an opportunity to recognize or be confronted by it.

[134

Even so. Poor Cod. "I overslept," she said. "I was at Ben's and I overslept."

He glanced up for an instant, then bent his head, hunched his bulky shoulders forward again and resumed his pedaling.

What next? He obviously expected or needed something satisfactory. She shouldn't have come home at all; it would have been better if she'd simply stayed at Ben's and given some reasonable or more palatable story the next day.

"What happened," she began, leaning more on the truth, "is that Ben had an opera going on his stereo, and opera sometimes bores me right to sleep. He loves it. And I try to put up with it." When her father did not respond to this, she heard herself add defensively: "The way you put up with Ben."

"I said nothing about Ben." And still pedaling.

"I'd rather you did," she said.

"Why? You know how I feel." For the first time her father stopped the machine. "And I feel more so this morning." Bitterness coarsened the texture of his voice.

Ann said: "You mustn't make the mistake of holding Ben responsible for my downfall. I know that's how you think of it."

"Let's not discuss it, Ann." The whir of the Exercycle commenced again.

"Why did you invite me down here then?" she said. "I mean, I don't see the point in our ever talking about Ben and me. I really don't, Father. You'll never loosen up. You're like this about any problem or situation that is tough to lick. You just tighten up and put on that hard chill face. I know you've had to do it, a habit in the company, it's how you play the old game. The auto business is played like that, isn't it? And now you can't act in any other way, you really can't. But I just can't take it anymore, I absolutely refuse. You know how it is between me and Ben. And that's how it is." Immediately remorse seized her. Her father had ceased his pedaling, caught himself, then resumed at once. But her outburst had stung him and she regretted it; she needn't have let it happen like that. Some parents could take a time like this. Jemmy's could. But not Ann's. "I'm sorry, Father. I didn't mean to get you all shook up."

He dismounted. His normally cool countenance was stippled with sweat. "I'm not all 'shook up,' Ann. I am disappointed."

"In me?" Ann said, and because his words had wounded her more than she'd expected, she went on: "Or is it that you're disappointed that I chose someone who can't fit into your ideal of dynasty? Like Tony or Dean."

"Ann."

"That is how you feel, it conditions everything you feel and do," she declared. "I understand. I mean, after all, you've been with Bellgard—you *are* Bellgard—since 1934. That's before I was even born. Now you find you've got a Ben Nodina on your hands and he's not interested in Bellgard or automobiles or anything else in Cartown. And that's not the kind of son-in-law you want."

"He's not the kind of man I'd want in my family *or* my business," Cod stated.

"Why bother to make the distinction," she said. "There isn't any anymore. Bad times for one is bad times for the other. A stain on one is a stain on the other. Our Father Who art at Bellgard. That's the prayer I must have learned first."

"This has nothing to do with what we are talking about," he said.

"It has everything to do with it," she retorted. "My being with Ben is no different than if one of the maids here were caught stealing. To you that would be a reflection not only on the family but on Bellgard too. They're indivisible now."

He would deny this, of course. An emotional tangent, a subterfuge of her guilt. He could not see himself as he was, as Bellgard. Not really, not fully. For Bellgard was no longer a privately held company. Its founders—Hiram Bellton and Jacques Gardeau—were long dead, and their heirs had sold out their holdings in 1928. That was the year, she knew, when Cod had been with Vanguard Motors, the year he had made the change-over from the four-cylinder engine to the six and eight. He could not have been as cool and inflexible then as he was now, and when he went with Bellgard in 1934 he could bend with the times, he had daring and vigor; prejudices hadn't yet calcified in him.

But now. Now the deeper Bellgard sank into difficulties, the calmer and more confident he had disciplined himself to be. That was all right too. That was how he had to run the show. He ran it straight, his honesty was legend; his principles were unshakable. Almost a handicap. For now the company he'd pushed to prominence was slipping; he had lost something, he had been unable to bend with the times, or unable to see their shape; administrative duties and politics had drained him of the magic he had once had. If he knew this, he resisted it. Just as, as a father knowing what her relationship with Ben was, he resisted that knowledge. And even when she had to spell it out, admit it, his comment was *I am disappointed.* Hurting her, wounding her, yes. But she realized now that he could have said something worse, crueler. He'd refrained because he hoped she would retract or qualify her admission; he'd hoped she might merely be trying to shock him. Now he knew otherwise. The blemish, the stain, was on him now. She could see this. This is how he was. People in the industry patently ascribed these qualities of his to the fact that he had had a stern New England indoctrination. Yes. But Cod himself—and how often she'd heard him say it—said: "Half the kids I grew up with are in jail today."

Wasn't this perhaps another reason why he was so blindly intolerant about Ben, Ben's father having been in prison once?

"I think I'll get some more coffee." Ann started out.

"Just a minute."

She turned. Her father's eyes, hard blue crystals of regret or sorrow, wavered, softened. He sat down in the leather chair near the exercise machine. "Nothing. Get your coffee."

"What is it?"

He withdrew his gaze. He looked up to the darkly paneled walls, undecorated except for a few prized and framed letters sent to him by Franklin Roosevelt, Eisenhower, Kennedy; there was the photograph of Cod taken at the plant with Robert P. Patterson, the Secretary of War in the early years of World War II.

Abruptly then he flung out his arm in a compulsive gesture of despair or bewilderment: "I don't know, I just will never understand, Ann. With all the interesting people around, how you ever let yourself get involved with—"

"Name one!" she cried.

"What?"

"Name *one* of these interesting people around." She moved back to the billiard table. Furiously she said: "And don't say Scott Quinnley!"

"I was speaking generally," Cod said. "Though I certainly see nothing objectionable in Scott."

"I know you don't." Then: "Even last night at the club, when we played that game that got everybody so damn nervous, even then you didn't complain. Why? Because I was playing it with Scott. And Scott can do no wrong. Isn't that the truth? I mean if it'd been Ben, I'd never have heard the end of it."

137]

Silence.

Then Cod rose, mounted the Exercycle and, as if to pump out all the burdens, he hunched low over the handlebars and began to pedal at a steady, grinding speed.

"It's true, isn't it?" Ann said again. "Scott can do absolutely no wrong. Well, he's still new. Give him more time." She walked out, her feet thumping lightly, futilely, on the tile floor. She felt relieved and even triumphant. Not until she reached the hallway upstairs and retrieved her green pumps, did she admit that she had gained no ground for herself or Ben, and that she had only quickened the pain her father did not deserve.

13: Scott Quinnley

IN the brilliance of the young June day, Scott Quinnley saw the double-deck trailer trucks, like great mobile cornucopias, nearing Quinnley Corners to discharge the new quota of new Bellgards. The deliveries had commenced yesterday.

He stationed himself by the second service entrance to watch. Three days ago he had walked away from the third floor with assurances from Kerwin's office that they would meet the demand to cut the quota of new units by a third. A negative victory, but a needed one. Advance word of what had happened had already infected the personnel of Quinnley Corners with a spirit of relief, even renewed hope.

Presently Kellog, in his white service coat, and holding the familiar clipboard, joined Scott at the entryway: "We've got a few three-legged dogs as usual, Scott," he said wryly, going on to report that some of the factory-new cars had arrived with missing parts or equipment dumped on the car floors, or windows that wouldn't lower, doors that wouldn't close, windshields that leaked. "But at least we'll be able to slap 'em in shape without clogging the entire shop."

Even Marty Calhoon had left the showroom to put in a word: "How'd you do it, kid?" And then some of the other salesmen, among the best: Dave Toff, Artie Bernstein and Al Fogarty. They stood around watching the unloading, saying nothing but clearly come to witness for themselves what they'd doubted could ever happen.

After a while, Scott turned to Kellog: "How many have we checked in now? Must be close to the end—"

Kellog nodded.

"How many exactly?" he asked a few minutes later, seeing another trailer truck nearing the intersection. "Maybe you'd better go out back and check with Leo."

Kellog went to the rear outdoor area of service to see his assistant.

When he returned there was a marked frown on his narrow face: "That's peculiar—we're up to a hundred and thirty-one—"

"A hundred and thirty-one?" Scott repeated. "You sure?"

Yes, Kellog said. He looked at Scott quizzically.

Marty Calhoon lit a cigarette, stepped out to the curb and peered to the corner. "I don't know," he muttered as he came back.

"Say, Frank—" Kellog's assistant, Leo, hurried up. "I don't know how I goofed on this, but we all just assumed there'd be a hundred and thirty-five units—" He looked at Scott, then went on: "But here it is, right on the covering invoice: two hundred units." His stained finger pointed to the figure stamped on the sheet.

Scott went out to the corner himself and saw with dismay two more trailer trucks waiting to negotiate the turn at West Main Boulevard and Timber Trail Road. He stared in a kind of stupor, puzzled, unbelieving.

No way to reconcile this with what had transpired only three days before when he'd gone to the third floor to see Tony Kerwin. He had laid down his protest. At first Kerwin had been brisk, cool, no evidence of smiling camaraderie. Then he had turned Scott over to another section of his office, where Scott had had to confer with a tableful of junior executives. They had listened in silence, had nodded at his demand that the quota be cut until further notice. They said they'd see what could be done, but since the request was highly unorthodox, they could not promise anything definite.

Not accepting their response, Scott had gone back to Tony Kerwin. But the vice-president seemed harried and preoccupied by more major problems, and then one of his secretaries had intruded to announce that a Mr. Sam Kyssin was waiting outside. Kerwin's darkly handsome features had become ruffled, yet he summoned what must have been the full quotient of his charm and tact, and in his eagerness to be rid of Scott, smiling his visitor out of his office, he had said: "Don't get yourself too exercised about this, Scott. I know it's hard to get a quick answer up here, but I'm going to get this squared away once and for all. We'll call it a special case. A hundred and thirty-five units? Right. You've got it. For now." In the anteroom he'd told a secretary: "Get me McGregor, please. I want him immediately. Goodbye, Scott, all luck to you." And then, swinging around: "Delighted to see you, Mr. Kyssin, sorry to have kept you waiting, this is one of those jammed-up cloverleaf days—"

That had been three days ago, and between then and now there seemed to be no connection, an abyss bridged idiotically by the unwanted procession of trailer trucks.

Scott felt the warmth in his cheeks and neck, incensed not only by the collective gaze of the men upon him, but by the factory's indifference and deception. If his own men regarded him as naïve or inadequate, he must have seemed to the executives at Bellgard like another demented kind of Don Quixote poking at the windmills of an entire industry.

Then the next trailer truck backed up for the turn into the garage entry.

Abruptly the sight of the new Bellgards acted to shake Scott loose from his inertia. He stepped just inside the service entrance, pressed the flat brass button. The heavy metal overhead door came groaning downward and clanked into place. Quinnley Corners was closed to all further deliveries.

Immediately from out on the street came the protesting blasts of the truck horn and the shouts of the driver. Kellog hurried forward, reached up for the door release. Scott stopped him. "That's all we're taking, Frank."

"What?"

"That's all we're taking. The garage is closed. You'd better go out there and tell the drivers to go back, tell them we aren't accepting any more new units."

"How's that?" Kellog said as if he might have heard incorrectly.

Scott repeated the order. Kellog looked at him for an instant, then nodded hesitantly and made his way out to the street. Chaos then ensued, for traffic became congealed as two more trucks blocked all circulation amid a cacophony of horns and cries of drivers.

Mrs. Bowsley, Red's secretary, was at Scott's side then, her birdlike face stiff with consternation: Red, she said, was on the telephone and wanted to talk to Scott at once. Scott returned to the main office and took the call at his father's desk. He had obviously been notified.

"Hello, Red." He braced himself. "Where are you?"

He was at the golf club. "What the hell is going on?"

Scott told him, still braced for the rambunctious protest that would follow, but there was only silence for a while, and then Red said: "Well, maybe you did the right thing." And Scott even thought he detected a slight sly smile in his voice. "We'll know how right it was before the day is over. I'll be in at two. Hold down the shop."

Red's reaction came like a fortifying tonic. The day passed without word from Bellgard. Nor were there any telephone messages at the house that evening. And after Red had seen Susan to bed, his father said: "Looks like maybe it'll stick."

"Yes."

Silence marked the second day until late afternoon when Scott received an enormous box of roses from a downtown florist. The card was signed *From an anonymous friend,* though the handwriting was Ann Smith's: *You must be either crazy or crazy. What kind of Company Man are you? Don't you want to eat? Don't you want to succeed by trying? What kind of true blue American boy are you?*

Red Quinnley studied the card. "Well, I think that's a goddam good omen."

"Why?" Scott said.

"I think maybe the third floor is buying it. I think maybe it'll stick, son."

As it turned out, the roses from Ann were but the first of several other manifestations. For the newspapers had come upon the story, making of it much more than it could possibly warrant, and the following day Scott received a note from Tony Kerwin's office stating that the special showing at the styling lab to which he had been invited "had been canceled."

Scott had undoubtedly lost his amateur standing. His professional virginity had been taken. The courtship was over.

As Red had said, the votes weren't all in yet.

By the third day, the silence from the factory ended, replaced by nothing less than the Regional Sales Director, Halister McGregor, who marched into the office late in the afternoon. He was, as on his earlier visit, asmile with ebullient humor. Except that this time he removed his white linen jacket, loosened his white silk tie, and sprawled back in one of Red's chairs.

"Whew!" He whistled. "Ninety degrees in the shade today. Hotter than a B-girl's box on Saturday night!" He paused, then looked directly at Scott. "Scott, I chased down here just to see for myself if you were on the other end of a butterfly net, or if maybe my old friend Red was functioning with a case of D.T.'s." He laughed good-naturedly. "But I'm happy to observe that the Messrs. Quinnley seem to be copacetic, as my dear departed dad used to say. Back on the third floor the impression they gave me was that you boys might have lost your buttons. Joking aside, I just looked in to have a friendly talk, I don't get hysterical like some of the brass. In fact"—he brought the blaze of his bright blue eyes upon Red—"in fact when some of our executives who shall be nameless, started talking about what to do with your franchise, I—"

"Listen, Mac—" Red cut through. "Listen, Mac, you must have the wrong goddam address, you're not talking to one of those tin-front, twenty-unit-a-month shops. Almighty Christ, if you want a fight, say so, but don't insult my intelligence or my rating with that horseshit of yours about my franchise!"

"As I was saying," McGregor continued, unruffled, smiling broadly, "it was I who told them, not so fast gentlemen, after all Quinnley Corners is like—"

"—a historical landmark," Red finished the statement.

"That's it, Red. And I said let me chase down there and see if maybe there hasn't been some error or some—"

"There's been no error," Scott said.

"No?" He turned to Scott. "Now that's peculiar. I could have sworn there was, or maybe you didn't realize it, my boy. Or maybe you forgot what we pay our P.R. people just to keep Bellgard's image right up there. We don't pay them so that Mr. Scott Quinnley can pull a stunt, make a splash for himself. Or maybe you didn't know that by refusing to take the full quota allotted you, you committed a dishonorable and malicious violation of the franchise."

McGregor's customary tone of robust humor had taken on a grimness as he mouthed the legalistic words, and even Red failed to rally the kind of rough response that usually marked exchanges between the two men. "Mr. McGregor," Scott said then, "I told you when you were here the last time, I told you then what our situation was, and you ignored it completely. I told the factory also. And they ignored it. There was nothing left to do, and I'm certainly not going to reverse what I did."

"This boy, Red," McGregor said, "ought to dip his balls in a basin of ice water."

Red said: "Scott's running the show now. We're standing pat." He paused. "He did this without consulting me, but now that it's done, I think it was a goddam good sensible idea. I stand pat."

"Oh?" McGregor said. "Well"—the zone sales manager tugged his white tie into place—"let me just say that I admire your stand, admire it. You and Scott are going to be a tough combination. Yes. Scott, my boy, you almost pulled it off, didn't you?"

143]

"Almost?"

"Yes. Almost." McGregor softened the volume of his voice. "After all, you sold Kerwin, who doesn't sell easy. When he tracked me down, he passed on the word for me to put you down for one-third less quota. Well, you know that didn't sound pretty to Halister McGregor. I argued the point, but he said it was an order. I lost that round. But I'm not a good loser. I told myself, well maybe Scott here packs a little special pull with the factory. However"—he paused to moisten his lips—"there were two things none of us counted on. First, that splash in the newspapers—"

The Detroit papers, perhaps for lack of anything better at hand, or because in the area no event, however small, is overlooked if it concerns the automobile industry, had picked up the incident, blowing it up to outsized value. *One-Man Revolution* was the way one of the dailies labeled the case in its lead.

"Well, that's over," McGregor went on. "And P.R. has sent out a covering release. 'Due to alterations,' " he quoted, " 'Quinnley Corners was unable to accommodate their usual quota of cars. But by the fifteenth of this month, Bellgard officials have been informed, Quinnley Corners will have their premises ready again to welcome their full quota of new cars.' " He waited, and then very quietly: "Welcome spells two hundred units. Or more."

Again Scott could only stare at the man in astonishment.

"Christ, Mac," Red spoke up, "you people never know when to stay dead, do you?"

"Red, you and I know what happens when a man lays down for the count, don't we?" Then, turning back to Scott again: "You've got the picture now, Scott? Quinnley Corners rolls along to the fifteenth, and then fulfills its quota to the letter. The letter. That spells two hundred units."

"Not here it doesn't! Why in hell do you think I did this?" Scott's voice rose in anger. "The quota stays as is. The factory can unload those cars somewhere else, but not at Quinnley Corners!"

"Not the factory. Those are my cars, my boy, *my* cars!" Halister McGregor almost leaped up from his chair, his thick index finger like a pistol. "Halister McGregor is the one who accounts for his own zone! Listen, my boy, do you know what happened after all that play in the press? Do you know what happened? Our switchboards, our mail centers, got swamped with calls and wires from a lot of Bellgard dealers, mostly in the sticks, who wanted to know why couldn't they get *their* quotas reduced too. Imagine those mushheads asking a thing like that? And then what happens? Tony Kerwin throws the ball right back in my lap. That's right. It's my department carries the ball. I'm the one answers to the factory. And you answer to me. That's how it plays, it plays according to the rules!"

"Whose rules?"

The man turned his indestructible face to Red, and after an instant during which he sat down again as if to calm himself, revise his strategy, a half-smile now softening his features, he said: "Of course you know how the boys in the trade are, don't you, Red? One of these winds starts blowing up and right away everyone wants to know if Quinnley Corners is still flying the flag. Naturally I told them it takes more than a little fart of a wind to shake Quinnley Corners."

"You can say that out loud," Red stated at once.

"That's just what I felt like telling Max Wilkerson."

"You can tell him for me." Red, in his gargantuan pride, had automatically risen to snap the bait McGregor had held up for him, for if his long loyalty to the factory might waver now and then, his bitter rivalry with Wilkerson was unshakable; Wilkerson was the only Bellgard dealer in the zone who had developed a greater volume than Quinnley Corners. But now Red, perceiving belatedly what McGregor had attempted to do, said: "Listen, Mac, don't dangle that old red herring in front of me. I was selling Bellgards big when Max Wilkerson was still stuck with his Edsel franchise. He's only holding out now because his father-in-law is rich enough to carry him. The quota," Red went on, as if to prove he had not been unsettled by McGregor's taunts, "stands as is. What else is on your mind, Mac?"

"Nothing much, Red, just trying to protect your good name, that's why I told the third floor I was penciling you in for the rest of the units in the middle of the month. Red, strictly *sub rosa,* that's what I told Wilkerson too. I had to, to protect your good name in the trade."

Scott watched his father, knowing his vulnerability, finding himself in the center, needing to combat McGregor while at the same time countering the weakness: his father's pride. "Red," he said, "I don't see the point of this long hassle. Mr. McGregor knows damn well how we feel and there's no sense in going on with it. The factory," he added, "will just have to struggle along with one less sucker for a while."

At once McGregor was on his feet again: "You know your trouble, my boy?" he said harshly. "Your trouble is you're making a two-bit villain out of the company, an all-out, black, two-bit villain. Shows how little you know yet, shows how green you are. You forget that the factory made your father a rich man who could send you to a good college and you forget also that today there are no more villains in this industry. The factory is in business, just like the corner candy store. The factory sets its tooling volume in advance, based on scientific statistics, surveys, the factory has its own quotas to meet, all the way from the steel tonnage we need, to the number of cars per dealer. It's a chain, and if it snaps, if any of the links break, the whole kit and kaboodle breaks, the whole country feels it, it touches everybody, the housewife stops buying steak, the family wardrobe gets raggy, it all goes right up and down the line, including the U. S. Treasury feeling the pinch. This industry does more than make cars, it keeps the entire country in business. Now what happens when just one dealer slows down? Let's say a dealership like Quinnley Corners —it's always been a pace-setter. Like the mechanical rabbit in those dog races. If the rabbit starts to stumble, slow down, every pooch on the course starts to poop out. People in this business go by the pace-setters, by the Quinnley Corners. Nobody is a villain, the company is just an ordinary business enterprise and it runs on ordinary arithmetic!"

The zeal, the conviction, of McGregor's speech did not conceal to Scott the fact that, like Red, he *had* to believe in the ways of the industry no matter what measures the industry took, so that to this end he could justify half-truths, lies or unfulfilled promises or even blackmail.

Red was silent.

"Let's not oversimplify, Mr. McGregor," Scott answered. "The arithmetic can get a little one-sided. That much I know. And I also know that no matter how many colors the company tries to wear, as far as I'm concerned, they're still black, and—"

"All right, Scott," Red said, "this isn't getting us—"

"Wait a minute, Red." McGregor's great paw was up like a policeman's waving traffic to a halt. "I want to show your boy how wrong some of his ideas are, they maybe sound good in a little magazine back East, sure, but here in the everyday world they don't hold up. As a matter of fact, he interrupted me before I could finish. I was just going to tell you what the 'villainous' factory is doing about the Quinnley Corners—situation."

[146

"It's not a 'situation,' " Red corrected him. "It's a—"

"Yes, yes, I got you, Red." McGregor said. "But what I was coming to, is that the factory despite what your good son might think, is reasonable, even generous with its family of dealers, that's why they are going to allow you an additional two percent for every unit sold."

"How's that?"

"You heard it, Red," McGregor said. "Two percent extra on every car, so that you can get over the hump. Naturally, this generous concession only applies to the full quota. That's why I know you'll take on the rest of the delivery by the fifteenth of the month." He paused, and confronted Scott. "Yes, Bellgard is a pretty villainous outfit, isn't it?"

"I didn't ask for a bonus," Scott answered, "that's not what we need—"

"What's the string, Mac?" Red said. "Are you people going to pack that two percent into *my* price?"

"Red, shame on you, you shock me. How can you say a thing like that? But look, if you don't want to snatch on to it, we can just forget it."

"I just wanted the word, that's all." Red said. He glanced at his son, a faint gleam of triumph in his eyes. "Well, that's fair enough, I'd say—considering what bandits we're dealing with, eh Scott? Who knows, we might unload the entire goddam quota yet."

In astonishment Scott looked at him: whether or not his father believed in the validity of the factory's last-minute concession, he had seized this moment as a way of saving face.

"Red . . ." Scott began, then stopped, blocked by the mysterious fraternity that now seemed to have united his father and McGregor, by the many years' bond between the two men.

"All right, boys." McGregor again slapped his slab of a hand down on the desk, as if to celebrate the end of the battle. "So what are we going to do about it? What do we do? I'm here to help, I'm not here to throw you out in the snow. Let's put on the brain beanies, chew this over. I want to help, be constructive, I'm not here to blow my silver horn, as my dear dad used to say." A pause. "Bellgard has a bagful of answers we can always dip into, supercharged sales boosters for dealers who are in"—he halted, as if to spare his old friend the ignominy of hearing the unpleasant word he'd almost uttered— "dealers who are in the mood for a change of pace."

147]

But Red, Scott saw, was not listening, he'd become preoccupied. He tilted far back in his chair; he'd taken off his hat and he kept running his hand through his thick russet hair.

"We've had results with the giveaway campaign," McGregor was saying. "We had a dealer in Peru, Indiana, who offered a hundred gallons of gas with every sale, and there was a nice booster in St. Joseph, he made a tie-up with the airline and gave away a free trip to—"

"Mr. McGregor," Scott finally broke in, after he had listed several more aids which Bellgard recommended, but which, of course, were paid for by the dealers. "Mr. McGregor, it seems to me that's only trying to cure one ailment with another, and—"

The sharp creak of his father's swivel chair intruded. Red thumped forward and buzzed for Mrs. Bowsley. He rose, and when the elderly secretary entered the office, he said: "Mrs. B., put up a Quinnley-gram in the sales hall: Meeting of all salesmen in this office closing time tonight." As soon as the woman had gone, Red turned to Mc-Gregor: "Good-bye, Mac, take your gab horn and stick it up Max Wilkerson's ass. I've got business to do. Maybe I'll see you around the fifteenth. Good-bye, you chrome-hearted sonofabitch."

Late that afternoon, Red stood up by his desk, his blue double-breasted jacket hanging limply, his wide-brimmed, cream-hued hat tilted back, surveying his salesmen.

A powwow of blue-clad Indians, Scott thought.

"Fellas," Red began, a fresh but unlit cigar in his right hand, "you all know my son gave the factory a little shaking up." He glanced at Scott, as if this opening tribute might, perhaps, be a kind of truce offering. "Well, we shook 'em up all right, but now we're going to shake 'em up again. In fifteen days, or less, we're going to tap 'em for the rest of the delivery, in fifteen days, no more, I want every goddam unit out of the shop, we're going to complete the full quota. That's right, you're hearing me right. My son," Red continued, pointing the baton of his cigar at Scott, "had a method in his madness, he knew what he was doing and now we're getting concessions from the factory they never gave us before. That's why I'm going to tip 'em over." He paused. "Beginning this weekend, we are going to put on one of those old-fashioned Quinnley Car Carnivals!"

From some of the blue-clad warriors there arose a faint moaning.

"Yes, I know you'll be dragging your tails, and I don't give a good goddam. I want you to know this: any man who doesn't pocket a take-home check of a minimum of a hundred and ninety-five dollars gets his notice. This operation is going to cost Quinnley Corners, it's going to sponge up the till, but it's going to pay off. By the fifteenth the tent has got to be cleaned out. That includes our inventory of optional extras, safety belts, radios, arm rests, white walls, tool and power kits, that includes everything including your gold teeth—"

On Friday in the Detroit, Oak Park and Southfall papers there appeared the advertisement:

ANNOUNCING
THE
MIGHTY QUINNLEY CAR CARNIVAL
TWO WEEKS OF WILD AND WONDERFUL CAR BUYS

RED QUINNLEY, YOUR FRIENDLY BELLGARD DEALER
IS READY TO GIVE YOU TOO MUCH FOR YOUR OLD CAR,
AND SELL YOU A NEW ONE TOO CHEAP!

WHY?

BECAUSE YOUR FRIEND RED QUINNLEY IS SICK.
MY DOCTOR CALLS IT ENLARGEMENT OF THE HEART.
THAT'S HIS DIAGNOSIS. ANYONE GIVING AWAY NEW CARS
AT PRICES LIKE THIS MUST HAVE A HEART TOO BIG
FOR HIS OWN GOOD.
MAYBE THE DOC IS RIGHT.

BUT THERE IT IS FOLKS.
NOTHING DOWN.
NOTHING UP.

ALL OUR BEAUTIFUL POWERPACKED BELLGARDS MUST GO!
COME TO THE CORNER OF "BUY AND SAVE."

YES, MY HEART'S TOO BIG AND MY PREMISES TOO SMALL.
IT'S TURNOVER TIME, VOLUME TIME AT QUINNLEY CORNERS.

PLUS
FABULOUS FAVORS FOR ALL!
PLUS
FREE MOVIES!
PLUS
FREE BARBECUE!

149]

In addition to the costly newspaper advertising and the buying of spot time on television, Red sent out a small army of kids to distribute special handbills which were wedged in windshield wipers of all automobiles within a five-mile radius of Quinnley Corners, offering trade-in and sale offers which, to Scott, were nothing less than insane.

But, as Scott discovered, the reservoir of Red's resources could at times be nothing less than prodigious:

FREE MOVIES? In the pine-paneled Repairs Waiting Room, Red ran a series of short films called *American Holiday*. The films, in color, showed beautiful views of pastoral landscapes, seaside, mountains, forests, valleys, streams, villages and great cities. Since they were made by the factory, it was of course, no accident that the automobiles seen in the pictures now and then happened to be a variety of Bellgard models.

FREE BARBECUE? Red's long-time friend Sophie Terraza sent over from her Tavern the sliced beef, sauce and buns, along with her brother-in-law and three waitresses (all relatives). The cost was no more than the wholesale price.

FABULOUS FAVORS? Here again the cost to Red was minimal: Eddy Capper, owner of Capper Novelty Company, supplied an assortment of paper streamers, whistles, balloons for the children, and plastic compacts for the ladies. Favors for the men were to be new hats, these supplied by Red's good friend Joe Laird on a consignment basis, the low price to Quinnley Corners being in exchange for the gratuitous advertising Laird Hats would receive in the showroom display.

All of it, the aura of Chautauqua and midway, and the attendant flamboyant sales methods, was of course exactly the kind of atmosphere which Scott felt Quinnley Corners had to get away from. Also, it seemed to him that the entire presentation of the Car Carnival must be too patently phony to lure a sales-resistant public.

But on that first Friday evening he saw that he was wrong. Quinnley Corners was thronged with a crowd of citizens, all manner of people arrived in all manner of vehicles from Vespas to 1940 Fords, Chevvy Trucks, Edsels, Bellgards and Lincolns. One man was even pushed in a wheelchair, and soon children were all over the premises, blowing whistles, popping balloons, gobbling sandwiches.

For five days the public continued to respond, though only ninety-one new units were sold. After that Scott noticed that the *esprit* of the crew, reflecting the falling off of the crowds, began to languish.

[150

By the ninth day the Car Carnival seemed to have reached low ebb. And then, unhappily or inevitably, Wilkerson and another Bellgard dealer chose the final weekend to launch gigantic specials of their own. Red was forced to buy extra TV time to soup up sales. This brought in a measure of business, though not enough. As the Carnival neared its finish, Scott could not escape the closing in, the oppressive climate in the showroom: if they had been edgy before, now all of them had become tenser, tempers were more brittle, egos raw.

"All right, boys," Red announced at the meeting on the morning of the eleventh day, "we've been doing good, but not big. Starting now not a goddam customer gets out of the tent until he's signed. I posted a revised list of prices, but it's up to us to pack in enough daylight to brighten up the till. But nobody, you understand, nobody gets to walk away from the tent without the key to a new Bellgard in his fist. Nobody! You're on your own, the pitch is yours and I don't care if you throw it low or high, all I know is Wilkerson is throwing 'em lower and closer, and the factory doesn't care a good goddam as long as all the dogs are out of the kennel—"

If, in the past days, the sales methods had been freewheeling, they now became almost fraudulent, and though Scott thought he was familiar with the devious gambits a salesman could use, he discovered as the Carnival soared to its frantic climax that he still had much to learn about the range and art of sales ploys.

One day, as he worked in the showroom, two customers came up to him, a Mr. Dempster and his wife, and asked to see Dave Toff. Mr. Toff, Scott explained, was home sick. Laryngitis.

"Maybe you can help me." Mr. Dempster was a tall, sticklike man wearing smoked glasses. Occupation: nightwatchman at a nearby college. "I came to close my deal."

Scott glanced at the sales agreement: the "deal," he saw at once, was a dubious transaction known as "unhorsing"—a specialty at which Dave Toff was a consummate master. The trouble was that the master was not there.

Mr. Dempster had succumbed to Toff's seemingly irresistible offer. Eleven days ago he had driven off in a new Bellgard sedan, leaving behind his old car. Toff had assured him that the Used Car Market, according to inside word, was due for a jump in prices, and if Mr. Dempster waited a week or two, Quinnley Corners would be able to sell the old car for nine hundred dollars instead of the then current listing of six hundred, which would be the down payment.

From there on, the procedure was supposedly simple: you merely apologized, explained to the customer that the Used Car Market had gone *down* instead of *up,* and that they were all lucky to salvage anything at all. However, since you knew the man had been driving the new Bellgard while waiting to complete his deal, you knew enough time had elapsed for him to become too attached to his new possession to back down on the sale.

Simple.

Scott studied the contract (which was not yet signed by Quinnley Corners) while trying to decide exactly what direction to take.

"Mr. Toff," the man was saying, "told me to come by today."

"I see," Scott said. The process would be simple, he reminded himself. Any articulate salesman could talk his way, leading the trapped customer around the first impact of shock, and going on to complete the negotiation.

The trouble was not only Scott's queasy feeling about this kind of practice, but that in trying to reappraise the customer, he saw that Mr. Dempster and his wife could ill afford to lose money on their trade-in, that in fact they probably had no right to be buying a new car at all.

"How'd we make out?" Mr. Dempster took off his dark glasses. "I want to know how we made out on the old car—"

"Yes, of course." Scott led them back into Toff's sales booth. He found the manila file and saw in dismay that the old car had been unloaded to an Auction Dealer for five hundred and forty dollars. "Won't you sit down?" he temporized, groping for some way to lead the couple around the unhappy news. But there was no way. "Well . . ." He hesitated once more. "According to Mr. Toff's file, I'm afraid we didn't quite have the luck we'd—"

"What? What's that?" Mr. Dempster's voice came in hoarse protest; in his long stringy neck his Adam's apple moved as in spasm. "What do you mean?"

"It was sold for five hundred and forty dollars," Scott had to say.

"Didn't I tell you, Carl, I told you!" Mrs. Dempster reproached him at once.

"Now wait a minute—" Dempster turned to Scott. "What kind of a double—"

The glass door had been flung open. Red stood there, impatient. Then he moved in, his hand outstretched, his features congealed into that visage of folksy goodwill that marked his "public face." "Mr. Dempster, sir. I am Red Quinnley." To the woman: "Madame, I'm mighty glad you are both here together. I was just talking to Mr. Toff on the telephone—poor fella is pretty sick. He told me the story and —" A pause, a hasty nod at his son. "Scott, would you hop out to Service, there's a customer waiting to sign out for that new blue convertible—I'll look after these good people."

Not long afterward Scott saw his father leading Mr. and Mrs. Dempster out of the showroom, he presented the man with "a new chapeau, courtesy of Quinnley Corners," and the woman with a white-boxed compact. As soon as they had left, he swung around, the great smile gone from his face. He motioned for Scott to follow him. In the office, he snatched up his half-smoked cigar from the ashtray.

"Scott, goddammit, where were you when those people came in? Where were you?" He paced around to the back of his desk, standing now beneath the framed picture of himself and the mayor, taken after the 1948 election. "Where were you? Where were your goddam brains, your goddam education? Where were you? Why, when I happened to listen in and heard that mumbo jumbo you were stuttering out, I knew you were losing 'em, but worse, I had to move in for the T.O. before you handed 'em a goddam lawsuit on a platter!"

"Look, Red—this was sprung on me, I wasn't sure how to get out of it, because—"

"Almighty Christ, it's not your job to get *out* of anything! It's your duty to sell! What's the matter? You think Toff or I threw a low one?"

"I think those people were taken."

"*They* were taken?" Red rolled his pink-veined eyes upward. "Almighty Christ, in order to close that deal and keep 'em happy, we took a loss of thirty-nine dollars and fifty cents!"

"You took a loss and the deal was rotten from the ground up. That's very bright, all the way around, isn't it?" Scott didn't even try to contain the sarcasm which burst out happily, almost cruelly. "You took a loss, you risked a lawsuit, but it was worth it because Halister McGregor can chalk another unit off another chart, it was worth it because the factory, the poor suffering factory, will be proud of you, and after all they gave us that fantastically generous gift of the extra two percent—which they were forced to do—but nothing matters as long as Quinnley Corners keeps its flag flying bravely and stupidly!"

"Goddammit, Scott, don't give me all this gab because you goofed on that deal. There was no excuse for fading out on that sale, no excuse, not with your qualities, you've got more brains than that entire crew out there lumped together, but you've got to get over this goddam campfire gospel like a goddam Boy Scout. I don't know what the hell it is."

"Listen, Red—"

"Sit down, sit down, you're going to end up like your old man—" He waved Scott to the chair beside his desk.

"Listen, Red." Scott remained standing. "We're losing track of what I wanted to do here, we're heading right back into the same hole we were in when I arrived. The entire point of my action with the factory was not just the—"

"I know the point," Red interrupted, "fine, fine, I know the point. But it didn't work out that way. I hoped it would, I was with you, but it didn't work out like that. Now we've got an emergency on our hands. That's how it worked out, an emergency. And you're giving me theories. Forget it. Forget everything. We are going to clean out the tent. After that we can stand up to Bellgard in the right way. But now I want results. I don't want any more of your theories, all I want is results. Get out to that tent and let me see results!"

"For what?" Scott refused to leave. "Results to show the factory? Bushing people, unhorsing them and losing money? I don't call that results, I call it taking up the factory's blackmail—and even that, if the product was first-rate, if we were selling a new first-rate car—"

His father's hands jutted upward. "Whose side are you on? Goddammit, if you're going to talk like that, I—" He floundered, his eyeballs distended as he glared. He was half standing in his chair.

"Red—"

"What?"

"Please sit down, Red," Scott said in alarm.

"All right." For an instant Red flattened his hands against the surface of the desk.

"I'm sorry," Scott said.

"All right." Red looked up. "Are you going out there or not?"

"Certainly I am." He saw how his father looked; he had to retreat, to placate.

"And let's see what you can do. Christ, some of my boys out there must think you're a—"

"A what?" Scott said.

Red did not answer.

"I know what," Scott said. "I know what they think of me. And it doesn't matter." Or did it? It had become very plain that the men were staying away from him. When he made a sale it was resented; commission out of their pockets. If he failed to make a sale or tried to discourage their sales methods on the Take Over, they put him down, betrayed their fury, even their contempt. And none of this mattered to him? Of course it did; at least it mattered more than he realized. Nevertheless, he said: "Is that what's worrying you, Red? What the sales crew thinks?"

"No, not at all," Red answered. "But you *are* my son. And you've got more brains than any of those guys out there. I just hate to see them getting the wrong ideas about you. Hell, I see how they steer away from you like you're bad luck or the goddam plague. How do you think that makes me feel? Look, we're in a hell of a spot here, and my own son puts a damper on everything that goes on." He paused. "I don't know. Maybe you'd better not go out there. Maybe you'd better stay the hell away from the showroom."

"All right, Red. Don't give me that."

"Give you what?" he answered. "All I said was maybe it's better all around, if you can't go with the pitch, it's better if you stayed away. That's better than killing the spirit of the organization. I don't like to see them looking at you the way they do lately. Bad for you. Bad for them. With me it's different. I don't know any other way. Tell you the truth, Scott, maybe we got the wrong approach. Maybe I ought to get out to the tent and you take over in here full time—" He rose from the desk.

"Red, will you please sit down! You don't have to give me any of that! Not again. I assure you I can get out there and pitch with the best of them!" Scott's voice rose sardonically. "Be glad to, if you think that'll get you immortality in the Bellgard heaven!"

Scott left. Had he been had? He wasn't really sure.

Yet Red *had* looked stricken, he *had* betrayed a deep concern or fear about what the other men thought of his son. Could you blame his father? If their roles had been reversed, wouldn't Scott himself have been seized by the same concern and shame?

155]

On the last day of the Carnival, Halister McGregor came by. He surveyed the chaos in the showroom—the shining floor now a mosaic of torn paper streamers, cigarette butts, balloons; a spectacle of children climbing in and out of cars, of women inspecting upholstery of station wagons, of men fondling quasi-sports models with concupiscent fingers—all of it, however, brought to McGregor's enamel blue eyes a joyous gleam. "Scott, my boy, I just chased down here to see how it was going and if there was anything we could do. What can I do for you, my boy? Reminds me when I was in college—would you believe I was a campus man for a year? I always remember this diner where I used to go for hot sugar buns and coffee, and the counterman always used to say: 'Everything okay? Anything we haven't done for you, Mr. Dunn?' " McGregor's laugh was sweet and loud with reminiscence.

Scott's nerves were too tight to respond. "We're doing all right, but not all right enough."

"It's not closing time yet, my boy. And from what I see here, Quinnley Corners is hanging it up. Hanging it up. I think we're going to give them second thoughts at the factory, second thoughts. Ah—" He turned as Red Quinnley appeared. "Red—bless you, this is more like it, this is the Quinnley Corners I used to know, the Quinnley Corners that used to help me pay for a mink stole for Mrs. McGregor. What's the count, Red?"

"Not too bad," Scott's father said, his fatigue plainly visible. "We still have about a blockful out there."

"Twenty-one units left," Scott said.

"It's only three o'clock," Red said. "I'm bushed—but Scott here is just getting his second wind."

This tribute to Scott's sales record came, he knew, because in the course of that day he had sold two cars under hard-sell conditions.

"Yes," Red was saying, "my boy sure as hell blitzed 'em today."

"Well." McGregor regarded Scott with a new, downright sentimental look of welcome. "Well, a little blitz now and then is relished by the best of men." (It was his way of paraphrasing what Scott had once read in the monthly Bellgard Bulletin: *There are times when a dealer might have to blitz, and though the company does not encourage these methods, it cannot dictate to the dealer who, after all, is responsible for the sales volume which will keep him in good standing.*)

It was at this time that Al Fogarty, accompanied by a young cou-

[156

ple, approached Red Quinnley. He held a sales contract in his hand, which Scott was very pleased to see, though he suspected from the way Fogarty avoided him that he might be playing this deal close and private.

"Pardon me, Mr. Quinnley—" Fogarty addressed Red in his finest showroom manner.

Scott saw that his father was still talking to McGregor, and so he stepped forward: "Can I help you, Fogarty?"

The chunky, blue-suited salesman turned, at once startled and suspicious, and then he turned back to Red: "I need this contract signed for Mr. and Mrs. Lozett here—"

But as Red brought his attention to the salesman, Scott heard himself intervene: "I'll take care of this, Fogarty."

Fogarty drew back, hesitated. Scott reached out for the paper, which the salesman reluctantly relinquished.

"Thank you." Scott examined the contract, his father now peering over his shoulder.

Scott saw at once that Fogarty was working "the Bush." He had deliberately written in the wrong price for the model, making it a hundred and forty dollars less than it should have been.

Scott was holding a highly dubious document in his hands. He knew it, and his father, standing beside him, knew it.

Red stirred as if wanting to relieve Scott of the responsibility of cadging the customer, or as if fearing the sale might be lost. Yet, because both McGregor and Fogarty were by his side, Red was reluctant to intercede. He was too proud. And, like the two men at his side, he waited, directing his gaze at Scott.

No choice. Scott knew that.

No choice now. He'd made his commitment to his father three days ago after the near-loss of the Dempster sale. And since then he'd carried out his bravado threat in only the most modest way. (Or was all this a rationale for his present determination to show his audience now what a pitchman he could be if he so chose? Was all this a justification built on Red's shame of him and the lowly opinion the sales crew had of him? Was it only Red he wanted to appease now? Or didn't he himself crave just a bit to regain the esteem of the other men? Answer: yes.)

So that now he found himself deliberately reaching for, snatching the opening gambit of the Bush:

Just what, Mr. Fogarty, Scott demanded sternly, was going on

157]

here? "There is a price error of one hundred and forty dollars. We can never let this car go at that price. How did this mistake happen, Fogarty?"

Chastising the salesman and embarrassing the customer was the way it was supposed to go. And Fogarty, having regained his composure, played right along. However, the buyer, Mr. Lozett, did not.

"Hey," the young man said, "what kind of jazz is this? I signed that contract, and if the price is wrong, that's not my funeral. I can go over to Wilkerson's and—"

"Now, Mr. Lozett—" Scott broke in and, following the ritual, led the couple over to the red sports model, so that while he talked to them they would have near at hand the car to which they were emotionally committed.

At this juncture Scott was supposed to confide in them, to lament the difficulty of getting responsible salesmen these days, and that yes the error had been regrettable, but after all it had nothing to do with the reality of the price tag, and as a matter of fact Quinnley Corners would be taking a slight loss as it was. Yet, what a pity to let a mere hundred and forty dollars stand between the Lozetts and that red beauty of a Bellgard.

The young man looked at his wife: for an instant Scott was sure he'd come through.

But Lozett said: "I'm not paying for somebody's else's mistake."

"I realize how you feel," Scott began in his disappointment, wishing to God his father, McGregor and Fogarty would stop watching as if he were struggling to reach the Twelfth Station of the Cross.

"Look," Mr. Lozett was saying, "I can't take on a deal like this. I was stretching it at the price Fogarty gave me."

Scott offered him a cigarette, which he declined. He dug deeply into the sack of tricks and ploys, scrabbling for some way to turn the sale.

"Well." In a sudden movement Lozett took his wife's arm. "Seems to me, honey, we better take off. I've got to get back to the office. I'm late now."

Fogarty, recognizing that fatal movement, had already bent his bulk to Red, his lips in urgent talk.

Blindly Scott reached to the bottom of the sack. "See here," he said, "let's not give up, I'm sure there's a way—let's have a look at your old Bellgard."

"What for?"

"Where is it?"

"Out there." Lozett nodded vaguely toward the side street.

As forcefully as he could Scott hurried them outside. He was relieved to see that Lozett's old Bellgard was in surprisingly clean condition.

"I think," he said, like a veteran salesman who seems to strangle as he makes an offer against his better judgment, "I think we might raise your trade-in price. It's going to pinch us, but what would you say if we added an extra fifty dollars. In other words, instead of seven hundred and fifty, we'll credit you with a full eight hundred dollars toward the new car. Is that fair?"

Young Lozett again consulted his wife.

"That's it, though," Scott added. "I don't see how we can be fairer than that. I'll take the responsibility for it, but it has to be now. It won't hold next week."

A great stream of relief began to course through him as he saw the first glimmer in Lozett's eyes. For, like many other men, he regarded the compromise as proof to his wife that he could not be as easily duped as she might have feared, that he'd forced a victory.

Quickly then, Scott led them back into the showroom, directly to the shining red car.

It was over. He felt flushed with triumph; he'd forgotten all considerations except the crucial one of making this sale.

"It's a deal," Lozett said. "If—if you can get this car ready for me by eight tonight. I'll come by from the office and pick it up. Can you get it ready by then?"

Yes, Scott told him, before even consulting Kellog. "Certainly. Eight o'clock." Then he guided them toward the office. He looked back just once, nodding to his father and the others, unable to resist signaling the results.

The papers of sale and financing were signed. And as soon as the Lozetts had left the showroom, Red came over to Scott: he looked ten years younger. Even Fogarty, who would receive half the commission, extended his muscled hand in a gracious, if still rather startled, gesture of congratulations. Halister McGregor's comments were nothing less than rococo in their eloquence.

Scott did, however, point out that they would still not unload all the quota by tonight. But Red, who was in highest form, said never mind, there was a Texas "bootlegger" in town. If need be, he'd sell the remaining units at the factory price. The cars, their speedometers disconnected, would then be driven to Texas and sold as "Almost New Dealer-Demonstrator Cars."

For Scott, however, the sun of victory did not shine very long.

He was the last one to leave that night. As he was preparing to go, the telephone rang. It was Ann Smith.

"Scott, I'm here with Jemmy."

"Where?" He was to pick up Jennifer Thompson before going on to the party the Rothes were having.

"I mean at the house," Ann said. "It's Tony Kerwin's birthday, and we're here *en famille*. But what I called about is Ben has to work all night, of all the ignoble things, and would it be all right if I came along like a fifth wheel?"

"Certainly."

"Thanks," she said. "I shouldn't really be seen in public with a traitor like you, but—"

"Ann—I forgot to thank you for those flowers. I'm sorry. They were wonderful, just what the funeral needed."

"You sound awful," she said. "Is anything wrong?"

"Not a thing, Junior."

When he hung up, Scott hurried out to his car which was in the Used-Car lot. He looked forward to the Rothes' party. He needed it. For already as he thought back on the Car Carnival, his old misgivings were creeping back.

And more. A new crop today. Gulling a decent citizen like Lozett.

As he crossed the vast lot, he happened to see the old Bellgard which Lozett had dropped off on his way home from work. Something about the car seemed different, peculiar. Scott went over for a closer look, and discovered that Lozett had switched the rubber. He'd replaced the good tires with secondhand retreads. He had also replaced the radio with another.

At first Scott was appalled, shocked. But almost at once he could have laughed.

The laugh, of course, was on him.

And driving back to Greenwood Park, he tried to see the incident by itself, as a joke, a private, unfunny joke between him and Lozett. But that didn't hold. Something else kept working inside him, he kept trying to sort out all the elements, think back, put together all the pieces that might account for, or justify, what had happened. He then began to see beyond himself or Lozett—to see how, as Marty Calhoon had once speculated, it was possible that the chicanery which

[160

now and then held together the chain of business between factory and dealer might have gone a link farther to extend to the consumer himself.

And so he could see, or tell himself, that a freewheeling, loose code of ethics was no longer the sole privilege of the business community alone. Now the public had moved in on the action.

Maybe it was true. But small comfort.

So where, he asked the ancient and maybe answerless question, do we go from here?

14: Scott Quinnley

THE party that night should have been welcome. Scott had shut himself off from even the most commonplace pleasures since the beginning of the Car Carnival; since, in fact the morning he'd acted to block the invasion of trailer-trucks.

It was fine to see Lorie and Phil Rothe. And moving into the living room, along with Jemmy and Ann, the prosaic sight of men drinking and talking, of women in party plumage, gave him the absurd, grateful feeling of a man returning to society from a jungle.

Maybe, he thought, it wasn't so absurd. For beyond needing to flee from Quinnley Corners, he knew there was something else. He'd discovered during the Carnival that in his descent from protest to capitulation, with the subsequent goodwill his father then showed him, he'd been trying to gain from Red something that could never quite be had. At the Carnival's end, they were closer than they'd ever been before, but only because, as his son, Scott had pleased him, had come through. The joyful glow had suffused Red's features only because, in truth, he saw Scott as an extension of his own ego, a potential symbol of all he had once stood for. In a way Scott now represented his victory over Scott's mother, a prize Red had long ago given up hope of winning but which he now had within his grasp. So that in his oversentimental way Red believed he loved Scott and that his son believed it too.

It was knowing more clearly where he stood with his father, as well as with himself, that gave Scott his disproportionate desire to flee from the past weeks. The party that night should have been like an open gate to fresh country.

Except it wasn't.

Phil Rothe embraced his old friend, and in booming melodramatic voice, cried out for all to hear: "The tiger, wounded and bleeding, returns."

"Forget it, Phil." Since Scott had not had the chance to tell him the full and unromantic truth which would have canceled out the glory of the newspaper accounts, his discomfort grew as he moved with Phil on the rounds of the introductions.

"Forget it?" Phil's hefty arm was still around him. "Listen, as far as we're concerned, you've just come back from orbit. We want to hear everything."

There must have been at least a dozen people in the room whom Scott didn't know.

Earlier in the week when Lorie Rothe had spoken to him on the telephone, she'd said she'd been wanting to give him a party for a long time, and that they'd invited the elite of their friends for tonight. And Phil, taking Scott around now, said that some of the men there were a bright and unsquare gang and didn't belong to the current regime in the industry. Maybe there'd been too much of this kind of talk, for Scott had begun to build up a resistance to the party even before reaching it.

During his initial foray into this group of Phil Rothe's friends, Scott tried, but failed to generate a spark of spirit for the occasion. And now, escaping from one of the guests—an engineer named Sturges—Scott crossed the crowded room and poured himself another drink. Presently Phil joined him. "Listen, Scott," Phil said, his air serious, almost conspiratorial, "I know you've got your back up, but there was another reason for this party besides introducing you to society. It's one friend in particular. Steve Sturges." He nodded toward the man at the other end of the room. Sturges, he said, was a young engineer not many years out of M.I.T.; he was employed by an automobile-testing laboratory near Detroit. "You were talking to him before—"

"Not much," Scott said.

Phil frowned. "No, you've got him wrong. He's quite a guy. I want you to get to know him."

"He's such a self-opinionated horse's ass."

Phil said: "You're no shrinking violet, you know." Then: "That's just his way. Scott, listen to me." He leaned toward him. "Let me tell you what he's up to." And Phil went on to describe the advanced work Sturges was doing in private on the development of electric-powered motors. "I know this is something you've been hot on too. You ran a series of articles on it last year, didn't you?"

"Not a series. Just one piece." But Scott recalled with satisfaction the mounds of mail the magazine received from readers around the country, and how the article had been reprinted in *National Automobile Digest,* and that it had been read as a paper at an S.A.E. meeting.

"Yes," Phil said. "Now the thing is, Scott, no one around here has licked it yet. The big companies are paying lip service to experimentation on electric cars but mainly for publicity purposes. Right now they're trying to blow up a storm with the gas-turbine engine, as you know, but that is still buggy. I tested a turbine and it takes off with a whine like a jet. By 1970 or so, the electric car's got to be the answer to basic transportation. The public may not know it yet, but they've had it with the gasoline engine, and they've had it with the carbon-monoxide fumes. Hell, even now in some states you have to put filter systems on the exhaust units. It's a law. The more the population explodes, the more cars on the highways and streets, and the more poisonous the air. How long can it go on? Sturges has an electric powerplant in the works, it's got less moving parts, less noise, it's poison-free. He's spent two years on fuel-cell studies—" Phil paused, jabbed Scott with his fist. "You look like you're coming alive now!"

True, and Scott had virtually forgotten the antipathy Sturges had aroused in him earlier in the evening.

"Now listen, Scott, when this thing breaks it's going to be guys like Sturges the big companies are going to buy into. But right now the problem is capital. He needs capital to set up his own organization, to get *all* the bugs out. And there are a lot. I'm putting a little money in —it's one of the reasons I needed the Bellgard job—I wanted extra cash. And Johnny Winters over there is putting money in too. Winters is dirty rich and so it's an agonizing process to part him from a really big chunk of lucre." Phil waited before going on: "I know you're having rough going with Red, I know Quinnley Corners is no gold mine anymore. But if you can see your way to get into this now, while it's still a baby, you can't afford not to. You'll get it back ten times. I'm convinced of that. But I want you to talk to him and even if you want no part of it, you've got to at least listen to what he has to say. I'll grant you, Sturges is peculiar, he's fussy, he won't just take anyone's money. But I want you to hear him out, I want you to go with me to his lab. But hear him out. Will you do that? I'm asking you because—"

"Phil, I'm up to my ears now in this goddam dealership situation."

"I know. But you're licking it, aren't you?"

"No."

[164

"Don't give me that, daddy. Not after that performance with the Bellgard brass."

"Phil—I tried to tell you before. It didn't work. My 'performance' didn't add up, I had to back down, way down. Now we're right back in the same bed with all the rest of the poor misbegotten dealers. If I was really in the clear—"

But Phil wasn't listening: "Scott, will you talk to him?"

"Certainly. But as long as I've got Quinnley Corners on my back —" He stopped. The spiral of excitement that had begun to rise inside him, gave way to the truth. In dismay he thought of the responsibility which had overtaken, smothered him, of the way he'd lost his hold on what he believed in; of how, in fact, because of his recent capitulation he'd reached a point where he had almost come to detest what he'd always cared for most: cars.

"We'll have to forget it," Scott said. "I'm pinned down. I wish to hell I could be free enough for something like this—God knows it's how I'd like to ride—but that's out. There's no way I could even allow myself to play with something like this, unless I—"

"Unless what?"

He hesitated, at once depressed by the thought that had suddenly possessed him: *unless I were free of Quinnley Corners.*

Even later when the party got up a good head of steam, Scott found himself unable to give himself to it. Though he had to admit, as Lorie, Phil and Jemmy had hoped, that the company was for the most part lively and refreshing, he still couldn't lose himself, shake off his mounting raging discontent.

And so, as Scott realized later, it was almost inevitable that he succeeded in wrecking what might have been a fine evening.

Near midnight, after the colored maid had brought out the cold buffet and the hot coffee, he found himself sitting on the floor with Phil and Steve Sturges, noticing with some surprise—and relief—that Jemmy was being given a concentrated campaign by Johnny Winters.

Highball in hand, his narrow head tilted slightly back, his sandy hair neat, flat, fixed, his narrow black knitted tie a stiff straight eel down his white shirtfront, Steve Sturges spoke, addressing Scott, but keeping his cool blue eyes partly closed. Frequently he used his glass like a baton to emphasize certain points.

"You see, Quinnley, it's necessary to understand, before even con-

165]

sidering the potential of electric-powered motors, why the gasoline engine as we know it now has failed to stay married to the times, if you follow me—"

"It's difficult," Scott said with less elegance than he'd hoped, his early prejudice against Sturges' smug, doctrinaire manner returning in spite of his resolve, "but I'll try."

Phil Rothe tried to intercept Scott's attention with a glance of warning.

Sturges went onward in that Olympian style of his, as if his audience were an apprentice mechanic or a dude of an executive who had never lifted the hood of a car, ticking off his opinions as if no mortal had ever uttered them before. Did Scott know the waste of money the industry expended on road-testing methods? Or the ridiculous extravagance of building proving grounds whose true worth lay not in testing new models but rather as fodder for advertising copywriters?

And horsepower?

With sardonic derision he revealed how phony the horsepower figures could be when engines were mounted in a laboratory free of air resistance and the brutal shake-up of ordinary road driving.

Still Scott held his peace—until Sturges started on a long preamble about the basic lack of progress in the gasoline-piston engine since its inception in France and America in the nineteenth century, and how "though this might sound like treason at a place like Quinnley Corners," the fact remained that the gasoline-piston engine belonged in the Smithsonian Institution.

Now as he wrinkled his sharp, freckled nose in a grimace of arrogant contempt, Scott suddenly broke in and to his astonishment heard himself springing to the defense of the powerplants of today's cars.

Phil was stupefied.

"Never mind, Phil," Sturges said, "I don't need a heavy battery of protection, you know." Adding then in his thin nasal voice: "Everyone is entitled to an opinion. But I'm afraid Scott might be looking at this somewhat from the dealer's perspective."

Phil raised his arm in a gesture of truce, staring at Scott from behind his spectacles.

"No," Scott interrupted, "he's right, Phil. That's how I'm looking at it. I'm just another square, ignorant dealer, very satisfied with the status quo. Sturges is way above me on a lofty plane, looking down.

But I'm enjoying this. It's instructive. I'm hanging on every word. Please go on."

"I'm afraid this is getting a little pointless," Sturges retorted and lifted his glass, taking a prim and measured sip.

"Why?" Scott pushed the point. "They all laughed at Galileo, Pascal, Edison, Ford. I'm merely another ignoramus laughing."

"For Christ sakes, Scott—" Phil said.

The hassle had now drawn several onlookers.

"I have no intention of making this a world issue, you know," Sturges was saying. "I was merely trying to outline—"

"You were trying what?" Scott said. "You were merely beating your ego like a drum."

"Now see here—" Sturges began.

"You might not be selling this right, did that ever occur to you?" Scott said, though he could see Jemmy signaling wildly to him from across the room.

Johnny Winters and Phil Rothe spoke up at the same time, but now Scott succeeded in making himself well heard above the din. "It's hard to sell an idea from way up on that throne, patronizing the peasants. You have to remember that none of us poor slobs have ever heard of the electric car, very esoteric stuff—"

"Now see here!" Sturges' face was stained crimson, he jutted out his hand in which he was holding his highball. "I wasn't *selling*, I don't have to *sell*. I'm not a car dealer, and I'll thank you not to—" His whiskey glass jiggled in front of Scott.

"Keep your pedantic goddam paw out of my face!" Scott's arm shot out and his open palm clapped the glass, sending it hurtling in a glittering curve to crash against the fireplace.

There followed a hasty rallying of voices, as Sturges' wife came to his side, as Phil Rothe sought valiantly to make a joke out of it, as Ann Smith padded to Scott in her stocking feet and asked him to give her a light.

Scott was looking at Sturges. "I'm sorry," he said.

Sturges did not answer, and his wife said they'd better be leaving.

Yet no one made a move to leave. As Scott turned to light Ann's cigarette, she said: "I don't know why everyone is in such a tizzy, I think a battle like this is the healthiest thing I've heard in these parts in a long time. Hey, Phil, I thought you were going to take us out back to see your jewel."

"Yes—" Phil seized her suggestion gratefully. He said he'd gotten his Duesenberg in show-shape for the *Concours d'Élégance*.

Ann Smith said: "I'm dying to see that relic. Come on, Scott. I haven't seen the Duesenberg since Tony Kerwin owned it. Old cars seem to have a way of luring young men, don't they? Like older women—all wisdom and mileage—but it's really only shacking up with Mom, isn't it?"

Someone laughed. Johnny Winters said: "Let's go." Winters, like Phil Rothe, was also a Classic Car collector. He was very rich, having inherited the income from his family-owned tire factory near Flint; a studious young man, he ran, in conjunction with the public library, a department of Automobile History—a hobby of his which he'd turned into a vocation. He turned to Steve Sturges: "Come on, Steve."

Sturges and his wife started out, followed by Johnny Winters and Jemmy, the Rothes and the others. Ann Smith took Scott's arm, and as they moved out to the driveway she said with calculated sociability: "I suppose when I finally get to Athens, the first thing I'll hear the Greeks talking about is disk brakes and air scoops—there must be someplace in the world where one can get away from this outhouse of civilization." They were the last to reach the garage, and she squeezed Scott's hand, and in a low voice said: "Keep slugging, pal."

Inside the garage, Phil Rothe took over, or tried to, but even the examination of the shining old Duesenberg failed to pull the evening together. It was too late.

And presently Steve Sturges, stiffly polite, left with his wife. Shortly afterward Johnny Winters and the others dispersed. Scott saw Jemmy moving on to say good night to him—Jemmy in the short dinner dress and the long black hair profiled darkly in the driveway's floodlight. And then she looked back and waved and went into the house with the Rothes.

The party was over.

"Do you have a minute, Scott?" Ann Smith had paused to make up her face; she was leaning against the polished olive flank of the Duesenberg.

Absently he nodded. He stepped outside to the short ramp at the entry of the garage. The night air was warm, there was the dry fragrance of geraniums and the faint hiss of mosquitos. At least, he thought then, I'll soon be out at the lake with Jemmy. Save best for last: sleeping with Jemmy was all that would remain of a disastrous night.

"Scott." Ann was beside him; she touched his arm tentatively. "Can we talk for a minute? I . . ." Her voice too, seemed tentative or embarrassed, as if she wanted to say something that was not easy for her. She touched his arm again. "It can't be all that lousy, can it?"

"No. Everything is at its maximum finest."

"I mean," she said slowly, "I know pretty much how you feel, how it's been for you and . . ." Another hesitation. "Well, you had to take it out on someone and I suppose Steve Sturges was handiest— not that I blame you, God knows he had it coming."

He moved uncomfortably, and she said: "That's true, isn't it?"

No answer. He looked down at her, surprised that she'd read him.

"Could be," he said, yet as he looked at her, he felt a grudging gratitude for her concern. "Thanks," he said. "That stupid battle with Sturges was the nicest thing that's happened to me in weeks."

"Oh, I'm sure it was."

A moment then.

"What I was trying to say, Scott," she began hurriedly and halted, and as she turned, peering out to the garden, she reminded him of one of those early nineteenth-century English portraits—the light hair piled up, the faintly Roman nose vivid above the irresolute softness of her mouth, the bare shoulders and the bold swell of her bosom in the décolleté dress. "I know how it's been, that is, what you've been going through at Quinnley Corners—because God knows I've heard it batted around at the house and at Dean's and Tony's. But really, Scott—" A hasty pause, going on then: "But really, Scott, you can't let yourself fall apart. That's how it is here. That's why I tried to warn you in the beginning—even though you wouldn't listen—natu- rally you wouldn't. Any more than I wanted to listen to you that time in Paris."

"That wasn't the same," Scott said, though the connection was plain enough. He'd met the Fulbright boy she'd been engaged to then; very attractive, yes, but looking for the maximum chance with the minimum risk. His interest in becoming a teacher of history was pat- ently less serious than his desire to fall into the Bellgard hierarchy, and as far as Scott could figure out he never spent much time at the Sorbonne. And once when Scott had gone to a party at Reid Hall and

169]

waited for Ann in the garden courtyard, he happened to overhear him making his pitch to another young and financially endowed inmate, and it played back like the same scenario he used with Ann.

"Well," Ann was saying now, "it may not be the same, except that when you tried to warn me about him, I was just as snotty at first as you were when I tried to warn you what you'd be up against here. Anyway, Scott, it's my turn now to talk like a Dutch uncle—I mean, aunt." She laughed a little and the laughter made her seem more at ease. "What I mean, Scott, is that I do know why you're in this awful swivet now—you think you've sold out—that *is* the proper cliché, isn't it?— But what I'm trying to say is that you *did* try, God knows you tried to buck it, and when you shipped back all those monsters to the factory, I was so carried away I had to go out and buy you a bag of roses, didn't I? After that though, when I saw how you had to backtrack and let them push all those dear old Bellgards right into your lap again, I knew it couldn't be helped, I knew you couldn't do anything about it. How could you?"

The sting of all those ill-starred days at Quinnley Corners was even deeper as Ann called them back, but at the same time, Ann's knowing how Scott felt, comprehending all of it, gave him a kind of painful relief.

"There was nothing more you could have done, I know that Scott," she said, looking up at him again. "But even so—well, I suppose the plain truth is that I was disappointed, I mean, I hated to think you'd had to become sort of McGregorized or Bellgardized."

"It wasn't a question of—"

"I must have felt that way because I knew how you used to be, I knew your whole history of—"

Scott interrupted her: "Listen, Ann, it doesn't matter what I might or might not have been, not under those conditions."

"What it is, I guess, is that nobody likes to see how someone else can change," she said.

"That's right." Scott answered defensively, too sharply since there was no trace of malice or the familiar irony in her voice. But going on nevertheless, lashing out at her unreasonably: "We can't all be perfect or consistent, can we? You're just the same as you were five years ago—little Orphan Annie, not a penny to her name, in tennis sneakers and beat-up blue jeans to mix it up with the rest of the cats on the *Boule Miche*."

He saw the sudden spark of protest leap to her eyes. But it burned out almost at once. "Do you really think I'm that different now?" she asked. "Oh, I'll admit I don't play poorhouse kid anymore and maybe I'm less phony and better dressed—" She dropped her cigarette and flattened it beneath the sole of her Chanel shoe. "Oh hell, we're getting all lost, what I'm trying to say, Scott, is that knowing how far-out stubborn, contrary, you used to be, I must have kept thinking, or hoping, you'd beat the old game anyway."

"Is this turning out to be a pep talk?"

"God!" Her smile erupted again. "It does sound like that, doesn't it?" And then the gray-blue eyes grew puzzled: "I don't know, Scott. I mean, you have to remember when you first came back, after Red's illness, the way you were snorting around like a white knight in a red Ferrari, and then after all that wonderful noise, I felt awful for you, having to see you end up in the ditch."

Once more Scott found himself caught up in a rush of gratitude for this small voice. He put his arm around her. "Thanks anyway, Junior."

A silence: the buzz of a mosquito grew suddenly closer.

"It was stupid of me to open my—" She stopped. "What's funny about it, I just realize, is that it isn't really funny at all—here I am wanting you to keep slugging away as if this sink of a town could be worth slugging for at all. I don't see how I—" In confusion she stepped away. And then abruptly: "Look, can I tell you something, Scott?"

"Yes. But make it nice and pretty."

"Oh, it is—I mean—what I was going to say was that my father is a kind of fan of yours."

"Come on, Junior. You don't have to go that far," he said.

"It's absolutely true," she said. "Your name comes up every time my father tries to put Ben down. That's the giveaway. It would probably be okay for me to sleep with you. But with Ben, it's an unforgivable sin. That's how Father is—I mean," she added now, "that's how he *was*. The morning that story about you popped into all the papers I saw him at breakfast, and I saw that the fan club was disbanded. You are no longer the court favorite."

"Surprise."

"The point," Ann said, "is that this nasty subversive act of yours might, by comparison, just possibly make Ben look like a real chrome angel. And selfishly speaking, I wanted to thank you."

Before Scott and Jemmy went out to the lake, they drove Ann Smith back to Kent Hills, through the curving lanes of the residential landscape. Most of the estates were dark, for it was almost two in the morning, and though Saturday night was Country Club night or Party night, the threshold of frivolity was never too high in Detroit. It was a production-line society at heart, and most of the people retired at a reasonable hour to conserve their energies, their health, for the day-time battles.

As they neared the house of the Tony Kerwins, Ann suddenly asked Scott to stop: "My God," she said, "the cottage is lit up like the Fourth of July. Tony's birthday can't still be going on. Why don't we all just march in and bust it up?"

"I've done my share of busting for one night," he said.

"Oh, come on, Scott."

"I'm not on easy speaking terms with your brother-in-law," Scott reminded her.

"I just want to see how poor Phoebe's holding up," Ann was saying as they drew into the driveway, parking before the sprawling gabled and timbered neo-English house. "You know she rarely drinks, but when I left earlier this evening she was downing the champagne like yogurt. That's practically historical." She turned to Jemmy: "Jemmy, can't you persuade your friend here—"

Jemmy said: "I think we have a date, Ann."

Scott opened the car door and escorted Ann to the front of the house. "Good night, Junior." He leaned down and kissed her. "Thanks again for all the good words."

"Oh, look Scott, please don't chicken out on me, come on in for a drink. You've got a date, but I'm stranded, I'm Ben-less and I want company."

"I don't think I—"

The house door had opened: Tony Kerwin stood there. "Ann—well, come in, come in, darling." Kerwin seemed eager to see her. And his smile, as he saw Scott, wavered only for an instant: "Why—hello there, Scott. Can't we give you a nightcap?"

As the two shook hands one would have thought they were fraternity brothers in happy reunion. Tony's hazel eyes seemed keen, his face had a feverish glow; the mole on his cheek was like a dark jewel in a roseate setting; his black hair was slightly roughed, the jacket of his suit was open, there was the gloss of the gold chain spanning his tattersall waistcoat. And then he was peering over Scott's shoulder.

[172

"That Jemmy there?" He stepped out. "Jem—you're expected in for a drink."

Scott was surprised to see him hurry to the car, open the door, and bring Jemmy back. It was as if he not only welcomed their late intrusion but needed it.

Ann, noting this also, said: "The hospitality around here, Tony, seems to be reaching a new high."

"Well, you know," he said, "when I see how the boys my age are dropping right and left, a birthday seems worth celebrating now."

And now into the foyer came Mr. and Mrs. Codman Smith, and Cod Smith kissed Ann. "Honey, we're just leaving. Shame you couldn't have got back earlier."

"Can't you stay?" Ann said to her father.

"Yes, no need to rush off now, Cod. We—" Kerwin began.

Cod Smith was consulting his wife, and Mrs. Smith said no, it was much too late. Smith nodded, glanced at his watch.

Ann said: "You might at least say hello to my friend." She smiled at Scott, and then resumed. "You have to look at it like this, Father, you might have lost a good ballplayer, but at least you've gained a troublesome dealer."

Codman Smith transferred his agate-eyed attention to Scott: "Dandy ballplayer, without a doubt. Good evening, Scott—or rather, good morning."

They did not shake hands.

The Smiths started for the entry and as Mrs. Smith stepped outside, Codman Smith paused, his stalwart, big-shouldered frame in the doorway. "Scott"—he tilted his head toward the driveway—"like a word with you." His voice was crisp, though amiable enough.

Scott followed him. After he had helped his wife into the long black Bellgard, Smith turned to Scott: "Scott, it might be an idea if you dropped by my office next week." His manner remained firm, distant and Scott felt a vague alarm or embarrassment. Smith detected this at once, for he said: "My secretary will get back to you, and we'll see if we can't sneak you up when no one's looking."

His dry laconic humor was, however, more welcome to Scott than Tony Kerwin's overhearty, overgracious greeting. Yes, Scott said, he'd come and Codman Smith nodded and got into the car.

When Scott returned to the house, the foyer was empty. He listened for sounds, and then turned into the wide passage on his right: it was a kind of trophy hall where the walls held, in recessed glass cases, silver cups, ribbons, medals and documents testifying to Tony Kerwin's preeminence as golf player, tennis player, yachtsman and car collector.

Scott moved on into the living room, enormous and paneled in somber wood. Above the stone fireplace was a portrait of Tony Kerwin in fox-hunting attire. Flanking the fireplace were two long divans in quilted chintz; a settee and several English Windsor chairs closed the circle around the hearth.

He saw Jemmy on the settee, and he saw Ann, her shoes off, standing by a cabinet examining the label on a bottle of champagne.

As he crossed, the stillness of the long room made Scott's movements conspicuous. The others seemed to be waiting, like figures on a panel or frieze grimly commemorating American exurban life. Tony Kerwin was directly beneath his portrait, his wife Phoebe beside him in white evening dress, her pale hair looking dry, faded, her eyes dilated, misty as she stared into her glass; her sister Myra Stratler sat on the divan, her blond hair puffed high into a pompadour, her slender legs crossed, her attention focused nervously on Ann; her husband, Dean Stratler, less conservative in his attire than Kerwin, and sporting one of those narrow, abstract-figured cravats he liked to design, sat alongside his wife, his straight ashen hair brushed sleekly, his head leaning back against the sofa, appearing every inch the Chief Stylist of Bellgard, the always restless eyes now contemplating the beamed ceiling with the remote gaze of the "artist" withdrawn from his more prosaic companions.

As soon as he seated himself beside Jemmy, Myra Stratler stirred: "Annie—" she called, "aren't you getting the champagne? Do stop dawdling. Phoebe's run dry and so have we." Then: "Whatever happened to your love? He couldn't still be working at this hour, could he?" She let the faintest sarcasm peep through this show of sisterly banter.

Ann swung around, but before she could make any kind of reply, Phoebe Kerwin said: "Come on, Annie, let's pass it around." Then, her voice less steady and speaking to no one in particular, she went on: "It's such good champagne. I've never cared for it, but I think I'm getting to like it, I do really. And Tony"—with effort her eyes widened as she glanced at her husband beside her—"Tony is furious with me, I think he thinks it's not suitable for me to drink. But why shouldn't I?"

"Phoebe, for God sakes," Tony Kerwin murmured. He ran his

finger across the gold chain of his waistcoat, and Scott noticed the almost furtive flashing glance he gave to Myra Stratler.

And there was another gap of silence, and then a burst of talk as Myra Stratler and the others plunged in to redeem the quiet.

Dean Stratler got up and moved to the arm of the settee. "Sorry about that showing, Scott. We had to put it off, but you've got yourself a raincheck. I'm sure you understand."

Yes: how well Scott understood.

"Dean." Myra Stratler sauntered over, moving so casually as to suggest a certain constraint, and in the faintly British cadence which often marked her speech, said: "Before you get bogged down in business, hadn't we better think of tooting off?" To Scott: "So sorry we couldn't have seen you earlier, Scott. You mustn't be such a stranger, you know." She stood there slim and elegant and poised, though her violet-shadowed eyes betrayed agitation; she glanced up to the mirror across the room, and as she spoke she kept consulting her reflection almost as if she were alone in her own dressing room.

"Now listen, Myra"—Tony Kerwin moved toward her—"you needn't take off in such a rush, after all you can put up with me on my birthday, can't you?"

"Oh, of course she can." Phoebe Kerwin came over hurriedly, unsteadily. Addressing her sister then, she said: "We're all just settling down to a cozy family evening, we don't have them too often, do we? Oh my, but it really *has* been cozy tonight, hasn't it?" Her pale misty eyes still held on her sister's. "Hasn't it, Myra?" And then seeking her husband's face, confronting him, "It has, hasn't it, Tony?"

"Now Phoebe . . ." Tony Kerwin began, but abandoned his attempt to placate her, turning quickly to Myra. "Myra what are we going to do about your sister?"

"I'm afraid we're keeping you up, Phoebe dear," Myra now said in a tone harsh with impatience. "I do think you ought to get to bed and—"

"Bed?" Phoebe said. "I'm not an invalid." She turned to the rest. "You'd think I was an invalid wouldn't you?" She wavered: "Why don't we have some music?" She walked rigidly as if counting the steps of an exercise, to the stereo set which was artfully concealed in a Jacobean chest. She lifted the lid of the chest, reached down absently, pressed a lever, and with shocking suddenness there came into the big room the wild snorting roar of a car motor.

"Oh no!" Ann's voice came in protest.

175]

"Oh, sorry—sorry." Phoebe had turned back hastily, as now the engine sounds rose in violent shattering fidelity, a car motor accelerating from takeoff to maximum speed.

Phoebe had stopped the machine now, leaving in the wake of the terrible roar a stillness that seemed even more thunderous. Yet the aftermath brought with it a certain respite, a nervous titter, even a kind of comic relief.

"Good God." Ann crossed over to the machine. Phoebe stepped aside to let her set up the proper records.

And Tony Kerwin, recovering his composure, said, by way of apology, that they had been listening to the record earlier, it had just been especially recorded for Bellgard and he'd played it for Codman Smith. He brought the disk to Scott, saying the company would be sending them out to dealers next year as part of a campaign to push The Bellstar, the still-secret sports model.

Scott read the label, *The Racing Sounds of the Bellstar,* and there was one of those streaky, glamorous sketches of the car with which the company hoped to compete with the sales of the Corvette or T-Bird. It would be a free booster gift, Tony said, given to each buyer of a Bellstar.

"I see." Scott did not mention what he already knew: that each dealer would be billed for a certain number of records, after which he would have to add the cost to the price tag of the car, or, failing that, simply take the loss.

By then the room was athrob with the beat of a dance orchestra, and it sounded somehow foolish as well as embarrassing with its brassy demand for gaiety in a room where gaiety had long fled.

But at least it would be easier to leave now, and Scott peered over at Jemmy. Jemmy drew the signal and she stirred, opened her bag and took out her compact.

"Isn't anyone going to dance?" Phoebe was saying. At first no one responded.

Then Myra Stratler turned to her husband: "Dean, why don't you look after my little sister?" She indicated Ann. "She seems completely undone tonight without Ben."

It was the second time Scott had noticed the way she taunted Ann, and it occurred to him, recalling other occasions, that if sometimes Ann seemed overaggressive or exhibitionistic, there might have been some justfication for it.

"Come on, Ann." Dean Stratler went to her. Bellgard's Vice-President of Styling seemed the only person in the room who maintained calm.

"Delighted." Ann in her stocking feet began to dance with her brother-in-law.

Perceiving this, and as if he feared being outdone, Tony Kerwin was quick to put on his Host's smile again. "You're not going to miss the *Concours,* are you?" he said to Scott. "Because this is something we're all very proud of around here. One of the finest in the country, I think."

Yes, Scott said, he looked forward to going. They talked about the event for a short while, and then as Scott was about to rise to leave, Phoebe intervened. She stood before him, her thin arms held out, and asked him to dance.

Scott rose hastily.

"You won't mind, Jemmy?" Phoebe said.

Jemmy looked up, she palmed back her long black hair. "Of course not, Phoebe."

With the thinnest enthusiasm Scott began to dance with Kerwin's wife. She held him almost tenaciously, trying to do her best, making small talk but rambling discursively, telling him about the evening and how there had been several people here from the company to wish Tony well.

"Anyway," Phoebe went on, "I'm so glad you and the girls stopped by, we don't usually have a party that goes on to—" She stopped, drew back; she had stepped on his foot. "I'm sorry, Scott." Then, with more effort, she tried to make a joke about how the men tonight had held only two business conferences, which was something of a record. "Oh—" she turned her head—"excuse me, that champagne does catch up with one." Her laugh came a little hysterically. "Tony!" she called out, peering over Scott's shoulder, "You're leaving Myra twiddling there. Spread your charms around to"—she hiccoughed again—"all the girls."

Tony Kerwin, standing by the fireplace, frowned, shook his head.

"Mean, that's mean of you, Tony, leaving Myra there—" Abruptly her arms slid from Scott; he caught her as she slumped down.

"Phoebe—" Ann said.

Kerwin hurried over: "Knew it was coming," he muttered, and he and Scott carried her to the divan.

And Ann appeared with a water-soaked towel and the brandy. Phoebe Kerwin's face was bleached of all color, it was moist, and her breathing was irregular. Ann raised her head and tried to give her some brandy, but it dribbled down her chin, and then Phoebe suddenly cried out "Tony—" only to fall back again.

Dean Stratler said: "I'll call Herley."

"No," Tony Kerwin said. "She'll be all right. I told her not to have any more to drink, she just can't take it and—"

Again Phoebe stirred, brought her hand to her mouth, and Ann said: "We'd better get her upstairs, Tony." She bent down and pressed the cold towel to Phoebe's forehead.

"Yes." Kerwin looked over at Stratler. The two men carried her upstairs.

"How is she?" Myra Stratler asked when they returned.

"She'll sleep it out," Tony Kerwin said. "Ann got her clothes off."

"Poor thing," Myra said.

"Sorry we had to put you through this, Scott," Tony Kerwin said. "One of those things, you know."

When Ann came downstairs, Myra said: "Is she all right, Ann?"

"I hope so," Ann said, and added, facing her sister: "It wasn't very bright of you to keep loading her with all that booze."

"Me?"

"Yes, you know damn well Phoebe isn't used to it." Ann did not conceal the reproach in her voice.

"I did nothing of the sort, wherever did you get a stupid idea like that?" Myra said. "If Phoebe told you I—"

"All right, Myra." Dean Stratler took her arm. "We'd better go."

"Well, let's have this understood." Myra drew away from him. "I was merely trying to help out. Phoebe takes these parties too seriously, she can't relax, and I was only—"

"Now let's not all get exercised about this," Tony Kerwin interposed. "Neither Myra nor anyone else had anything to do with this, it was simply that Phoebe was way out of her depth. She'll be all right in the morning. This is still my party, let's not desert me. Scott, let me pour you a—"

"No thank you. I've got to get Jemmy back."

"Good night, Tony." Myra shook Kerwin's hand rather formally. "Let me know in the morning how she is, if there's anything I can do."

"Certainly, but nothing to get exercised about."

"But do let me know, Tony, if I can do anything," Myra said.

[178

"I think," Ann peered at her sister, "I think you've been helpful enough for one night."

Dean Stratler quickly took his wife's arm again, and there was a flurry of movement as now all of them moved to the entry hall.

Ann came out to the driveway with Scott and Jemmy, and she kissed Scott and apologized for having pushed them from "the frying pan into the ignoble family pot." Adding: "But anyway, Scott, thanks and I couldn't be more sorry."

Nor Scott. And conscious that during the dying hour of the stopover at the Kerwins, he had unwittingly lost his status of outsider; unwittingly he had been drawn into the ring of Kent Hills, closer to its center.

Ann waved them off. Scott saw her standing beyond the doorway, her light hair trapping the moon's radiance: an unenviable figure. The thought unsettled him, he had always let her rest in the niche to which he had patently consigned her, so that now he had the disconcerting sensation of an easy, long-held judgment suddenly becoming invalid.

Driving back through the curving lanes of Kent Hills, Jemmy was quiet, uncommunicative. Finally Scott said: "Been quite a night."

She nodded remotely.

"What's the matter, Jemmy?"

She didn't turn from the window. "Nothing at all, Scott."

"Are you sure you want to go to the lake?"

"Yes."

As soon as they turned into shore road, clean and carless now, Scott pushed the Bellgard almost flat out and soon they were bombing down the narrow road to the lake cove, and he saw the familiar fir trees—last survivors of a once prodigious forest—bold shafts against the diamond galaxies of the sky.

They went into the coy house of Jemmy's cousin, into the familiar alpine ambience of the bedroom, a room Scott had come to dislike and tonight he cared for it even less: he could have wished for it to be downright sinister or furnished with Grand Rapids Gothic.

But no.

Scott wondered if Jemmy sensed or perceived how he felt and if she would vary what had come to be a kind of routine. She didn't. On the contrary, even the practiced routine seemed to lack spirit; and soon she was tugging aside the little curtains to let in the moonlight, and then she was in the bed waiting for him, naked and somewhat rigid, her lustrous hair dark on the pillow. The pallor of her face had given way to a faint stain of color, and her vivid mouth was not parted in that drowsy half-smile of anticipation.

Lights out. Moonlight in. And Scott lay down beside her, drew her to him, and it was better then, though a long way from what he seemed to want or need tonight.

Tonight he wanted nothing less than some celestial and unholy ride; instead he found himself lumped on a hammock in a field of edelweiss. . . .

What had happened? It hadn't been quite like this in the beginning, not even like this two weeks ago. In the beginning Scott had liked what he thought was a certain sullen, aggressive manner about her, that kind of sleepy-eyed, sensual-mouthed allure he'd found in her on that first Sunday morning on the terrace of the Smith's house. But somewhere along the line Jemmy had lost it—unwittingly Scott thought of his wife, yes, and how Ellen too had subtly altered, losing abandon for comfort.

Or maybe he was imagining all of it, or maybe it was just the long silence in which they lay too closely locked, the feel of her seemed desperately close, as if she wanted to make any interplay impossible, and Scott felt cheated of her body, the fine milky tint of her middle and her thighs.

He decided to get up. He moved to the small window and looked out to the lake, to the path of gold the moon inscribed on the water's surface: a vision of pearly calendar art that left him wanting thunder and wind.

He heard her leaving the bed, and she came to stand alongside him, and there was the unexpected delicate grazing of her body to his, and he turned and embraced her, a loose slow embrace at first and then feeling her breasts cool and hard and tasting then the upthrust offering of their buds, and feeling the curving length of belly stir, stiffen. And all at once he felt intensely happy, wanting her, appreciating her, and they fell back onto the bed again, and then it was not the same as the other recent times.

Not until afterwards did Scott wonder why it had been different, what the source had been. They were smoking cigarettes, lying beneath the sheet of the disheveled bed in the chill mildew of the lamp-lit room, and soon he became aware that the lazy warm aftermath of lovemaking was not with them. Jemmy lay there too rigidly, unlike other times when she might have rested, propped up on one elbow, the gray eyes untroubled as she talked. She almost always talked afterwards, as if the act of sex, however relaxed or familiar it might have been, had unloosed the thoughts held captive all week, and she would dwell on her tendency to let her life slip by and how she should have felt more guilt for not putting her mind to some serious pursuit—"Why, I don't even try to cut down smoking," she would say, "I keep putting it off, the same way I keep putting off starting on some postgraduate work. I don't know. I suppose my trouble is I haven't got anything to protest against—that's what Ann always says. Of course she's got good reason, but me—I really haven't got much to get worked up about."

Tonight, however, the outgoing confidences seemed choked off; the hand holding her cigarette hung alongside the bed lifeless.

The smoke of her unsmoked cigarette curled up and she moved at last, stubbing out the cigarette in the ashtray on the bedtable. She said: "I suppose we should have come out here earlier, I mean—you're more human now. You were all bristly tonight."

"Yes, I know."

She moved again, pulling up her knees. "We could stay out here tomorrow if we wanted." The offer seemed tentative.

"Tomorrow? You know I can't, Jemmy. I have to be with Susan."

"Yes," she said. "Or maybe no. Maybe you'd be a better father if you didn't worry it to death."

"Maybe. But that's not the answer either. Sunday is the one day Suzy counts on."

"I think I'll open the window." She got up and flung open the small casements. She said: "Can I get you anything, there's some beer or bourbon, I think—"

"No thanks, Jemmy."

She picked up her white slip and put it on; for a moment she stood near the bed, she was biting her lower lip, and then absently she moved to the bed's foot and fussed with the sheets, rearranging them, a now familiar domestic ritual, and as she worked, her long hair kept falling, partially blocking her sight so that she kept pushing it back, and as he watched her Scott found himself again thinking of his wife: like Ellen there seemed to be lurking beneath Jemmy's personality some sort of demon, poised on some invisible brink, ready to leap out.

Scott said, a last effort against the weight of sleep: "I was thinking maybe next Sunday I'll take Suzy along with us to the *Concours*."

Jemmy tucked in the sheets at the corners, saying yes, she thought that might be a good idea, but speaking almost mechanically now, going on about her work with frenzied fingers, mechanical fingers, separate instruments of toil, having no connection with her mind or body. Once she looked up: "I got the impression you invited me along more out of habit or duty—I mean it doesn't matter that much, Scott. And—" She did not finish. She sat down at the end of the bed.

"No, not at all," he said.

"Well anyway, I spared you," she said hastily. "I'll be going with Johnny Winters."

"Winters?"

"Yes. Besides, he's richer than you," she joked, but her voice sounded labored. "He asked me tonight and I thought it would be better all around."

"Now look, Jemmy . . ." he began and ended.

"What?" Sharp interest marked her question, and when Scott failed to answer at once, she said: "What were you going to say?"

"Nothing immemorial," he said.

She studied the pale carpet. "I—I'd hoped you would."

"Would what?"

"Say something immemorial—no, not actually. I actually didn't expect you to." A flicker of smile, weak, disturbed, and she busied herself putting back in place one of the ribbonlike straps of her slip.

"Come on over here, Jemmy." He tapped her pillow.

She peered up, as if to examine his expression, but she did not speak.

"What the hell is it?"

"What?"

"You haven't been at all like—"

"Like what? Oh hell, have you got another cigarette?" But without waiting for it, she rose and moved back to the window. Abruptly she turned then, palmed back her hair: "Listen, Scott, I wasn't even going to mention this, believe me, I wasn't. But—" She shook her head once more.

He sat up at once, alerted by the alarm in her eyes.

"Oh, I'm so furious I could spit!" The words burst from her; distractedly she came to the side of the bed and lit one of his cigarettes, exhaled: "If I'm pregnant, I think I'll go out of my mind. I've never

[182

been late like this before and—" She turned as if wanting to shield him from the sight of her.

"Jemmy—"

"Never been late like this."

Scott swung to the edge of the bed. "Are you sure?"

"I'm sure all right." The words tolled out. "It's four days, five tomorrow."

Sinking deeper in him, the dismal apprehension came to rest like an anchor in the silt of his stomach. He saw the faint droop of her back, in contrast to the squared thrust that had accompanied her persistent show of independence earlier. "Four days?" he echoed it stupidly.

"Oh, I'm so damn furious I could spit!" she said again.

Scott rose then and went to her. Too clumsily he put his arm around her.

She stepped back. "Oh, it hasn't actually happened yet and I don't expect you to make all the honorable sounds, it's just that I'm scared as hell, I don't know what I'd do if—"

Scott didn't know either; he didn't want to know. But he reached for her arm again, and he drew her to him and held her. "It's still a little too soon to worry."

"I hope so." She let him hold her. "Oh, Scott—" Her sudden sob was muffled against his throat. "I didn't ever want to mention it, I wanted to wait, but it's—"

Her flesh was chilled and Scott could feel the goose pimples cold and prickling on her bare arms and shoulders. He took his shirt from the chair and draped it around her. Then he went into the little kitchen, half filled two glasses with bourbon and brought them back.

She looked deceptively small, sitting there on the side of the bed, the white buttondown shirt falling below her knees like a nightdress. Looking down at her, Scott thought how the freewheeling candor of their relationship of the past months had within a few seconds evolved into something else, and how with all their intelligent guarantees of mutual freedom, they were no longer free at all.

"I suppose I might as well have some more." Jemmy held out her glass. "It tastes so awful it might be good for me." A pause. Then she said in a sudden spurt of cheer: "Actually I keep thinking it has to be a false alarm, it just can't happen to us—I mean, to me." She corrected herself.

"I'm sure it's a scare, Jemmy. No more than that," he said staunchly.

Later he went to the kitchen with their empty glasses. When he brought in the drinks he asked if she'd said anything to her parents yet.

"No, that's the least of it actually. They're—you know how they are, Scott. Oh, I mean they wouldn't rush out and get it published on the front page of the Ann Arbor *Herald*. They'd be good about it—" A reconsideration then: "Or maybe not. Maybe if it actually happened and I had to tell them, maybe in spite of all their liberalism and parental psychology, they'd fall apart just like any other parents—I don't know." She studied her glass, drank more of the bourbon and made a face. "But oh, Scott, wouldn't that be a mess though, oh Christ, what a mess!"

The anchor lodged deeper. "It still hasn't happened."

She nodded numbly. "Why *now,* why in hell right now—it's terrible enough, but with you, you're the one I—"

"What?"

"Nothing. Nothing. Oh Christ!" She kept looking at him, searching his face. "As terrible as it is, if it wasn't you, I'd—"

"Stop worrying about me." But Scott perceived then for the first time what he should have seen sooner: she had put him in the kind of spot to which she was vehemently opposed. And he saw what was behind her behavior during the entire evening and why she'd gone out of her way to encourage Winters' attention, as if she needed to prove to Scott and to herself that she must not be regarded as a desperate female, clinging and trapping him in this banal and classic predicament.

But trapped he was. And all her good intentions could not soften the hard core of his resistance. Worse: the very fact of her fear of trapping him came now as the oblique admission that love, which she had always denied, had for her, come to exist.

"Will you believe me, Scott? It—I mean, it just can't happen. But I mean it, whatever happens, I don't want you to think I'm trying to—" A sigh of exasperation.

And Scott saw that his feeling had been right. As he looked at her now, sheathed in the white shirt, her wide pale face softened, narrowed by the fall of black hair, rendering her younger, more vulnerable, he felt himself yielding to her in spite of himself, dropping weakly into the trap.

[184

"Look, Jemmy, for God sake, it hasn't happened yet, and even— even if it did, you know damn well I'd—"

"Oh Scott—please!" Her hand rose in protest and he saw in her eyes how fierce the protest was. But it was generated from her mind, her intellect.

"That uncle of mine in California," she went on, her voice suddenly dry and toneless, "he's in Los Angeles. Believe me, if I have to face this, that's where I'm going. He's a doctor, he'll know what can be done. He's always writing to me to come out there. California—" She broke off. "Oh, Christ!"

Scott held her then, for how long he didn't know. He found himself admitting, in an unforeseen light of pure reason, that if it had to happen, there were worse fates than marrying Jemmy. If it had to happen. He at least had the honest consolation that from the point of view of Suzy and his own inadequate role in her life thus far, there was nothing but a high score for Jemmy. She had been out to the house many times, and it had become clearer than ever that, unlike Ann Smith, she seemed to have an easy, natural way with children. She had certainly been marvelous with Susan; even Red had not failed to mention it. He could see all this now, he was forced to see it. He knew he'd been evading the problem of Suzy, keeping himself in mid-track, never letting himself near where the rails force a decision. And now there was the dubious comfort of knowing the problem was suddenly riding with him.

More bourbon. And exhaustion overtaking them. When at last they fell asleep they beat the sun's rise by less than an hour.

When Scott awoke, the dreadful squeaky cry of the cuckoo clock having done its work, he probed through woolly semiconsciousness, his arm crept out to find only the faint body warmth where Jemmy had been. Slowly, as daylight touched him, and with it the kitchen sounds, he opened his eyes, his mind unfolding slowly like a morning flower stiffening to the sun.

New hope took life in him. New day. Exit the demons of last night. He listened: the kitchen sounds seemed brisk. He swung out of the bed, thrust on his gray trousers, going shirtless and shoeless toward the kitchen.

Jemmy was dressed. An unsought tenderness held Scott as he saw her, though she looked not her best—the sockets of her eyes showed darker depths and her long black hair was unbrushed. The answer was there, taking with it the euphoria his first hopes had induced. She looked up and said good morning, and he heard himself asking why didn't she come home with him for the midday Sunday dinner.

She paused in her work, glanced at the knife with which she'd been buttering the toast. She said, as if needing to batter his small attempt at gallantry: "Thanks, Scott. But no." Then, answering the question he hadn't asked, she said, well, the fifth day and nothing had happened yet.

And she turned with a compulsive movement as though to ward off anything he might say, but her arm struck the chrome percolator and it toppled over, falling onto the counter, and then the clean Swiss kitchen floor was suddenly awash with the murky steamy liquid. "Oh, great!" she muttered in rage, and ran for the sponge.

Afterward she improvised, stirring some powered milk into a pitcher of water, and they had the toast, and it seemed suddenly that they couldn't get out of the little house soon enough.

At least the day was fine. Scott drove her back to Ann Arbor, along the highway already dense with Sunday drivers. Nothing was altered or accomplished between them, except that Scott got her to agree to kill the engagement she'd made with Winters for next Sunday afternoon.

When he returned to his father's house in Greenwood Park—a drive of more than thirty-five miles—Scott had had enough time to sweat out, to sort out, the onrush of burdens. In twenty-four hours all his former concerns had become not secondary but less immediate. Now there was the primary concern, the one least expected, least likely, yet most overwhelming: Jemmy.

He didn't have to feel that way, nothing was forcing him to do anything he didn't want to do: Jemmy had made that vehemently plain.

Free as the proverbial bird was he. California was a good distance. The kind of luck a man can rejoice in.

Except that he knew how Jemmy's feelings had changed. She'd betrayed that last night, not wanting to admit love even to herself, and hence letting it fill the room. Detesting this sort of trap, she wanted to divert him from it with her gift of freedom, her determination not to impose any of the rules.

But if he had the luck of her offered freedom, he somehow couldn't take it: with someone like Jemmy, constructed as she was, you didn't have to make "all the honorable sounds," but you did. If it became necessary, you did.

True: though not in any way lessening the burden. Neither Jemmy's decent qualities nor his awareness that he had to act soon one way or the other to give some kind of completion to Suzy's life— none of this could lessen the fact of the burden.

15: Scott Quinnley

As the week began at Quinnley Corners, Scott discovered that the Car Carnival had left its casualties, two salesmen fallen in the campaign: Dave Toff bedded down with a throat infection; Marty Calhoon absent, his wife calling in to say he was "indisposed." Scott too could qualify as a casualty, though of a different kind, and he took a certain solace in knowing that veterans like Toff and Calhoon had been cut down. It was his father, however, who suffered the most severe strain: he had not stirred from the house since last Saturday night, imprisoned by helpless exhaustion.

By Wednesday Toff was back, though there was still no word from Marty Calhoon. And by Thursday even Red appeared for a few hours in the afternoon.

First on Red's agenda was Calhoon. When his repeated calls brought no response, he became alarmed. He quit his swivel chair and moved to Scott's desk. "Listen son, I sure as hell don't like this. I want you to track it down. Today. I don't like it." He pulled at his veined cheeks and paced back to his chair, standing there below the framed photograph of himself and the mayor at the Firemen's Annual Barbecue of 1948: the contrast between the Red Quinnley of that time and today made Scott want to look away.

Later, as he prepared to leave, tugging his creamy hat over his forehead, Red said: "Keep calling Marty, will you? And tell that long lump of Irish I want him back on the floor. We're getting into the dog days and we have to have him." He opened his humidor and removed a fresh cigar and studied it wistfully before thrusting it into his mouth. "I've been carrying Marty for a year, but I can't carry him forever just on a past record. We can't afford it now. It's that goddam wife of his. I want you to get to Marty and I want you to make it clear to him that unless he gets over here on the job and starts delivering, we'll have to let him go." But Red, as he said this, seemed to lack heart: Scott knew he would never dismiss Calhoon despite the man's declining sales. "You'll take care of that today, Scott?" Then: "You lay it down."

"Yes."

"I'd go see him myself—"

"I'll take care of it."

But Scott dreaded the encounter. On his second try, Mrs. Calhoon answered the telephone: Yes, Marty was still out but he was sure to come in by dinnertime. He decided to see Marty on his way back to Greenwood Park.

He remembered he had to call Jemmy in Ann Arbor. However, just then Mrs. Bowsley came hurrying in. The elderly woman's face was taut with excitement. "I just received a call from Bellgard, from Mr. Codman Smith's secretary. He would like to see you next Tuesday afternoon."

"Codman Smith?"

"Tuesday afternoon. I've put it down for you." Mrs. Bowsley, in her agitated pride which suggested that Scott had been summoned to the White House, had not even consulted him before confirming the appointment.

"Thank you, Mrs. B." he said.

She peered at him as if in disappointment, and as she left he saw that the pulchritudinous receptionist Miss Mergenfreed was standing just outside the door, and he heard her breathless query: *What did he say when you told him?*

Obviously Scott had failed the women: obviously this had been the only time when the president of Bellgard had become real for them, reaching down from his lofty realm to recognize one of the minor satellites of his empire. But belatedly he too was caught up in the command, recalling now the nip of Smith's words as he called him aside in the driveway of the Kerwin residence, and belatedly he felt again that same sense of alarm that had held him at the time.

Tuesday next. He jotted down the date and the hour.

Then he called Jemmy. He waited, hoping for the lift of her voice, that pitch of tone that might tell him at once if her situation had changed.

It hadn't.

She said she'd decided to write to her uncle in California. "I don't think there's any doubt now, Scott."

"Listen, Jemmy"—he stared down at the glass surface of the desk

189]

—"I still say we should wait, I don't want to see you redballing all the way out there, it's still—"

"Oh, I appreciate the gallantry, I do, Scott. But there's no point kidding myself. Or you."

He said he'd already told Suzy about Sunday and how she was looking forward to it, and that they'd pick her up in Ann Arbor, going on then to the *Concours*. "Let's at least wait until then, maybe by then—"

"I doubt it."

"What did you do today?"

"Swimming again," she said. "My family must be wondering what gives with me, I've suddenly gone 4-H, you never saw such a healthy character. I'm going out again tomorrow. High dives. I haven't tried that yet." Her laugh was throaty and she coughed.

He said why didn't he pick her up and they'd go to dinner.

"Jack Winters called me this noon, I'm, going out with him tonight."

"Oh."

"Oh what? You don't mind that much do you?"

"Well—I—"

Her tone rose to a nuance of cheer: "Well anyway, you're very sweet."

"What about Sunday?"

A hesitation: "All right."

His anxiety had taken another turn, an ignoble one, as Ann Smith would have said. He was now reaching out for superstitions: he kept hoping that by accepting his responsibility in the highest honorable way, he'd be rewarded for his virtue by a miraculous reprieve—just as a man long unemployed finds that as soon as he takes the one job he deplores, another offer will come along for something much better.

At seven o'clock he drove to Marty Calhoon's ranch-style home which was near Greenwood Park, on a street of other ranch-style homes not as large, imaginative or luxurious as the residences of Greenwood Park (which in turn were but expensive imitations of the manor's of Kent Hills).

Vera Calhoon opened the door. He'd seen her several times when she'd come by Quinnley Corners to pick up Marty; she'd seemed stiffly polite, and the only thing he'd noticed about her was that she must have been about twenty years younger than Marty.

[190

"Come in, won't you, Mr. Quinnley? My husband just got back from—that tavern—what is it—Sophie's?"

He followed her into the living room, a clean pathetic sort of room with its wagon-wheel lighting fixture suspended from the low ceiling, its Western Frontier bar in one corner, and its three other pieces of Machine-made Rustic. There was a fleecy white throw rug in front of the sofa. Marty stood up.

Vera said well she'd go in and dress. She walked, her posture carefully controlled, into the bedroom. Quietly Marty fixed him a drink.

"What is it, kid?" He confronted Scott; he spoke quietly, even sluggishly. "The heat on? Red send you around for the Big Take Over?" Moistening his lips: "I would have gone to see Red myself, but I don't want to rev up that ticker of his."

"Marty, we can talk some other time if you—"

"Take it easy, kid." He slumped down on the couch. "Sit down." When Scott seated himself, Calhoon said: "It was dead over at Sophie's, none of the boys around. I'm glad you're here." His glance went to the bedroom door. "I'm quitting, kid."

"You're what?"

"Sent you a letter when I went out before, sent it to you, not Red. What they call a letter of resignation." The slow, heavy measure of his speech made Scott see how serious he was.

"Marty—" He leaned toward him. "You're not quitting, you're not doing anything like it." But he was suddenly stung by a sense of loss, suddenly he knew how his father felt, how they needed him; despite his decline, they needed him. His presence now seemed crucial, as if the loss of him might somehow loosen, undermine the already unsure structure of Quinnley Corners. "Listen, Marty—you know damn well you go with the lease."

For a flash, a particle of time, Calhoon seemed to shed that weary inwardness, to take on a bloom of life. Then: "Let's say the lease has expired as far as Marty Calhoon is concerned."

"Marty," Scott pushed it now, grateful that the prime issue was out in the open. "Marty, you know I'm on your side, I've always been. Otherwise I wouldn't be here."

"Sure." Without warning Calhoon laughed, a laconic laugh, startling, out of place. "Sure. Now that I'm quitting I can talk to the boss's son." He seemed reasonable, taking simple refuge in his teasing.

"Not that way, you can't," Scott said. "You're not quitting, let's get that straight. You're needed. Badly now. I certainly need you." Then, attempting to reach him with a lighter hand: "You're still my professor."

"Come on, kid," he answered. "I'm not worried about you anymore. You're gonna come through, you gave a real performance for that Car Carnival of Red's. Got your spurs. Not going to be too long before you're gonna score the kind of record your old friend Calhoon used to peg."

Scott reached down to the coffee table and picked up his glass; he drained off a third of the martini, needing to wash down Marty's unwelcome tribute. "Let's not get hung up on that, Marty, and let's not get hung up on that letter you wrote. If you're going to quit, pick some other time, not now. The way we stand now, we need all the experience we can get. You're still the man who—"

"Naw, not quite, kid. Used to be. But I lost it. Or it lost me. I don't know." He studied the backs of his big, brown-flecked hands. "Haven't got the feel anymore, Scott. And this summer I ain't getting it back, doesn't come that way."

"This summer"—Scott called up Red's words—"is when we're going to have to push the hardest. That's what Red's concerned about," he went on, falling back on the cushion of his father's condition. "I know Red's been riding you now and then, but I also know he can't run the shop without you." He paused; he saw he wasn't gaining on him. He heard himself say: "What I—what we were thinking, Marty, is that for the next quarter, I want to up the commission. For you, that is. It'll be worth it all around."

Marty seemed to consider this: a tangible offer, not a valentine. He shook his head, however, and said: "Thanks, kid. But I ain't bucking it, not this summer, that's for sure. Did you see the spreads in all the magazines came out today? You see them? You see that issue of *Time*?"

"Yes."

"You saw it then, huh? You know what it means?" Abruptly Marty seemed to acquire new energy. "You'll find out soon enough, kid." He went on then, as though he were not only eager but relieved to expound, break into the long self-imposed fast of silence: "Christ, they used to spiel up the publicity but not until the end of the summer. Now Bellgard's got twitchy pants, they're scared to hold off. So what happens? They're getting the public all hot for the new models

[192

way in advance, and so no one but a deadhead or a bargain-basement piker is gonna want to buy the leftovers of this year's line. Mr. Dean Stratler shoots off his load and makes all the magazines and papers. Fine. But you're gonna feel it beginning tomorrow. Tomorrow Quinnley Corners is gonna be a graveyard, believe me, kid, the next sixty, ninety days are gonna be deadville. And who's gonna be stuck with the tab? That's right. Red Quinnley Your Friendly Bellgard Dealer at the Corner of Buy and Save."

They were on other ground now. His sardonic prophecy, however much exaggerated, left Scott chilled. But he said, trying once more: "Marty, what we have to talk about is personal. It doesn't concern Bellgard or—"

"Bellgard is what I'm talking about," Calhoon broke in. "Bellgard is my pocket—it's a lot more than that. I was going to quit anyway, but all that shit flying in the magazines today made it easier for me."

Grayly there rose in Scott's mind the prospect of facing his father, reporting to him Marty's decision, his particular despair, and knowing even now that Red would not accept this and would only put it down to Scott's failure. He said: "Marty, you've been up against a hell of a lot more than this and anyway, if what you say is true, that's all the more reason why I—"

"Forget it, kid. I'd pitch in if I thought it would help. But I know better. Can't put myself through it anymore, not the way I feel. I've lost it. I can't sell those dogs anymore, don't ask me why, and don't ask me to tell Red why—I'm not like him, I can't keep on hypnotizing myself into believing I've still got something to sell. And I'm not up to the haggle with this crazy new breed of customer. They used to come in to buy an automobile, now they're shopping around for a rainbow with a big pot of gold hanging from it. You don't sell those creeps—you may think you do—but you don't. They sell you now, they lay out the deal. They've got ten thousand different models and colors and more optionals to choose from than the Maharaja of— Listen, they've got every dealer kissing their asses any way they want it. For what? For those four-wheeled dogs?" The words kept spilling from him, erupting with some fierce joyous need: "You wanna know something, Scott? Just between you and me? I think the automobile's getting to be a joke— Sure, it's dressed up better now, no more stupid tail fins or all that spaghetti, the boys are hot on saving their souls with simple lines now, like they got religion. But it ain't religion, it's just a new gimmick to sell, just like they're selling safety belts or the

193]

torsion bar. But you look at the highways and streets, and then look at those jobs they're blasting up to the moon, and you see we're selling a joke, a horse and carriage that fools you because it goes fast, a racing car with no place to race—" He stopped. "Naw, don't let me hand you that, kid. I'm just feeling lousy, is all, and I like to hear myself talk like one of those stupid old-timers—or maybe I've pulled so many fast ones on people that I don't like to see 'em pulling 'em on me." He got to his feet. He looked at Scott as if awaiting protest or agreement, but there was not a thing Scott could say to him.

Calhoon lifted his head, stretched, touched his fingertips to his temples. And though he had scarcely touched his first drink, he strode to the bar and poured another. He called out: "Hey, Vera! What the hell you doing in there? Are we going out for that Chinese food or are you getting all dressed up to call on Mr. and Mrs. Ford?"

He saw Scott rise. He said: "You see, kid, I'm spoiled. That's the trouble. A man starts out selling a first-class product and he thinks he has to have it all the time. You see what I mean, Scott? You see?"

Only partly. Yes, Scott saw. From Marty's position. But none of this could be communicated to his father.

"You see it, kid?" he demanded again. "No, I can see you don't—look, I'm not blaming you. I like you. I understand. I know you got a hard-on for cars, and that's how it has to be. But not for yours truly. Not anymore." Marty looked away and his eyes were like stones. He hunched forward and walked into the bedroom.

At first Scott waited, alone, uncertain, reluctant to leave, fearful of staying, anticipating some terrible outburst that would come from beyond the door.

Nothing. He listened again just before he left.

Only the sound of his own breathing in the stillness.

The instant he drove off he made the decision, or rather he reverted to the same impulse he'd wanted to act on after the Car Carnival.

Leave. Return to New York. To the magazine.

Quit Cartown.

He had never quite picked himself up from his fall from grace—from the showroom floor of Quinnley Corners; nor had he quite recovered from some of the other unpalatable events in his recent life. As for this evening, he was crushed by what he'd witnessed, felt, in Marty Calhoon's household.

[194

He wanted no more.

Couldn't he say that Red was now in condition to carry on again? Yes. And couldn't he tell himself Red had never really let the dealership slip from his control, his influence, his power? Yes.

Red wanted him around; he liked the idea of it; he was pleased, even flattered now and then. He admitted he was learning fast, he liked much of what he'd done, or tried to.

But it could no longer be said Red's need of him was desperate.

So Scott believed. Now, in this impulse. And as soon as he reached the house he telephoned New York, Russel Farington, the acting editor of the magazine.

"Russ—I want to apologize for hanging you up . . . yes, I got your letter." His last communication of a week ago had stated that he and the other two men to whom Scott turned over the magazine had found a source of capital, and were now anxious to buy him out if he intended not to return East. He hadn't even considered the offer; the mere prospect of relinquishing it caused him to hold on. For which he was now thankful. "I couldn't give you a quick answer, Russ. I've been putting it off—"

"Of course. Understand that, Scott."

"But the situation is changing."

"Oh?" Farington's voice rose in sharp expectation.

"I'm thinking of coming back, Russ."

"You are? Are you sure, Scott?" The young editor's disappointment was eloquent: you would have thought the magazine was a gilded property, whereas it was at best only modestly successful, and still had among its rivals *Road and Track, Motor Trend, Car and Driver* and *Car Life;* not to mention the excellent English *Autocar.*

"I'm as sure as anyone can be in this town," Scott said. Never had the prospect of reclaiming his brainchild seemed so desirable, joyful, necessary.

"When? How soon, Scott?"

Scott hestitated. He had in his haste not even given this thought. "I'll need—let's say a month. Possibly longer. Probably not until after the fall season gets off." A pause. "Let's say for the Christmas issue."

"I see."

"I think I'll get my clumsy hand back in and cover the *Concours* here next Sunday," Scott said.

"I'll pass on the news," he said. "This is final?"

"Yes it is, Russ."

"All right."

"I'm sorry," Scott said.

"Well—we only thought it was kind of pointless going on with the present arrangement if you were definitely not coming back."

"Yes."

"We'll be in touch of course," Farington said. An interval, then: "Sorry it didn't work out for you out there, Scott."

16: Tony Kerwin

THEY'D come from all around, they'd converged on the grassy saucer of valley dominated by the town of Bridgeton where each year the *Concours d'Elégance* took place.

They'd come driving their showpieces. Like Tony Kerwin: Tony at the wheel of the gray 1926 Bellgard Touring Car, Tony attired in the style of the period, in cap and a kind of Norfolk jacket and bell trousers; Phoebe beside him in a fringed sheath, the black cloche clapped over her light hair, looking, he'd thought, a bit like a flapper past her prime, but making a pretty picture, complementing him, embellishing the entire package. Now and then he'd waved to some friend on the road, though not all the participants worked in the industry; many drivers were doctors, professors, lawyers, accountants. On the same route he'd seen Philip Rothe and his wife, they'd passed him in the olive Duesenberg which until eight months ago had belonged to Tony. As they neared Bridgeton, the procession of vintage cars had become denser, and he'd recognized more friends: they'd come from Kent Hills, Greenwood Park, Detroit, Pontiac, Grosse Pointe, Highland Park, Cranbrook, Bloomfield Hills, Dearborn, and all the other centers which formed the sprawling wheeling heart of the automobile kingdom.

It was an almost cloudless afternoon which heralded the event, a time, a rare time when at least among the auto society, an air of felicity often prevailed. Friend and foe, rival and associate, were more closely bonded by nostalgia. Current sales figures, tooling costs, labor problems, styling changes—all this was to a degree lessened on the day of the *Concours,* muted, rosily hued by the spectacle of the cars of days gone by.

At the site itself, once a polo field and clubhouse but now the property of the Bridgeton Automobile Museum, several thousand people had gathered, fanning out on all sides of the green-and-white striped tent which had been set up in front of the brick museum. Here beneath the tent sat the judges; at the rear were long tables on which the punch and sandwiches would be served later.

Like any sporting event, the occasion was an exhilarating one for Tony. Though the *Concours* did not represent a unique joy in terms of the cars themselves—he wasn't one of those buffs like Philip Rothe or others, who reveled in pride of car, working weeks in advance to restore, clean and polish their vehicles (he'd had all that done for him by men from the plant)—no, it was rather the festivity of the event, the challenge of winning, that held his zeal. That, and the sporting picture, which most titillated him.

A charming sight, his milieu, this view of top-echelon elegance, the spectacle of fine old Packards, the Pierce Arrows, the Cords, the Bugattis, the Duesenbergs, the earlier T's and Stanley Steamers—the drivers and their wives, many of whom were in costume, in large hats veiled or festooned with flowers, the men in linen dusters and goggles, others attired in top hats and striped trousers. And everywhere the spectators mulling around, talking, inspecting the cars.

So tonic was this day that he could almost push from his mind all other considerations. Almost. Yes. And if it hadn't been for Phoebe, he might have given all of himself to the almost sensual pleasures at hand. But as he drove the splendid old Bellgard into position—the area designated for *Classic Cars*—he noticed Phoebe in a flurry of nervousness tuck the strands of her pale hair into her black cloche. Yet, he thought, she was certainly in better form than she'd been a week ago.

"I feel so conspicuous way up here," she said. "I'll never get used to it."

"Come on, Phoebe—" He reached out for her gloved hand. "You know you always say that in the beginning." He knew that her present discomfort came mainly out of a natural reticence for any kind of public display. But he found this charming; to him it was a mark of breeding.

"Yes, I suppose," she said.

"We're going to walk off with this one," he asserted with vigorous optimism.

"Yes." She was looking past him.

And he saw approaching, Myra and Dean Stratler, along with Mr. and Mrs. Codman Smith: time for the well-wishers.

"We're going to walk off with this one," he said again, and leaned over and kissed her on the corner of her mouth, as Myra reached the

[198

car. Myra slim in the white shantung silk dress, her blond hair drawn back into a chignon—without doubt she looked splendid, the mauve-shadowed eyes adding that interest to her partrician features, though somehow she failed to make the impact on him he'd come to expect.

This had held true, he supposed, ever since the disastrous night of his birthday. Without doubt that had been a freakish cross-up the way Phoebe had come along the hall, and passing the small guest powder room, had seen him through the partially open door, bent over Myra, the two of them standing very close together, between the basin and the john, doing what? Nothing.

Nothing. Myra had got something in her eye and he had taken it out, and when Phoebe had looked in she'd been startled, shocked, staring at her sister, then at him, and what could you say? The very innocence of the incident made it absurd to explain. It was so absurd, getting hung for something like this, when you thought of all the times he'd been with Myra and no one the wiser, yet this time hanging himself, the irony of it was almost funny. Even so, it might have passed if it hadn't been for what happened later, and then Phoebe having to buoy herself up with all that champagne and then that hapless collapse, a damn nuisance, a dreary capping of the party, and worse, with Ann there, along with Scott Quinnley and Jemmy. Thank God the Codman Smiths had left earlier.

He'd awakened early the next morning, he'd looked over at the twin bed to see that Phoebe was still out, still in a fitful sleep. By the time he'd dressed and breakfasted in the dining room, Phoebe had still not come to life. He could have left the house without confronting her, putting it off until evening. He had a Policy Committee meeting at nine-fifteen. Nevertheless he did not leave. He went into the living room, sat down on the divan by the fireplace. With something less than his customary gratification he glanced up at his portrait, and then he opened his dispatch case to study the notes he'd made at breakfast preparatory to the meeting. He'd no sooner begun when he heard the familiar sounds: Cora, the maid, carrying the tray upstairs. Phoebe had awakened.

He rose hastily. He'd get up there at once, see how she was, talk to her, get it over with. It wouldn't be easy. Innocent or not, it wouldn't be easy, and as he mounted the stairs all he could think of was how she would look, sitting up in her bed in her white lace-bordered night-gown, and that reproachful, wounded gaze in her eyes that would greet him. It would be a backbreaker.

But when he reached their sloped-ceiling bedroom, the curtains in the dormer windows were open, sunlight was streaming in, and the flowered wallpaper struck him now as offensively gay. Out of habit he moved to Phoebe's bed as he did each morning when he would kiss her before leaving for the office.

Her bed was empty, and he was surprised to see that she was standing by the door of her dressing room, attired in a beige summer suit, transferring the contents of one handbag to another. The unexpectedness of the sight disarmed him at once.

"Phoebe, what are you doing up?"

She only glanced at her watch.

He said: "I came in to see how you were."

"I'm all right."

"Where are you going?" He asked.

An appointment, she said.

"Oh. This early?"

She looked at him for the first time. Her face seemed masklike, unfamiliar in its cold determination. "I have to be in Detroit by half-past nine." She turned and put her handbag down on a chair. "I'm meeting Father later on."

"Meeting Cod?" He had to clear his throat.

"For lunch."

"Oh." His anxiety sharpened. "I don't think I heard him call."

"I called him," she said.

He brought out his gold cigarette case. Cod Smith seldom gave time to personal matters during the working day; he even used the lunch hour in the Executive Dining Room like another conference or meeting. "Well." He tamped a cigarette against the back of his suntanned hand. "Well, must be quite an occasion when you can get Cod out of the shop." He spoke casually, though in a way that would demand an answer, any answer.

Phoebe merely moved to the dressing table and picked up a cinnamon-colored scarf.

Unsettled, Tony watched her. He would almost have preferred seeing her as he'd expected to see her: in bed, looking reproachful and helpless. Instead there was this. And that luncheon with Cod. He said: "I didn't want to leave—you were in pretty bad shape last night, darling. Though you're certainly looking much better now." Silence as she tied the scarf around her neck. "Much better," he said again. He felt somewhat stranded, at a loss. He certainly couldn't resurrect the incident of last night; he'd been through all that; to go over it again would make his innocence seem questionable. "Well," he said, "I'm afraid you'll live, darling. You look—"

"What?" She glanced up. "Is that what you came here to say?"

"What did you expect me to say?" He paused, and when she failed to respond, he had to add: "You're certainly still not getting yourself exercised over that silly business last night—"

"Silly?"

"I don't know what else one could call it, Phoebe."

"You don't?"

This uncharacteristic bluntness of hers caused him to flounder once more. He saw that her breakfast, a single cup of black Sanka, had gone untouched. Brusquely then, he said: "Have your coffee, Phoebe."

Absently she moved to the bedtable, her hand was unsteady as she lifted the pink and gray Spode cup.

"For God sakes, Phoebe, what is there to say, we covered it all last night. It's absurd." He waited, but Phoebe held her ground, waiting too, as if all he'd said thus far had been utterly meaningless. Irritation began to scratch at his nerves. Unbearable to think that the one time he might claim total innocence, he had to skirmish his way through like a criminal, but even more irritating was the inescapable fact of his past guilt. Loftily, he said: "You know, giving first aid to your sister Myra is scarcely my idea of one of life's greatest experiences." He hadn't meant to remind her of the long-cultivated enmity between Myra and himself, but it seemed necessary.

"It isn't?" Phoebe peered at him.

And he was stung by sudden anxiety. For the first time she wasn't buying it. Why? Why should she suddenly question it—unless she'd heard something somewhere, so that the incident of last night had verified what she'd heard.

But what?

Who could it have been?

He and Myra had been careful, he hadn't been with her since the dismal afternoon Vince Eames had discovered them. Unless Vince . . . maybe last Wednesday night at the Kent Hills Country Club, Vince, being as gauche and insensitive as he was, might have implied something, however inadvertently. No, that would have been impossible. Vince was still his ally no matter how coldly you cut it. Vince had been awarded his contract for another year.

Yet, looking at Phoebe now, you couldn't mistake the fact that for some reason she had chosen not to buy the legend. He had no alternative but to call her on it: "What do you mean by that, Phoebe?"

"Maybe you can tell me," she said.

"Tell you what?"

"I would just like to know, if all this is so innocent, why did Myra act the way she did afterwards?"

"What is that supposed to mean exactly?" he said.

"I would just like to know why Myra was suddenly so sweet and solicitous, waiting on me with all that champagne, and then asking me wouldn't I go with her to the opening of the Cranbrook art show, insisting on it—she's never done that before. After all, Tony, I'm not a fool, all that sweetness from Myra did nothing but show how guilty she must have felt."

"For God sakes, Phoebe, Myra was stoned. You know that."

"But she's never come falling all over me like that, you've never seen her like that, have you?" Phoebe said.

But he detected at once that Phoebe had thrown this at him not as a firm statement but rather as a tentative question.

He noticed too that she was watching him with an almost trembling intensity. He said: "Phoebe, you've always had a chip on your shoulder when it came to Myra and naturally you saw a lot that wasn't there. You forget how sick you got and Myra did no more and no less than anyone else, she was probably only trying to get your mind off yourself. You could say the same about Ann. How often has Ann fallen all over you like a little mother? No, Phoebe, you're way out of line on this. It's understandable, but—"

He saw that even before he had finished she was looking at him in a slightly different way, her gaze seemed less implacable or positive, as if she were trying, trying somehow to believe him.

"Listen, Phoebe—" He spoke at once, sealing off this first breakthrough, and going on quickly in another direction: "Let's at least try to be sensible about this. Let's say for argument's sake that you're right about Myra or me—and I don't have to tell you how preposterous that would be—but let's say it was true." He smiled and shook his head as if to underscore the very preposterousness of the situation. "Do you think for a minute that I'd try it right in my own house, right under your nose? After all, I don't think I'm quite that stupid, that wouldn't be very bright of me, would it?" Going on then: "Good God, that would be about as logical as our taking a new prototype over to General Motors Proving Grounds for testing."

Something of the conviction with which he spoke (and within its own limits, he *was* convinced) seemed to reach her, touch her with what could pass for the appearance of truth. For Phoebe stirred; that film of resistance in her eyes had wavered.

He saw what he had detected earlier, that she might be wanting, waiting, hoping for any additional evidence or logic of his innocence, any kind of new peg on which to hang her belief in him.

Though she still had not said a word, he saw that her features were softening, and as he watched her putting on her white gloves, he noticed how she'd glance over at him now and then, and there was that fugitive shy look of trust or love that he'd known so well so long. Except that now he found himself appalled by the thought of how close he must have come to killing it.

It was true that her trust and confidence in him was something he'd come to take for granted, but he needed it, it was very important to him.

So that now he felt rising in him, out of this new gratitude, a renewed warmth and esteem for her—not that he'd really lost it, but the thought that he might have, made him know exactly what it meant to him.

This had nothing to do with his affair with Myra. For he'd never confused the qualities of the two women, there'd never been any doubt in his mind that it was Phoebe he wanted to be married to. Even after the affair had started, and God knows he couldn't have resisted it, even after that, he'd never really let himself be deluded by its enticements.

A man like himself needed to have the complete faith and trust and honestly of a wife like Phoebe. For nine years he had had it. Of course he knew that he was, in effect, the sole foundation of her life. He'd seen from the beginning that she'd wanted, needed, to regard him in that way. (Even now he could not shake off the remembrance of the night when he'd taken the risk of trying to prepare her for any trouble or disaster which might befall him in the future, and though he'd deliberately tried to exaggerate the truth, making it appear like a grim fantasy, he'd seen all too plainly the shattering impact it had made on her.)

He'd seen from the beginning how she needed to find her life in his life, and he'd encouraged it.

He'd seen soon enough when he'd married her, not that Phoebe was less loved by her parents, but that she'd become outdistanced, overshadowed by her sisters. He'd seen how it was: Myra with her compulsive need to star in the civic firmament, Myra who would enlist Phoebe's help in a committee, having Phoebe do most of the dreary preliminary work, knowing how conscientious she was, and then of course Myra would correlate all these efforts and present them in a manner that left people thinking she'd accomplished miracles single-handedly. And there was Ann, the one whom Cod loved, who most stimulated him and hence the one he spoiled; though sometimes her outrageous antics might enrage him, he could never totally suppress his admiration for her spirit. The point was, however, that in all the interplay of the family, it was Phoebe who seemed to have got lost, trailing the field, turning instead to Tony, finding what she wanted in him. Sometimes he would try to warn her, tell her she was foolish to slave away for others, and once or twice when he'd found her in the library involved in the dull spadework of one of Myra's committees he'd raised hell about it, urged her to let someone else do the digging, and why didn't she step out on her own, shine on her own?

But he'd learned that Phoebe couldn't function like that. He'd made the mistake of wanting her to conduct her life the way he conducted his. And of course he should have known that was impossible.

"That's silly, Tony," she would say. "What difference does it make who does the work? The point is it has to get done."

"But people—"

"Oh people," she would answer. "What difference does it make as long as the job gets done? And anyway, I wouldn't be doing it unless I enjoyed it, would I?"

This simplicity or honesty of hers, however removed from his own easy cynicism, was something he'd come to respect, and this respect had never been challenged. He might get himself exercised over her flaws, her faddist diets or lack of exotic personality or her blind dull dedication to family, home and garden—but always there was this total faith in him which, like her reticence and guilelessness, gave him reassurance, even comfort, as if these qualities of hers might more securely weld the framework of his own character.

Before he'd left that morning, having gained at least her willingness, readiness, to believe him, he felt what any man might feel who has warded off the loss of something of incalculable value, and once more he was surprised by the extent to which this touched him, and in a curious way he was also touched by the unexpected show of her toughness, so unlike her, yes, but nevertheless raising his regard for her. It left him feeling this new warmth, even tenderness for her.

She did not mention the matter again. A hopeful sign. Less hopeful, however, was the fact that she scarcely mentioned the luncheon with her father. He tried as artfully as he could to discover the reason for the meeting, but Phoebe never did tell him. She hadn't been evasive about it really, merely passing it off as something she enjoyed doing now and then: a daughter who seldom had her father to herself, and he chose to be relieved, not pressing it further, though he could not resist asking: "Is Cod still hot for that Florida junket?"

"Oh yes," Phoebe had said. "But please don't ever talk about it, Tony. You know how he is."

Yes, he knew how it was, and again the prospect of the top chair going empty the next year shone bright and irresistible before him.

Another corner had been turned.

He commenced the program to solidify his gains. On the following afternoon when he'd been in Detroit on business concerning next October's "World on Wheels" automobile show in New York, he'd gone afterward to the jewelry store on Washington Boulevard and bought an antique gold brooch, an oval studded with minute diamonds, and that night he'd given it to her. Antique jewelry was one of her few extravagant passions. And on Friday night he'd canceled out a card game scheduled with three fellow members of Bellgard's Board of Directors, a sacrifice for him since the game was incidental to matters more crucial. And on Saturday afternoon he'd turned down a last-minute invitation for tennis, going instead with Phoebe to the regatta sponsored by the Detroit Yacht Club. He'd found this new companionship with her agreeable and free of the stigma of duty, so that what he felt was communicated to her.

He might have been acting against the grain of his true nature, but if he was, it had to be admitted that the experience was novel and, for what it was, rewarding. At any rate he felt he was bringing in the payload. The Kerwin luck was back in his pocket.

Now, as Mr. and Mrs. Codman Smith and the Stratlers came up to the vintage Bellgard car for the ritual of well-wishing, the sight of Myra immediately disconcerted him—not for any of the reasons that might have stirred him a few weeks ago, but because it might spark again in Phoebe the very apprehensions he had succeeded in smothering.

"Phoebe—" Myra's eyes were wide and sparkling as she addressed her sister—"you look marvelous, that cloche really does it." She turned to her mother: "You know Phoebe looked all over for it and no luck, and then I got the bright idea of suggesting the Scarab Club, and sure enough Phoebe found it there." What made this performance of goodwill seem so valid was not Myra's interest in her sister, but rather something else, something within Myra herself, a certain exuberant self-satisfaction which, Tony surmised now, might have had its origin in her husband's recent coverage in the national press. For it had certainly been Dean Stratler's week, and Myra showed it, being able to bestow on Phoebe an almost dazzling benevolence.

Mrs. Smith, admiring the hat, said: "It's charming, Phoebe."

And Codman Smith stepped forward and kissed her. The sun of all this attention, thought Tony, came at a good time for Phoebe, warming her, bringing that measure of shine to her reticent personality. He was glad for her, glad for himself.

Yet now, as the movements of his brother-in-law Dean Stratler crossed his vision, he was at once drawn back into the anxieties that made up the daily scramble.

Dean Stratler. Look at him now. That drama in full play. The thin ashen hair and black sunglasses, the black linen blazer and one of those avant-garde ties of his and the narrow cuffless trousers—Dean, his sharp features softened by complacent authority, as if he were still aglow from the flashbulb bursts which had brought his face to the pages of national magazines; yes, and moving more closely, cozily, along with Codman Smith. (But for how much longer? A year or less, a year from now Cod would be boating in Florida waters.)

Now, driving up alongside the Bellgard, there came a 1928 Stutz Black Hawk. The owner, a moustached man, an officer of the Chevrolet Division of G. M., called out his salutations to the group, and then peering at the old Bellgard, joked in the tradition of the day: "Best-looking job you people have put out in years, Dean."

"Yes." Dean Stratler smiled, surveyed the Bellgard and, returning the jest, said: "Yes, I think we've got a real barn-burner here, all right." Addressing Codman Smith then: "Haven't we, Cod?"

The G. M. man chuckled, pushed his goggles upward. Dean Stratler moved now to accompany Cod Smith; the two men strolled around the old Bellgard, Dean eying the vehicle with his appreciative gaze.

"Don't know how we ever turned them out like this." Codman Smith stepped back, hands thrust into the patch pockets of his houndstooth tweed jacket, his voice taking on a rueful sort of admiration. He kept studying the seven passenger V-12, its open body mounted on a 143-inch wheelbase. Bemused, he looked over at Tony. "What crankshaft is this, Tony?"

"What?" Tony touched the mole on his right cheek. "Well, let's see, this is—" But he could not remember, and before he could say anything else, Dean Stratler spoke up.

"Nine-main bearing, I think," Dean said. "I think we borrowed that from Studebaker in the old days."

"Right. You're right," Codman Smith said.

Dean nodded, as if indifferent to the small point he'd just scored on his brother-in-law. It was one of Cod Smith's little games to take the wind out of the sails of his subordinates by testing their technical knowledge now and then. "You know, Cod," Dean said now, "I'd like to see this job in the New York show this fall. If we could spare the space, like to see it alongside the BBX." Referring to the prototype of the Bellstar, the sports model now being rushed through Engineering. "Make a hell of a display, don't you think so, Cod?"

But Cod Smith's marble-cool eyes glinted with sly humor. "No, wouldn't risk it, Dean—might show up styling weaknesses on the BBX."

Tony laughed to accent, underscore, the moment. "You asked for that one," he said to Dean.

Two other Bellgard executives had come up, and then Tony saw, with no trace of pleasure, the chunky silk-suited Vincent Eames moving toward the car, Vince emerging from the line of spectators, glistening like a seal who had just flipped out of the water, Vince now gripping his hand. "You got that trophy cup feeling, Tony?" Then: "How are you, Phoebe? You look right out of that musical show—what was it—with Carol Channing?" Not waiting for a reply, he nosed forward: "Cod—greetings to you, sir!"

Codman Smith reached down to give Eames his famous fish-shake, a masterpiece of glacial politeness reserved for such as the importunate peddler.

And Tony saw Myra, in a hasty gesture, take Dean Stratler's arm and saunter off. And he felt Phoebe stir, stiffen beside him, as if the mere sight of the supplier had rung the alarm which Tony had made the mistake of first sounding on that unhappy night last spring.

Did Vince leave now? No. Not Vince. There he was by the rear of the Bellgard, lowering his hulk to peer at the muffler, rising then, shaking his balding pink head to announce: "An exhaust system like this would cost a pretty buck today, eh?"

Tony in exasperation pressed his tongue hard against his teeth. You would have thought that Vince would have made himself scarce, you would have thought he'd have the good taste to let matters sit after that touch-and-go tug with the contract . . . but no, not Vince; no different here than he was on those upland game junkets, using a heavy shell load for birds at short range.

Fortunately Tony hailed a friend, a young man, a new executive with Jefferson Motors, and after they'd exchanged small talk, he broke off and called Vince over and introduced him to the new man. It was in order, he thought, to create a diversionary picture, to show Vince Eames in social fraternity with an officer of another company, thus making more natural his own association. And he was relieved to see that Vince, scarcely missing a beat, moved off with the man, Vince already gesturing, his sausage wrists jutting forth in animated talk with the Jefferson executive.

"I think it's going to start now," Phoebe was saying.

Tony glanced to the green-and-white striped tent. "Yes." And he saw that Ann Smith had arrived, accompanied by Ben Nodina, and then he saw Scott Quinnley nearby, Scott with a little girl and Jennifer Thompson.

Your attention please! A voice rasped across the summer air.

Tony straightened his cap, sat more erectly, his sorrel eyes straight ahead now, focused on the glittering silver figure on the crest of the Bellgard's grille. His entire concentration, like an electronic impulse, went out in a single direction; a tight exhilarating concentrated force worked inside him: to win, to place first in his class.

17: Ann Smith

"IF he doesn't place first," she said to Ben Nodina, "you know he won't be fit to live with." It was lip service only, her way of trying to divert, subdue the secret excitement inside her, though it didn't quell her desire to tell about it, share it. She glanced past Ben to Jemmy and Scott closeby among the spectators flanking the left side of the tent.

"Who?" Ben said.

"Tony," she said.

"He's got more than a good chance," Ben said.

"Yes." But she wasn't really giving much attention to Tony and Phoebe anymore. Now the charade was on and the Kerwins, costumed and aboard the old Bellgard touring car, presented for the community that almost too perfect picture of conjugal harmony, what ten years ago when she'd been a freshman at Smith had been known as "togetherness." The horror of a week ago must have passed, though how Tony had ever regained Phoebe's goodwill was something she could still not figure. Unless she'd been wrong, unless what she'd perceived that night of Tony's birthday had all been wrong. But whatever it had been, Phoebe had come out of it. More than that, she seemed improved, surprising, a violet sprouting forth like a snapdragon.

More power to her, Ann thought.

And to me.

As of now it wouldn't be more than two or three months before Cartown would only be a place to which she'd be sending postcards from Greece.

She hadn't known about the new turn of events until late last night; Ben had told her nothing until then. Which was like him, a last-minute man. Leaving her now high with the greatest expectations—and no one to tell them to.

If she could only have let loose now—not to her family, not yet, but to someone like Jemmy. She looked over at her again: no, not a chance. Jemmy seemed decidedly low, all locked up, in a swivet, standing there by Scott and Scott's little girl, and looking like the very last rose.

No, you couldn't even tell Jemmy. It was bad business to lavish your high feelings on someone who was obviously in no mood or condition to share them; it would be callous, if not downright cruel—like rushing up to your rommate who has just flunked out and telling her you've made the Dean's List. (This had happened to her and it was still one of her most awful remembrances of Northampton, the only saving grace being that her roommate had gone on to New York, married a Phi Beta Kappa, had two children and then had started, on a veritable shoestring, an art gallery, and now at twenty-eight was on her way to becoming one of the most prominent, younger dealers in the city—a record which made Ann view with an unsmug eye her own scholastic achievements.)

Until Ben, until last night, what had she had to show for her life?

But to tell someone now.

Scott. It would have been nice to tell him. Yes. It would be safe with him. She peered across: he did not look or seem as low as he had last week at the Rothes' party, or in the garage. Now, however, he was studying the file of automobiles lined up before the ramp of the tent, and you could see from the way his lanky frame was hunched forward that he was high on a happiness of his own, lost in that same misty world of bygone cars that seemed to hold all the other nuts at the *Concours*.

So you couldn't intrude, break in. Scott was out, no telling him now.

"Miss Smith—" She turned to see one of the news photographers.

"Oh." She clasped Ben's hand and put on a smile that, she felt, must have been as dazzling as all the lamps on the Place de la Concorde.

"Thanks a lot," the photographer said when he'd flashed his picture, saying then as he put in a fresh bulb, "Great day, isn't it?" He was the same one who'd taken her picture several times before . . . yes, last year's Detroit Auto Show and . . . he was the folksy one, mumbling away all the time with that barnyard gabble but never missing a beat, getting his shots. As Myra and Dean approached he was ready, and he said: "Guess this is always a high spot for the Smith family, eh, Mrs. Stratler? I notice you're all right here Johnny-on-the-spot—"

"Oh, quite." Myra's reply was crisply chipped from the bedrock of Great Britain. She said to Ann: "It is a decent turnout, isn't it?"

"Most piss-elegant crowd I ever saw, Myra," replied Ann.

Her sister threw it off. There was the indulgent smile, and she became very busy being grand and gracious, distracting the photographer's attention now, linking her arm with Dean's and showing her profile, her left side, the best side, the side she always turned to the mirror. Oh, she was a smasher, wasn't she!

Dean and Myra were then immortalized for the newsprints, and the photographer, still chatty, hastened on to the Chrysler executive who was tilting back on a gleaming shooting stick—half of Kent Hills was here with shooting sticks, looking like robust invalids with silver crutches.

No more than two more months, she thought again, and there'd be none of this. What would there be in its place? Whatever it might be, it had to be better. As if to confirm her hope, she glanced up at Ben. He was watching the scene, his face held slightly sidewise, the eyes dark as teakwood, intense and dreamy, though unlike Scott, you couldn't tell if he was really enjoying what he saw or if he was regarding it as a composition in the finder of his camera.

"Are you having yourself a good farewell look at all those good old cars?" she said.

"What?" Ben turned. "Oh, no—just torturing myself, thinking of all the film work I'm going to lose after we leave. And for what? For love. Greece. No more nuts and bolters, no more pressures, no more having to good-guy myself around. Maybe we'd better not go. Look what happened to Gauguin when he went to Tahiti. He fell apart, nothing to show for it except masterpieces."

"Gauguin didn't have a rich wife," Ann said. "That's where you'll have the edge." A slip, she shouldn't have let that slip out.

As always when she joked in this vein, Ben grew uneasy or irritated. If there was anything she could find about him that didn't please her, it was this reluctance of his to discuss her money. That was why she sometimes tried to humor him out of it. Like last night. Last night when she'd been with him at his apartment she'd nearly wrecked the entire evening when she'd said it would be stupid for them to stay at anything less than the most attractive hotel in Athens.

211]

She had her own gold reserve, she'd said, and she had every intention of using it and living accordingly. She'd only said it because she knew what a hazardous venture he was getting into and what a sharp drop there would be in his income. But he couldn't see it like that. It was really his only flaw: the view of some men who seemed determined to treat a wife's wealth like an unmentionable disease.

Until that moment of money talk it had been another of those free and wonderful evenings. Ben's place, a suite in an apartment-hotel on East Jefferson Avenue, had a fine view of the river, and there was excellent room service though Ben preferred to cook when there was the time, and last night he'd put together a spectacular Indian curry— he'd worked his way through school as a short-order cook and you would have thought he'd never want to face another skillet as long as he lived, but instead he'd gone on with it, on a more complex and refined scale of course, and it had become one of his most pleasurable pastimes. Ben seemed to hold on to, cherish, rather than abandon, the grim experiences of his life. He wasn't even bitter about his home-town, a small, mean, besooted city in Pennsylvania, where as a little kid he surely couldn't have had it worse. His father had once been a bootlegger and had, as Ben put it, "graduated" into the slot-machine racket. When Ben had been nine he'd seen his father picked up by the police and sent to jail, and Ben having to take the terrible taunting of his schoolmates, yet going on, working his way through the local college, writing and staging the annual campus show, going on to radio and television and producing several documentary films, and then taking the job near Detroit to make industrial films for automobile companies. During the past five years of his rise he'd been pulled down by his sickly and pathologically jealous wife, unable to leave her, for whenever he tried she would fall ill, playing her deathbed harp, plucking on the strings of sympathy. Until this year when, not knowing how else to get away, he simply said one day he was going out for a pack of cigarettes and he never went back. She'd refused to divorce him at first, and then she'd yielded, though as it turned out she'd really not done anything about it, forcing Ben in the end to take the final action himself, though he had said nothing of this to Ann.

Not until last night during dinner, telling her only then how he'd had to go about it, a fantastic story and one which she would have liked to tell to everyone, particularly since her family had taken pains to point out that he was using his wife's delaying tactics as a way of not committing himself.

[212

The suddenness of the news last night had sent her into such a fit of happiness that she'd been unable to eat another bite, staying with the wine instead, and then at the peak of her new exaltation she'd made the error of talking about money.

Ben's reaction this time had been curious, or maybe not so curious when you thought about it. For that passionate nature of his simply froze, congealed, and the lovemaking that normally would have happened looked like it would never happen at all. Instead, he'd swung away from the table muttering something about how they had to do more boning on their Greek, and he'd brought back the two books, and with an almost savage determination he'd started in on the practice conversation, questions and answers from the books of phonetic phrases.

It wasn't until much later that he began to thaw out or show signs of boredom with the lesson, and then he became more like himself again, suddenly throwing aside the books and going to her and kissing her and after that it was all right again and she hadn't got back to Kent Hills until past three this morning.

Now, as the voice from the loudspeaker system announced the start of the *Concours,* she turned to him. In a half-whisper she said: "I'm just absolutely dying to tell everyone, it's awful having to keep it to myself—it must be like being pregnant and never having the baby."

"It'll have to wait," Ben said. He consulted his watch. "I've only got about an hour left." He was leaving for Pennsylvania.

"I wish you wouldn't drive there," she said. "Couldn't you take a plane? I don't trust automobiles, not the way you drive."

"I'll keep it under ninety except at the toll stops on the turnpike."

"Call me as soon as you get there."

"It'll be too late for that, Ann."

"Yes."

"I'll call you noon tomorrow, I don't want to call until I've got the papers locked in my suitcase—" There was in his voice that last trace of doubt, as if he too shared her fear that the necessarily devious way he'd had to get the divorce might in some way backfire or not be valid. As it stood now, all he had to do was sign his name and come back, and it would be unlikely that his wife would try to have the case reopened, it would be too late for that.

Twenty-four hours more.

Of course she knew that even after he had the papers there might be other delays. Business delays. Knowing Ben, knowing how he worked, knowing that even though he was rushing to complete his current assignments—he had just finished making the film for Bellgard which would be shown at the Eastern Dealers convention—he wouldn't take off for Greece leaving the work to others, he'd stay on doing all the final work himself, supervising the cutting, rewriting the narration, altering the sound track, even reshooting if necessary. She knew she couldn't count on a specific time for leaving, that until they were on the plane or ship he'd be here working around the clock. A last-minute man.

The loudspeaker again.

As she turned to bring her attention to the file of cars starting up for review before the judges, she heard Scott's voice: "Suzy!"

She saw him and Jemmy looking all around, and then she saw the child, who had apparently run behind the line of spectators and who now ducked between two of them and was scrambling out to where the cars were.

She ran out and quickly retrieved the child. She brought her back to Scott.

"Oh—thanks. Thanks very much, Junior." He turned to the little girl. The child said she couldn't see the cars and she wanted to see them. Scott shook his head, suddenly distracted, irritated.

"I'll take her," Jemmy said.

"No, it's—"

"I want Jemmy," the child protested.

"Here we go." Jemmy took her hand and went off through the rear of the tent toward the other end of the field.

Scott was left happily free to watch the *Concours*. And when Ann looked at Ben she saw that he too had become totally absorbed and, like Scott, seemed lost in the automotive past.

Scott did not even notice that his father had arrived, Red Quinnley now making his way along the thick fence of people, his smile as big as if he were greeting an audience, though everyone was looking out to the field. And reaching Scott now: "Decided to come over for this one, haven't seen one in years." Red Quinnley spoke a fraction too loud, and several people turned around then, and then turned back to the show.

Ann saw the older man grip his son's arm, and Scott's surprise showing darkly on his face as he edged away to make room for his father, poor old Scott obviously not expecting him here and trying to welcome him now, though unable to conceal his impatience, as if once again he was being deprived of what he'd come to see.

Ann said: "How are you, Mr. Quinnley?"

"Why, Ann"—the old man looked up—"how are you? I'm tiptop, had to get out to this junkyard and see how the scrap looked." But he hadn't really looked out once.

"Why don't we just have a drink first?" Ann said. She saw that Red Quinnley welcomed the suggestion; she also noted that he must have had a shot or two before getting here. "Ben," she said, "I'll be back."

As she and Mr. Quinnley moved back to the rear of the tent, she heard the great burst of applause from the spectators and she looked around: Tony and Phoebe had just driven the vintage Bellgard up the ramp before the panel of judges.

18: Scott Quinnley

"How do you like it, Scott?" Nodina's voice pierced the backwash of applause for the Tony Kerwins.

"A lot of very tasty stuff here," Scott said, but he didn't feel much like talking. He'd had more than his share earlier that morning—another battle with Red, and once more it had been impossible for Scott to tell him of his decision to return to New York.

He brought his attention back to the ramp. Like former times. He'd covered other *Concours d'Élegance*, in Long Island, California, Connecticut. Almost like former times.

Watching in silence now. And now seeing that Phil Rothe was driving his Duesenberg up the carpeted ramp. The old car looked superb as it drew up before the line of judges—the Duesenberg S J, its olive flanks shining, that masterly Murphy coachwork, the cowls like silver pythons. (And Scott's Pierce Arrow stored in dust in New York.)

Phil drew a good hand. Important. For this was a Drive-Up show, and the point system was different from most other *Concours* in that the tally was partly based on spontaneous appreciation of the car and occupants, with a separate detailed inspection to be conducted later. Scott supposed Phil did not look as glossily groomed as Kerwin or some of the others, but he had that authority at the wheel and an exuberance on his robust face which brought real shine to his presentation. Lorie, sitting beside him, dressed in the period, was rosy with excitement, and Scott realized that all her protests of Phil's devotion to the car must have been more or less academic.

The old S J, so lean, showed all the muscle and love Phil had given it, as he drove slowly onto the sloping descent of the ramp and onto the field to await the team of judges who would make their close-up examination.

Now up the ramp there came a coffin-hooded Cord, an 810, while moving into place behind, near the base of the ramp, was the gothic-grilled Sport-Phaeton Packard Super 8 of 1933, a real beauty of a

[216

landboat, bright red as a new fire engine. Now there was a wait, and Ben Nodina, nodding back to the tent, said: "I think your father's snatched my girl." He consulted his watch.

"Looks like it," Scott said. Red and Ann were drinking. "That'll be Ann's good turn for the day." And he thought, yes, Red was going right after the punch, there being no bonded booze around. He'd need it, Scott knew. He'd just come back from Marty Calhoon's house.

That morning at breakfast when Scott invited him to the *Concours,* Red had said no, it was nothing but a lace-pants cocktail party, not for him. "No," he'd said, only to surprise Scott by adding: "Where I'm going is straight over to see Marty."

"Red," Scott had said at once, "it's pointless, you have to forget it."

"That's where I'm going. You got nowhere." He poured more coffee into his cup. "It's ten days now Marty hasn't showed up."

"Yes, I know," Scott said, fearing he could no longer conceal the truth from his father, "but we can spare Marty. He needs the rest, let him have it."

"I want him back on the job!" Red thumped the flat of his hand down on the table with such force that the china and glassware jiggled.

It struck Scott then that it wasn't really Calhoon the salesman he needed, but something else. It was Calhoon's presence, as if the salesman's absence after all these years would deprive Red of something as reassuring and familiar as all those old pictures and testimonials on the walls of his office.

Impatiently Red said: "Listen, Scott, I've seen that big lump of Irish have his ups and downs and if you baby him along it's the worst thing you can do. I need him and goddammit I'm going to have him back at the Corners if I have to roll him there on a grease dolly."

"I'm trying to tell you, Red, it won't work. He's shot. I know. I was there. He can't take it now."

"The hell he can't. I know what's wrong, it's what I've always told you, that wife of his—"

"No, you've got that part of it all wrong." Scott's voice rose. "She's a silly dame but that's not—" He stopped.

"Not what?" Distracted, Red looked away and then he poured himself another cup of coffee—his third, two beyond the prescribed limit. "But what? You didn't answer me!"

"Why don't you listen then?" Scott said.

"You're not leveling with me, goddammit, what're you trying to say?"

Scott hesitated. "Try to listen to me, will you, Red?" Unhappily he paused again, probing for some way to edge up on the truth without quite touching it. "What you've got to see, Red, is that this thing has gone much further than even Marty knows, I mean—well, let me put it like this. Marty, as we know, was losing his grip, his selling power, and that began working on him, he couldn't stop brooding about it—how could he, a man like that, what else has he had in his life?—but all the time keeping it inside him. He must have been hard to live with, setting up awful tensions in the house, and his wife felt cut off, isolated, as if he no longer needed or wanted her, she doesn't know how to cope with it any more than Marty knows how to cope with himself, and now it's gotten so out of hand and they're like strangers, enemies and Marty's lost—"

"If that's how it is, goddammit, then why doesn't she at least try to help him, can't she forget herself long enough to—Christ, that's when a man needs help. But I can tell you how she's helping, she's running around town, getting it from someone else, instead of trying to pull him together, a bitch like that."

"For God sakes, Red, I keep trying to tell you it has nothing to do with her, not basically. It's Marty himself, it's in *him* where the—"

"Marty himself!" Red half rose from his chair: "Don't you tell your father about Marty! He's been with me for almost sixteen years, don't you think I know him?" He was on his feet. "And I'm not letting another day go by, I'm getting over there right now and when I'm through, I'll guarantee you I'll—"

"Sit down!" Scott outshouted him. "Haven't you heard a word I've said? Will you please sit down. You won't listen because you can't see anything beyond Red Quinnley—you're so worked up you won't see how goddam rotten the—"

"Worked up? *I'm* worked up? Look at yourself!"

"Listen, Red. Listen. Marty's not coming back. He's never coming back! You know why? Because he's through, he can't sell, he can't sell because he doesn't believe in the goddam car. Not anymore!"

It was the crushing way the silence dropped between them that made Scott stop, aware only then that he'd said precisely what he'd striven to keep from Red. And seeing him then: his watery eyes murky, dilated, as he stared at Scott, his mouth open, frozen as if he'd suddenly broken off an utterance midway and couldn't remember what he was going to say.

And so quiet that when his father swallowed, Scott could hear the dry cracking sound deep in his throat.

Miserably, Scott watched him: the head lifting at last, the tendons of his neck firming, a hand roughing through the thick mane of titian hair. He whirled around and made for the hallway, snatched up his wide, cream-colored hat; there was the slam of the front door which brought Mrs. Coombs in running, followed by Suzy, and Scott heard the car start and the violent roar as it spun out of the driveway and the wild double acceleration resounding along the Sunday street.

When he'd turned up so unexpectedly at the *Concours* Scott saw immediately—he didn't have to smell his breath—that he'd come away from Calhoon's house with what he hadn't wanted to hear—a confirmation of what Scott had had to tell him.

Though not a word about it, only that same bluster of his, not wanting his son to see how he felt, if he believed it or if it had cut into him as it had into Scott, and as he watched him now under the tent drinking there with Ann Smith, Scott experienced that too-familiar bleak stab of despair and remembered how sensibly he'd tried to look at this change in his life, seeing it as a dutiful mission, one that might even be ultimately worthy of serious effort—and, failing that, how he'd hoped he would at least serve the purpose of helping his father regain his health and his place in the one world he knew and needed.

He looked away.

He'd be going over there shortly, as soon as the first stage of the *Concours* was over. At least Ann was with him now, and for that Scott couldn't have been more grateful, and if Red was tanking up a little, God knows he needed it.

The past week at Quinnley Corners had been, as Marty Calhoon had predicted, a dead one. The mirage of all the new models soon to come seemed to have turned the current inventory into a wasteland into which few buyers wanted to venture. At a time when the rest of the industry was tooling up for their biggest volume year, Bellgard was lagging behind, not that you would have suspected it from the looks of its executives: they were everywhere around Scott, their professional manner like gaudy banners proclaiming *all is well*. He could see with nothing less than awe Codman Smith carrying on with that same cool confidence, he could see Kerwin and Stratler and the others and he wondered how they could swagger around in the face of the public's apathy, and if so, for how long? And always beneath there was the more personal concern: how long could Quinnley Corners survive? Yet other dealerships seemed to be weathering the storm—the figure of Max Wilkerson came into Scott's view now, Wilkerson not more than nine miles from Quinnley Corners, selling the same cars—Max now sauntering over to the tent with the cocky strut of a big volume Chevrolet or Ford dealer. How was this possible? Yes, and Wilkerson waving to Codman Smith and Smith giving him the good nod. Next Tuesday—Scott thought of the appointment with Cod Smith, and of his recent opposition to the factory. There would not be the good nod next Tuesday.

He decided to cut out for the other end of the field to join Jemmy and Susan; the first phase of the Drive-Up was nearing its end. But then Ann Smith returned. "Scott, I think I must be losing my touch. Your father took off. Suddenly. Just like that."

When Scott glanced back, it was true, there was no sight of him. "Thanks anyway, Junior," he said. Had it been the nearness of Max Wilkerson which had sent Red on his way?

Ben Nodina looked at his watch again. He had to leave. Ann said she'd be back and left to accompany him to his car. It occurred to Scott then that something about Ann had altered. She was wearing her hair differently, not piled up, but hanging very full, curving like thick gold parentheses around her cheeks. She seemed almost feverish with good humor, there brimmed in her eyes a goodwill toward all, even the denizens of Cartown, and as she moved away the white pleated skirt, short and elegant above the fine legs, took on a swirl of movement.

Junior was making it, it was a lovely sight.

Scott made his way behind the throng of spectators. Beyond the far wing of the brick museum he was glad to discover that Suzy was busy playing with another little girl. He saw Jemmy then, though she wasn't alone: she was talking with Jack Winters. It put Scott off, this way of hers, trying again to prove she was not bent on holding him to "the decent thing."

It was wrong somehow; not false, yet tipping the balance of Scott's feelings. Like moving the center of gravity of a car.

He decided to move his own center of gravity, and turned back to the tent to get himself something wet. Let Jemmy act it out, let Johnny Winters have his moment. Winters was a nice enough guy and in addition to being rich, the work he was doing as an automobile historian was first-rate. In a way it seemed a pity he hadn't come along before Scott had. In his own shy or cautious way Scott knew, as did Jemmy, that Winters had this real itch for her.

The green-and-white striped tent—it was called a pavilion by way of snobbing up the event—was almost empty. As he reached the long punch table Scott recognized Mr. Max Wilkerson: his being here, he thought again, might have been the reason for Red's sudden departure. For though the two dealers, as rivals, played the game of good fellowship in public, no love was lost between them, at least not on Red Quinnley's part. In the past seven years Wilkerson's Bellgard dealership had come up fast, cutting into Quinnley Corners' revenue; even now during the dog days it seemed to be holding its own, a fact which was remarkable, granting, as Red never failed to point out, that Wilkerson's wife was wealthy enough to carry him.

Personally, Scott held no active animosity toward the man. He'd met him several times and they'd talked shop and Wilkerson had been extremely agreeable; if anything, too agreeable. Middle-aged and of middling size, a bland-faced man except for the thick-bristled eyebrows projecting like craggy ledges from his ivory forehead, he was neat and natty and a bit suave, scarcely a super-pitchman. Or so he'd always impressed Scott. Unlike Quinnley Corners his operation was not homespun: you had the feeling he might be selling oil stocks instead of cars. What got Red's nose out of joint was that he sold cars, and it was true that when a potential buyer slipped away from the Quinnleys', he would often find a deal at Wilkerson's (It's Always Open House at Wilkerson's House of cars). His ethics, Scott supposed, were no lower or higher than Red's, yet he had a way of conducting himself and his enterprise which seemed to disarm the Better Business Bureau and charm the public into his showrooms.

He was in the process of lighting a short, very thin cigar when he saw Scott. He clicked shut his lighter to shake hands. "Scotty"—he invoked the nickname Scott had always run from—"good to see you, you look fresh as a daisy before plucking, as one of my crew likes to put it."

And Scott said, as if it were obligatory, falling like a veteran into the custom of joking with one's most deadly competitor: "How is it you're not open today, Max? It's only Sunday."

"Closed for church," he retorted. He lit his cigar then, still regarding Scott as though he were his most favorite citizen, or more accurately perhaps, as if he had just stepped into his showroom as a potential buyer. With great good courtesy he had the barman pour a punch and handed it to Scott. "I just saw your dad. He seemed in excellent shape— I mean for a man saddled with all that real estate."

Blatant though the statement was, he made it seem soft, easy, friendly.

"Red's doing all right," Scott answered stoutly.

"Tell me something, Scotty—" Wilkerson was settling down, the overture almost ending and the major melodic theme about to begin. "You've had a peek at the new line. Like your opinion."

No. Scott had not had a peek. But Phil Rothe had.

The forthcoming models of the "new line" would show certain improvements: there would be a little more built-in quality, notably in the suspension system; the steel stampings of frames would be better, the torsional strength upped about 25 percent, and there would be a modified, slightly superior muffler (at long last). But the styling, in its attempts to meet and beat the competition's current craze for "classic simplicity," looked like it would fall midway between contrived plainness and gimmicky innovations. Scott feared most of the series would end up as yawners, neither fish nor fowl for the pampered appetites of today's market.

But of course you didn't say this. What did you say?

With some dismay he heard himself snatching Dean Stratler's gambit: "I think we'll have a few barn-burners, Max."

"That's for sure," Wilkerson said, and what was more he seemed to believe it. Like Red. Unlike Marty Calhoon. Or Scott. Then this brief spasm of religious fervor passed and Wilkerson, after predicting a Bellgard boom, said, as if in afterthought: "But if you people find yourselves overstocked this fall, Scotty, don't hesitate to Bell me, we might be able to take a few units off your hands."

"Very generous of you, Max," Scott commented with the proper sardonic inflection.

"No, I mean it. We're still an old-fashioned dealership, we just keep taking on the monthly quota as it comes," he said, adding, as he regarded Scott with pointed jocularity: "We're too chicken to buck the factory, we just let them throw the full quota at us—the more the monier, as one of my crew likes to put it, bless him."

"Yes." Scott, irritated with himself for keeping up the pretense, gazed out to the field, seeing a team of judges inspecting the tool box at the boot of an old Rolls Royce, the trays of tools all slotted in place and as clean and shining as jewels in a Cartier window.

[222

"Well, see you around, Scotty." Wilkerson put down his glass on the white table. "Give a shake to your dad, we didn't have much time to talk. You can tell Red for me, if that corner gets to be too much for him, let me know—"

Scott realized it was the second or third time their competitor had thrown this at him, these arrogant feelers. Yet the message was there for Scott to read, and even as he read it a notion possessed him. He couldn't quite tell how serious Wilkerson was, but he'd given him the word.

"Red will never sell," Scott stated, though already he was thinking, yes, this is what I should have considered earlier. Red would have recoiled from the idea as sheer treason, but to unload Quinnley Corners would have been the wisest move, not only freeing Scott, but leaving Red free, unburdened, with only a daily quota of eighteen holes of golf to contend with. However, Scott was too conscious of Wilkerson's gaze to betray what he felt. "No," he said again, "Red will never sell, you know that, Max."

"And his son?" Wilkerson kept peering at Scott, impassive except for the faintly raised eyebrows.

"The same."

"Well, see you around, Scotty." Wilkerson was already strolling away.

Scott watched him. How foolish, he thought, to have closed the door that tight. Who knows what might have happened if he'd given Max enough daylight to see even the smallest possibility in some future negotiation? If Wilkerson could swing it, and he probably could, Quinnley Corners might be off Red's back. *And Scott's.*

"Max—" he called.

He turned, his darkly vivid eyebrows in an arch of voracious interest. "What?"

"Nothing . . ." Scott hesitated, naked in his unpreparedness, saying then: "I just wasn't sure if you got this straight."

"Like?"

It came to him then: why would Wilkerson want to buy their franchise when he knew its value was not as great as his own? No, what lured him was the real estate, his father's lifelong lease for that location. "I don't think we were talking about the same thing," Scott said.

"Oh?"

"What I mean, Max, is that we both know that Quinnley Corners has a lot more than just a Bellgard franchise to offer."

"It has? You fascinate me, Scotty." But the eyebrows remained fixed in their hungry curve; Wilkerson stood there for a moment looking alert, bright, almost boyish or more like a conservative member of the junior Board of Commerce. "Well, been nice talking to you, and anytime you fellas get too lonesome out there in orbit, just Bell me."

He saluted farewell with his little cigar and sauntered off. If Scott had scored you would not have known it, and Wilkerson's parting shot came like the exhaust fume from a car snorting away from the line, leaving Scott behind to breathe in the blast.

Once again he started out to the field. Now the vehicles of participants were everywhere, grouped by class, and the crowds of people were milling around moving in clusters from one automobile to another—it looked like Clearance Day at The Dream-of-Heaven Used-Car lot.

When he glimpsed Susan she was running (did she ever stand still?) and scooping up pebbles and throwing them in the air and laughing when innocent bystanders ducked to avert the shower of stones. He hastened over to her to find that she was still playing with the other child. She'd lost the blue ribbon on one of her pigtails and her knees were smudged, and the blue and white dress Red had bought her looked ready for the heap. She smiled up at her father like a cocotte and asked did she have to go?

Yes. But she was quick to grasp, take advantage of the indecision in his voice, and she and the other girl darted off again, scratching up pebbles.

"Suzy!" This time a firm paternal command.

Back she came, and Scott said they were going to look at some of the cars now, and she said did she have to and you stay here daddy. She spread her fingers and the pebbles dribbled to the ground. "Where's Jemmy?" she asked then.

"Sarah!" A man's voice.

"I'm playing—" The other little girl was confronting her father: it was Steve Sturges.

Then he saw Scott and there was that squint behind the glasses.

Scott said hello to him, and there were a few stiff words about the children. Steve turned to his child, then bent down and retied the dangling lace of her shoe.

The same Steve Sturges, though as Scott watched him squatting there tying the child's laces, as he looked at him, recognizing the same thin face, the same rather pointed, freckled nose, the same thin lips, he found little trace of the aggressive hostility he'd felt toward him the night of the Rothes' party.

As soon as he'd finished, the little girls ran off again, leaving the two men on the island of embarrassment.

Scott said: "I'm afraid I owe you something of an apology."

The squint behind the glasses. "Oh—well—"

Scott waited, half expecting him to finish by saying "forget it." But he didn't.

"I was in foul shape that night, Sturges." Scott led the way again, not with zeal, but wanting to get it over with. "I'm afraid I took it out on you. I'm sorry."

"It's okay." The young engineer parted reluctantly with the truce.

"I got to thinking about it afterward," Scott said, "and I saw pretty much how—" Stopping then, conscious of a queasy feeling in this extended apology. He said: "Well, I guess that pretty much covers it."

Sturges said yes. He seemed relieved. There was a rigid moment or two, and then he said: "To tell you the truth, Quinnley—I'd been coming up against so much resistance on that project of mine I might have been a little on the scrappy side myself."

Scott nodded. Over the hump. Yet another silence. He reached into the pocket of his jacket and brought out his pack of cigarettes. He offered it to Sturges. No, he didn't smoke. But the small talk helped reduce the strain.

"How's it going now?" Scott asked.

"What?"

"That project."

"It's—creeping along." Though Sturges spoke matter-of-factly, discouragement clung to his words, dampening them like mildew. Scott recalled his arrogance, his patronizing tone that night, except that now he found himself more willing or able to understand the reason for what had happened.

"Well," Scott said, "it's always rough trying to get new converts when the old religion is still bringing 'em in."

He nodded, but squinting at Scott again as if perhaps he'd slipped him a glib one. So that Scott couldn't help tell him, just for the record, that last year in the magazine he'd run two pieces on the potential of the electric-powered engine.

225]

"Yes, I know." Sturges nodded once more. The thin sandy hair took on luster in the angle of sunlight. "Yes, I read them," he acknowledged. "They were good, though rather elementary."

But Scott saw that a faint grin had grown on his face. "I'd like to have a look at your project sometime," Scott said, "if that's all right with you."

Yes. Phil Rothe and a few other guys were coming to his lab some night next week, and Scott was welcome to look in.

"I'll check with Phil," he said. "Maybe I'll tag along." He could not deny the subtle current of excitement—as if the week ahead might now be broken by a different kind of rhythm, one which he was suddenly anticipating with an interest that was keen and outsized.

"Okay," Sturges said. He looked around. "Well, I think I've had it here. I've got to get back. I've got a pregnant wife at home, you know."

Yes. Scott knew. And he found himself turning to look back at Jemmy. She was still talking with Jack Winters.

When Sturges had gone off with his child, Scott gathered up Suzy and they went out to where the action was. Something of his old verve for the *Concours* was with him again. Now that it was almost over.

When Scott neared Phil Rothe's Duesenberg, six judges had already arrived and were going over the S J, pads and pencils in hand, inspecting Phil's treasure with the scrutiny of surgeons studying the X-ray of a crucial case. Scott let go of Susan's hand and she sprang away like a puppy released from the leash.

In the dense circle around the Duesenberg, Scott waved, caught Phil's eye and called out good luck. But his attention quickly returned to the judges who were compiling their score. The inspection tally for this kind of Drive-Up show was based on a total of 300 points: for elegance and conception of design, 50 points; paint and finish, 35; plating and glass, 25; seating and upholstery, 25; engine and compartment, 50; instrument panel, 12; floor covering, 12; boot, 15; chassis, 20; with miscellaneous points for extras, mileage and age.

After a while Scott left to round up Suzy, and he saw her approaching with Jemmy, and then the three of them made their way back to the tent. Jemmy, he noticed, seemed to have lost the will to gaiety which she'd shown coming in earlier from Ann Arbor. Her untanned face was grave, rather nervously she kept palming back the strands of her long black hair; and she didn't talk much except to Suzy.

[226

The pavilion was massed with people. The roof of the tent caught, deflected, the flashing diadems from the glassware on the punch table and the chrome-plated shooting sticks. The sound of conversation was rising like the approach of summer thunder.

But then the voices began to subside and the judges were filing back to their table in front of the tent.

There was another announcement. The Chairman, a tall, horse-toothed man wearing the official green and white badge in the lapel of his tweed jacket, rose; he walked with a slight limp as he moved to the microphone.

It was time for the awards.

They were pressed, swept forward toward the edge of the tent; the thousands of other spectators were hastening in from the field, forming a crescent around the ramp and pavilion. Scott had to hoist Suzy onto his shoulders so that she could see.

"Ladies and gentlemen, members of the board of Bridgeton Museum—" the Chairman began, and you could tell at once that a windy preamble was in the making. He explored at length the history of the automobile museum, he spoke of how the *Concours d'Élégance* had become a tradition here and he cited figures showing the rise in the public's attendance. He concluded with some pretentious thoughts on the "significance" of the *Concours* to those people —"and that means most of us"—in the industry who found "in this evocation of our past, not only inspiration but a chance to pay homage to the craftsmanship and genius of our automotive ancestors. The automobile is not only the hub around which the nation's economy turns," he reminded the listeners, "it has reached a plateau of technological performance, beauty and safety undreamed of in the past."

The Chairman's voice rang with solemn emotion, as if he were pledging allegiance to the flag during wartime.

A restiveness had set in among the spectators. But now as the Chairman brought his speech to an end, one of the judges handed him a sheaf of papers. He cleared his throat, edged closer to the microphone. Stillness again held the field, and within the tent everyone turned once more to watch, listen.

Scott shifted Suzy on his shoulders. He looked out to where Phil and Lorie were waiting in the Duesenberg, seeing Phil, his robust frame at the wheel. He had a good feeling, a foretaste of how the Duesenberg would score; it was the kind of hunch hard to put down.

"—and with a total of 289 points—" the voice of the Chairman of

227]

Awards was in full oratorical cry—"first in class, Classic cars, goes to Mr. and Mrs. A. J. Kerwin of Kent Hills, with particular mention for the outstanding—"

Scott looked away from the Duesenberg.

"—and second, with a total of 281 points—" It was the Bugatti.

Phil's Duesenberg was judged a close third with 277 points.

Later there was the parade of winners and the awarding of silver cups, and then the crush in the tent reached its noisy zenith, and the bibulous celebrations and postmortems were underway.

When Phil and Lorie finally joined their friends, they were trying not to wear their disappointment. "We're holding a wake at our house, Scott," Phil announced. Ann Smith had come over and presently John Winters was there. "Ann, you can come, can't you?" Phil asked.

No, Ann said, she was afraid she couldn't make it tonight. She wanted to stick close to the telephone at home in case there was a call from Ben Nodina. "I'm not even going to my dear old brother-in-law's—"

"Well look," Lorie Rothe was saying then, "who's coming? Scott, we can count on you and Jemmy, and—"

Scott said yes, they'd be there.

"I can't." Jemmy stirred beside him. "I'd love to, Lorie, but I—I have to get home and pack tonight."

"Pack?" Scott said.

"I'm leaving for Los Angeles," Jemmy stated quietly, but with that level gaze as if to warn Scott.

"Los Angeles?" Ann Smith said to her. "Are you serious, Jemmy? Since when did you—"

"My uncle invited me, I thought a change might be nice."

"Listen, Jemmy, you might at least have said something about it," Scott began.

"I told you about it last weekend, didn't I?" Jemmy answered.

"Yes, but . . ." Scott halted, looking at her as though he'd been deceived.

"I found out this noon. I got space on the first flight out in the morning," Jemmy said. "I have to get home to pack."

Scott said he would drive her back. He was too unsettled to fight it out here.

"It's not necessary, Scott. After all, you've already made one round trip to Ann Arbor today."

The shy, dry voice of John Winters: "I'll be glad to take her, Scott."

"No," he said.

"It's not much out of my way," Winters said.

Jemmy turned to him: "Are you sure, Jack?"

"Come on, Jemmy." Scott took her arm, and with his free hand reached down for Suzy's.

"Will someone please tell me what goes on?" Ann Smith looked at them.

But Jemmy only shook her head, and they started off for the car.

The *Concours d'Élégance* was over.

19: Scott Quinnley

Iт is a long and ugly run to Bellgard Motor Company.
Except for one exotically modern edifice designed by Yamasaki, the
landscape is a monotone of mean streets, reconstituted slums and
housing tracts until you near the open plain where recent industries
have settled.

And the heat. On this Tuesday afternoon as Scott was on his way
to keep the appointment at Codman Smith's office, the sun beat down
ferociously, its blaze sucking the moisture from the earth and singeing
the leaves of trees. Now Scott slowed the car, drew over to the side of
the road. He rolled down his shirt sleeves and put on his seersucker
jacket and tugged his black knit tie back into place. He felt the airless
weight pressing his flesh, wilting his spirit. He thought of a professor
he used to have in Comparative Religions; when the weather got too
hot, the man would always begin his lecture with the same whimsical-
ity: "Well, it looks as if the Chief Celestial Engineer has turned the
thermostat higher—"

A foul day to be confronting Cod Smith.

Except for the unexpected call from Los Angeles from Jemmy this
noon, the day had held defeat and discouragement. Ever since his
encounter with Max Wilkerson at the *Concours* Sunday he had been
working up a way of approaching his father with the proposal to unload Quinnley Corners. And today, after lunch, he got around to it,
tenderly, delicately feeling his way around the curves and hairpin
turns of Red's resistance. Naturally he had not mentioned Wilkerson's
name, but it didn't matter. Red jumped in almost at once and blasted
the entire proposal. When he was dead and buried, and not until then,
would he ever consent to selling the enterprise. It should not have
surprised Scott. But he'd been living with the new hope that he might,
by encouraging the sale, get himself free enough and monied enough
to become part of the project Steve Sturges was organizing.

But no. That hope had died today even before the first lap had been run. He was ready for the pit when the call had come from Jemmy:

"Scott—?"

"Yes—"

"Can you talk?" she said.

"What?"

"Can you talk now?"

Scott glanced at his father. "More or less."

"I'm sorry. I had to call you, Scott."

"Of course." He dug into his pocket for cigarettes.

"But I had to tell you what's happened to me." Her tone was excited, hoarse, throaty. "When you hear this you're going to fall flat, it's horrible and funny, but—"

"What?"

"Scott—honest to God, wouldn't you just know it? I'd only been on that damn plane—it couldn't have been more than two hours or so, when—it happened! Can you imagine? Two hours after we took off and there I was thirty thousand feet up in that damn plane—" She was speaking so rapidly, the words tripping over one another, that Scott still wasn't positively certain if he'd understood.

She said it again. Then: "Of course I should have listened to you and waited—or maybe not—maybe it was the altitude—I don't know. But whatever it was, I feel terrible and wonderful, and I only waited another day to make sure. But I had to call you now, I couldn't bear to think of you stewing all this time, you looked so awful yesterday at the airport. God, I think I'll get myself looped tonight!"

When at last Scott hung up, the perspiration was cold on his face and neck, but he thought he must have wanted Jemmy at that moment more than any woman in the world. And his esteem for her took on the wildest proportions.

How close, he reflected now as he resumed the drive to the factory, how close he'd been today to a new freedom. The straightaway had almost been within sight, he could have cut out into the open. How close.

Onward now to Cod Smith.

The fan club is disbanded. You are no longer the court favorite. Ann's warning caught up with him again.

At least, he thought, if Smith was going to blast him, he was prepared for it.

231]

Fast now. The car sliced through the flatlands. It seemed limitless, this territory, but soon he made out the stacks and towers of the Bellgard powerhouses in the almost blinding whiteness of sky; and soon he was nearing the plant, the sprawling complex of buildings modern and superannuated.

An overpass spanned the highway framing much of the vast acreage, the units of the plant, long and low, slab-roofed or skylighted, beneath which flowed the mighty river of production—the coils of sheet metal to be cut into body panels, the chassis units journeying along assembly lines, engines swinging down from overhead conveyers to join the frames, draw presses shaping the hoods, suction cups poising plate glass above windshield openings, car bodies deep-dipped in monster tanks of rustproofing paint, and the body-drop lowering the exterior for that final marriage to the chassis.

A second underpass, and now Scott turned right, passing the railroad siding and the Bellgard bus station and the first parking area—cars sitting there row on row like geometric pastries glazing in a giant outdoor oven.

Another mile and he was at the road-bar and sentry bunks to have his identity and purpose of visit confirmed. On his way again, to park, a long esplanade of lawn flanked by the most recent (1947-1956) of the white-stone buildings which housed the brain of the corpus Bellgard—Engineering, Research, Product Planning, Advertising and Public Relations, Auditing and Cost Control and, recessed from the sidewalk, the security-guarded Styling Studios.

Parking now in the area specified for Visitors. He started for the massive Administration Building but as he neared its lofty glass doors, Codman Smith stepped outside.

"Oh, Scott—" He shook Scott's hand. "Come with me, have an errand to do. But I thought you might want to see this—" They had walked to a car parked among others nearby. "Hop in," he said.

If Scott had been mildly startled to see Smith at the entrance, he was even more astounded when he got into the front seat of this car, an ordinary V-8 Bellgard sedan.

"Naturally you'll keep this to yourself," Codman Smith said. "It's dream stuff, a long way off. This is the only one we have."

There was no evidence of a steering wheel, no sign of gear box or clutch, no instruments and no familiar dashboard.

Cod Smith reached out and from where the steering wheel should have been, he pulled into place a panel which adjusted itself before

[232

him like a kind of small breakfast tray. It was the console, and on it was everything needed to run the car.

A touch of a button, a flick of a lever and they were moving. The steering wheel consisted of a dial the size of a fifty-cent piece. Codman Smith drove and did not say a word, though across his iron features there was the faintest play of mischief (as Scott had often seen in Ann's eyes). The drive ended less than a hundred yards away, in front of another building.

Smith excused himself, hastened into the building and returned a few minutes later. "Why don't you take her back?" he suggested in the most casual way.

They changed places. Scott could not wait to take over. He had studied the console carefully; he had also noted Codman Smith's performance. Now he drew the console toward him, adjusted it to position. He was ready.

Smith sat back. Nothing was said. Scott was on his own.

Reversing the car was a totally new sensation, for though Scott turned his torso and his head, looking back to see exactly where he was going, there was no familiar and reassuring steering wheel for him to hold on to; instead he directed the car with thumb and index finger lightly on a dial.

When he got the car back to its original parking place, Codman Smith opened the door. "Well," he said, "I guess you know your way around a car."

Scott handed him the key, and Smith said for him to go on up to his office; he'd left word to admit Scott, and he'd be back in no time. No reference to the car was ever made again.

But Scott was still in it, walking then to the Administration Building, still in that car, still absorbed by the performance, the kicks he'd had, and still feeling almost light-headed from an experience which had lasted no more than a minute or two.

He made his way into the court of the Administration Building and passed the glass-sheathed Exhibition Center where all the models of the current line moved in circular display: an automotive carousel. Into the air-cooled lobby, lofty and marbled: in the middle sat three young women, pretty and earnest, circled by the splendid marble desk.

"Codman Smith," Scott said.

Another telephone call for verification. A buzzer sounding. A young man appearing: his guide for the perilous safari.

Presently in the elevator and then once again, as on that dismal day he'd gone to see Tony Kerwin, he was walking the sacrosanct corridors of Mahogany Row.

Except this time Scott was led to the corner of the right wing and delivered into the handsome reception room. A secretary then led him into an inner chamber, also handsome. And paneled. Here one of three secretaries ushered him into the spacious, anticlimactically plain-walled office of Codman Smith.

The room was empty. The secretary asked him to sit down. Mr. Smith would be along shortly.

But it was a wait. Scott rose and walked around. Beyond the large uncluttered desk the corner was formed by glass: you could see much of the sprawling plant in the distance; closer by you saw the long vista of the esplanade. But from up here you could also see the many secondary, older, bleaker buildings tucked behind the principal structures like poor relatives standing obscurely on the fringe of their more elegant and illustrious family members at some formal garden party.

Scott waited. Knowing Cod Smith, however superficially, he should have felt at ease. Yet the instant he strode in he was conscious of a certain tightening of nerves.

There was another cordial handshake and how are you, Scott? How's your father? It was as if the incident downstairs had never happened. Scott was no longer dealing with the sweatshirted Sunday ballplayer or the affable clubman or simply with the father of Ann Smith.

He moved to the desk, the tall figure with the brisk stride. His pewter-gray hair was rendered silver in the sunlight, and as he looked at Scott the blue eyes held a reserve as if to balance the friendly smile.

Business. Work. He was at the plant now. It was natural that this Codman Smith might not appear the same.

Yet Scott kept trying to see him as the man he'd known only socially. What he saw, more forcefully this time, was how much of him had been born into his daughters: the once fair hair was now carried by Ann and Myra and Phoebe, the blue eyes also, and the finely modeled faintly Roman nose—all three daughters commemorated him (except that their personalities were so opposed that they might have been strangers to each other, which in many ways they were).

"Well, Scott—" Smith began. A telephone call from New York. He asked Scott to excuse him.

Scott moved beyond his sight, stepping to the side of the window wall to wait there in a sudden upsurge of apprehension.

The telephone clicked into its cradle.

Scott moved back to the black leather chair by the desk.

Codman Smith said: "I wanted to talk along lines of the future, Scott. The immediate future. I'd like to see you make a change. I'd like to see you come with Bellgard. On this end."

20: Codman Smith

". . . I've had this in mind for some time, Scott. And now that Red is functioning again—I thought he was almost looking his old gingery self at the *Concours* Sunday—I think it might be in order for you to move into a place that is, let us say, more on a level with your abilities or potential, particularly after the stint you've put in with your father. There's a place for you here." Cod often sprang a proposal straight and swift; it gave him a chance to test the reflexes of the man with whom he was dealing.

But in dealing with Scott Quinnley, this habit was more automatic than necessary, for he knew Scott, or believed he did.

He felt an esteem and warmth for him. The reasons were plain enough. For one thing, Scott's way of infighting when he'd bucked the Bellgard monthly quota had been something he himself might well have done; he hadn't approved of it, and in the early flush of anger he fumed bitterly and condemned it. Only later would he admit to himself that, from a purely personal point of view, he admired Scott's action.

He had also followed Scott's early months of operation the way you follow a bush league player's record before recruiting him into the majors. He saw him in terms of the reorganization and reforms now in progress at Bellgard.

A reorganization that was long in coming, overdue, needed, if not desperately imperative. He had waited a fraction too long to get it underway, slogged and sidetracked by the day-to-day problems which had kept him from pushing the plan into action.

Now it was underway, new blood was beginning to flow, stir through the hardening arteries of the plant's life. In time—just in time—to get it off the ground before the next stockholders' meeting.

New men, young men like Quinnley. This was needed to put juice into the team, bring it up in the league.

Never too late, even though he suspected it might be too late for him to quit next year, head for the Florida waters.

There was something else about Scott. A minor consideration, but personal, and one which had obviously spurred his interest in him.

True, when he'd first met Scott in Paris at the Automobile Show, several years ago, he had been somewhat indifferent to him. Scott had seemed like another of those young dilettantes with a flair for competition racing, and holding the familiar highbrow and limited attitude toward the industry.

However, last winter when Scott had turned up in Kent Hills, he'd been struck by the marked change in him, the sobered visage, the tautness beneath the voice—the loss of his wife and near loss of his father would have been enough to ripen any man. But this too might have gone unseen if Cod hadn't begun to notice the special rapport between him and Ann.

Immediately then, Cod had gone out of his way to be friendly—he'd tried every imaginable idea that might divert Ann from her involvement with Ben Nodina. No results. So that when he'd seen Scott this time he'd taken hope that his being here might just be providential enough to break the unfortunate pattern of Ann's life. He'd drawn Scott into the circle, had him to the house as often as possible.

But it hadn't quite worked, and Ann had been quick enough to see what she called his "ignoble machinations."

Notwithstanding, he'd held on to his hope. Until today.

Until this morning.

This morning at breakfast, that hope had evaporated like the vapors of his first cup of steaming coffee.

Ann had burst into the sun-warmed dining room, her eyes pale from sleeplessness yet brimming with unconcealed joy and a little defiance as she announced, first off, the news he had never wanted to hear: Ben Nodina had returned from Pennsylvania and he had his divorce "in his pocket."

Although he'd more or less prepared himself for it, he found himself unready. The punch rocked him.

Refusing to show it, he tried to look for an opening. He thought he saw it when Ann seemed to lose some of the quick defiant brightness. She stood by her place at the table looking at him, hesitantly, not following through.

Then it came: "I know it's an ugly word, Father," she said it softly, but she said it, "about the wedding. I mean I don't want one. Not one of those monsters. When I think of what you and Mother went through with Phoebe and Myra's weddings, I shudder—I mean with that mob, everyone and his wicked stepmother tramping all over the grounds, sopping up all your champagne, tons of caviar, the production with bridal gowns and that godawful rehearsal with Reverend Cass. I just couldn't expose you to that. And with me it would be worse, knowing some of those creepy characters talking behind your back, saying anything to spice up the day, including some jazz about how your precious daughter Annie is probably just making it a split second ahead of the shotgun. When I thought of all of it, I just shuddered. I just couldn't put you through it. So what I thought was we'll just take off for some J.P. I want to make it as painless as possible for you—" She'd stopped, she'd watched him as if looking, hoping for some sign that he might be softening.

But all he saw was that she would be leaving, going to Greece on a dubious adventure with a man he had never been able to accept.

He'd sat there rigidly, he could say nothing. He had to contain himself somehow. To protest would only strengthen her determination.

"Look, Father," she was saying, "you've never even given yourself a chance to get to know Ben. That's true, isn't it? If you knew the way I feel, you'd know what Ben means to me." She stepped back, her hands clasped behind her.

He looked up to meet her glance, to see reluctantly, and not without pain, the happiness and anxiety plain on her face.

She was demanding some acknowledgment, any kind of recognition of what she felt. He couldn't bring himself to give it to her.

No matter how often you reminded yourself that a child's life could only be guided up to a certain point, no matter how braced or prepared you were for the disastrous day when it comes, the blow still cuts deep.

Ann moved to him. "Oh, I"—her glibness was fading—"I don't know how to tell you how it is, I just don't, Father. Except . . ." She paused again. "Except you've got to believe me, that's all. Trust me. Otherwise it will be awful for me."

He could say nothing.

She bent down, touching his cheek. Not with her customary ease or boldness, but almost shyly, she said: "I mean, after all, you know you're my original pinup man, and I couldn't bear to lose you—"

The sweet closeness of her only sharpened the pain; he knew that the joy she was trying to express and have confirmed was being killed by his resistance, his refusal or inability to yield.

[238

All his love for her gathered into rage. He said: "There's no point trying to put a good face on it, Ann. You know exactly how I feel, how I've always felt. You have no right to come in here and ask for something you've always known I couldn't give you."

"You've never given yourself a chance to feel anything except prejudice."

"Ann, I won't go along with this, I resent it, I think it's a terrible mistake. I'm thinking of you and how—"

"You're not thinking of me!" she reproached him.

"I'm not?" Abruptly he stood up. His resolve had collapsed completely. For him to lose control was as rare as it was, in this instance, stupid. "You think I don't understand how you feel? Certainly I understand it. And a lot more. I won't have Nodina destroying your life!" He heard himself uttering all the wrong and ancient cries. "You damn near destroyed it yourself I don't know how many times before. But this time it's going to happen. I won't have it!"

"You can't stop me, I can't believe you'll do that to me!" Ann exclaimed.

"I'll do anything I can to keep it from happening!"

"There's nothing you can do except make it worse!"

"Don't you tell me what I can or cannot do! You listen to me this time! I've never interfered before, but now I'll be damned if I take—"

"Do you think"—Ann's voice had become suddenly hard as his— "do you think I'll ever settle for what Phoebe or Myra has? You know me better than that."

"That's not what I'm asking of you. That has nothing to do with it —" He halted, conscious of the false air of conviction. There were two truths in him and he couldn't reconcile them: he did want Ann to join and be part of his life, he did want her to be part of his community like Phoebe and Myra were; he did want to keep her in the nest —yet, he also knew that the very qualities he most cherished about her, her spirit and imagination and enterprise, were the qualities which made her fight, resist the way of life around him.

Into the silence Ann's voice came bitterly: "It's what you're trying to say, isn't it? Why don't you come out and say it? I used to think, I used to be stupid enough to think you at least had some comprehension of how I felt, I used to think you understood *why* I wanted no part of what Phoebe or Myra have. I used to think you at least knew *why* I refused to let myself get flattened by the 'good life' of Kent

Hills. But when the chips are down, all that counts with you is keeping me here. I used to think you were very smart, but if you were you wouldn't be hoping—no matter how unconsciously—for me to get myself another Tony or another Dean. That's what it amounts to, doesn't it? But I suppose even the smartest man can't be that smart. I don't know why I worried so much about hurting you, when you—"

"That'll be enough, Ann! It's not necessary to try to get around me like that." But he spoke without rancor: she had touched him. Yet he went on: "Perhaps that might work with your mother. As for your unsmart father, let me say, though I'm sure you won't believe it, that I've always hoped I'd never have to stand in your way, that something like this would never happen between us. But it has, and the handwriting on the wall spells out nothing but ruin for you. I'm forced to try to prevent it, I've got to. And all I ask now is that you wait. You've waited this long and—"

"Wait for what? I'm twenty-five. If I wait, what then?" She stood before him, her legs splayed in a stance of aggression, her lower lip trembling. "What can you do? Call your lawyer, change your will? Put Ben out of business?"

"Ben Nodina is not in business, and his history is too mercurial for—"

"What in God's name do I care?"

"I care," he said.

"We aren't talking about the same things, are we?" Without warning she hurried to the double doors, leaving him, and at once he felt the lifelessness of the house, being deprived of her.

"Ann!"

But she had not come back.

When he'd reached the plant it was past nine o'clock. It was the first time in a long time he'd been that late.

Thus the day had begun.

On the great expanse of his desk, set aside from the mass of morning memoranda and reports, was the secretary's note: Ann had called.

Ann. Then it wasn't over. He telephoned her at once.

"Sorry to bother you." Her tone was not apologetic but a little softer. "I called because in all that nasty ruckus we had, there's one thing I forgot to tell you, Father."

"Oh?"

"We're—there'll be no announcing, no shouting from the rooftops right now. We want to wait until Ben has cleaned up all his work. As it stands now we plan on getting married just before we fly to New York. So I'd appreciate it if you keep this between us, I mean I'm not saying anything to Mother or the others."

His relief, temporary as it might be, came like a reprieve. "Of course, Ann."

"All right. That's all I wanted to tell you." Then in hasty afterthought: "But everything I said still stands—"

"Yes."

"Including that I still love you," she said.

The temptation to keep her on the line, seize the unexpected truce, rose strong in him. But as much as he wanted to let himself bask in the moment's warmth, he couldn't permit the indulgence, he couldn't weaken his already weak position. "Thank you, honey," was all he managed.

However, for an instant, after he'd hung up, he allowed himself the false luxury of renewed hope. Then he brought his attention to the day's business.

The day's agenda.

An hour lost already. Already several officers of the company waiting outside to see him.

But having to scan, check the many reports.

Reports from Automotive and Parts Division.

Engineering. Experimental. Products Planning.

And Committee reports.

Audit Committee.

Salary and Bonus Committee.

Cost Control Committee.

Policy Groups Committee.

Distribution Policy Committee.

And always picking, snatching out small items that can grow into big griefs:

106 employees in Audit Control given their notices, their services to be replaced by newest electronic BC Ledgexel Computer System.

Or:

Belated investigation of paint blistering on bodies.

Secretary's voice: Mr. Dean Stratler called. Five o'clock showing, Stage 3, Styling Studio.

Secretary's voice: Engineering has arranged a second filming of Kyssin Muffler tomorrow, 3 o'clock. Would he wish to attend?

No!

At last coming to what always had to be first: report from Sales Division.

Yesterday's sales: off 17.3%. Previous month, off 15.6%. Total drop thus far for model year: 13.2%.

Down. Down.

(And Fred Gordon, Chairman of General Motors, saying at the last shareholders' meeting: *Over the next ten years we anticipate seventy-eight million cars and thirteen million trucks will be sold, or more than nine million units a year.*)

Cod stared down at Bellgard's downward figures. A death warrant. To be converted into a birth certificate. Rebirth certificate.

Next year. He'd be sixty-five.

He'd been through many rebirths. He'd created them. Today he was in the process of midwifing yet another, except this time it would have to be the last, and it would have to be lasting. He couldn't quit, retire.

To quit this year would mean having to live with the pointlessness of his life.

Pushing aside the papers, rising, rubbing his forehead. It wasn't possible to feel tired this early, was it?

But as the morning went on, as he moved through the air-conditioned day, his energies seeped back. When at half-past two as he stepped from the Executive Dining Room, a sturdy lunch inside him, a good meeting on the progress of his Reorganization Program behind him, his pace had bounce. How did he feel? Dandy. Or almost.

Almost three o'clock now. Scott Quinnley before him, the office soaked in sunlight, but cool and dry behind the Thermopane glass.

Cod said: "Well, how does it strike you, Scott?"

Instead of answering, Scott Quinnley was lighting a cigarette.

"Don't tell me we caught you off base?" Cod said.

"I'm afraid you did," Scott said.

"Why?"

"I suppose I expected something else, that is, something pertaining to Quinnley Corners."

"I see." Cod smiled. This task of reorganization he'd delegated to other officers, but in particular cases, such as young Quinnley, he wanted to do the recruiting himself. Undoubtedly this too had surprised Scott. "As it happens," Cod went on, "this does pertain to Quinnley Corners. Indirectly."

"Oh?" Scott moved forward in the black leather chair.

From the single drawer of the desk, Cod drew forth the report—one of those detailed reports known in the company as a Green Paper. Any new project or proposed new policy was green-papered along to those committee members concerned. "This is something I'd like you to look over, Scott. Take it with you. It is still classified material and I'll have to ask you to keep it that way."

He handed over the bound and stapled document, Part II, which dealt specifically with the total overhauling of Bellgard's dealer system, a reversing of many of the traditional methods and laws between the company and its franchised dealerships. An allocation of fifty million dollars was the muscle behind it: to rehabilitate and finance the shaky part of the sales network. Certain dealers would be dropped, new ones would be added; certain dealerships in fading areas would be relocated, and wherever necessary would be built and financed by Bellgard.

Cod Smith said: "Some of this material may be familiar to you."

Scott was leafing through the document. He looked up then: "It is." His smile was wry. "Very familiar."

"Your brains, along with quite a few others, have been thoroughly picked." Cod was recalling some of those afterdinner talks at Kent Hills when Scott in a spurt of passionate candor born of his grievances had stated his feelings about the dealer system being antiquated and a financial waste, and why, he had asked, was it necessary for an auto company to depend on a middleman to sell the product? It had seemed to him that a dealership would be much healthier if, instead of being a harassed and competing dependent, it would be integrated within the financial structure of the company.

Scarcely a revolutionary theory, and one which was already underway at Vanguard and Chrysler. However, Quinnley's feelings coming when they did, and being those of a comparative outsider, happened to coincide with discussions Cod himself was conducting with other men in the company.

"I'm afraid I'm still in the dark." Scott put down the Green Paper. "Obviously it's a project I'm for. But I—"

"What it represents," Cod said, "is a hell of a lot of work ahead and I'd like you to consider moving in on it." He went on to discuss the salary plus possible bonuses and, after two years, stock option privileges.

Scott would be part of a team of men, several of whom had been sales executives. "And we're getting in a Relocation Expert from another company which shall be nameless for the moment."

Scott Quinnley was frowning now, his head tipped sidewise, the dark straight hair showing the thin mottling of gray. It might well get grayer in the months to come, Cod suspected.

Scott said: "You really caught me off base."

"There's no rush," Cod Smith said dryly, "you can think about it for a few minutes."

Scott looked up at him.

"But the program itself gets underway this fall," Cod said.

Scott said: "I'm going to have to stick it out at Quinnley Corners for a while. And then I—"

"Why?" Cod said. "You're beyond that now."

"I can't walk out on Red."

"Why not? Red's all right again, isn't he? That's the word we've been getting."

"It's the word *he's* been handing out," Scott said.

The buzzer sounded. Cod spoke into the intercom: "Yes?"

"Three o'clock, Mr. Smith," the secretary's voice announced. "Policy Committee."

"Thank you." Then: "Sorry, Scott, I'll have to run for this one." He rose, a fraction irritated by the time it had taken to accomplish little. "As I said, there's no rush. I understand your situation. If you like we'll have a talk with your father. I doubt if Red will want to stand between you and something that is considerably bigger than the operation at the Corners."

He saw Scott get to his feet. "Aside from that, Mr. Smith—"

"Start thinking." Cod left him briefly, stepped out to his secretary's office and asked her for "my poker hand." She had it ready, the thin deck of filing cards with which he armed himself for certain committee meetings. These cards contained pertinent figures and facts of problems to be discussed. He put the deck into the inside breast pocket of his light gray suit. Returning to his office, he resumed: "Right now all I'd like to know, Scott, is if your interest in this is definitely positive or negative."

How could Quinnley even hesitate? There he stood, still frowning, still knitted in frowning concentration.

And Cod, thinking of his own long past and how different the milestones of a man's life had been in his time . . .

(Here was Scott Quinnley holding this valid, first-rate offer which had been presented to him, yet standing here giving no answer.)

. . . nothing like this in the early years of Codman Smith: in 1919 when he'd come down from Massachusetts to Michigan, with one army year behind him, he'd had no gold-plated offer dropped in his lap, he'd been lucky to push and sweat his way into a machine shop, an apprentice at 18¢ per hour. He'd come down with his mother and father, following the success of his grandfather who'd been among the first New Englanders to settle here. That tire store on East Bush Street which his grandfather operated had seemed to the gangling Cod Smith like the wonderland heart of the automobile industry . . .

(Here stood Scott Quinnley unable to commit himself, yes or no.)

. . . and in 1923 when Cod Smith had gained a tenuous foothold, moving out to the old Ford plant at Highland Park, he'd had to stand in line two days just for the privilege of talking to the Hiring Office . . .

(1923—that was eight years before Scott Quinnley was born.)

. . . there'd been the jump to General Motors in 1926. A production man, Cod had still not known what it was to go home at the end of the day without the blackness of grime beneath his fingernails . . .

(The Scott Quinnleys of today often seemed as though they were still being sheltered by ivy-walled campus halls.)

. . . Cod Smith had never had to hesitate about accepting an offer that looked right. From G. M. he had gone to Bellgard. 1934. A vice-president, still a production man, though by then his fingernails seldom got soiled . . .

. . . at heart a shopside, shirt-sleeve carman. During World War II, even then, there'd been that old direct life with the making of machines; not auto engines, but propeller shafts. Yet it was that, the smallest of incidents, that had transformed his life: that argument with a snotty vice-president. Cod had aired his exasperation by the repeated failures to machine the propeller shafts to the close tolerances specified by the government, and he'd brought the V.P. with him into the shop; he'd told the worker to step aside; he'd proceeded to machine a shaft himself, and when he'd finished, checked the dimensions with a micrometer to find they were hairline perfect, he'd turned to the executive: "That's how I want the job done here."

. . . the Shop Steward was already on his neck, running over to

245]

cry out that he was violating union rules, and so Cod had picked up the newly machined shaft and hurled it to the floor, ruining it. "Okay. Now we haven't broken any union regulations either."

. . . the commonplace incident brought him unwarranted recognition. But such were the ways of the trade that he found himself thrust higher into administration, upper-echelon management.

. . . from that, in 1944, to Executive Vice-President of Bellgard; in 1946 he became President.

. . . Shirt sleeves down, cuffed, his machine his desk, his concerns turning to Index Volume and Tooling Volume and Capital Expenditures and Plant Expansion and Automation and Distribution and Public Relations and Advertising and Styling and Products Planning . . . all in Committee . . . his boss the Stockholders, his goal: profit per share of stock . . . a far detour from the heart of his first passion . . .

. . . no longer face to face with the real process of car manufacturing, except now and then, except now and then when he would accompany some guest, a cabinet member, a senior senator, a president of some foreign country, guiding the visitor through parts of the plant . . .

. . . Tired, growing tired if he'd admit it. Which he wouldn't. But no heading for the Florida coast until he brought the company back to within reach of that 11% gross of the total automobile market . . .

. . . by next year?

To succeed him? That would remain open, though it would give him natural pride to know that Phoebe's husband, Tony, might get voted in on his recommendation. Possibly Dean Stratler, given an alternative . . . or . . .

. . . Nothing counted, however, except pushing the company up into its rightful share of the market.

(Scott Quinnley lighting another cigarette, still not leaping at the offer.)

. . . it had taken Tony Kerwin less than ten seconds to give the word; as for Dean Stratler, he had initiated his own deal . . . they were older than Scott, of course; just enough older to belong to a generation that hadn't come under the subsidy society, the age of the built-in opportunity, the corporation job doled out with the college diploma.

"Put it in a letter, Scott." He fired the parting shot with curt impatience.

[246

He was late, he moved off, out into the corridor.

"Mr. Smith—"

He turned: it was Scott.

"Yes?"

"I really can't put it in a letter," Scott said. "It isn't a question of yes or no. I'm certainly all for the idea of the project, but"—a pause —"I can't break away from my father. And when I do, my plan is to go back to New York."

"Are you trying to talk about more money?" Cod broke through the customary bounds of his courtesy.

"No."

Cod waited, irritated.

"Well . . ." Scott seemed distinctly uncomfortable, if not embarrassed. "It's not easy to lay it out simply. But what it is is that if I stayed here, if I worked here for you, I'm afraid of getting hung on current problems, I think I might get sidetracked." Then: "I'm being sidetracked now out at the Corners. That is"—another hesitation—"I realize this is a damn fine offer, but—for itself alone, no. Unless I thought it would lead to something else."

"For example?" Cod found his patience threading thin. He saw several executives filing hurriedly into the conference room.

"What I'm getting at is the future stuff, what's going on in product planning. I couldn't think of making a move unless I thought something like that might lie ahead for me."

"I see." Cod spoke flatly. This boy not only wanted to toy with the offer, but a guarantee for a top chair in Product Planning. Normally Cod would have walked off, canceled out the entire proposition—except that you couldn't do that. For Scott Quinnley's earnestness was inescapable. And Cod found himself bemused by the nature of this interview: he'd given Quinnley more time and certainly more emotion than the occasion deserved.

Why?

What had prevented him from nipping the talk off, ending it, instead of . . .

No. If he looked back, put together all of his talks with him, all he'd sensed and observed, he would realize what had kept his patience or tolerance from cracking; he would see that an underlying, invisible bond had come to draw him close to Scott, a bond which, though it had never been quite articulated, existed between them, and which, if he wanted to admit it, he did not fully have with his two

247]

sons-in-law—that central, pure, and serious concern for the automobile.

Of course, you could have said that every executive in this building held serious concern for the automobile. The difference, however, was that to many of his associates the producing of cars was essentially a medium through which they could gain greater self-aggrandizement; these same men might have dedicated their energies equally to the making of washing machines or cereals or missiles.

With Scott Quinnley it wasn't like that.

It was this quality, more than anything else, that Cod Smith wanted to buy. He said: "In the meantime, why don't you read over that material. We'll get back to you next week. Good-bye, Scott."

Not until Cod returned to his office after the Policy Committee meeting did he discover on the chair where Scott had been sitting the Green Paper.

Scott had forgotten it: an oversight? Absentmindedness? No. It showed more clearly than anything Scott had said, the real nature of his feelings. To Cod, however, this negligence was inexcusable, irresponsible.

Without doubt Scott was still valuable talent for the Bellgard team, but for the new dealership program he wouldn't be worth the price of a secondhand retread.

On the other hand, he had not failed to detect in Scott's eyes the spark of reaction at the prospect of salary and bonus which the offer held.

Even so, the negligence was inexcusable, an affront on his judgment and his time. Irritably he buzzed for one of his secretaries and dictated a note, a very brief note, to Scott.

And now the remainder of the day's agenda closed in on him:

The P.R. boys were already on hand. Before him now was the Vice-President of Public Relations, along with the junior executive who had ghost-written the speech which Cod would have to give at the convention of Eastern dealers shortly before the opening of the Automobile Show in New York.

As was the custom, the V.P., a former lawyer and hence not without a flair for drama and acting, would read the speech aloud to Cod.

"I'll run straight through it, Cod." The V.P. took the center of the floor, facing Cod's desk. "We'll just tune it in for sound."

As the man began to read aloud from the manuscript, the junior executive listened to his creation, eager and worrisome, his mouth moving now and then.

Cod leaned back in his chair.

"Gentlemen—" The V.P., an urbane man, had already taken the informal stance, the informal, folksy manner he felt appropriate for the audience of dealers. "Gentlemen, this is not going to be a speech." He looked up from the manuscript, pausing for the anticipated burst of cheers. "This Get-Together is too important for speechmaking. I just want to have a sort of personal talk with all of you, want to tell you something about the new policy we're commencing with our dealer family. After all, we *are* a family, and so we're not going to pull any punches." A quick confident smile over at Cod. "Well now, about that new dealership policy. What is it? Why are we adopting it? What are its objectives?"

The junior executive leaned forward as if he were about to offer a suggestion, but the vice-president hushed him with a discreet sidelong glance and proceeded with the presentation of the speech.

Cod listened attentively. He did not interrupt. No time for that now. When the two men had gone, he put the speech into his attaché case; he would take it home, work it over tonight; it was a good speech, professionally and adroitly done, the product of thorough research, studded impressively with pertinent figures and facts. But Cod would put his own hand to it, slugging out certain of the overfolksy touches or overrhetorical flourishes.

At five o'clock he left Administration, walking via the underground passage beneath the Esplanade, to the vast Styling Studio building. Elevator to the fourth floor. Down the corridor to Stage 3. Walking more rapidly, accelerating his pace as if to hurry the fulfillment of his expectations.

The two Company Security officers were stationed outside the doors. As soon as he entered, one of the men followed him in.

At once, as he moved into the white, soundproof, wedge-shaped room—a kind of laboratory-theatre—he felt that throb of nerves, that excitation which, no matter how often he participated in these showings of new or future models, always stirred inside him.

The sensation, his love of seeing, shaping, directing the early life of a new model, was heightened always by the awareness that he and his associates would be gambling their judgment against the odds of public taste. But more than that, today, there was the grim knowledge that for Bellgard the odds were grave and much greater.

He saw sitting in the tubed folding chairs the dozen officers, his friends and associates, the heads of different departments or divisions. They were waiting for him and as he greeted them, he only allowed his excitement, not his apprehensions, to show. His confidence had to be communicated to the others. The men here were so absorbed with their own departments, their own egos, that they had come to rely on Cod as the collective conscience of the company.

He moved among them now, but the smalltalk was limited. Even Cod wasn't quite up to it.

Tony Kerwin had placed a chair for him, and as he seated himself, he glanced to the platform-stage. It was like a signal: quiet seized the room.

"Anytime you're ready, sir," called Dean Stratler from the dais near the canvas-shrouded clay model of the new Bellstar, the prototype of the restyled, advanced version of the sports car which was to be shown at the Automobile Show this fall, but which would not be produced until the following spring. Behind Dean stood several technicians in their long white lab coats.

Cod nodded up at Dean.

"All right," Dean Stratler called to the guard at the rear of the room. "You can lock up now." Dean, his jacket off, the knot of the tie he'd designed—a rough strip of fabric of olive and black abstract figures—was loose at the collar of his white shirt. His gray-blond hair was unkempt today, the straight strands in disarray. These presentations, Cod knew, were a trial for Dean. Understandably. You had to please yourself and your department; and if you met the specifications of Engineering you might not meet the approval of Cost Control; if Distribution was pleased, Codman Smith or others might not be.

Cod folded his arms. Waited. He could feel the accelerated pulse in his wrist.

"As you all know"—Dean's preamble was underway—"we've had to crash-program these changes. . . ."

Crash program had indeed been the story; Cod could not forget the frenzy that had marked this project.

Six months ago the push began. Dean Stratler and his team started designing the body, shape and flow; Chief Body Engineer Fred Fox, along with Ernst Kamber, began experiments with plastic bases; and the chassis engineers bore down on new suspension.

Embryo chassis was drawn up for tentative weight, height, width.

[250

All sketches went into the mold shop, and there, directly from the drawing boards, they put together a chassis in wood and styro-foam, while Styling transformed its design into the first clay mockup, modeling it, working over the clay on its wooden lattice frame, pressing, scooping, smoothing the malleable substances into sloping hood, vents, side panels, roof, fender wells.

Nonstop until seventeen days ago for the first showing, at which time in this same room objections were raised and discussed. Now these changes, Dean said, had been completed.

"I think this ought to be it—and I hope we can wrap it up today." Dean's voice carried strain. "There's less than two months left before we have to have this baby on the floor of the New York show. I don't have to tell you how close that's going to cut us." There was a pause, and then he nodded to the white-coated men who then removed the canvas covering.

Imperceptibly Cod bent forward to study, reappraise the full-scale clay model of the coupe.

From pointed snout with concealed quadruple headlights, to the glass sloping rearward, the tapered fastback hiding the new independent suspension, the two-seater came close to thoroughbred (152 mph —with open exhausts) rating. The wheelbase was now reduced. The contoured shell, already checked out in wind-tunnel tests, was perforated by twin side vents and a nonfunctional hood vent. The doors extended into the roof panel for added entrance height—yes, a beauty. What a pity they couldn't have got it out for the fall line.

(Italian influence in the design? Without doubt. What Dean had seen, nosing around Turin two years ago, turned up on the drawing board this year. But what you didn't borrow from others, they would borrow from you.)

Cod's reaction was still positive. He still felt the full thrust of his pleasure as he studied the clay car, knowing it was more than an experimental job, that it represented their first G.T. sports car for the luxury market, knowing the reason it was being rushed to the New York show was to lure, titillate the public's appetite for Bellgard's products, knowing also that on the public's response, certain elements of this design would be abstracted for use in the standard passenger models of the future.

But slowly pleasure diminished, second and third thoughts now blunting the show. For his personal taste the Bellstar still seemed a fraction too tricky, a little too much—even though, in this case, he was yielding to Dean Stratler's department and to the most recent surveys of public opinion.

He had no choice. He had to move with the tide. He hoped the others would be proved right.

"First," Dean was saying, stepping to the rear of the car, "I want to call your attention to the changes here in the configuration of the fastback. And here"—he indicated the rear window—"we've enlarged the glass area to—"

"Dean!" Cod spoke up then. "It still looks a little pinched to me. Very handsome, but we might get kicks on the limited vision." He turned and glanced over at the Chief of Safety Engineering; the other officers swung around to give their attention to the man. (Even two years ago they might not have been so attentive, but Ned Gillman commanded new regard now; back in 1957 he had been deep in the doghouse. He had had safety belts installed in that year's models and almost every buyer had ripped them out; complaints came from all over the U. S. A. Today the safety belt was being pushed into law by most state legislatures: Gillman was now an honored prophet.) "How do we stand here, Ned?"

But before the man could answer, one of the telephones on the wall cabinet buzzed and the small red light at its base blinked. Dean Stratler shook his head: "That'll be your office, Cod."

Already Tony Kerwin was bringing the telephone over, the long white cord trailing behind him.

"Yes?" Cod said.

It was Fenley Roberts, president of Wolverine National Trust, the principal banking connection for Bellgard and for Cod's personal business. "Gather I'm getting you at a poor time, Cod," Fenley Roberts said.

"You are." But knowing that when Roberts called this long past banking hours, it signaled news crucial, disagreeable.

Cod rose and moved, holding the phone, to the side wall beyond earshot of the others.

"Sorry, Cod. But I got onto something I thought I'd better pass along."

"Yes?"

With that familiar show of solicitude, good manners, Tony Kerwin put down a chair for Cod.

"Today," Fenley Roberts was saying, "a sizable chunk of Bellgard stock was acquired by a party representing Ed Holtsbridge."

[252

"Holtsbridge?" Cod spoke very quietly. Tony was still standing by, lighting a cigarette now. It didn't matter, however, Tony was in the family.

"That's Holtsbridge Construction of Cleveland," Roberts said.

"Oh? Well good for him." Cod saw that the others in the room had resumed conversation.

"It turns out," Roberts said then, "that he's also the new money behind Kyssin Mufflers. Sam Kyssin—"

"Kyssin?" As he said it, he noticed Tony Kerwin's hasty or surprised glance.

"And I wondered if it might mean anything to you. Can you put any special light on this, Cod?"

"Don't know him," Cod said. "Can't make anything special out of that, except that somebody obviously believes Bellgard is going to be a good place for his investment dollar."

"Yes," Fenley Roberts replied affably enough. "Well, I wanted to check with you, Cod. After all, there hasn't been too much activity on the board, Bellgard-wise."

"Let's wait. The year's not over." When he hung up he said: "Tony, you ever hear of Holtsbridge Construction, Cleveland?"

"Vaguely yes," Tony said.

"He seems to be tied up with this Kyssin," Cod said. "Who is he exactly? I got a call this morning about some film of Kyssin's—"

"Oh, that?" Tony touched the mole on his cheek. Then: "Sam Kyssin is all right, just a vendor," he added almost with indifference. "One of those bright new boys who's going around town trying to open doors. He was pestering Engineering a while back. He's peddling a decent enough product, I understand, but he's got some idea he's selling platinum spacecraft instead of muffler systems. Why? He's not trying to get a foot in your door, is he?"

"No," Cod said, "nothing that simple. Can you have your office send me a memo on him?"

"Will do." Tony's helpful smile came as if he were indulging Cod in a minor whim, yet the shadow of a frown persisted on his face. "But I can't imagine anything about Kyssin to get yourself exercised about, Cod."

"Have your office run down the information," Cod said, and preserving a confident calm which didn't quite exist, he moved back to the group, back to the chair. "Sorry, Dean—"

253]

Dean seemed ruffled, nervous. "I don't want to rush anyone, but we *are* getting pushed for time."

The call from Fenley Roberts kept intruding on Cod's concentration. For all of Roberts' casualness, Cod detected the faint alarm or urgency beneath it. He rose again, pushing back the chair.

He saw that Ned Gillman, bald, small, spry, was up on the platform still studying the twin windows. "How does Safety feel about that, Ned?"

The engineer said: "We've been chewing on it, Cod."

"Can't we sweep that glass around more?" Cod said.

"Well," the Safety Engineer said, "we can check her out as she is now. But fuller vision would be advised." Tactfully he consulted the designer: "How about it, Dean?"

Reluctantly, Dean turned to one of the white-coated technicians. "Want to see how much we can lose there?"

The technician, using a metal straightedge, bent over the sloping twin windows. Deftly, with a sculptor's skill, he began to shave off thin margins of clay from the frame of the rear window.

"Hold it," Dean called. "I don't think we can dare widen the glass area any more than that. The entire design concept can get fouled. You need more balance if you want to keep the fastback contour right—"

The critique, the changes went on. By the time the window bugs were killed, by the time the asymmetric vent on the hood had undergone surgery, by the time all the final definitions had been agreed upon by the different departments, the meeting had gone an hour over scheduled length.

The clay model was once again sheathed with the canvas cover.

It was past eight that evening by the time Cod, weary, distracted, reached his house.

Ann was not there: out to dinner with Nodina.

It was just as well.

He dined with Mrs. Smith. He said nothing about the breakfast scene he'd had with Ann, he made no mention of the call from Fenley Roberts. He was glad to be dining alone with his wife. He discussed the forthcoming trip to New York. But immediately after dinner, he went into the library. He would work on that speech.

Yet, he couldn't settle down to the task. The voice of Fenley Roberts was still audible. He laid aside the manuscript. He telephoned the banker at his home in Kent Hills.

21: Tony Kerwin

IN New York, on this harassing autumn afternoon, coming upon Myra alone in the hotel lobby was a sudden gift; the first turn in his luck.

A tonic. A blessing.

The first time since the New York junket began three days ago that either he or she weren't flanked by family or friends or associates. He saw her now in the hazel wool suit, studying her reflection in the reflection of the bronze elevator door.

Alone.

No one around: his wife Phoebe in Kent Hills; no Dean Stratler; no sight of Ann Smith, married as of last week and undoubtedly bedded down with Ben Nodina around the corner at the Carlyle. None of the Bellgard troupe; and he'd left Scott Quinnley at the Seventh Avenue offices; and no Vince Eames breathing down his neck now, Vince daytiming around for business among the Automobile Show crowd, nighttiming it with some deluxe Call Girl.

But a pity time was pressing him now. That conference upstairs in Cod Smith's suite.

Christ, how he needed a respite. And here was Myra, alone, standing there, jiggling the lizard bag nervously, and looking at her, he was mindless of the tight ache in the core of his stomach.

Never been in a condition like this—nerves and muscles shot—it had begun back in the summer, specifically it had begun with that telephone call Cod Smith received during the styling conference. And no letup since. He'd tried in every way to bring himself out of it; this noon he'd even canceled a business appointment to have a steam bath, a rubdown. But that hadn't done it, of course.

As he crossed the marble floor of the lobby, however, his step grew more buoyant, the tightness around his jaw lessened—all the worry dogging him these past weeks since the Holtsbridge stock maneuver had first come to light.

No respite. It had been a small storm in the beginning, a private matter threatening him, encroaching on Bellgard. But since New York, the storm of rumor, gossip, had erupted into gale force. The vast auto industry could be so small. No way to escape it anymore. No way for him. Except to lose himself even for a while.

But to be with her. For half a night, half a day, even half an hour —now.

"Oh, Tony—" She turned in surprise as the elevator doors slid open. He followed her in. He pressed the button on the panel, shutting the doors.

Myra had stepped into the corner of the car, her glance severe, distraught.

"On my way to Cod's," he felt obliged to explain. "Where's Dean?"

Dean, she said, was still on the floor of the Automobile Show supervising technicians and workmen for the last details of the Bellgard display. Three hours before the auto show had its private prepublic opening.

He felt the pinch of envy: Dean Stratler was well out of it, his hands clean, all the rumor and gossip not touching him, at least not impinging on him in the way it was on Tony.

Twenty-ninth floor. He and Myra got off.

"For God sakes, Tony." She hastened her pace along the broad, thick, carmine carpeting of the hallway. "I'm late. I have to dress. I'm meeting Dean at eight—"

"It's not six-thirty yet."

She turned right, taking out her key from the handbag. "I'm sorry, Tony—we'll be seeing you later—"

But he followed her into the sitting room of the suite. Quiet in here, the ceilings noble, the gray walls paneled in palest gray.

"Please leave, for God sakes you can't stay here." She paused to confront him, the large, shadowed eyes staring at him in anxious appraisal. "I simply don't know how you can think of anything like this now, of all times—"

"I have to see you."

"You've heard something? Is there something new?" she said at once, uncomfortable, stiff, little trace of the Myra of those delicious enclosed afternoons.

"Why this freeze?" When she failed to answer, he said: "No, I

[256

haven't heard anything except the same drivel. Nothing to get exercised about."

"Well, *I'm* exercised about it." She glanced at her watch and hurried to open the double doors to the bedroom, dropping her lizard bag and gloves on the dressing table. Then in a compulsive movement she turned around: "You're sure you haven't heard anything?"

Was that all anyone could say? What have you heard? And if they didn't ask it, they said it with their eyes, there was that same unfailing, unspoken question in the look of almost every executive you ran into wherever you turned.

But in Myra, this lack of poise, this obsessive anxiety . . . Unless she knew more than he did. But that was unlikely.

"I still don't quite see the point of this sudden chill. We're not in Kent Hills, darling." Close to her and heedless of anything else, only Myra, only the heavy quiet, the muted, rich-textured stillness of the hotel room. . . .

Standing behind her, his hands rested tentatively on her shoulders, the fruit of his need, heavy against the thin woolen skirt.

"For God sakes, Tony, this is insane, you can't stay here, you know that." Yet, though she stirred, she did not leave.

"Myra." The sound escaped him, whispered and melodic.

She cut through: "If you've heard anything, please say what it is."

"I told you!" Exasperated, furious, shaken, he had to go on, dogging through as if he were with Phoebe: "It's nothing startling. I'm sick and tired of it, it's become a bore, do we have to talk about it now? Why now?"

"There isn't anything that—"

In desperate answer he slid his arms around and under her suit jacket, pausing only long enough to watch her face in the mirror, waiting for, anticipating, that look, familiar and rousing, when the cool eyes would grow opaque, heavy, glazed. It didn't happen. He lifted his hands to her bosom, and ah, there was the feel of the fullness beneath the blouse, and he bent down and kissed the hollow at the side of her throat, and stroked her breasts, but astounded by her still rigid unyielding stance, her failure to respond, so that abruptly he swung her around, curving her body into his: only then, without warning, feeling her mouth and the sudden thrust of her tongue.

All else closed out. Rediscovering, tasting her, he was beatifically isolated—and already projecting himself into that delicious, silent, palpitating chaos, the swift silent undressing and sinking down onto the bed with her.

So that he didn't even hear the sound from the sitting room. And when Myra broke away from him, he was breathless and uncomprehending.

"Yes—"

Alert now: Dean. Dean in there.

"Yes—?" Myra's voice. "No. Later please." She returned. "The chambermaid," she said, not looking at him. "Of all the—"

"Come here." Relief charged through him.

"Of course not." Her breathing was still erratic, her cheeks dull as clay beneath the makeup.

"Come here, Myra."

"You'll have to leave, Tony. I mean now."

He said: "We're in New York. You can get away, you can get over to the Berwyn, we can make it tomorrow, late in the afternoon." He retained an apartment at the Berwyn, on upper Park, it was one of those luxuries, tax-deductible, but indispensable to his way of life, even without the tax consideration. How many times had Myra been there in the past . . . ?

"I wouldn't think of it, you know that. Not this time. I'm late, Tony."

He sat down on the bed; he peered at her, puzzled, resentful. The moment, the rhythm had been lost. "What's happened to you?" He hurled the reproach at her. "Since when do you have—"

"Tony, for God sakes, will you leave? I only let you stay because I thought you had something to tell me."

Back to that. Why? Still on it. Why? Apprehension grew in him again.

Fighting it back, seeking a familiar, lighter diversion: "Certainly I have something to tell you."

She turned, attentive, anxious.

"You're meeting me at the Berwyn tomorrow," he said.

She caught it, she even smiled. "I—I don't see how I can—" There was equivocation in her tone, her eyes.

"I'm counting on it." He reached out from where he sat on the side of the bed and drew her against him. She stood there and for a short still interval he pressed his face against her stomach, wanting her so much and conscious again of her puzzlingly rigid resistance. Yet he did not move his face, letting himself savor her closeness, the texture of her skirt, as if he might muffle, bury, shut out his newly aroused fears, close out all else except the dark, rich sensations he'd always known with her.

Wanting it so, he lifted her skirt and the white slip, and now that satin warmth of her flat belly soothing to his mouth, his spirit, soothing and violent. He was sure he felt her with him at last.

She'd be lying before him again, arching that mossy need for the feel of him.

The fantasy of past overlapping present could not have been for more than a second or two, though he wasn't aware that it had really ended until the ruffling movement. She was tugging down her skirt and slip, stepping away.

She was standing irresolutely, nervously, near him but beyond reach, murmuring "Tony." And again, though more severely, gaining her composure: "Tony—"

Hung high, gritty rage worked in him. "Myra, what the hell is this?" His voice unclear, hoarse.

Nervous fingers touched the ruffled blouse of her suit. "Tony, I'm sorry—will you please leave? Quickly."

"Of course not." He stared at her. He could not relate her action to anything that had ever existed between them, he could not, or would not, bring himself to move. "What's wrong with you?" Then: "Or is it me?"

She said: "You know what it is."

"I only know this kind of bitchiness isn't what I expected from you. Since when—?"

"Oh God." She glanced around. "Give me a cigarette."

Mechanically he offered the gold case. Mechanically he got to his feet, clicked open his lighter.

She said: "Do you think I like this any more than you? I'm simply too damn worried."

What had hovered in the air, intangible, ominous, had abruptly congealed into something almost visible. He didn't want to talk about it. Yet he had to.

"You mean Dean?"

"I mean all of us."

From the way she said it, it was plain that she assumed he knew what she was talking about. He studied her more carefully. "All of us?" he repeated. "Since when does that have anything to do with you and me?"

"Isn't it obvious enough?"

"I'm afraid not."

"Oh Tony—" She was still regarding him with that same frowning concern. It was almost touching in a way, this concern for him. But why? Why? What was she holding back from him? And if she wasn't . . . no, she assumed he knew.

"Can't we forget it?" he said. A feeble shot in the dark.

"I can't," she answered at once. "I don't see how you can, not the way things are now, it's never been like this, not in all the years of the company's history."

Back to that. "Listen, Myra," he said brusquely, needing to say it for her as well as for himself, "you ought to know this industry by now. How can you let yourself get swamped with all this—"

"The talk everywhere is—"

"Of course there's talk now, rumor. Always happens like that when a company is getting pushed against the wall." He paused. "But memories are short. After the war they were all burying Ford, the wreath was hanging out in Dearborn. Until they came out from under. The same with Vanguard. And with Chrysler. All that mess with the stockholders. But now they're all doing business, and all is forgotten, forgiven. No different with Bellgard. If the new model year gets the kind of public response we expect—"

"If." Myra moved distractedly to the dressing table.

"We'll know within forty-eight hours. If the show gets off the ground, the uptrend begins."

She looked at him, a sudden look as if searching or hoping for a more significant meaning beneath his spurt of optimism. He said: "As a matter of fact, it doesn't even take the entire series. If people really go for the Bellstar, if it really looks like a real barn-burner—that in itself can kick off the uptrend we need." He knew his optimism was only partially justified, yet look what happened when G. M. at the last minute, at a single automobile show, slipped in that plain, classic little Corvair, and the sudden landslide of sales interest that followed.

Myra said: "You sound like Dean in his better moments. But even Dean admits how dangerous it is to put all your eggs—I mean, as far as I can figure out, that only shows our weakness, it only makes worse all the talk, much worse—"

"Myra," he broke in, almost thankful for what amounted to another chance to speak loudly against the current of his deepest anxiety. "Listen, Myra, you're being undermined by everything you hear. That's exactly what a guy like Holtsbridge wants. The more gossip, the more the stockholders get agitated, the quicker they'll go over to him to protect their interests. So he gets their votes. And this, plus his own big bundle, can give him a big enough voice to throw out the present management. . . ." He paused, not wanting to, but faltering for an instant. "That's just how he's playing it. Not that it'll work out like that. He's still a long way, a hell of a long way, from getting that many votes." Tony made the statement with what he hoped was swaggering assurance, at once presenting the dangers and dismissing them. But he was beyond believing it; he'd been saying it too often lately; nothing he could say could rid him of what lay hidden, threatening him; it wasn't talk, gossip; it wasn't the discontent Holtsbridge was stirring up.

It was himself, his own beloved hide.

Again he tried to resist the demon thoughts.

Again he reassured himself: his private arrangement with Vincent Eames was virtually impossible to uncover. Tight as a safety deposit box, wasn't it?

Who could dig into it?

No one.

Who could dig up those figures? Or know exactly how much? The money got there too indirectly.

He was covered. Vince was covered.

Yet . . . if it was . . .

Accepting gratuities for favors rendered was common practice between friends in business. Yes. Everyone knew that. But common practice or not—it was still Anthony James Kerwin.

His hide.

He went toward Myra. "All right, can we drop it now? I didn't come up here to analyze every move Holtsbridge makes." Lightly then: "Are you going to listen to me? The Old Master who knows whereof he speaks?"

"He does?" Myra said. "I wish Dean felt that good, but he doesn't. Holtsbridge is much too chummy with Sam Kyssin—or doesn't that trouble you either?"

"What?" Unwittingly he touched his cheek. "Oh, that." Quickly he brought his hand down, reached into his pocket for the cigarette case. "Why should it?" He put a shrug in his voice.

261]

But alarm rang in him like a siren's blast: Kyssin. Again.

"Don't think Dean hasn't been in a stew about it. And so am I. I begged him not to tell Father," Myra said.

Tony lit the cigarette. "I wouldn't worry about Cod."

She said: "It's you I'm worried about, Tony."

Her sudden, level tone froze through him.

"Not only you, all of us, for that matter," she said. "Why, Dean claims Sam Kyssin is the one who started all this talk about collusion —payoffs—" Something like a spasm accompanied these words, and she turned away to stare out the high windows. "And if that's what he's telling Holtsbridge—"

"Sam Kyssin—" Tony had to interrupt. "He's one of those peddlers, a really objectionable pest. He lost out to Vince Eames' bid, and he can't lay down, can't take it. He's out to sew up every muffler contract in the industry, but that's no way to do it. No one wants to do business with a man who goes crying around and—"

"Holtsbridge is apparently willing to listen to him," Myra stated in a dull voice.

"I doubt it," Tony asserted. Kyssin, the name kept ringing through him: remember how many times Kyssin came back, losing the contract, but coming back, showing that film glorifying his product, his exhaust systems and auxiliary products; getting Engineering all exercised to reconsider his bid. Still, after the turndown, still Kyssin came back, film in hand, graphs, figures, pressing his way into Bellgard: even Cod Smith had been invited to that second showing. . . . "I doubt it seriously," Tony said again, but more carefully now, going on, moving in the dark as if he knew his way, as if what Myra had inadvertently revealed was something he too had known. "And with all due credit to Dean, I'm afraid he's too quick to believe everything he hears—"

"Dean didn't say he believed it," Myra answered, "he only learned about it today, he only said that if it was true it could make—oh, I simply die when I think about it, and I can't stop thinking about it—I mean these things can *look* so bad—after all you *were* part of Vince's company, and he *does* make that same equipment for Bellgard and— it simply looks so—people are bound to see some kind of connection, once the idea has been aired, and—" She paused, with effort continued: "And I keep asking myself if—" She looked away again.

"If what?"

[262

"If all this has any real foundation." Another nervous hesitation. "And if it has, who could it possibly concern?"

"Are you asking *me* that?" Tony said.

"Well . . ." She turned to face him once more. "Yes, I suppose I am, Tony."

He could not avert her gaze. He knew from the quick steaming warmth suffusing his neck and cheeks that the nausea, the fear which had been working in him, had stained his face.

He detested her for confronting him directly with her miserable suspicion.

And all this concern for him. It was what? Concern for herself: if scandal touched him, it would touch her husband, her family. *Herself.*

Myra, with that long-cultivated image of herself: civic-minded matron, counselor of culture, ranging from Kent Hills to Detroit to Grosse Pointe to Bloomfield Hills—this image might end up how?

And look at her now: watching him, the violet-ringed eyes staring at him with that reproach, even loathing.

And as if unable to endure what she saw, she swung around and slumped down into the cane chair of the dressing table.

For the misery of another second, as he stood there, he tried to summon some word, some phrase, that might sting her into shame or denial of what she had implied.

Nothing came to him.

Except the need to leave. Yet he couldn't. He saw her raise her head now, peer at herself in the glass; then her gaze lifted to meet his, and she shut her eyes at once as if all she saw in his rigid features was death.

The room was so soundless. Like an empty stadium.

Without warning she stirred. "Tony—"

Immediately he stepped closer to her.

But his movement seemed to rouse her like a threat. She bent her head down, her shoulders stiffened. It was suddenly impossible for him to look at her. And this brutal silence between them seemed to intensify, coalesce, to contain in it all her recrimination, all his guilt.

Escape it.

He turned away. What was left? A futile hope that his now-purposeful and furious departure might come as some sort of final statement.

He reached the sitting room door. He opened it. How short a span of time existed between how he'd felt when he'd seen her in the lobby alone, when he'd craved her so, to this moment when all he wanted was to flee from her.

Down the wide corridor, along the scarlet carpet, past the blank gray doors, he strode his rapid sportsman's stride. The meeting in Cod Smith's suite, yes. But late. Yet, unlike all the other times when neither personal chaos nor emergency could slow him from his mission, he found his step faltering, the will to hurry draining from him, and this curious, meaningless looking-around, looking rightward and then leftward. . . .

Looking for what?

22: *Dean Stratler*

HE saw her there alone, the Bellstar, at last alone, mounted on the black velvet turntable, unmarred by any Bellgard personnel, no one around. The P.R. people were due back soon, but the others gone, and the workmen, technicians, gone; no one but a handful of porters moving sluggishly among the other displays, sweeping, vacuuming, feather dusting. Dean's jewel now free, outstanding amidst the standard passenger lines, outstanding, he liked to think, amidst all the competition of this automobile show, a jewel of a car shining white in the astral radiance of the vast exposition hall.

His baby.

His sugarplum.

Bellgard's chips on her. On him.

Outstanding, wasn't she? Living, real, almost as sleek as one of those oversleek airbrush renderings he used to make back at school.

His baby: he'd sired her. More or less. But for this one instant he felt too euphoric to let doubts niggle him, he was too high with hope now to even admit or recognize how much he had borrowed from other designers. (Where had the fine Italian hands of Pinin Farina, Bertone, Vignale, or the American flair of Mitchell, Arkus-Duntov, Bordinot, Engel, Exner, Loewy, or Teague left off and where had Dean Stratler begun?)

For there she was. Alone now, shining, dustless, the roof raked back, the flanks sculptured to slither through wind; mobile beauty, born out of paper and clay and sheet metal, born despite the niggling badgering of Engineering or Cost Control; now a living form which could give him this feeling, indescribable, a visual orgasm.

A motorcar for the armchair racer. Like himself.

He didn't need to drive her; he didn't need that seat-of-the-pants joy of the cockpit; what inspired a Cod Smith, a *Grand Prix* man like Sterling Moss or Phil Hill, was unnecessary to him.

265]

He lived by his eyes. This final private view was everything, the highest plateau of visual experience.

There weren't many moments like this in your life. If you looked back, what had there been? Nothing comparable. That first prize at the Academy of Industrial Art; or that design solution for the portable TV; or that first sketch which won the refrigerator account; or those early days as consultant to Bellgard, the starring success his '53 station wagon gained in the Bellgard line?

Rare times at best. Derived from objects.

Not people.

Except Myra. Admittedly. Going back how many years now to that first visual excitement, the first midnight of their honeymoon, checking into the island hotel, going for that short beach walk.

Dean shut his eyes. He shouldn't have let that come back to him— too many other pictures patched his memory, a collage of recollections of nights which had not quite risen to what they'd had in the beginning.

Not that he could blame Myra; it was his own doing, his own nature. You couldn't drain your energies at the plant and still know the kind of love he'd once known with her. He couldn't quite reach or match in performance what her beauty demanded.

He'd look at her sometimes and see a vignette, a portrait, but when he roused it to life, his lovemaking too often left him feeling inadequate; what he had, felt, hoped for, seen, was never what it had been before he touched her.

Errors, failures, you couldn't compensate or revise. No erasures, no revised sketches, no reshaping clay, no midyear modifications . . . He stirred. Footsteps nearing him. A respite.

"Dean—we're ready to tie this up if you are." The voice of Ralph Alsop reached him. He turned to see that the Public Relations man had returned, along with another of his men, and the two girls, the models, dead-eyed and golden-legged, their hair glittering like mica— these models who would alternate every hour, sitting, smiling, sparkling at the wheel of the Bellstar to lure the crowd away from the smiling, sparkling models who might be straddling the show cars of Ford, G. M., Chrysler, American, Studebaker.

"Sorry to keep you waiting, Dean. Been giving the girls some early spinach, but they're ready to do a job." Ralph Alsop's long, saturnine face now shone with that glorious expense-account glow which junkets like this always endowed him with. A bachelor, a car buff, a good man whose imperturbable good nature could only be ruffled if you called him "Ralphie."

Yet Alsop's eagerness was somehow unwelcome now. Dean hadn't had enough time to himself.

"Okay, Ralph," Dean said. He looked at the models. He would have preferred to show the Bellstar off without the human decoration, but of course he knew the girls were indispensable: one more minor badgering irritation in a designer's life. "Let's see if we can get the run-through over quickly." He noticed that the models were smoking; one of them, the tallest, seemed indifferent to the inch-long ash on her cigarette. "Ralph, would you tell the girls no smoking on the turntable?"

Alsop nodded. The rehearsal began. The first model, however, could not open the door of the Bellstar, and Dean hurried over, unduly furious at this inexcusable failure. Needed a drop of oil. He'd have it taken care of later.

After the girl was seated at the wheel, Dean took out his handkerchief and polished the chrome door handle which showed a cloudy smudge from the girl's moist hand.

By six o'clock the work was finished, and Alsop and his aide took the models off again.

Alone once more. Belatedly realizing the models had been so dead-headed they hadn't even commented on the car: the Bellstar might just as well have been a refrigerator or a brassiere, just another object to pose with.

Unsettled. Nerves.

He studied the car, but this time torment ruined his view, the old torment: what would people think of it? What would the reaction be? Unanswerable until tomorrow. The unpredictable swing of public opinion, taste; or the unpredictable success of some other designer's stroke.

Some other designer. That was stupid: after all, he knew what the competition was presenting, it was all around him. No surprises. He'd known for months. Despite all the hush-hush and security around styling studios, you always knew more or less where the other designers were going. Six hundred different suppliers making parts and units for all the companies; the tightest secrets were bound to leak out; men in the machine shops talked; bosses talked. And you always had your own people around picking up loose ends of information.

Not so easy with the foreign contingent, though the imports no

267]

longer niggled the industry; that ten percent inroad they'd once made was whittled down. Tide turned. Now if you went to Europe you'd see bits and pieces of Bellgard or Chevy or Ford improvised onto Simcas or Fiats.

The fact was he'd been so occupied with the home product he hadn't even taken time to examine the foreign exhibits this year; there was a reversal for you.

He smiled. He whistled, but the sound reverberated hollowly within the huge hall. Still it was good to be alone.

But no: someone else now. Again.

He saw Scott Quinnley hurrying through the entrance doors, Scott moving like a damn unstoppable arrow into the reserve of Dean's needed solitude.

What in hell was he doing here at this hour? Dean consulted the mighty globe of a clock which hung suspended from the dome of the hall. Five past six. Wouldn't you have thought Scott could have waited until nine tonight?

But no. It was to be expected. All that zest was natural enough. Like most new executives, Scott was gunning for all he could see and do. And he'd never seen the Bellstar, at least not as she stood now.

He waved to him, but Scott didn't seem to notice; he'd veered off course, stopped way over left near the fire exit at the Italian stand, lost from sight. Why the detour?

Dean lit a cigarette. Absurdly nervous, keyed up. Anxious, overanxious, for another opinion. Scott's would be head-on and knowledgeable, but . . . He stepped closer to the sandpot, fearful that a spray of ashes on the floor would muck up the clean tableau of the white Bellstar on the black turntable.

Absurd. (Myra liked to call him "Nastyneat"; he could never tolerate untidiness of any kind; at home or office he was always emptying his ashtrays; he could not even see a cushion on the couch out of place without righting it at once.) He stubbed out the cigarette and moved off impatiently, pacing around, moving away from the Bellgard stand, seeing Scott then: Scott messing around that Italian job, that cigar-snouted import, the RV 277. Even from here you could see that Scott was having trouble pulling himself away. He reminded you of Ed Cole of G. M., with that same zesty, getaway eagerness when Cole got near one of his special new babies.

And now Scott was hastening over, and when he reached him,

Dean, joking above his delicately honed nerves, said: "All that attention on Italy, that's disloyal. Didn't you sign the Bellgard oath of allegiance, Scott?"

Scott's smile seemed a little remote. "I was afraid I couldn't get in here at this hour. Wanted to case the cars before the traffic started later."

"That makes two of us," Dean said, turning then to regard the Bellstar, pride rising in his voice. "Well, how does she look to you? I'd say she doesn't have to be too bashful about meeting the competition—"

Scott squinted, studied the car on the turntable, his shoulders hunched forward, his hands in his pockets. "Yes," he said. "Looks very fine, and against that black velvet—"

Which, Dean figured reluctantly, was like having to give an opinion on a painting and saying how handsome the frame was.

Yet, so hungry was he for what he wanted to hear, even knowing that Scott was new and determinedly unbiased and knowledgeable, that he said: "Well, I grant you that does help show her off, though she looked awful pretty on the proving-ground track also."

Scott nodded. Could he take a peep at the engine?

Of course. Dean accompanied him to the car, released the hood, and Scott peered inside. After a while he said: "Haven't I seen this powerplant before—back last spring?"

"Why?"

"Almost sure I saw it, Dean. Except it was in one of the big standards. Parked in the driveway of the Smith's house. That first day I showed up, that first ball game day—"

Slowly it came back to Dean. "That's right, I think that's right. How in hell did you—" He peered at Scott.

And Scott recalled how he'd found the hood open and gone over surprised to see the beefed-up motor in the conventional chassis, and how the chauffeur had come along and quickly snapped the hood shut again.

"You've got the elephant's eye," Dean said. "We were testing it all over the place, though this is a modified version."

After a few minutes, Scott said: "Have you had much of a peep at that RV 277?" His gaze had drifted back toward the Italian stand.

"To tell you the truth," Dean said, "this is the first free time I've had to myself since we got to New York."

269]

Scott rubbed his chin. "The way they kept the height down on that rear end, that fastback contour is almost perfect, doesn't sit so high-assed off the ground."

Dean frowned, inadvertently glancing back in the direction of the other car. How could Scott have touched a sore spot right off? "Well, personally, I prefer that extra height we have here. Sassier."

When Scott did not answer at once, Dean could not restrain his irritation: "Of course you have to remember that I—we were handicapped by our package limitations. To crash-program this through we finally had to use one of the basic Bellgard frames, no way to cut down the height."

"Yes. That's true." Scott began to circle the Bellstar once more.

Actually, Dean thought now, it didn't look that bad, or was it that Scott's tallness gave the sports car a nice extra dimension of horizonality, even at the rear where the fastback might have been humped too high?

Yet irritation kept needling him. Even though Scott must have understood the engineering problems involved, there he was quick to trigger off a critique, forgetting what a designer had to put up with, forgetting a stylist had to work with only one hand, the other being tied behind him, roped by all the other departments, having to meet a thousand and one specifications: weight, wheelbase, height, seating, and always tooling and dies and budget-beating, doubling up with standard parts and units.

But what the hell choice had Dean had? Having to start with that basic frame to beat time?

True, the committee had green-lighted the program, yet that same committee, with the possible exception of Cod Smith, would be quick enough to back down if the critical heat was on, if the public didn't buy it.

Nonetheless, Scott had already salted down the sore spot, singled out what Dean himself had originally hoped to avert: that overhigh tail. All that damn committee niggling over the split rear window, vision safety . . . getting sidetracked with the shape of leaves when the tree trunk was out of line. . . .

But who knew?

And you had to stand back of what you did.

And the Bellstar did have a sassy contour. In fact it was Tony Kerwin, at that last private showing, who said the high fastback might mean distinction, a sort of status mark, like the whine of the first Chrysler turbine.

Suddenly Dean found himself wondering about the Italian job, that 277 GT coupe which had evidently solved all the problems in a single package.

"Hey, Scott—" He motioned to him. "Let's go have a look at that baby."

And as Scott accompanied him to the Italian stand, he felt a rush of gratitude and warmth for him. If he hadn't come in, if he hadn't shot that particular bolt of interest in the 277, Dean might have lost an opportunity.

Compulsively he put his arm around Scott's shoulder. "Between us," he said after they'd reached the foreign car, "I had the Bellstar laid out close to this 277—in the early stages. But you know what can happen."

Yes. Scott said he knew.

And already Scott had stepped away: he stooped down to peer beneath the Italian car.

Dean felt draining from him that last vestige of euphoria. He was already sliding down from that lofty realm.

Doubts. Self-recriminations. Again. A hundred hates and regrets.

And the Bellstar had been his most daring job. He'd always ridden through too safely on the conservative edge. This time he'd tried, within the limitations, to go all out. Far out.

Treacherous. Nothing so treacherous in a designer's life. It could be death if you were too soon. Or too late.

You had to come in at just that split crack of time, you had to sense, anticipate where the wind would blow from.

Slowly he shook his attention back to the 277: Scott was flat on his belly now beneath the tail assemblage.

"For one thing"—Scott finally eased himself up from the floor; there was a stippling of lint on his gray suit—this is a perimeter frame, transaxle too. How they got that low continuity of line, don't you imagine?"

"Could be." Then: "You better brush your suit off, it's all linty," Dean said, and already seeing other elements in the Italian design he hadn't noticed before. "They really snuck this one in, didn't they? I knew it was in the works but I never expected to see it on the floor here."

271]

Absently Scott began to brush off his suit. Dean's mind raced. The 277 was still not near production. Bellgard could beat it, or at least meet it by the time of the midyear model change. Much here he would like to incorporate if he could make modifications on the Bellstar.

He had to get it down. Now.

From his pocket he drew forth the show catalogue: not even a photographed of the 277, it had come in too late. Deliberately. But he could get it down, get it measured up.

Sketch it, yes. But that would take too much time, no time for drafting board rush. . . .

Get Scott out of here. Imperative to measure this job down to the last hairline of an inch, get the data he needed.

"We'd better take off, Scott," he said. "It ill becomes us to be snooping around. Can I buy you a drink?"

"What?" Scott seemed bemused.

"Almost six-thirty. Let's go."

"Already?" Scott said. "Thanks. A drink I could use, but I'm meeting Ann and Ben. I'm supposed to be at the Carlyle as of fifteen minutes ago."

Again his arm was around Scott's shoulder. He walked him toward the entrance way. The hasty good-bye was on his lips when Scott slowed down, stopped. He was late but he couldn't bypass the British stand; why didn't they go over for a peep?

And so for a while he and Scott inspected the English products. But Dean was not with it, not now, not with that 277 on his mind, and soon Scott was wandering ahead among the always familiar array of "Gentlemen's" motor cars, the Bentleys and the Rolls and the Jags and the lovely little Lotus.

Dean coughed; he checked his watch; the gesture failed to lure Scott back, and as he watched him, saw him swinging with all that verve, it brought back rueful recollections of his own first year with Bellgard. He supposed Scott would never have gone with the company if Quinnley Corners hadn't turned up on the edge of bankruptcy, or so the word was.

"Scott," he called finally, "afraid I'll have to be leaving."

There was the French stand to be seen, Scott said, but well, that would have to wait until later tonight, and so Dean got underway once more, this time they made it to the foyer, and he said good-bye, excused himself to go to the Men's Room.

Immediately then he returned alone to the Italian stand.

[272

Of course the 277 was locked. None of the crew around.

He'd have to get hold of the key. Somehow. He couldn't do that himself, that was out of the question. Keys were kept in the Auto Show offices.

He'd send one of Ralph Alsop's boys in there. But later. Around midnight, after the opening ceremonies, after the trade had gone. Late. When only a few porters would be left.

But he'd get that key, have the 277 calibrated thoroughly, slip it into the studio works, ready for presentation to Engineering. The changes could be made by midyear. If he got the green light, he'd be ready. . . .

Suddenly Dean, with the revised image of the Bellstar bright and taunting before him, decided he could no longer remain here alone: he couldn't bear the comparison between the two cars.

He'd clear out now. Get back to the hotel. Myra was there now. Dressing. They'd have a drink together.

In the taxi, hotel-bound, he gave himself to the needed, temporary distraction: see Myra, be with her in their suite, a stiff drink. Too bad, the thought crept up on him, too bad he'd stirred her up with all that talk he'd heard today, shook her in a way that had made him uncomfortable. At a time like this, now, with the rest of the industry gloating complacently, the Bellstar itself would be clouded by it. His baby born at a time like this, victim of what was a cold-war preliminary to a hot proxy fight. . . .

Into the hotel, the elevator. Scrutinizing his face in the mirror. He palmed down his hair: seemed more gray there, but blending in with the blond, not too noticeable. He tilted his head. Better this way. He even smiled. Was he acquiring Myra's vanity? Marriage could do that. You took on qualities, traits from each other without realizing it.

Twenty-ninth floor and almost at once he saw the man turn the corner from the other hall, and he could have sworn it was Tony Kerwin, except that the man did not walk like Tony, there wasn't that swaggering, athletic stride. . . .

But it was Tony. Dean called out to him. Puzzling the way he moved, sluggishly, as if he was swacked.

"Tony—" He reached him.

Kerwin stopped, his gaze dilated, unsteady. A secret pleasure touched Dean. You never saw Tony looking or acting like this, not Tony Kerwin with that constitution of his, a master at playing so many ends against so many middles. No matter how tough Tony's days were, he always seemed to develop power as he went along, he could function at the plant, he could ride, shoot, sail, golf and still get extra mileage late into a party night.

And looking, acting like this now, as if all the charges being shot at Bellgard top management were riding on his back. Was it possible that Tony had overplayed himself this one time? If the talk was true —and that was always open to question—but if it was true, who was involved?

Yet hard to believe or imagine Tony, with his boundless ambition, stupid enough to ruin himself in that kind of involvement.

That was the flaw. Those charges Holtsbridge's group were circulating were general enough to be unsettling, damaging, but they were not pinpointed, not yet. . . .

No tears if Tony got pinpointed, washed up. Unless that washed up the rest of the team, Dean included.

Which is what Myra saw in it.

"What are you doing in these precincts, Tony?" He presented that façade of amiability he and Kerwin always maintained toward each other.

"Hmm? Oh—" Tony seemed to have to focus his attention. "Oh, on my way to Cod's. Got in the wrong hall." He looked around. "Got lost. See you, Dean."

Puzzled, disconcerted, Dean moved on to his suite.

Myra seemed startled when he walked into the bedroom. She was undressed, sitting on the side of the bed, taking off her stockings. "For God sakes, Dean, you scared me." Her hand remained immobile on the clasp of the garter belt. "I was just going to shower. Aren't you early?"

"I decided we ought to have a drink before the fireworks."

"Oh—" She peeled off her stockings.

The sight of her came as a lovely balm to his nerves. "Ran into Tony out there in the hall."

"Tony?" she said.

"Yes," he said. He started toward her then. She'd taken her hair down, the blond strands hung flat and glossy and long, and he wanted to kiss her.

"Oh, wasn't that stupid—" Myra had already turned; she rose and moved to the bathroom door, but speaking so rapidly; "Wouldn't you think he'd take his troubles elsewhere? But not at all, he didn't know what to do with himself and so he came galloping in here. I had a

[274

hideous time trying to get rid of him, finally chased him out. I really think he—"

"He certainly didn't seem like himself," Dean said and stopped. It was curious, wasn't it, that Tony hadn't mentioned anything about having been in here? You would have thought he'd have said something about it . . . no, come to think of it, all he said was that he'd got himself lost, nothing else. Dean removed his jacket and placed it fastidiously over the back of the chair. "What did he have to say, baby?"

"Oh, just the— Look Dean, I'll only be a minute, I just want to shower." She opened the bathroom door.

"I'll call down for some drinks." Going to the telephone: "Tony certainly wasn't himself, couldn't miss that." He glanced back at Myra. "What happened, did he just barge in on you while you were—"

"Oh, of course not. I mean fortunately not. I'll be right out, Dean. I really want to talk to you about him. I'm really worried now. I'll be right out, darling—"

The door closed. Dean started for the telephone.

The door opened again and he turned to see her, one arm held somewhat demurely across her breasts. "Oh, I simply can't tell you how pleased I am you got back early." Her eyes held a benign tenderness.

"How long was he here?" Dean asked.

"Who? You mean Tony?"

"Yes."

"Oh—it seemed eternal—you talked to him, didn't you say you just ran into him? That's what I've got to discuss with you. We won't have a chance later. I won't be a minute, darling."

He nodded, moved back to the telephone. His reflexes seemed slow; he couldn't even order the drinks with simple coherence; he had to call down again: not two Scotches—one martini and one Scotch.

Nerves.

Pre-show jitters.

And that Italian 277.

Soon as he saw Alsop he'd fill him in, have him arrange to borrow or buy that key; no resting until the Italian car was thoroughly measured, set down.

Pacing around the bedroom, he straightened a chair, edging it back to its proper place; he lifted the ashtray from the bedtable, but saw that it was empty; slightly smudged but empty.

275]

From the bathroom came the hiss of the shower.

Curious the way Tony had been: that fugitive, almost desperate way he'd acted.

And not even mentioning he'd been in here.

Dean loosened his hand-blocked tie; carefully he untied the knot.

Ridiculous, an idea like that. Absurd.

Impossible.

What had Myra said? She'd had to chase him out. That figured. There'd never been any love lost between those two.

Ridiculous. Nerves niggling him like this.

After all, Tony Kerwin was no different from himself tonight.

All of us too nerved up.

The sibilant sounds from the shower had ceased. He went to the bathroom door: "Hurry it up, Myra."

23: Scott Quinnley

THEY had to hurry from the banquet at the Waldorf that night, Ann and Scott, along with two Bellgard executives. In a company car they started on the last lap for the private opening of the Automobile Show. But by the time the industry's convoy of cars, taxis and company limousines neared 57th Street, the procession clotted up bumper to bumper.

Scott nudged her: "Why don't we walk the rest of the way?"

"Walk? Don't you know that's a dirty word in this industry?" But her hand was on the door. "Yes, let's."

"Count us out, Scott, we'll do our fifty-mile stint at the Show," said the more portly of the two tuxedo-clad men, a group vice-president, Chester Ormond.

As soon as they gained the sidewalk and began walking westward up 57th Street, Ann said: "God, it's good to get some air."

"Yes. Foul as it is." Fumes from the long line of cars hung like a gray and lethal mist in the autumn night.

"Hey, not so fast." Ann lifted her black evening coat, which trailed the pavement.

"Sorry," Scott said. "I feel tight as a jack-in-the-box. I could walk all night."

"Me too," she said. "I thought you held up very well considering. Better than I did."

"You don't feel these things until afterward." He massaged his jaw and the corners of his eyes, conscious only now of the strain of the evening. Sitting immobile at that large round table with Ann and her parents and the others, he'd had to sweat out his altered status. Having been a friend of the family he had become a company official. In the conversation between and after the "inspirational" speeches by industry leaders, he had been on display, a new specimen to examine. Each word or idea uttered—and he had been sufficiently nervous to utter a number of unsolicited ideas—had been covertly appraised.

Ann said: "Did you blame me tonight for getting Ben off the hook?"

"No, you did right, Junior."

"But it *was* true, he did have that last-minute meeting with the Greek government people and it would have been wicked to let him cancel it. For what?" She turned slightly against the current of wind. "My dear sister Myra is reveling in it, did you notice? And my father isn't even *trying* to be civil to him any more. But Ben's been an absolute saint about it and—oh, I suppose none of this means anything —what it is, what it's always been, is that my father would never believe any man was quite good enough for me—short of Abraham Lincoln, the three Ford boys or Dr. Schweitzer."

"I'll probably be the same way about Susan someday," he said.

"Probably." Then: "I'm sorry to be unloading all this on you. It's just that—" She stopped, tilted her head downward. "Oh, this damn wind." She gave him her handbag and began to refasten the velvet band which circled the high crown of her hair, and as he watched her, he became more aware of the stain the evening had left on her spirit. Once she looked up at him, and there was a dim smile: "Oh, I wish it was tomorrow and I was to hell out of here on that ship." She took her handbag again and they moved toward Fifth Avenue. "Anyway, I'm glad Ben missed the whole dreary bit."

"You could have missed it too," he said. "I remember at the Auto Show in Paris— Is it five years now? Yes—you couldn't have cared less."

"Oh, I know, and I still don't," Ann said. "I've always wriggled out of these affairs, at least the last two. But Father keeps trying to get me to come. He likes me at the table among those present—like a kind of mascot. But this time I thought it wouldn't kill me to show up, I could be a mascot for once. Tonight was different, after all. I mean with my leaving tomorrow and—well, it's no secret the company is in trouble, and I just felt it's sort of dirty pool ducking out on him now of all times." She paused and peered distractedly into Tiffany's window. "Oh, to hell with it. Nobody wins, do they?"

"Sure they do," he said. "But—usually it's the wrong people. Come on—" The light had changed and they crossed the Avenue.

"I'm glad you're here at least," she said.

"What's left of me."

"We must promise to write once in a while," she said.

"Yes."

[278

"We probably won't though." She held on to his arm more firmly. "I'm lousy about writing and you'll probably be up to your neck in work—" An abrupt pause and she looked up at him.

"What is it?"

"Nothing," she said. "I'm going to miss your ugly craggy face. A couple times tonight I thought who would have thought I'd ever see you all tuxed up at a Bellgard table at an A.A.M.A. *soirée,* a model executive complete with flecks of premature gray and—"

"Cut it out, Junior."

"Okay." Silence. "But I'd have been lost without you *quand même.*"

"I don't know what help I was," he said. "I think I was very busy putting on my brightest face."

"You needn't have."

"But I did. I'm a corporation man almost overnight." Yet the feeling, the change, was obviously far more difficult for Scott to adjust to than it might have been for most of his friends or contemporaries. The men he'd gone to school with, his own generation, had been neatly swept up into the grinders of big companies, had had their lives laid out for them, their housing problems, medical problems, social life, even marriages—all these had been stamped out, processed like tape feeding into a computer.

But Scott had shied off, taken off alone, not only to ward off pressures of an ambitious mother and a disappointed and hostile father, but because he'd developed such an allergy to group life of any kind, to the orders or encroachment of others. He'd preferred to lose or find himself in competitive racing, and later in the magazine. Even Quinnley Corners, rough or corrupting as it might have been, was still a far cry from the new role as part of Tony Kerwin's organization.

"Scott—"

"What?"

"I've never asked you this because you made it plain it was none of my business."

He looked at her. "You're not going to ask me why I joined the company, are you? Because I'm in no mood for funny-funnies."

"What I mean," she said, "is not why you joined the company—but why Bellgard? I mean you must have known you weren't getting on a gravy train or a bandwagon."

"I had an inkling."

"I mean really. Why? What was it?"

"Long story."

"What was it though?" Ann said. "Challenge? Crusade? All that good old jazz?"

"Money," he said.

"Oh, I've got to buss you for that." She stopped. "I've got to." She pressed her arms around his neck and kissed him. Drawing away then: "All right, Scott. Money. But what else? How could you make the break? From your father, I mean? The last thing you told me was you were going to quit as soon as you could and go back to New York."

"I'm back in New York," he said.

"Seriously, Scott."

He told her some of it, though not all, as they walked toward Columbus Circle. He told her how it had been, the turn of events which had led him away from and then back to Bellgard; and he found himself working up a head of steam no less intense than he'd known at the time, less than six weeks ago.

The doldrums lay upon Quinnley Corners during that period preceding the new season, the new line. Several of the sales crew were on vacation. On that day Red had slept late. Scott had noticed that he'd taken to sleeping longer in the mornings, dozing more often in the afternoons—and the shop was Scott's to run.

Which was as bad as it was good. Bad because time was scratching at him, reminding him of his age (he had just turned thirty-three). Good because Red began staying away from him more, trusting him more, thus giving himself a better chance to make a sound recovery and giving Scott sounder hope of leaving.

Or so Scott was led to believe.

So that Scott did not tell him about the offer he'd had from Bellgard, not even that he had, in effect, turned it down. It was no time to unsettle him, particularly with the new season not yet begun and the old season dying without a final gasp of sales.

When Red had asked why Codman Smith had wanted to see him, Scott lied, telling him it was in connection with Bellgard's new interest in racing as a publicity ploy for creating an image of speed and durability.

"Oh. That's all? Thought it might be something else," Red had said in a curious, even disappointed way.

"No. That's all it was, Red."

[280

To his desk at Quinnley Corners the next morning there came the rather curt note from Cod Smith, along with the Green Paper on Dealership Reorganization—that same document which Scott had forgetfully but significantly left behind at his office. He put the document aside and finished up the day's correspondence.

Yet, Cod Smith's letter and the Green Paper kept imposing their existence upon him—a taunting distraction, not a lure, but that same scratching reminder of time slipping and opportunities unexplored.

Once, to escape his thoughts, he hurried out of the office to see if there might be any action in the showroom. But of course the same nine tail-of-the-year Bellgards still stood there, unattended and forlorn as gaudy flowers on a grave many days after the mourners have gone.

When he returned to his desk he stuffed the Bellgard envelope into a bottom drawer.

Fini.

Yet, as it sometimes happens, it was a negative deed that pushed Scott into a positive one. He picked up the telephone and called Steve Sturges. "Steve, is that meeting still on?"

"Yes. Tomorrow night. Why?"

"Is it too late to count me in?"

"Up to you, Scott, I wouldn't want you to rush into this too impulsively," Sturges answered rather huffily, though it was justified since Scott had been circling his way around the project without ever committing himself. It was, as Red would have said, time to get off the pot.

"I'll be there," Scott said.

The next evening, along with Phil Rothe and Jack Winters, he attended the meeting at Sturges' house. The original group had grown. Sturges no longer conducted the session; the fund-raising program was presided over by his lawyer. Nine other men were present, all young—two engineers and a chemist, five businessmen and Sam Kyssin of Kyssin Parts, whose interest in the young company encouraged Scott as much as anything else. By midnight when the meeting drew to its end, Scott had pledged twenty thousand dollars (partly his own capital, mostly back salaries he'd let accrue at Quinnley Corners) as his share of good faith and small financial interest in the organization being formed to develop, produce and ultimately market the electrochemical engine Sturges had been working on for the past two years.

On paper and in their heads the prospects were nothing less than glorious. But prospects they were since all of them were defectors from the traditional gas-piston engine and the more recent turbine.

For Scott, Phil Rothe, and most of the others, this would have to be a between-and-after-hours project in the beginning. And when they left the meeting Scott was swinging—exalted and maybe only a little scared. He'd broken the negative rhythm of his life, had done it of his own choosing. And he felt easier about having declined Cod Smith's generous offer.

On the following morning at Quinnley Corners there arrived the first of two unwelcome figures, the first being none other than that bull-hided master of gall, Halister McGregor, the Regional Sales Manager of Bellgard. McGregor, looking not unlike a prosperous ice cream vendor in his white suit and white tie, and carrying a bulging briefcase, strode into the office.

"Where is your dear dad, Scott? Third time in a month I've come here and no Red Quinnley to be seen, except the last time when I found him snoozing in his chair. Since when is he entitled to the easy life? If he's out of commission again, you'd better tell me. Or am I to understand you are definitely Number One boy now? Used to come in here, no matter if it's the A.M. or the P.M. and Red was always quick with a cigar or a wee drop of Chivas Regal. What's now? No, don't get up, relax, my boy. I was on my way to Three Forks, Michigan, and I thought I'd better look in again, because I've got some mighty grand future news, mighty grand."

"Oh?"

"That's right. And I'll come right to the point, Scott. The plant is going to shave off your quota on the first shipment. Looks like there might just not be enough product to go around."

"How come?" Scott waited, already suspicious.

"No idea. They are playing it very close to the vest. You'll have to discourage advance orders and concentrate on the rest of the line. By the way, you received your shipment of records?"

"Records? Oh. Yes." The shipment of the specially recorded disks *The Sounds of the Bellstar* had come last week, along with the invoice: as a lucky Bellgard dealer Quinnley Corners was entitled to the wholesale price plus 20 percent.

"Yes, we got them."

"Good. You play it yet?"

"I heard it some time ago."

[282

"Just checking." But McGregor's leathery, deeply suntanned face showed the first creases of constraint; he sat down now by Scott's desk and crossed his legs. A nervous forefinger played along the sharp edge of his white trouser.

"What's the trouble, Mac?" Scott asked.

"Trouble? Now that's a word never on this soul's tongue," he answered.

"About the quota on the Bellstar."

"Oh that?" McGregor laughed. "Shows you what a simple soul I am, had the idea this would be mighty good news here at the Corners and you call it trouble. Why, I went out of my way, Scott, to juggle distribution just to take the heat off you and Red next season. Is that the thanks I'm getting? Trouble? I'm playing your side of the street, my boy."

"Since when?"

"Scott, you're the one raised all the stink about the quota, aren't you? Well, I thought I was doing you a favor, is all. Let's face it, the Corners just isn't up on that plateau anymore— Oh, I'm sure the new season is going to be a banner yield, but as of now, I wanted to cooperate with you, give you a breather." He paused. "That's why I'm letting the goodies fall to the dealerships who keep their doors open on delivery dates."

"I see." Scott let the arrow stick in its mark. "All right. Thanks. I appreciate it. Except that since we do need a real boost why not give us the chance?" He felt the spurt of sudden anger. "If the betting money is all on the Bellstar now, why cut us down? Why, Mac? And then load us up with the dogs?"

"Dogs? Scott, is that fair? Why, you'll love those new beauties, you'll love 'em. But if you want to talk about dogs, then why don't you unload that kennelful you got in the warehouse and out front? Let's not defame the new line so soon." Without the slightest transition in tone, he went on: "Scott, have you given any thought to cutbacks?"

"Cutbacks?"

"Payroll. For example."

"Yes," Scott said. "Why?"

"Well," McGregor said, "payroll is only part of it, but I think we can help you all around." From his briefcase he brought forth a booklet. "Like you to look this over, Scott. Dynamic Budgeting, we call it, and it's just what the good doctor ordered. Of course I know

283]

you're already acquainted with the Green Paper on Dealership Reorganization—" He waited a moment so that Scott might savor the fact that his meeting with Cod Smith was not a classified secret. "Well, my boy, no use any of us looking the other way now, is there? You can tell your dear dad, or not tell him, but the horseshit days are over. In other words, and they're sad words for me to say, but you catch 'em the way we throw 'em, otherwise we're going to have to call the game off on account of darkness, if you savvy me."

"No, you're too subtle, Mac," Scott answered.

He laughed. "Joke over? Okay. Now my boy, strictly sub rosa, I know you're in a spot where maybe you can act, get your dear dad off the shitlist. Who knows, maybe soon you might be on the other side of the fence, huh?"

"I don't know what you've heard," Scott said, "But this is still my address. So let's not confuse the issues again. What I want to know is what's behind this latest pushing around? Now listen, Mac, listen to this: either we get our fair allotment of Bellstars or we don't take on the other—"

"Am I hearing you right?" he interrupted. "Is this the same fighting lad who once spit in the factory's face? You mean to tell me you actually crave your allotment of Bellstars? Can't believe it. That's not the scrappy quarterback of yore. Oh well, everyday has its surprises." He paused. "Good enough. I'll pass on the message, and who knows, we might still let you get your full share of the goodies. As soon as Gil Alberts gives us the nod."

"Gil who?"

"Alberts. Auditing Department. One of the best C.P.A.'s in the business." McGregor swung his arm around and consulted his watch. "He's late."

"Now wait a minute, Mac, you know goddam well we have our own outside accountant, and we have our own bookkeeper right here. Now what the hell is this?"

"Easy there, boy, easy. I forgot to tell you that this is a free service. Gratis. Part of the new program."

It reached Scott then. He recalled that section of the Green Paper which outlined the new auditing service Bellgard would use in the cases of dealerships of questionable risk. He looked at McGregor. "Well, I suppose I ought to jump at this, something free from the factory. Leaves me overwhelmed, Mac. But I doubt if Red will call in

[284

his thanks. He doesn't like any outside fingers in his pie. You know that. And as for me, this is one time when I—"

"I love Red." McGregor spoke with something curiously akin to honest emotion. "Love him. And you tell him that Halister McGregor will not let him down, as long as he—"

The buzzer of the intercom sounded. "Yes?"

"Mr. Alberts is here."

"Alberts?"

"Ah—that's Gil." McGregor was already on his feet, going to the door.

"Send him in, Mrs. Bowsley," Scott said.

But McGregor had flung open the door. "Come in, Gilberto, come in. This is young Quinnley, a mighty fine boy, not one of those old farts doesn't speak your language. Well, I'll leave you. Scott, a pleasure as always. You're a gentleman. And you give your dear dad a hug and a kiss from one of his greatest admirers."

In the wake of his departure Halister McGregor left Scott feeling outright panic, and already his exaltation of the previous night seemed wild and unreal.

"Sorry about this." Alberts' voice.

Alberts offered him a reticent smile as if in condolence. He was a youngish bespectacled man, an Eastener without doubt, in striking contrast to the Chautauqua personality of McGregor. He placed his attaché case on the chair. "If you'll bear with me," he said, "I'll try to be out of your hair in a couple of days. I'd like to see Mr. Waterman, if I could—"

Three days afterward, Gil Alberts telephoned and asked if they could have lunch. It would be better if they didn't meet at one of the hangouts of the trade, he said. At one o'clock Scott met him at the River Chop House, a restaurant patronized mostly by Downtown businessmen. In one of the dimly lighted oaken booths, Alberts removed his spectacles and wiped them. "This is not the happiest situation we have to discuss." He motioned for the waiter, ordered drinks and the lunch: oysters, Mixed Grill and coffee. "If you'd prefer we can discuss it later, but there is a great deal of—"

"Let's get it over with. The sooner the better."

"May I ask," Alberts said then, "exactly how familiar you are with the situation as it stands now?"

"As of now, I don't know how close I am. Waterman has briefed me from time to time, but yesterday when I tried to pin him down I didn't get much except what I already knew, that we're in on the deep side. Mainly I know it's our floor-planning system, and I tried to stop that months ago, but my father insists on continuing it, and Waterman assured me—" Scott stopped. The accountant's pale blue eyes, behind the thick lenses, had taken on a pained aspect. Scott drained off most of his martini.

"I'll just—well, this puts me in a disagreeable spot. I don't like to betray confidences—yet I don't see how I can be honest about this without doing just that."

"I understand," Scott said. "Obviously there's something I don't know."

"I'm afraid there are several things you don't know." Alberts waited until the waiter had put down their platters of oysters. He lifted his oyster fork but did not eat. "Chiefly what I'm afraid this is, is that Mr. Waterman is trying to be loyal to your father, too loyal. The result is that he's had to keep you in the dark." A pause as he speared his first oyster. "Now there's nothing wrong with floor-planning your cars, many dealers do just that—it's a perfectly valid system, you get your quota, your fleet delivery from the factory, and the banks pay the cash to cover you. But when Quinnley Corners, in its turn, fails to meet its obligation to the banks—"

"I know we're behind, but—"

"Mr. Quinnley, you're more than behind, you're swamped. Not only are you in default to the banks for the cash they've laid out for you, but there's the interest charge, that five-percent tab for each car. Now that's manageable enough if you move your inventory, but if you don't, the five percent keeps right on going for each unsold car." He put down his oyster fork. From his breast pocket he produced a sheaf of auditing papers. He detached one of the sheets and handed it to Scott. "I'm giving you the worst of it first," he said. "Total of cash owed, plus accumulated interest charges. This is the indebtedness outstanding as of the present time, that is, as of yesterday evening."

At first Scott was certain there must be some kind of error, there had to be. The indebtedness—over two hundred thousand dollars—could not possibly have been accurate.

It was, of course.

"Christ." He looked across at Alberts. He tried to swallow down that sudden knot in his chest, but the anger, futile and inarticulate, kept rising in him. "Christ—"

[286

"I'm sorry," Alberts slowly resumed his meal. "As I said before, I'm afraid it's one of those internal situations. Waterman is a good man, but in this case his loyalty to your father has been woefully out of order. He as much as told me that your father wanted much of this kept from you, that is, the *extent* of the trouble. If it had been any other dealer, the banks would never have played along. Even so, I'm afraid the situation is more serious than that. . . ." A pause. "I'm sorry. Not conducive to an enjoyable lunch, but we'd better eat it."

"Yes." Scott tried, though he could only down two oysters, nor was he able to do much better with the Mixed Grill.

"What else?" he asked when the coffee came.

"Quite a bit." Alberts then presented the other papers, the complete report.

What had been staggering at first now loomed as monstrous.

Despite the element of tax deduction, Red's "improvement of property" had been insane. In addition to the overelaborate and expensive air-conditioning plant and the sound system he'd installed, there was the overpurchase of new machinery for the shop; likewise the Auto Stock Parts Department was overinventoried, a deadweight loss. He had also bought too much land for the expansion of the Used-Car lot, and he had taken on a second mortgage to cover construction costs of the enlarged Service Wing and the additional showroom space and the new Customers' Waiting Room. To heal one wound by opening another, he had spent wildly on radio, television and newspaper advertising. . . .

The holocaust—it seemed nothing less than that—left Scott too stunned, too enraged, to know how to combat it.

He could not forgive his father, and he could not forgive himself, his own failure to see all the way through Red's deception.

Alberts took out a curved, chunky pipe and began to fill it, saying: "Now on the constructive side, for what it's worth—"

Scott heard him only dimly.

He knew, without knowing anything else, that his association with the Sturges project was dead.

And the money he'd pledged—that would have to be unpledged. His small commitment of twenty-thousand dollars had suddenly become enormous, and he knew he could no longer count on it.

"—to look at the constructive side," Alberts was drawing on his pipe, "there are certain possible steps that might be taken: first there is the—"

But here, belatedly, Scott knew the answers, though he listened to him courteously.

He could not get back to the office soon enough. But Red had not yet come in.

He called the house: Mrs. Coombs said he'd left an hour ago, after his nap.

As he hung up, Scott noticed more mail on his desk, particularly the airmail envelope, the handwriting Jemmy's.

Jemmy.

He slit open the envelope.

SCOTT DARLING:

Would you believe I don't have your address in Greenwood Park? Hence this letter to Q.C. And to think you were almost the You-Know-What of my Chee-ild. Anyway, first on the agenda is that I've decided that since I'm out here and the worst is over, I owe myself (and you, too) a respite from, well, from just about everything. And so I plan to stay on a while longer—instead of getting right back to our lakeside lovenest and striking while the iron is hot. Or has it cooled? You'd think after that scare I had, sex wouldn't interest me now. Not true. You spoiled me. But to get on with this. My uncle's house is very posh, complete with pool and exotic botanical specimens. He has much loot—being a dermatologist in Beverly Hills seems to be the biggest business next to automobiles and missiles. I feel ten million miles away from Ann Arbor and the groves of academe. Maybe that's what I need, though as I said I'm already beginning to miss what we had at our Edelweiss nest. I just hope I don't miss it too much. Compliments over. I've written to Ann about not getting back for her wedding. I'll miss that too, but even a professional bridesmaid reaches a point where it just ain't fun anymore unless you're on the other end. This is not meant as a hint to you, I hope you know me well enough to know that. You were sweet and honorable, and the novelty was lovely. But as I told you more than once, you're going to have to choose your own wife, you can't let your child do it for you. Period. Yesterday I went to a — — —

Scott put down the letter. Red had arrived. "I've been waiting for you."

"You have, huh?" He gave Scott a hearty, affectionate clap on the shoulder, but the gesture, which normally would have been welcome, somehow only recharged Scott's impatience and anger. Red moved to

[288

his swivel chair then, opened the jacket of his light blue summer-weight suit, pushed back his wide, cream-colored hat and exhaled a resounding sigh.

"How about that McGregor?" Red spoke first.

"What?"

"Ran into him at Sophie's Tavern, stopped by for an eye-opener on my way here, and there he was just leaving. Known that sonofabitch half my life and he's in a hurry, no time to talk, just says consult you. I said what about? He says we don't get our full quota of Bellstars, a special favor to us. Some funny humor, huh? That wasn't on the level, was it?"

"Yes."

"Yes? Well, you didn't let him get away with it, did you? I'd been here—"

"I called him on it, of course. I got nowhere. Because that was just his way of telling us that we . . ." Scott hesitated before Red's piercing, dark gaze.

"Telling us what?" Red said. "What'd he tell you? You look like a —" Without warning his defensive manner changed, and he said softly: "Son, you can go ahead and tell me, but I can save you the trouble. I know what's got you in this sweat. Waterman told me." An aggrieved sigh. "Well, I was just trying to spare you some grief. A mistake. I shoulda known how you'd take it. Well, I can tell you before you tell me. They sent in that little C.P.A., one of those new boys with a slide rule up his ass and a computer machine instead of where his brains should be. Is that it, Scott?" He peered at his son. "Sure. I knew it."

"If you knew it, why didn't you—"

But Red rode right over it. "Well, here's something you forget and something that C.P.A. couldn't figure with all his equipment, and that is that Red Quinnley doesn't always go by the neat little book, he never has and never will! Red Quinnley was doing a two-thousand-car-a-year-business before that C.P.A. learned how to hold his pecker in his hand. Sure, I know he threw the works at you, those boys are like the goddam medics, the one thing they do best is sign the death certificate!"

"Red"—Scott half rose in his chair, sat back again—"Red, why didn't you tell me?"

"What?" Weakly, like a man with poor hearing, he inclined his head.

"Why didn't you tell me, Red? How it was, how it really was? Why?" The reproach came harsh and clear.

Red turned away and snatched a cigar from the humidor on his desk. When he lit it, Scott saw the appalling unsteadiness of his fingers.

"Red, I wouldn't smoke another one if I were you. Lay off."

In answer he swung around away, thrust the cigar between his teeth.

"Scott—" The faintest smile, pitiable, yet somehow admirable, wavered on his flushed face. He took a very deep breath. "Scott, before you say anything, because I know what you're going to say, let me ask you this: you used to race, you know what makes a good racing man when you see one, you know what it's like sometimes. You're driving a contest, let's say you blow a tire, you lose a wheel, your oil system breaks down. You're in the pit when the other guys are making their laps. How do you feel? What happens? Do you chicken out, throw in the sponge? Or do you know you know your business and get your car on the track again and push for the flag? And even if you spin and crash, get your goddam bones cracked and no one's around to give you the cash for another machine for the next event, the wiseacres in the front office write you off—do you crawl in some goddam corner, do you forget your past performances, the records you made? Do you sign in at some goddam mausoleum of a home for retired drivers and sit your ass in a rocking chair?"

Scott watched him, astonished at first as he roared out this locker-room oratory. Twice he wanted to cut him off, yet somehow he couldn't. For however transparent it was, he spoke with a passion which Scott could not mock.

"Whew!" Red wiped his forehead and walked a little less firmly back to his swivel chair. "Not used to big speeches, I guess. Guess it musta taken something out of me—" He put down his cigar at the edge of the wood-top desk, and with his outsized pale blue handkerchief mopped his cheeks.

"Look, Red," Scott said then, "maybe we'd better talk about this later. It's gone this far and a few more hours won't—" Scott stopped, for as Red brought the handkerchief from his face Scott was sure he detected the smallest bead of a gleam, bright and cunning, in his eye.

"Hmm? How's that, son?" Red glanced up with the effort of a weary and brave soldier, though at the same time he pressed his hand against his chest.

[290

And Scott saw he'd been scored. "All right, Red." He held his gaze on his father. "If you're recovered, I'd like to finish this."

"Hmm?"

"Can we talk now? Whether we can or can't, we're going to try. Right now. And the first thing I—"

"Sure, sure, son, why not? I know what you've got on your mind, I was only trying to put you straight, so maybe you'd see how it is. I know better than you what kind of crape that C.P.A. was hanging on our door. Only I don't get scared like some people. That's why I didn't tell you, I knew you'd get scared, I knew you wouldn't be able to put your best foot forward if I laid everything out for you, that's why I—"

"You're right," Scott began. "Except that I'm not scared as much as I am . . ." He did not have the heart to finish it.

"Ashamed? Is that it?"

"Well—no. Disappointed," he answered. "I thought any man who built up a business, an institution as big as this was, couldn't possibly let himself get in a hole like we're in now. I made the mistake of trying to correct or change what I thought was wrong, both here and with the factory, but I still assumed you knew what you were doing, I assumed you were too smart, too experienced, to dig this kind of hole." Scott's voice kept rising with his anger. "I assumed, believed, too much. If you deceived yourself I couldn't believe you'd deceive me and I can't forgive you for it. And the figures—"

"The figures, huh?" For an instant as he faced Scott, a force powerful as sorrow seemed to ravage his features. "That's the difference between us, I guess," he said. "I don't scare that easy." He hunched forward: "Is that why you quit racing?"

"Because I was scared? Certainly I was scared, but I quit because Ellen wanted me to, and she happened to be right. I wasn't good enough to warrant killing myself, and—" But once more Scott recognized the tactic of diversion he had set in motion, and he veered away from it, infuriated that Red had led him this far off. "All right, Red, don't try rattling me or beating around the bush anymore. The only thing left now is to talk out what we're going to do." He swept up the papers of Alberts' report, rose and went to his father's desk. "Here it is, and maybe you'd better study it carefully before you try taking off on me again. The mess we're in is bad enough but never telling me about it, getting me to leave New York, change my entire life, working here all this time and not telling me—"

"Son—"

"Will you read that?"

"Son, if I'd known you better when you first came here—"

"Oh, cut it out, Red. You've never leveled with me and I don't think you ever will!"

"Is that what you think? You think your father is like that?"

"Will you please read that first?" Scott slammed his hand down on the papers. "It's all there, but you refuse to look at it. How long do you think you can go on hiding your head under the hood?"

"Hiding my head. That's what you think, huh?" He snatched up the report and hurled it across the office. "You think your father is hiding his head, got his eyes shut, you think I've got to read that crepehanger's figures? Now let's see how stupid Red Quinnley is—" He sat up, took another deep breath, and then began to recite item for item, dollar for dollar, the entire dismal contents of the auditor's report. When he finished he was breathless, though he scarcely paused before saying: "So much for that, so much for the man with his head in the hood. Now let me ask my son a question. He's very educated, smart. What does my son suggest we do?"

Immediately, and before he could reconsider, Scott said: "Sell out. That's one alternative. Sell out to the first reasonable offer, and that's probably Max Wilkerson's. He's got that kind of money and he wants this location, he's always wanted it. I know how you feel about him, I know he's a swine, but that no longer holds. You can go on a trip and leave me here to handle this and—"

"That's how you'd—"

"I haven't finished!" Scott cut in.

But Red was on his feet, possessed of a fierce energy whose source Scott could not fathom. "That's how you'd go about it, huh?" He clenched the dead cigar in his hand. "Then you didn't get what I was trying to tell you before, you'd settle for the rocking chair. You'd take this enterprise your father has built up for thirty-five years and you'd hand it on a silver platter, on your knees, to a bandit, a shithead like Wilkerson?"

"That's exactly what I'd do, Red."

Red's florid face stiffened and he tried to bring control to his voice. "Very good. Simple. Takes guts and know-how to do a thing like that, doesn't it? A Phi Beta Kappa man is the only one can come up with a smart solution like that. Very good, son. Any other suggestions?"

[292

"Yes. If you won't consider selling, then you've got to consider going to Bellgard and get yourself in on the new Dealership Rehabilitation Plan. At least that is the—"

"Ah, the new plan," Red cried out vehemently, "the Marshall Plan for Underdeveloped Dealers. I go to them after thirty-five years, Red Quinnley goes to them with his palms up, and says: Boys, seems like Red Quinnley has been a fraud all these years, a phony, and now you see, I'm bankrupt and would you please take over, bail me out, run the operation for me, I'll just hang my hat on the rack every day and follow orders. You see, gentlemen, I haven't got a cent left, not a pot to piss in." Red was no longer still, but moving in a frenzied path around the office. "Not a pot. Why? Oh, no good reason, just threw the money away on piddly little things like building more space, making Quinnley Corners the automotive showplace of the entire area, and buying all those cars per quota. Stupid? Naw. No more stupid than I was back in 1955 when I turned down franchises offered me by General Motors and Ford, turned 'em down because I believe in sticking with one company, got a lot of crazy notions like that, and never mind where I'd've been today if I'd gone with G. M. or Ford, or Chrysler. Let those companies ride high the way they're doing now —me, I prefer to stick with the factory I started with, a dumb bastard who is trying to hold on even if the goddam banks have to wait a little for their money. So maybe the product doesn't sell like it used to, maybe they lost some of the old magic, maybe two or three hundred other Bellgard dealers threw in the sponge, closed shop, but a dumb bastard like Red Quinnley has enough faith in the product and himself to pile more dough into the operation, spend even more dough on his own advertising, and even cash in insurance policies so he can put on those mighty Car Carnivals and keep a payroll going without firing a single man. What the hell, there's always a new model year, a new line, and a fella like Red Quinnley goes right on hoping the new line is the miracle he's always been dumb enough to believe in. Now they say maybe it's going to be the Bellstar starts a whole new uptrend and maybe then some of that talk you hear about corruption at Bellgard, maybe that'll all go by the board, soon as a real barn-burner hits the country, and then maybe the banks will be willing to come in with Quinnley Corners again!" At this point Red's machine was running on sheer nerve, yet he had to rest, grasping hold of one of the chairs near his desk, leaning on it, but never removing his wild and bitter gaze from Scott's face. "So why doesn't Quinnley

293]

wait? Why doesn't he wait until the customers start peeking into the tent again? I'll tell you why, gentlemen, because one blast from the C.P.A.'s whistle, and my son, my very educated son Scott, wets his pants and sends his father up here to see how's chances for a handout under this new Marshall Plan. And say, while I'm up here, and since my son is so popular with the big brass, maybe you could give him some kind a job, just to tide us over and—"

"Are you through, Red?" Scott said without calm or charity. "Whether you are or not, you've been in that cornfield long enough and I think you'd better sit down."

"Maybe you're the one better sit down."

"I merely wanted to say I *was* offered a job at Bellgard," Scott stated. "Cod Smith wanted me with the company."

"Cod Smith—" Red stopped. "You say Cod Smith offered—"

"Three days ago. That's what I was doing up there."

"This on the level?" Red made his way to the swivel chair and sat down.

"Yes."

"Why didn't you tell me?" Red said. "What the hell were you lying for?"

"It was pointless discussing it. I didn't want the kind of spot they had in mind."

"You say you didn't want it?" Red's demeanor altered. "You didn't want it? Well, that's all right, a compliment their asking you." Then: "I'm surprised you didn't jump at it though. Here you are saddled with your old man who—"

"Red, please, no more violins and heartstrings. I didn't take the job, as I told you, because it meant the kind of work I've had enough of."

"Sure. But even so." Red pulled at his jaw reflectively.

"Aside from everything else, I didn't think this was any time for me to walk out of here."

"Why not?" There was almost reproach in his tone.

"I have no intention of quitting here, Red," Scott said. "Not now, not in view of what's going on."

"Well now—" But whatever he was going to say, it never emerged. Instead he rose, came to Scott and thrust out a fist, thumping his son on the shoulder. "Well, now—" he began again, and once again seemed at a loss to go on. Then: "Scott, let me ask you something. You—you closed the door on it?"

"What?"

"You shut the door on that offer?" Red said.

"As much as."

"I see." Red knotted his shaggy eyebrows in a prolonged frown. "Maybe you shouldn't have been so quick, son. After all, if you had a chance like this. What'd he say exactly?"

"Who?"

"Cod Smith."

"Oh." Scott shook his head. They wanted me to take over the new Dealership Reorganization plan, but—"

"But you turned it down." Red wouldn't leave the track. "You're so rich and independent and Quinnley Corners is where you want to bury yourself."

"For Christ sakes, Red, will you let me finish what I'm trying to say?"

"What if you reconsidered?" Red leaned forward in his chair.

Scott shook his head again. He lit a cigarette.

"Scott—your father is not always the dumb bastrad somebody might think. Maybe you made a mistake."

"How?"

"How? Well, there are worse things in life than having to take an executive slot with Bellgard. They talk money?"

Scott told him of the initial offer.

"You're worth more."

"I am? That doesn't quite fit in with what you were saying before, does it?"

"Now Scott, we were both—not ourselves, lotta crap flying off the handle I know we didn't mean. Hell, son—you can't look me in the face and tell me you want to bury yourself here with your crazy goddam father."

"I want to get some action, Red. I want to clean this up one way or another. There's no choice now."

"Sure, sure." But that paternal glow which Scott had seen so seldom was suffusing his face. "What I mean is, I was thinking, when you think about it, kinda nice, the idea of your keeping up, staying in the family. Might have looked nice, you up there, topping your old man, but still in the family—"

"Oh." It wasn't until then that Scott got the message. He understood it then. "What I think I'll do, is try the hard way first. Go to the banks. I know that's what you'd prefer."

"Hmm?"

"Go to the banks. If we can hold out for five months, or six," he said. "And I know already, even if I can score with the banks, it'll mean our having to bootleg as much inventory as we can. But . . ."

Red smiled slowly, wryly: "You don't know A-B-C about bootlegging, Scott. And another thing, if anyone goes to the banks it's your father."

"Not this time, Red."

"No? Since when? You think it's too late?"

"I think you're not in a position to pack that much power, not at this time."

"And your weight?" Not derision but rather incredulity edged Red's question. "What kind of weight do you think you can carry? You don't know the banks. Sure they'll listen to you. They're very polite. But the answer I know in advance. You can talk better than your father but all your words won't mean a—"

"My words might mean a little more if I happen to be an officer with Bellgard."

Because his guard was up, Red's response did not come at once, but then his eyes dilated, softened, and slowly there came over his features that same joyful, soul-deep pride which had touched his face before when he had so readily grasped the image of his son at Bellgard, choosing to see it as a way of mollifying his own business failure, justifying his reputation and creating a kind of continuum of his name in the industry.

"Well now"—he raised a hand of feeble protest, as if he knew or suspected that Scott had read his mind—"well now, I don't want you doing anything just for the sake of . . ." But then he abandoned this tactic, and simply gave himself honestly and anxiously to what remained foremost in his mind: "You said you turned 'em down? How're you going to open the door again?" then: "By God, son, you're all right. You're all right."

Codman Smith was not available, his secretary said when Scott telephoned, but she had a memorandum on the situation and immediately put him through to Tony Kerwin. Apparently his call had been

[296

anticipated. Kerwin said for him to report to his office the next morning.

Tony's greeting cut through and eliminated much of what Scott had planned to explain. "Welcome aboard." He gripped Scott's hand. "We're all in a speedup here, Scott. Prepping for the New York junket. But Cod filled me in on this and I took the liberty of suggesting an interim setup—assuming you go along, of course. As I understand it, or rather as Cod put it, you evidently can't work up much power for the Dealership program, not the course you want to play, is that what it comes down to?"

"Well," Scott said, "that's true, but I'd be willing to tackle it if—"

"Oh? You would? May I ask why?"

Kerwin's eyes invited Scott's confidence, and, reluctant as he was to do so, Scott began to tell him of the insolvency of Quinnley Corners.

"Yes, yes," He did not wait for Scott to complete the statement. "We're aware of that, Scott. But we don't think that should determine which deck you want to work on." He paused; hastily, fondly, he surveyed his large office which, unlike most of the others, was not surgically modern, but like his house in Kent Hills, notable for the elegance of its English period pieces and the splendid prints depicting the sporting automotive life prior to World War I. "The fact is, Scott, I can use you here in my division, wouldn't want to waste you on the Dealership end. On the other hand, I'm afraid your interest in Product Planning will have to go by the boards. I'm afraid we'd meet too much resistance from P.O. right now. However, I did suggest to Cod and the committee that you would be extremely useful on my deck, so to speak."

"Oh?"

"What we need, what we've been scouting for for some time, is a new eye, a fresh hand, in Quality Control and Analysis. You're familiar with what we hope to do here?"

"Yes." Most of the industry was familiar with Bellgard's recent (and belated) attempt to create a new department dedicated to a careful examination and comparative analysis of all parts and units being built into the product.

"You'd be working out of this office, that is, through me, reporting directly to me," Kerwin was saying. "Naturally the best man to run a

297]

show like that is a man fresh from the outside with no ax to grind, no personal prejudices, nothing but a pure objective interest in seeing the job done properly. I'm very keen to express this program and score the results before the midyear model modifications." He glanced at his watch and stood up. "Sorry to press you like this, but . . ."

That same morning Scott's processing through Executive Personnel was begun. It went rapidly, not only because the *Word* had been sent down, but because almost everyone was preoccupied with the forthcoming Eastern Dealers Convention and the Automobile Show which would follow it. The currents of anxiety and excitement had reached all departments. They touched Scott too, despite all the reservations he held about both the company and the unwanted turn of his own future.

He was leaving Personnel shortly before half-past twelve when he heard Kerwin's voice directly behind him in the corridor. "They moving you right along, Scott? Good. You might as well hop upstairs with me and meet some of the team."

On the top floor of Administration the glass-walled Executive Dining Rooms—there were two, the large and the small—offered a view of the green Esplanade below. Kerwin, like a host, showed Scott the small dining room: a single Knoll table, long and oval, was centered in a pure white room; a single painting, that of the first Bellgard of 1907, was centered on the largest wall. In here lunched the chief officers and directors. In the large room, executives were served at small tables; there was a round "snack table" in the middle of the room; it was the biggest table—about twenty feet in diameter— Scott had ever seen. Here he saw executives standing, plates in hand, as they dipped into dishes of *smörgåsbord* variety. To make the system easier and more efficient, there were buttons around the table's edge which you pressed and which sent the huge electrically controlled lazy Susan spinning like a languid roulette wheel to the position you wanted.

Kerwin guided him through, pausing here and there to introduce him to certain men. They sat down at a window table and Scott was still conscious that some of the men were watching him. In a curious and magnified way it was not unlike his first day at Quinnley Corners, more gracious, more hearty, more subtle, but also more formidable.

They were midway through the lunch when Kerwin, whose unprecedented friendliness made Scott feel uneasy, looked up and said: "None of my business, Scott, but about your father. When I talked to

[298

you this morning my information was rather sketchy. Since then I've been filled in. I want you to know we're all extremely sorry to know the story. Now if there is anything we—I can do in any way—"

Scott thanked him and said no, the problem had fallen in his lap and he was going to try to stretch their credit enough to hold out through the first quarter of the new model year, the banks willing.

"Which banks?"

Scott told him. "I know it's going to be tough at this point, but—"

"It might have been tougher if you weren't connected with Bellgard. Of course," he added pertinently, "you know that."

"Yes."

"One of your banks," Kerwin said then, "Wolverine National, might be worth a call. I might call them, give you a little extra wind to tack in on—unless you'd rather sail in alone."

This time Scott seized the kindness. That afternoon as he was finishing in Personnel, a messenger brought him a note from Kerwin's office:

> SCOTT, if you will see Mr. David Dodds at Wolverine National, 10 A.M. tomorrow, he tells me he will give you his most sympathetic ear. He's a good friend of mine so I was able to sound off on your excellent qualifications. He knows you are on the payroll here, and that ought to help a bit in getting the carpet out.
>
> Best luck.
>   T.K.
> I'll expect you at my office at 11:30.

It worked. There was little doubt that Tony Kerwin's interceding had helped as much as Scott's association with Bellgard, and when the conference was over, Dodds said he would recommend a ninety-day extension to the Board, plus an additional credit to floor-plan one-fourth of the cars for October quota. On the basis of this, Scott was able to go to the other bank and get the promise of the same assistance, for the faith the first bank had demonstrated encouraged the second bank to go along.

There was but one other piece of business to attend to. That evening he telephoned Steve Sturges, having put off the call long enough.

"Steve? This is Scott. Are you going to be in later tonight? I want to see you."

"No, I'm on my way over to Johnny Winters. Something special, Scott?"

"Yes," he said. "Special and lousy." And as briefly as possible, Scott told him what had happened since the night of their meeting.

"In other words," Sturges broke in, his tone implacable, "you're opting out because as a fine Bellgard man now, you *dasn't* get yourself involved in a project like mine."

"Were you listening to me, Steve?" Scott said, and was forced into the longer explanation, telling him that the Bellgard offer was sheer expediency, if not desperation. "You know damn well, Steve, how I feel. I'm only trying to say that I—"

"Not necessary," Sturges came back with his familiar and defensive arrogance. "I know all the dialogue, I'm accustomed to it now. You're not the first one who's pulled his money out, for whatever reason, and you won't be the last. Though I must say, after your enthusiasm the other night, you had me fooled."

"What I'm trying to say, Steve, if you'll kindly shut up for a second, is that if I ever get myself squared away—and I know that'll take some doing—I want to have the chance to knock on your door again. Why the hell do you think I'm calling you? Do you think this is my idea of fun? I haven't got any more right to count on extra money, not a round red cent. But I'm going to try to change all that, and I wanted you to know exactly how I stand, how I feel, so don't get your silly goddam back up."

From his end there was an unexpected quiet, though it didn't last long. "You want me to understand, is that it? All is forgiven. Well, I can't and I won't. I'm sick to death of these dialogues, I've had them for over a year, playing on the same tape. So forget it, Scott. Keep your collar buttoned down, stick to your new teakwood desk and maybe *Fortune* will write an essay about you someday."

"God," Ann said after they'd reached Columbus Avenue. "That was a ringer and a half to go through."

"It'll learn you to ask personal questions," Scott said.

"At least you were absolutely straight about it—the money part, I mean." A frown as she added: "That's something I don't quite understand about Ben, the way he still won't admit about my money. He pretends I haven't two cents. I've got pots and what the hell is it for if not to spend on a good cause, or even a bad one? But no, Ben's got an absolute blind spot. The Frontier Syndrome, wants to trap the mink, skin it and put it on my back. I used to think everybody was inhibited about sex, but I think it's money that's the national guilt, and Ben is head man—" She stopped. "You know, I was thinking, I wonder what would have happened in Paris if you'd seduced me or I you—"

"It crossed my mind once or twice."

Ann smiled for the first time: "I don't see how. You were very busy screwing that little Scandinavian number who went to the Sorbonne."

"You were very busy too," he reminded her.

"Yes." She made a face. Then: "Anyway, what I kept thinking about was what if we'd had a real thing and wound up in the good old marriage bed—you might have come back to Cartown and ended up just like my two brothers-in-law. God forbid. But think of it, you might have saved almost five years getting to where you are now."

"And you?"

"Me?" she asked.

"Never mind. We know the answer to that one, Junior." He spared her having to admit she would have joined the ranks of Myra and Phoebe and the other Car Widows of Kent Hills. "So you see, it worked out. At least for you."

"Nous esperons," Ann said.

And presently they were part of the throng beneath the canopy of the floodlit building, moving, inching forward in the dense procession of people in evening clothes, pressing on to the great foyer.

Ann kept looking around. "I said we'd meet them here. God, how I don't envy my father tonight! Isn't that Tony over there? Heading for us. He looks awful." Then: "Your boss."

"Yes."

"Mind if I tag along?" Tony Kerwin asked. Despite his splendidly tailored dinner suit, he looked uncomfortable, and the familiar ruddy coloring of his cheeks had given way to a putty-like pallor. "Ann, how about giving your poor brother-in-law some moral support? Damn shame Phoebe couldn't be here."

Ann said: "You're certainly not your admirable self tonight, Tony. How come? Does it take a crisis to make you humble as the rest of us chickens?"

"Too much dinner, too much champagne. And let's have no sass from you, Mrs. Nodina," Kerwin said.

The change in him was even more visible now, and its source was that same anxiety that possessed all of the Bellgard crew. Yet, though he seemed distraught or unwell, he kept smiling, saluting, calling out to other men: "Hello, Lee—Howareya, Warren?—Hank!—Hi, Mitch, you boys got anything to show here tonight?" and "King Cole. None other!"

"Mr. Kerwin—would you mind, sir?" The first of several photographers from the press and the trade journals asked the question. Presently the photographers turned, shunting off in another direction like hunters alerted by the rustle of bushes behind them. They closed in on Codman Smith and Mrs. Smith, and Dean and Myra Stratler who had arrived, flanked by half a dozen other officials.

Codman Smith was a portrait of calmest authority. Bulky and pewter-haired, the glacial blue of his eyes animated by the merest smile, the more handsome in his tuxedo for the indifference to the black tie which was askew, almost folksily out of place, he alone of the Bellgard hierarchy betrayed no glint of anxiety. On the contrary he looked as if he were concealing the knowledge that the Bellstar would be a sure winner. And Ann, beside Scott, said with spontaneous admiration: "Look at him, he's absolutely supreme, isn't he?"

"Yes." And Scott noticed too that Dean Stratler in his olive-black dinner suit and olive cummerbund seemed to have grafted to himself some, if not all, of Cod Smith's show of confidence. Curiously, Myra was the one who appeared tense, though it probably went unnoticed, for each time she and Dean posed for a photographer her rather strained beauty took on remarkable shine, the eyes wide and sparkling, the straight blond hair in patrician chignon, the rich texture of the white evening dress—all composed into a vision which could have deceived the wariest audience.

It was only when Ann left Scott to join her father that he saw Smith's composure waver, that loving but sorrowful look as he watched her approaching. Yet, as soon as the group moved forward to enter the vast show hall, Codman Smith once more communicated that supreme authority of confidence to those around him, endowing them with firmer hopes for success.

As it happened, Scott never got into the hall to witness the Bellstar's reception. For as the party was edging ahead, Tony Kerwin suddenly gripped his arm, his weight lurched against Scott, he muttered something, turned away, stopped to look around him.

"Tony—what is it?" Codman Smith said.

"I think he's sick," Ann said.

"Scott . . . would you . . ." Codman Smith began. Scott caught up with Kerwin and led him hurriedly into the Men's Room at the far end of the foyer. In one of the booths he retched, and when he'd finished he stood leaning weakly, trembling, against the door, his flesh ashen and wet with sweat, his tuxedo stained.

"Thanks," he said once, and lowered his head into his hands. Scott asked him if he could wait while he tried to find the hall physician, but immediately Kerwin grasped his arm. "No—can we, if you can get me out of here—"

When Kerwin insisted, protesting that he felt better, they left by the side entrance, and as soon as Scott got him into a taxi and lowered all the windows, he said: "Decent of you, Scott, can't tell you how I—never been sick in my life, don't know what I—"

But he bent forward then, eyes squeezed shut, his head in his hands.

"We'll be there in five minutes," Scott said, and urged the driver to fire it up.

No sooner, though, had they reached the suite at the Berwyn when Kerwin cried out, clutching his stomach, groaning in anguish as Scott helped him into the bathroom.

He vomited again, only this time there was blood, a hemorrhage. He lurched sidewise and Scott reached out, breaking the fall, holding him. Deadweight. Kerwin was unconscious.

Automatically, and with a grim familiarity to his actions—for he was going through many of the motions he'd gone through during his wife's illness—Scott called Ellen's doctor. Less than half an hour after that he arrived, Dr. Milton Krayler, a wiry and vigorous man long of neck, and with crisp curly hair red as an autumn leaf.

He questioned Scott briefly and went to work. Then the telephone rang: it was Mrs. Codman Smith, calling from the Automobile Show. Scott told her exactly what he knew, passing on Krayler's diagnosis: ulcerous hemorrhage, and he told her an ambulance was en route from Presbyterian Hospital. Mrs. Smith was shocked; she warned Scott then that no one most notify Phoebe yet, for her health was not robust enough to carry news of Tony's collapse. Five minutes later, Ralph Alsop of Public Relations called and said in the event any newsmen turned up to get rid of them if possible; he would be sending one of his men to the hospital first thing tomorrow.

Scott followed the ambulance uptown, driving Dr. Krayler's car and once again thinking of Ellen and those last dreadful months with her; and thinking then of Tony Kerwin, and how his judgment of him seemed to be undergoing so many revisions, this man who had

303]

seemed at best a charming, dynamic operator in auto-gamesmanship, but who must have been more vulnerable than lesser men, and Scott saw in the nature of his collapse something beyond mere nerves or the fire of rumor and a failing product.

That night Scott stayed close at hand in the small adjacent hospital room, taking all calls, calls from the family and associates. He was shaving with Kerwin's razor early the next morning when one of the nurses came in. Kerwin had regained consciousness; she supposed his basic constitution was standing him in good stead now. Scott hurried into the next room. Kerwin's eyes looked out at him, glazed and dark in the ashen face. With effort he raised a hand and dropped it, and he said with a feeble voice that he felt he'd never get out of here alive; and he said if he ever did get out of there in one piece, he would always have Scott to thank for it.

After Dr. Krayler's appearance at seven-ten, no visitors were permitted in Kerwin's room. Scott returned to his cubicle and finished dressing. At nine o'clock Mr. and Mrs. Codman Smith arrived. Shortly afterward they were joined in the lounge by Myra and Dean Stratler, three executives from Kerwin's division, and a young man, very young, from P. R., who was carrying several newspapers.

Almost from the outset Scott noticed the change among the group, the blush of triumph and relief that tinted their faces (particularly Dean Stratler's), so that he received his first official, if unspoken, declaration on the success of the Bellstar.

The subject was in their midst, even though the talk was only about Tony, the gravity of his illness, the lab tests which were to begin. When that had been exhausted, Codman Smith said: "By the way, Scott, I seemed to have forgotten to thank you, it was very good of you."

Dean Stratler turned to the P. R. man: "I doubt if Scott has had much of a chance to see the papers—"

"No," Scott said, "I haven't."

The young man from P. R. handed them over, each one open at the page which contained the coverage on the show. Being early editions the reports were not comprehensive; nothing yet from Ingraham or Blunk of the *Times*. But as he scanned the different pieces Scott saw that the Bellstar had been singled out as notable news in the automobile world. The P. R. man was talking with enthusiasm and pride of accomplishment, however remote his own participation might have been: ". . . and we're getting top color space in *Life*,

Look, Saturday Evening Post—Life shot extra takes late last night—even *Road and Track* is expanding their story on it."

"Williams—" Cod Smith addressed the young man.

"Sir?" Then: "It's Killham, sir."

"Killham," Cod Smith resumed, "you'd better count on sticking here." To Scott: "It's just possible you might want to get some sleep, isn't it? Why don't you knock off, Scott—say five or six minutes," he added dryly.

Scott said he hoped to get to the Show and to the ship to see Ann and Ben off at eleven-thirty.

"Scott," Mrs. Smith said, "we can't tell you how much we appreciate what you've done."

"I happened to be the tow truck on the road when the accident happened," he said.

"Mind if we use that, Mr. Quinnley?" the P. R. man said. "We're sending a release out on this—"

Scott's fatigue spoke for him: "You couldn't be that hard-pressed for copy, could you?"

"No," the fledgling P. R. man came back unflinchingly, "but it would be even better if we could say you happened to be in a *Bellgard* tow truck." He turned to Codman Smith as if to seek some recognition in the president's face. Smith's laugh was mirthless, but the young man did not hesitate: a laugh was a laugh. He said: "Well, why not? The Hard Sell like Charity should begin at home."

"Say, Scott." One of the executives, the bald-headed and rotund Chester Ormond, called him aside. "Problem. Tony was heading a safari out to Gifford, Long Island, tomorrow, luncheon and demonstration we're throwing for the staff of that Negro newspaper, a goodwill powwow tying in with our Eastern Sales end—we have to start boosting sales, the colored population out there has been slow to buy the product, and we want to needle them into more interest. Could you come along? Obviously Tony isn't going to make it, and we want a full quorum. Important little junket."

"Sure, I'd—" A deep and noisy yawn escaped him. "What time?"

"We leave the Waldorf at noon, due in Queens at one. Like you to sound off a little on what our program of Quality Control will mean to the consumer. Important little touch."

Later, as he was about to leave, Scott saw the chubby, overelegantly attired figure of Vince Eames hurrying down the corridor toward Kerwin's door. The muffler manufacturer was perspiring and

305]

agitated. "How is he, Scott? Everybody gone? Have to talk with him."

Scott gave him the report. "But no visitors for the time being."

"A fact? That's what they told me downstairs. But he'll see me," Eames said. Puffy crescents of flesh shadowed his small eyes; he popped a capsule into his mouth and knocked on Kerwin's door.

When Scott reached the elevator, Eames caught up with him. "He's closed off, all right. Can't understand it, tell you, Scott, I know Tony, never been sick a day in his life, but this must be a slugger. I hear you got him that doctor not a second too soon. Can I drop you anywhere?"

Scott said he was on his way to the Show.

"Good, so am I. We'll grab a cab." In the elevator, he went on: "Well, looks like Tony has joined the club all right. I had my first operation seven years ago, and I can tell you, it's no picnic, nothing left of the good things of life except pussy." He laughed, but outside at the taxi line, his tone took on more urgency. "Like to know what brought it on. Understand he just collapsed—what? Nerves? Goes for all of us in this business." Then: "You were with him, did he—he didn't say anything, did he?"

"Not much."

"You sure?" More intently: "You can tell me, Scott. I'm his friend. I mean was he delirious, anything like that?"

"No."

"You can tell me if he said something, a man sometimes—"

"He was too sick."

Vincent Eames seemed relieved. In the taxi, he said: "Want to congratulate you, I know Tony spoke very high of you, you couldn't work under a finer character. I can say that. He's not a bum like yours truly. All I know is the muffler business"—without a pause he went on, while at the same time turtling his head forward and patting down his thin, black pomaded hair—"don't want to talk business, you got a bellyful of that these days, but just to inquire: you see our exhibit on the mezzanine floor?"

"Not yet."

"A must," he said. "Not to knock the competition, you understand, but you take that Kyssin display they got up there, right next to ours, all those pictures he's running, you seen them?"

"No."

"A must—if you've got insomnia, there's your answer, that nuts-

and-bolts movie, even in color, put you to sleep quicker than ten Nembies. I'd like you to see it anyway. Now that you're in Tony's office, somebody ought to warn you Kyssin'll pest hell out of you—you're new, virgin territory for him. I wouldn't open my mouth except nothing he does is kosher, got to watch him, he's the one behind that Holtsbridge stock grab and Holtsbridge is his chum. Two and two is what? You got the answer. He's out to move in on Bellgard's business if Holtsbridge gets control. But my product can stand on its own, the product we're engineering for next year will talk for itself. I'm a fella welcomes competition if it's fair and square, but you take someone like Kyssin posing himself like a super modern genius, he happens— just between us, Scott—he happens to be a prick. The minute we underbid him he shows himself for the prick he is. Well, you saw the papers, didn't you, you heard how it's going, the Bellstar copped the banner, and the Eames product is very much in evidence, I wish Tony had been there at the show last night to see for himself, it's Tony gets the dirty end of the stick that Kyssin and Holtsbridge are trying to slug him with. Sorry, I realize I sound like the blues, but I got all this on my mind—"

And more, Scott thought, for Eames had seized him, hungry for a wider or newer audience, overgrateful for some chance to let go, break the restraints and the snubs he suffered at the hands of others. Scott remembered that first Sunday ball game at the Smiths' in Kent Hills and how Eames had pushed himself into the play but how most of the others veered from his path as if he had had some communicable disease.

"Well," he was saying, "enough of the blues. By the way, when you get back give my very personal best to your father, will you, Scott? Red Quinnley was one of the all-time greats, used to set that town on fire. Where you staying here by the way? They get you the right accommodations? You at the Waldorf or the—"

"At the Park Madison," Scott said.

"Park Madison?" Eames said. "Okay. I want you to know, that as Tony's friend, I am grateful to you. When I had my first attack not a living soul was around, I could've died, just like that. What're you doing tonight, Scott? If you're free, I'd like to show you my appreciation on behalf of Tony, like you to come up to the hotel, where the action is— Oh, you're busy? Well, if you get unscrambled, I'm having a small party, don't hesitate to join, I know how it is in this town, a bachelor like yourself, like me, you can get lonely without trying."

He lit a cigarette. "My ninth so far, that makes eight too many according to my doctor. But this Show, keeps you too keyed up. Every year same deal. Nothing left for a man. Except pussy, and even that—"

The taxi had stopped before Columbus Hall.

"Allow me." Eames removed his fleshy frame from the cab and handed the driver two dollars. "You'll try to make it upstairs, won't you, Scott?" He pumped Scott's hand. "And thanks for lending an ear. I get to gabbing and the snapper won't stop yapping. Thyroid, maybe. Well—see you, Scott."

The supplier waddled off, dumpy and harassed, in his costly Italian vestments, the pockets of which must have contained, in addition to abundant cash, a dozen varieties of pills or medicaments, though, Scott supposed, his real malady might have been loneliness.

Scott walked through the moving mass of spectators, past the dense islands of people centered around the various displays—a public increasingly wary and pampered, yet seemingly insatiable, hooked on automobiles, a public ogling, sniffing, touching, comparing.

To the Bellgard stand.

There he had to elbow his way to the white Bellstar on the slowly revolving black velvet turntable. The crowd had congealed here, leaving barren the rest of the line, the standards, the bread and butter of the industry, the cars most people would buy, yet going begging now, losing out to the jazzy flash of the Bellstar.

And there, undulating around the steering wheel, was one of the models, her hair bright as chrome, a white plastic microphone peeping out from between her resplendent breasts as she whispered huskily to the crowd, intoning libidinously the miracles and wonders of the Bellstar.

Ralph Alsop tapped his shoulder. "How's it look to you? You just get here, Scott?"

"Just."

"Tragic, Tony Kerwin can't place this scene, huh?" Alsop went on. "We're really swinging here. Orders already piling up and the show is less than two hours old. We've got a survey team on the prowl here and all we're getting, reaction-wise, is plus plus plus. We're going to cut into the champions this time, running a close behind the Corvette and Mustang according to my poop. What's the info on Kerwin?"

Scott told him what he knew, though his eyes were already shifting their attention, swiveling about the mob of lookers. And soon, after Alsop had left, Scott's fatigue began to creep back again, the crowd became oppressive, the air-conditioned air seemed stale. He backed away and fought through to try to get a glimpse of some of the other displays, but like a cocktail party at the opening of a new art exhibition, he couldn't see the paintings for the people.

An hour before time to get to the ship to see Ann off. An hour and his legs felt like sandbags. He went upstairs past the display stands of myriad suppliers, past plastic seat covers, supercharger units, special wire wheels, headlamps, prefab carports, until he saw ahead, like an oasis, a kind of Quonset hut: "The Kyssin Theatre." About twenty people were inside, many of them asleep, and Scott saw the last half of the technical film, in color, showing the making and testing of the new Kyssin exhaust system, a first-rate film, because instead of dozing off as he was sure he would, he became alerted and refreshed by the way this antiquated product necessary to the antiquated gasoline engine was extolled. Not until the lights came up did he remember his promise to Vince Eames to look in on his company's display. But there wasn't enough time, and he had to hurry out.

In the taxi to the pier, Scott kept thinking of Kyssin's product and what it had to offer. For the first time he saw some daylight in the intramural war at Bellgard—not the general warfare between Engineering and Budget which went on almost all the time, but the specific, minor skirmish relating to the muffler units. You didn't have to be a member of S.A.E. to recognize the superiority of the Kyssin system.

Rumors, too many to ignore, had been leveled at Bellgard, yet not aimed at any one man. Some sources charged plain mismanagement, others outright corruption. Depended on who was making the charge. If you listened to Sam Kyssin, as Scott had one evening, he left no room for doubt that it was Kerwin's office or influence that was the offender, at least in the case of Kyssin's failure to win Bellgard's business.

But if it was Tony Kerwin himself who championed the Eames exhaust system for friendship or money, Scott couldn't quite go along: it had to be more than that. Six months ago he might have been quick to agree, but in his short, concentrated association with Kerwin he couldn't see it. Kerwin was too smart, too knowledgeable, too covetous of the top chair at Bellgard, too eager to place first in

309]

the *Grand Prix* of Cartown's social race, ever to risk a payoff or kickback manipulation, even granting that men of equal rank had risked it before.

Kerwin had been exceptionally kind and helpful to Scott, though when he had told Ann about it last night she had said, with her customary contempt for the varnished fictions about the industry or her own family: "Certainly he's been good to you. You're his boy now, not only because you've got quality brains, though that helps of course, but because he knows you've been one of the rosier apples of my father's eye."

How true or how false, it mattered not.

Scott had had no illusions about the offer. He had only known that he had to take it.

Nor did he have any illusions about Kerwin being a man whose heart was made of purest gold. On the other hand, he'd seen enough of him to realize his heart was not made of unalloyed flint.

Scott was also aware that Kerwin had shown little daring in setting him up to head Quality Analysis and Control. No engineer, no statistician, no accountant, was necessary for that post. Experts in those fields were aplenty. What was needed, and Kerwin had told him this candidly, was someone whose business virginity at Bellgard was intact, someone who had no alliances with the personnel and whose primary requisite was a serious concern for the nature and importance of the work, someone, finally, who could ignore all the conflicting egos and come out with clear, objective recommendations.

No. If Scott held any illusions, these were centered chiefly on the future—that future which to him was represented by men like Steve Sturges, Jack Winters, Phil Rothe or Sam Kyssin.

He'd lost his chance with Sturges, though his belief in the project was strong—even stronger now that he had to work in terms of the *status quo*. And that was the bug: He had put himself in the position of a man who, though in love with another woman, was compelled to make his existing marriage work. And suddenly and disagreeably he saw himself, like this same married man, needing to make the best of his union and seeking in his partner some hidden virtue or allurement —just as now he was already seeking in Tony Kerwin virtues or allurements which in reality might not be there.

Scott glanced ahead, relieved to see that they had reached the ramp descending to 44th Street. He saw the great ship at anchor, its curving prow rising in beauty above the debris of the dock.

[310

But the sight, so pleasing, brought him down: why? He did not know. Only that the immediacy of Ann's departure acted to depress him further. She had talked about it for so long that it had lost reality. Until now.

"Hey, tiger," the familiar voice boomed behind him.

"Phil—" Scott turned, surprised, delighted to see his friend. "I thought you weren't due in until tomorrow. Christ, I'm glad to see your ugly face."

Phil Rothe had made an earlier flight. "Knew I'd catch up with you down here. Do you know Ann's stateroom number?" They reached the escalator. "I've been to the Show already, even had a glimpse of the Bellstar—"

"What'd you think?"

"Looked better than you do," Phil said. "You have a bad night?"

"Not that kind. Unfortunately." Scott told him about Kerwin.

Aboard ship—a chaos of baggage, visitors and passengers—they walked to the Boat Deck. "Listen," Scott asked, "why don't we go to the Chanteclair for lunch? Been a long time."

Phil agreed. They stepped sideways to allow two women and a porter to pass. Phil said: "You know, Lorie kept telling me she'd take odds Ann would never take off."

"Based on what?"

"Hunch, I guess. Or past performance," Phil said.

"Looks like Lorie played the wrong hunch." Scott saw Ann down the passageway, waiting by the open door of the two-room suite.

Though she ran to meet them, though her greeting was warm, lavish even, as soon as they reached the door she looked back like a nervous hostess still waiting expectantly for the arrival of the major guest. "Scott darling, you didn't see my father anywhere along the line?"

"Not since the hospital."

"Oh. You poor thing. You've had a hell of a time, haven't you? It's so sweet of you to come, you and Philip. Here, let me get you some of this vintage French fizz." She filled our glasses. "Courtesy of Mr. and Mrs. Dean Stratler."

The Stratlers were sitting there, a shining Dean Stratler within the nimbus of his fresh success; and a Myra Stratler, shining too, though in a light more oblique.

Standing alone was Ben Nodina, looking, Scott thought, determined and independent, though it might just have been the fierce

311]

thrust of his recently grown beard. For a short span the talk was polite, general, and the Stratlers asked many questions about Tony Kerwin. After that Ann moved back to her post by the door, and while Phil spoke with Dean Stratler, Scott went over to Ben.

"Nice of you to come, Scott," he said with immoderate gratitude.

"Wouldn't have missed it, Ben. I guess I'm the last one here."

He rubbed his coarse beard, glancing over at Ann. "You probably will be the last—"

"No," Ann interjected from the door, "he'll get here. I'm positive he will."

"Of course he will," her sister Myra said. "Father'll make it somehow. He will for you Ann. We all know that. May I have a bit more, please?" She held out her glass.

For a few minutes, in counterpoint to the shoptalk between Dean Stratler and Phil Rothe, Scott spoke with Ben, though Ben did most of the talking. The Greek officials, he said, promised him full cooperation. "Anything I want, including interviews with the King and Queen, anything I need except good winter weather. It'll be next spring before I can get most of my exterior stuff," Ben said, going on then in a voice unnecessarily, surprisingly loud: "But at least there'll be no more deadlines for midyear model changes, no last-minute retakes because the headlights are going to be recessed three-sixteenth of an inch deeper. Farewell to nuts and bolts." Ben paused, turned his back on the group. "If this Greek film pans out, I've got a couple of art cinema people ready and waiting for it, and some serious TV interest. A hell of a market for this kind of picture if I can unstiffen it, keep my footage free from documentaryisis. If I can lock it up without the corn, I'll be home."

"Home? Who's going home?" Ann left her post by the door. "Did you say something about coming back, Ben?"

"No, we were talking about my—" Ben's words were lost in the brisk but measured English of the Italian voice over the loudspeaker system: first warning for visitors to go ashore.

Scott saw faint consternation come into Ann's eyes.

"Well"—Myra Stratler rose, held up her glass—"here's a last one to the bride and groom." They drank. "And while we're at it," she looked down at Dean Stratler, "why don't we drink to my husband. Why be modest, this is his day too, isn't it?"

"Let's wait on that one, dear." Dean Stratler was speaking more out of caution than modesty. Neither he nor anyone else in the company could forecast how much of the Bellstar's potential sales gold would rub off on the standard passenger series.

Myra offered the toast over her husband's protest. And they drank again. Then to Ann: "Darling, for heaven sakes, smile up. If Father doesn't make it, it's only because he's swamped today, and—"

"Balls," Ann said.

"Oh Ann, really," Myra said. "I mean it, it has nothing to do with you or Ben."

"Of course not," Ann said.

"Well," Dean Stratler's voice cracked through the stillness, "we'd better pull out before the ship does." He shook hands with Ben Nodina, and embraced Ann.

"Annie—" Myra went to her. "Have a wonderful crossing." She kissed her; she drew back, and then in an unusual onrush of tenderness, she hugged her sister again. "I still can't believe you're really leaving. Oh, I suppose we've had some nasty moments, but I'm going to miss you more than I—well, good-bye, good-bye, Annie darling—"

When the Stratlers had gone, Ann said to Ben: "What do you suppose came over her? She seemed all shook up."

"Not from this angle of vision," Ben said.

"Oh, I know she hung around long enough to see if I was getting the freeze-out from Father, but somehow . . ." She glanced back to the doorway, and then rather nervously she lit a cigarette. "Scott, I'm sorry. Unfair to expose you to all this again."

There were sounds of raucous farewells in the passageway.

Phil said the time was up, and he shook hands with Ben and Ann, and then Scott went to her, and the disquiet he had been feeling gave way to something else. "Well, good-bye, Junior."

"Oh, don't run out on me, Scott."

There was the blast of the ship's horn.

"Bye, my old buddy," she said; she squeezed his hand hard. "Hold down the fort, keep your shoulder to the wheel and your nose to the ground—"

He bent forward to kiss her, but she'd turned away: Mr. and Mrs. Codman Smith appeared at the open door.

"Sorry to be late, Ann, we're going to have to rush right off again," Codman Smith said after Mrs. Smith had made her greetings.

"Oh but you fooled me!" Ann exclaimed in joyful contrast to her father's reserved manner. "I was absolutely positive you'd come and then I gave up, and now here you are!"

313]

"Only for a moment." Cod Smith turned to Nodina. "Wanted to wish you a good trip."

"Thank you." But Ben's face had reddened and there was that thrust of his bearded chin. "Thank you. But since we all know where we all stand, I don't see the point in going through the motions of—"

"Ben—did you have to?" Ann broke in.

"Well there's no point in—" Ben resisted her imploring tone.

"For God sakes Ben this is no time for—" Without warning, Ann's voice cracked and there was a sudden angry shimmer of tears.

With as little awkwardness as he could manage, Scott said his good-byes again. As he followed Phil out, he heard Codman Smith saying:

"Well, Ann, no use my putting on my happiest face, is there? It's just as well there's no time left—"

In silence the two men bucked the passageway and stairs clogged with other visitors hastening to leave the ship.

As they reached the gangplank, a man, obese and bulge-eyed, jostled against Scott. "Watch it, will you!" Scott's voice was rude and rasping.

Phil looked at him. "What's the matter with *you?*"

When they gained the street, Phil said: "You're in great form today, aren't you?"

Scott did not answer.

"Listen," Phil said then, "can we spare a few minutes before lunch? I'm looking for a pair of old rings for the headlamps of the Duesenberg. Know a good place?"

"Yes." Scott said. He flagged a cab and they drove to the battered store on West 40th Street where he had acquired many of the parts for his Pierce Arrow. Phil found the rings he wanted.

In the taxi afterward, Phil said: "That was some Bon Voyage, wasn't it?"

"Hmm?"

More like a funeral than a farewell," Phil said. He shook his head. "Poor dame. Did you think she—"

"Let's discuss it later, Phil." The cab turned into 49th Street and drew up before Le Chanteclair.

"Maybe," Phil said, "you better drink your lunch today."

Into the restaurant and losing, for a while, the bitter aftertaste with which Ann's departure had left him, Scott felt home again, taken back to former times:

Through the bar and seeing again the wall of photos of racing drivers, great and ungreat, alive and dead.

Reunion with the proprietors, the brothers Dreyfus, talking with René Dreyfus, himself a racing man, one-time driver for Bugatti, Alfa Romeo and Talbot, and who in 1930 won the *Grand Prix* of Monte Carlo.

Sitting at the table with Phil, seeing again those wall panels, those misty Paris landmarks, the Place de la Concorde, the Tuileries.

The heightened flavor of premarriage martinis and dinners with Ellen.

Back again.

No, no martinis today. Stick with the wine, yes, a Pouilly-Foussé. Needing rust remover for his French.

Seeing again, like a familiar mural of the past, the faces, costumes, manners of the clientele of the off-Madison Avenue restaurant, except here an edge of difference, this being a kind of H. Q. for racing drivers, automotive writers, admen, and assorted car buffs (here even the ashtray's design celebrates the Bugatti).

And hearing the familiar crosstable music:

"Ja go to the Glen?"

"Ralph's going to cover it."

"Got all bent up in one of the cars *you* people make."

"Ya see Denise?"

"We also picked that agency because they had a P.R. department right in the shop."

"It reads nice but will it sell car wax?"

"All night, Lime Rock to Detroit."

"Bartley did the piece."

"He's going to enter the Formula One Ferrari."

"Purdy wrote it."

Back again, again seeing himself dicing around these same tables talking to anyone who would listen to him expound on how fine and big his little new magazine was going to be.

Yes. Back again.

And seeing Ellen again, pregnant with Susan, belly protruding and his having to push the table back to accommodate her, a table there against this same wall where he was sitting with Phil.

The waiter now putting before him the swordfish garnished with slivered almonds; the curry of chicken for Phil.

315]

"You feeling a little more human?" Phil said after they'd begun to eat.

"Yes. Certainly."

"Because for a while there, after the boat, I wanted to paste you up with brightwork, give you a phony glitter—of course that was a depressing farewell if I ever saw one."

Scott nodded, not answering, not wanting to ride with the subject anymore.

"Too bad," Phil said. "Leaving like that."

"How's that curry?"

"Delicious," Phil said. "And I'll tell you this, Scott, if I'd been Ann, I'd never have taken it. Poor kid."

"Her own damn fault," Scott had to say.

"Her fault? I don't see how you can blame her. The way Ben blasted off, and then the old man frosting up like a—"

"For chrissakes, Phil, I don't know what you or anyone else expect at this point."

"Look. I'm only discussing it, I don't want to slug it out," Phil said. "How can you say it's her fault?"

"I merely meant," Scott said irritably, "that after all this time, the way Ann's been making that loud pitch about breaking away from her family, Cartown, et cetera, and then when Ben finally does take a stand, she cries out and falls apart."

"What are you in such a steam-up for?" Phil said.

"I'm not."

"She happens to love her father, what's wrong with that? How many kids today love their fathers? It's a novelty, it's wonderful—"

"It's so wonderful," Scott broke in again, "that she couldn't wait to put Greece between herself and Daddy and the rest of them."

"Well, when it came to actually going, naturally it wasn't so easy for her. Not for Cod Smith either. And if he was sore or hurt, or even jealous, that was a—"

"She made her bed, she ought to lie in it. With Ben."

"That's not the point, Scott. The—" Phil peered at his friend, frowning, squinting behind the thick glasses. Then he grinned and shook his head. "For a minute there, tiger, you were—" But he stopped.

"I was what?"

"Sounding worse than her father."

"Oh, for chrissakes, Phil!"

[316

"That's how it sounded, as if you were the one who—" Phil shook his head again.

"For chrissakes, Phil, what kind of noise are you trying to make?"

"Nothing. Let's enjoy this food."

Scott stared at him: "You can't be serious."

"You're the one who's getting serious."

"All right, Phil. Joke over. I can't be all that square."

"Why not?" he said.

24: Scott Quinnley

THERE were two parties that night: the major one, at the Manhattan-Plaza, was a dinner-dance and floorshow for Bellgard's Eastern dealers and their wives; the other party, the one at which Scott found himself and which took place at another hotel several blocks East of the Manhattan-Plaza, was for the Lonelyhearts. A less conservative affair, of course. Here men could enjoy fraternal car-talk and booze with other men, or other pleasures with the girls at hand. Or both.

Scott was late. He'd run far beyond his normal lap time at lunch with Phil Rothe, and he'd overextended his afternoon tour of the New Jersey assembly depot. (Random checks he'd made of cars finished and stamped for shipment showed a discouraging count of goofs: a window running out of its channel, a broken distributor cap, a speedometer needle that never left zero, directional signals that wouldn't cancel, front wheels out of alignment, a loose, rattling tail pipe, a door that wouldn't latch, a radio fuse which blew whenever it was turned on, shimmying wheels.)

When he reached his hotel that evening there was a call from Chester Ormond. "Scott," he said, "can you get over to the hotel here, we're having a little goodwill fun, same old thing, but you might as well partake and then we can have a little talk, want to start briefing you for tomorrow."

"Tomorrow?" Scott was flat on the bed; since Kerwin's collapse he couldn't have had more than four hours' sleep.

"Tomorrow noon," Ormond said. "The safari out to Long Island. We're throwing that little lunch and demonstration for that Negro newspaper—"

"Oh yes." Dimly he recalled having accepted the assignment.

Scott said he'd be over soon. But it was already past seven and he wanted to telephone home first, talk to his father and to Suzy. He put in the call. He must have fallen asleep only a few seconds after he'd finished, for when he awoke, the telephone was still beside him on the bed. It was nearly ten o'clock when he rose to dress for the party.

One entire wing of the thirty-first floor in Ormond's hotel was given to the Bellgard festivities, and by the time Scott arrived the party traffic was thick. Chester Ormond, his tuxedo already looking a bit soggy, greeted Scott in the reception hall and led him through the private dining room and the oval room where couples were dancing, to a long barroom. "Let's get you squared off with a drink first," he said.

They sat down on one of the divans and a waiter took their order. The room was paneled in oak and the lighting was minimal. There were pockets of shadow. You could hear the uneven wash of voices, bright, guttural, murmuring; now and then a man would cough or you heard a girl's laugh, quick and hard as the crack of glass; men sauntered in and out, others huddled talking at the bar, others, with girls, passed through to rooms beyond.

"About tomorrow, Scott—" Ormond began. "Here's the story—"

Scott had finished a second Scotch by the time the vice-president neared the end of his outline for the program of the luncheon-meeting and the new-car demonstration to be given for the Negro newspaper people in Gifford, Long Island.

"Chet," a man called as he approached. "Can we see you a minute? A problem."

"Excuse me, Scott." He put down his glass. "Be back with you pronto."

Ormond never returned. Looking around the smoky barroom as he walked to the bar, Scott felt thankfully removed from all that had happened since the night before—had it only been twenty-four hours since he and Ann had walked up 57th Street to the Automobile Show? And no more than twelve hours since he'd seen her off at the boat this noon, and later leaving Phil in front of Le Chanteclair, in that uncharming mood, touchy at his well-meant and unwanted counseling?

Scott noticed now, close by, an elderly man and a young woman step from the bar and start to dance, borrowing the diffused sounds from the orchestra in the adjacent room. In the spray of light from the bar, the girl was attractive, her dark auburn hair thick and shining, her breasts prominent (justifiably) in the low-cut and sleeveless dress.

"Well, Scott—" Vincent Eames sat down at the bar beside him. "I see you're checking over the new fall line." He waved, wiggling flaccid fingers at the girl. "Howya, doll."

She glanced over her partner's shoulder and acknowledged Eames with a severe smile.

"Still mad?" Eames said. When she did not reply, he turned back to Scott. "She's been giving me a hard time, on the way over here from my hotel she got her nose out of joint over some little thing I said, can'ya imagine? At those prices? I goddam near clobbered her—" Cruelty cut into the soft fatty texture of his voice. "Never used her before, but there are plenty more where she came from in case you want the number." A considered pause: "Or haven't you ever had to pay for it? No, I guess you haven't." He obviously offered this as a compliment. "If I was in your shoes I sure as hell wouldn't pay for it, or maybe I would, maybe I like pussy best when it comes that way. Other guys, they can't even get it up if they know it's going to cost 'em."

Scott turned to watch the girl again, he saw a man sitting at the other end of the bar, a Bellgard man; Scott had seen or met him, though he could not place him until he heard Vince Eames call: "Howya, Ernie, didn't know you knew where the action was."

Ernst Kamber. Yes. Assistant Chief Engineer at Bellgard. (The joke Scott had heard around the plant was based on punning his name so that if you wanted to dismiss or walk away from some engineering problem, you would say: "Too much understeer, let me try a little less negative Kamber on the rear.")

Ernst Kamber made a frail, dutiful gesture of greeting, then shifted his almost-skeletal figure on the bar stool, so that his back was half turned away. When he lifted the drink the barman had given him, his bony hand had a noticeable tremble.

Scott saw that Vince Eames was still watching him rather intently. Then he said, "Does these guys good to get away, relax. Hey, you need a fresh one, Scott."

"No thanks, Vince. I'm on my way."

"Don't rush off." He touched Scott's arm, edged closer, hunched his shoulders as if to readjust the fit of his ribbed-silk tuxedo. "Scott, this morning when we left the hospital, there was something I wanted to discuss but—with Tony so sick I was too, uh, exercised, as Tony says, to think about it. What I mean, if you won't mind my talking to you like a father—" A short laugh. "No joke intended, but it's about

[320

your father I wanted to talk to you; after all, I've known Red a long time and I know how he is, what he's like. For Red, there's nothing I wouldn't do. And that's straight from the heart."

Scott thanked him, stirred on the stool and glanced with excessive interest toward that auburn-tressed and slender-armed chick who was still dancing, her face in a freeze of boredom.

"Listen," Eames said as if having to rouse Scott from his distraction, "I'm not looking for any red-ribbon honors. This was meant only for you, Scott, I just wanted you to know that if your dad finds himself in a tight corner, please don't hesitate to call on me, I mean if it's a matter of picking up—uh, any loose ends— What's the trouble, Scott?"

"Nothing. You just threw me there for a moment." What had in fact thrown him was not that Eames should propose this sort of bribe or payoff, but that the practice was obviously so common that it never occurred to him that Scott might balk.

"Hell," Eames resumed blithely, "I only wanted to show you whose side I'm on, is all. I know what a responsibility you've got on your hands now, carrying this whole Quality Control program, but I also know there are people going to buttonhole you, try to bitch me, downgrade my product. Scott—now listen to me, keed, I don't expect any favors, but if your department decides for some reason Eames mufflers don't measure up or something's wrong, all I ask is they tell *me,* personally, not buck it through Engineering or make a federal case out of it in some committee meeting, that's all I'm talking about. In my business the competition are all barracudas, a guy like myself gets clipped because he wants to do things the right way. You're new at Bellgard, and Tony told me you're the kind of guy gets his nose out of joint pretty fast sometimes, but I just want you to know whenever anyone shows me ordinary decent consideration I always show my appreciation. What I said about your dad, that still goes. In this industry, a man like your father is someone we all respect, and if any of us can help . . ."

There was no point in leaving indignantly with his honor bruised; that would have made too much of it. Instead, Scott deliberately let his attention rest on the auburn-haired girl. "Who'd you say she was?" he asked Eames.

"What? Oh her?" Obligingly he called: "Hey, doll. Come here."

Her partner turned to Vince Eames scowling, his mouth in a belligerent pout. "Now wait a minute—!"

321]

But the girl had disengaged herself swiftly. "Been nice." She dismissed him with a sure, icy charm. She came to the bar. "I know he's a friend of yours, honey, but what a creep."

"Forget it," Eames said. "He shouldn't even be here. He's from Scranton, it's his brother who's my friend. Doll, how would you like to meet this gentleman?"

"I would." She broke in. "How do you do?" she said. "The name isn't Doll, by the way. It's Faith."

"Faith. That's right," Vince Eames said cheerfully. "Well, what's in a name? This is Scott."

She appraised him with cool glaucous eyes. From her white bag she brought out a cigarette, as Vince was saying: "What'll you have, Fay?"

"Not Fay. I told you. It's Faith. Orange juice."

Vince Eames ordered the drink. "That how you keep that chassis of yours? On orange juice?"

"One of the ways." She turned to Scott. "Do you have a light, please?"

" 'Scuse me, will you, I have to look after a friend over there." Eames began to speak with the engineer, Ernst Kamber, at the far end of the bar. And shortly he reached out to net a passing girl, his stubby arm around her waist as he introduced her to Kamber.

Faith seemed preoccupied and drank her orange juice and smoked her cigarette, not speaking, the gray-green eyes staring blankly like those hollow-eyed girls you see having breakfast alone at the counter in Schrafft's.

Yet Scott was glad he hadn't left. She might not have been as attractive as he'd first thought, and her skin was coarse, but she looked good to him at this point in a long, dry season. He liked her kind of slimness, the way her slim leg showed through the slit at the side of her white dress, and the less subtle view of her breasts curving above the scooped neckline.

It wasn't until the silence between them became burdensome that Scott asked her to dance. She responded with animation, even sparkle, and they went into the oval room.

"This is more like it," she said after a few moments, and with a kind of spontaneous, yet impersonal manner, she slid her arm tighter around Scott, curved her body into his. As far as he could tell she wore nothing under her dress except panties. "Love this," she said. "That creep I was with before didn't know what was going on, all he knew was, well, who cares? What gives me hangnails is he kept calling me Fay, he'd heard Mr. Eames calling me that."

"It bothers you that much?"

She didn't answer, giving herself totally to the music. A natural dancer, her movements were instinctive, sure and delicate as a cat's. Her feet, thighs, hips, twined themselves in flawless rhythm around the base of the melody. Once she said: "Rather dance than anything. But you never get much of a chance, not like this, when you're working." Another show of joy, her pelvis firmer against Scott, not in any special sexual way, but rather as if she wanted to weld them into a perfect and fluid union.

Scott was reminded, as he held her, of Vince Eames' attempt at a compliment, his surmising Scott had never had to "pay for it." Which was true. He had always lived with the feeling that he couldn't or wouldn't function in sex if it was offered commercially. But this little conceit of his did not seem to hold together now.

When the set ended and they walked back to the barroom, she said: "That was great, honey, loved it. Dancing always makes me turn on. But when I started work tonight, I was so tired, you know all I wanted in the whole world? All I wanted was a can of Campbell's tomato soup and sleep sleep sleep."

Scott said he might call her before he left New York, and she said: "I'll give you the number. The Car Show in town keeps me booked. Tomorrow there's two cocktail parties, and one serious one."

"Serious?"

"Well, not just standing around. That kind. They're all right, if there's no freakers. I cut out if there are any freaks or if they want a show. Don't have to take that in my position."

"Orange juice?" he asked her.

"Thanks." She put her white handbag carefully on the bar top.

The bar was busier now. The girl who'd been with Ernst Kamber and Vince Eames was no longer there. The two men were talking, arguing.

"Miss my wife? I sure do, I'll be honest, I miss her," a man was saying to a young woman, his voice growing thick, "just talking about her I get a catch in my throat. You take last night, I took out this girl, a kid, eighteen, nineteen, just for dinner, just because I'm restless, not because I want to lay her—wouldn't know how to make a pass at a kid her age—anyway, as I told her, there going to be any passes they'll have to come from her. She was all over me after that, but as I was saying, you take in my case, it's not like most fellas they get away from their wives—"

Scott recognized him as one of the men who'd been at the Bellgard banquet the night before; he was sales manager of a Delaware dealership.

Faith tamped a cigarette on the bar, and in that opinionated way of hers, she said: "Anything gives me hangnails, it's one of those *sincere* husbands."

She leaned forward, cigarette between her lips; as Scott reached for his lighter he saw the flurry of movement at the other end of the bar: Kamber pushing Vince Eames' arm away, and Eames, his cheeks red as cranberries, jabbing out at him, grasping him then, shaking him in a rage of temper, and then the two men locked, clutching, jabbing, on their feet, and now a barstool knocked to the floor. . . .

All crosstalk, even drinking, had ceased. Scott looked around for Chester Ormond. He saw Faith shake her head as if in disgust or impatience. Finally, since no one seemed to want to stop them, Scott rose, and after a clumsy scuffle he broke it up, spinning Eames away, getting his arm around Kamber's shoulder and walking him—he was rubber-drunk and atremble—into the main corridor. There one of the waiters signaled him and held open the door of one of the private party rooms. Scott ordered black coffee; he kept Kamber upright on the sofa and got the coffee into him, but Kamber wouldn't let him leave, he begged him not to leave, and all the time holding Scott, clutching his sleeve, and then as if an emetic had been given his very soul, he spewed out an awful bile of confession, part confession, part protest, until finally having unburdened himself, he fell back into a snoring sleep.

When at last Scott returned to the barroom, all he wanted was to forget what he'd heard. Vincent Eames had gone. And with him, Faith.

Scott had a last drink before calling it a bad night.

Not a word Kamber had said would leave him. And back at his hotel, all the while he was taking a shower, brushing his teeth, Kamber's face, gaunt and pitiable, was close before him, vivid and awful as the bile of his anguish.

In the other room someone was knocking on the door, and at first Scott didn't even hear it, he was still hearing Kamber:

"You saw me, Quin—Quinnley, you saw me, you know I was doing, doing nothing, that true?" he had said in that initial outburst.

[324

And then Kamber, who was a New Englander of German descent, told him much more, as if to draw Scott into his own miserable affairs:

Remember him, he urged, kept urging, remember him tonight, like any man who dropped in to have a drink or two and talk with others in his field, he'd only stopped by because he was tired after a long afternoon at an S.A.E. meeting, no reflection on the S.A.E., and he had not, despite Vince Eames, bothered with any of the girls present at this party tonight. . . .

Remember him, he begged. Witness to the truth.

But something else: last year, no, the year before, when he'd been in New York, he'd met a girl at his hotel, at the bar, and yes, he'd ended up sleeping with her in her room. Only time he'd ever picked anyone up. Except that he hadn't even done that: she'd been sent there with the explicit purpose of meeting him. A week afterward, at the plant, at a meeting, he'd vetoed the acceptance of the Eames muffler system; on that same evening, as he and his wife were playing Scrabble in the living room, the telephone rang: "It's for you, Ernie," his wife said in a curious or unrecognizable voice, "some girl, a Miss Molloy, she says."

The name registered at once. Of course. A man like Kamber is without a little black book, the range of his female acquaintants is encompassed by a single name: Molloy. At the telephone then and cutting her off frantically, acting like an idiot, but a guilty one, and his wife, her suspicions aroused, gave him such a bad time, not believing anything he said, yet because his record as a foolish, faithful husband had never been challenged, she ultimately relented, but Kamber had been left shaking, loathing himself, the circuit of his nervous system shorted, broken. . . .

Not ending with that night, for the next day in his office mail there'd been the envelope marked *Personal:* there he was in the photograph, asleep in the bed with the girl, his silly guilty mouth open. "If anything happened this time, anything, never face my wife again, and my boy, he's a freshman at Ann Arbor, what would it do to him?"

But nothing, Scott told him, nothing had happened this time, had it?

No. But he was scared nevertheless.

Eames?

Not only Eames. All of it was too much for him to cope with.

325]

Even so, Scott found himself out of patience with him: he was a mature man, an intelligent one, and for all his alleged love, and his loyalty to wife and family, his protests seemed thin, just a fraction thin. He'd had himself a night with some tasty tart and he might readily have thirsted for it again except for the fact that he had been scared, and his so-called puritan conscience, long fallow, had bestirred itself too tardily, ignited only by the sheer force of blackmail.

What got under Scott then was not the engineer's plight alone, but what it mirrored: this kind of subterranean climate in which a man like Kamber had been working, living. (And what about a man like Scott Quinnley?)

"Yes," Scott called out. At last he heard the rapping on the door. Hastily putting on his dressing robe, he went to the other room, hurrying in sudden alarm, suddenly hurrying, out of indefinable alarm: a telegram. Red.

"Hello. I wake you up?" Faith, in her lustrous fur coat, came into the bedroom.

"Where did you . . ." Scott began.

"Mr. Eames told me."

"Oh. What happened to Eames?"

She shrugged. "Changed his mind, we went out for something to eat. He was in a terrible mood."

"That I don't doubt." Scott knew what Kamber had told him. "Would you like a dri—no, you don't drink, do you?"

"You go ahead." She glanced around. "Is there a hanger anywhere?"

"Oh. Certainly." He helped her off with the coat. Its heft was impressive. He took it to the closet, hung it, and closed the door.

She was standing in front of the mirror now, combing her thick auburn hair, her weight shifted to one leg, her flat belly curving out. Such a pretty-assed stance.

"How is it you decided to come up here?" Scott said.

"Why not? I'd rather finish up here than take on one of those late tricks, they're usually freaks or spooks."

Scott rolled with the tribute. "You'll never get rich like this."

"That's for me to worry about, isn't it, honey?" she moved to the bed and sat down. She took out a cigarette, then as an afterthought offered him one. "Or don't you feel like smoking now?"

He felt like it, yes.

Still, hard to believe that she was simply being gracious, a cigarette and conversation. Unfortunately, in view of what he'd seen and heard on this night, he knew he wasn't going to avail himself of what Mc-Gregor would call the goodies. So that a cigarette and conversation was what it had to be. And after all, he was still an amateur, and like most amateurs he was alive with curiosity about her, if not as a type, then as this one girl. He'd keep it all talk: one cigarette, maybe two, and then he'd give her the flag.

"Look," Faith peered at him not without intolerance in the cool, cloudy green eyes, "if you're worrying about how much it is, forget about it, everything's been taken care of."

"It has. By whom?"

"Mr. Eames," she said.

"I see." But hearing it, having it laid out for him, shut off any possible interest in her. Conclusively. He was not taking the Kamber circuit and he was not taking the track of any of the other nignogs on the team. "Well thanks, Faith, but I'm going to have to opt out tonight. It's my loss. But . . ."

"You like the lights on?" She rose, put out her cigarette. She took his failure to reply immediately as the answer, and smiling faintly, her astral gaze fixed just above and beyond his shoulder, she unzipped the long white dress and let it drop to the olive carpet. No pants. She moved back to the bed.

He tried, with some success, to see her with detachment, to admire her slender nude body. Then he got up, tugged the sash of his robe a bit tighter, and cleared his throat. "Faith—"

"What is it, honey?" Adroitly her hand darted inside his robe, parting it. "What's the matter, honey? You're not interested?" She lowered her hand, touched it, slipped her fingers around it. "*He* is, isn't he?"

No answer from Scott Quinnley. His throat throbbed, and his teeth and gums went numb and he felt as if his blood had hurtled downward to swell and break between his legs, and that is how it happened that he slumped back on the bed, there being no support from his sensible resolutions of thirty seconds ago. Principle? High purpose? Even caution? Where were they? Where was that warning image of Negative Kamber and how many others? Or the gross, corrupt and generous benefactor, Mr. Vincent Eames?

Where?

Here.

She was straddling his lap, and the only principle or purpose or image there was, was the bold milky thrust of her breasts directly in front of his face, her nipples darkly pink and erect.

"How's that, honey?" Her murmured, solicitous question came after the lifting of her haunches, and then slowly coming down, sinking down on it, enclosing it, letting it rise in her, holding back then, savoring the instant, keeping it unhurried as he could, and she stayed with it, a silken vise. Soon there was the change, and she began to move, drawing him into her spiral, and she took on a noisy excitement, or the sounds of such, for he wasn't quite sure, and he found himself wanting to make it sound real (like how many other clowns before him?) but pleased now as he thrust deeper, all the way, to hear that fine feminine gasp—at once, however, feeling it might again be part of her performance.

She knew her business. She paced Scott, anticipated him, that silken vise ever tightening until the final swelling spasm quivered, spattered out of him into her waiting warmth.

Joylessness so soon, and knowing it was over much quicker than he had wanted it to be. And here she was now, the cigarettes out, offering one, and talking, acting how? With some kind of remote tenderness? Maybe. Except that Scott happened to notice in a few moments that her gaze, like a magnetic ray, shot to the closet door: dark haven of her mink coat.

He could see or imagine seeing in her face exactly what ticked in her mind: Yes she had made short, shrift of him, a job well done and finished, and now a decent night of sleep. . . . *A can of Campbell's tomato soup and sleep sleep sleep.* . . .

Why he began to resist this will of hers to leave, he did not know, unless it was that being an amateur, he still had this determination to raise her or bring her down to the exact level of sexuality he had felt. What the amateur cannot admit is that he is little different from the Vincent Eameses or the Kambers or all the other anonymous and faceless men—even with a pro like Faith who might have been cantankerous and coolly honest, but who was still coolly graceful, and who still possessed a sculpture of flesh that sat prettily splayed across a man's lap.

Yet, whatever his shortcomings or failings, Scott persisted in believing himself a cut above the others with whom she had to do business. So he would keep her there, ignore the quick glances to the coat closet, keep her there. Prove something. The hallmark of the amateur was plain upon him, and he cared not: he had to turn it into a contest. Let's see if Scott Quinnley can make out where others can't. A contest, imagine, even with someone like her. (Not even with Jemmy had it been much different, had it? Always a contest of a kind. And with Ellen, loving her, or believing he loved her, he'd expected to make out differently, no scratching hostility or belligerence, no gladiators in bed; though in truth he never found that great sweet essence which love is said to distill from sex.) Was Ben Nodina finding it with Ann; Ann with him? And what did it matter?

Let it rest here, take the cigarette. Talk. Even the most untutored amateur should have known that sex with Faith was perfect only if you enjoyed it for itself; and that being the case then why couldn't Scott look back and take joy in what he'd had, admitting that her custom-built commodity was available precisely for a time like tonight.

Yet, as for her, what was there? Nothing? Really nothing? Ever?

"What's with you, honey?" Languidly Faith reached out and extinguished her cigarette. "Didn't you like it?"

Scott nodded, but did not hold his amateur's tongue: "I was thinking how it was for you."

"For me? What's the difference, you're the one who . . ." She paused; she was bored. "What do you want to know? Did I come? Is that it? Look honey, I want to make *you* feel good. Me, if I want kicks, I'm just like you, I pay out too."

Kicks. You couldn't tell from that what she meant, if it meant no more than that or if it was her way of summing up her love for someone. From the opaque gray-green surface of her eyes, you suspected that love might be a word she could not or would not utter.

She turned, and there was that glance, less fugitive now, toward the closet door.

How was it for Ann? Sex with love, love-sex? Again the question. More sharply and with some pain. Ann and Ben in the bed of the ivory-walled suite on the ship. . . .

"Look." Faith frowned at him. "If you want to take a little rest or sleep, don't worry about me, you can go to sleep, everything's been taken care of, honey."

"You told me that before, Fay—Faith, you told me that," he cut in irritably.

"Are you trying to put me down?" She pounced at once.

"No. Sorry. Forget it."

"You said it on purpose."

329]

"Just to get a rise out of you." He resorted to gallantry.

She said: "You worry about getting your own rise, honey. Okay?"

"Why does it bother you? I don't know why that should bug you—"

Exasperated, she said: "It bothers me because Fay is, was my name. I changed it when I quit high school."

"Oh."

"It wasn't my idea. My girlfriend's. She thought men would go for Faith."

"Do they?"

"No, they don't. It's too nice, reminds them of their sister or some angel cake in the family or who they're married to. But I don't care. I got so's I liked it, and that's how it's going to be." Faith spoke with that same lively, intractable impertinence. "And if anyone doesn't go for it, too bad. That's how it is."

Now a silence and into it Scott's yawn came helpless and wide and condemning, and she said: "If you're tired, honey, why don't we just tuck you in?" She rose from the bed. "Okay?"

"No," he answered obstinately. He muscled back another yawn. "Why don't you stay over?"

"Are you trying to snow me? You are, aren't you?" She measured him with a glacial eye: "You're not going to turn into one of those mean bastards, are you? I thought you were cute."

Scott got up and went to the bureau. He brought back his wallet. "I never asked you how much it was, Faith. Forgot to ask about it."

"Mr. Eames—"

"Yes, I know. But I'm picking up the tab for this round," he said.

"It's paid. He paid for everything from five this afternoon including for me to come here," she said.

"How much, Faith?"

"Two hundred. That is for everything, not for—"

He opened the wallet. A hundred and thirty dollars. He put down a hundred on the bedtable. He wasn't paying for Mr. Eames' earlier pleasures.

"I told you it's been paid. Keep it, don't be crazy."

"Can't help it. Runs in the family."

She peered at him and shrugged. "Look," she said then with a certain weary logic, "if I'm getting the money twice, then you've got more time coming to you." She stacked and folded the bills and placed them carefully on the bedtable. Then she said: "Listen, honey, if you're . . . if you want it some special way, tell me. Only I don't go for it too freaky, people don't engage me for that."

"I'm sure they don't, Faith." He sat down alongside her on the bed.

"Because," she said, "if there's something, some little way you like it better, just say so, you're paying me and you didn't have to. What's so funny?"

Funny?

He hadn't thought of it as funny, but of course it was. He'd reached a point where, among too many people, including himself, he kept finding too many things lacking, and where even the simplest probity or rectitude came as a kind of surprising bonus. And here closeby was this girl, this coarse, cool, pragmatic and naked girl who could make him grin with embarrassment because he couldn't tell her what was funny, when all it was, was his recognizing that it had been she, Fay-Faith, who possessed a code, however limited, of honor.

25: Scott Quinnley

THE exodus of the Bellgard camp began the next afternoon. How palpable already was the current of optimism; already the Bellstar was seen by some as a meteor streaking across and illuminating the whole brooding firmament of the company's fate. Yes, and already people seemed less concerned over the Holtsbridge stock maneuver and more indifferent to the tide of rumor and defeat which had swamped them on the eve of the Automobile Show. Dean Stratler and some of his staff were among the first to hurry back to the plant; Codman and Mrs. Smith and several directors departed in the evening in the company plane, to be followed early the next morning by many other officials.

Scott flew back twenty-four hours later, along with Chester Ormond, Ralph Alsop, Mrs. Stratler and others.

Yesterday in New York he had done what had to be done to break the last links with his old life. He had gone to New Canaan to have lunch with his mother-in-law, a drab and cheerless occasion, since he could see more clearly than she how soon they had gone on their forgetful ways. (Here was Ellen's mother, spry, cosmetically restyled, whose sorrow at the time of Ellen's death seemed as if it would really be nothing less than eternal, yet fluttering about the gay saltbox house, piping away on the telephone to her gaily widowed friends, and later coyly laughing, obscenely flirtatious when the youngish man next door stopped by to return her last week's issue of *The New Yorker*.) Scott had hurried back to Manhattan and, after arranging for the shipment of his vintage Pierce Arrow, attended to the signing of papers making legal the transfer and finances of the magazine to Russel Farington and his group.

Afterward he was intensely conscious about what lay ahead, what he was returning to, had to return to. Even if the continuation of bank credit for Quinnley Corners had not depended in good measure on his association with Bellgard, he would have wanted to return. He could almost say he felt happy about going back, though he didn't know why and wondered about it all the way out to the airport early the next day.

The sun, shy and pale in the early morning, had now boldly cracked through the marbled sky as he reached the ramp of the jet liner.

Scott was the last to get aboard. Myra Stratler was alone; she waved to him as he started down the aisle.

"Scott—" Chester Ormond detained him, "soon as we're airborne we'd better have a little talk on that Gifford situation."

Scott nodded: the Gifford situation was Ormond's way of referring to the ill-starred junket they had made to Queens to woo the goodwill of the Negro newspaper.

As Scott sat down beside Mrs. Stratler, Ormond turned around, presenting to her a solicitude, a charm, that seemed almost genuine. "Man's work never done, is it, Myra?"

"But never, Chester." She settled back, crossed her legs and consulted her face in the glass of her gold compact. She fastened her safety belt. She inclined her blond head toward Scott: It *was* a relief to be getting back, wasn't it? Too bad Dean had had to rush home ahead of her, but wasn't it really marvelous the way his baby had gone over at the auto show? Yes, and even she had had some small good fortune in New York; she'd arranged with the director of a museum to bring a show of Pop Art to Kent Hills late in the spring, and it would really be a smasher, all the big, that is, major names in the movement— Well no, no, to answer Scott's question, she didn't care all *that* much for the Pop stuff, but it *would* lend itself to her purpose, she'd make a charity occasion out of it, very steep admission, the money going toward the building fund of the new Kent Hills Fine Arts Center, and too, it would be fun, all those Coca-Cola bottles, hamburgers and cartoons on the walls, with the Grosse Pointe crowd thinking she'd gone mad; they *were* square, always took them time to catch up with the doing at Cranbrook or Kent Hills, didn't it?

The takeoff then: the jet dicing out the runway, the sharp nosing upward, the leveling out for cruising altitude.

"I meant to ask you, Scott," she was saying, and her hands no longer resting on her lap but working in small nervous arabesques, "about Tony. How is he? You saw him yesterday, didn't you, with Phoebe?"

"Yes. Last night." Kerwin's wife, Phoebe, had finally been notified and had flown to New York despite her own poor health.

333]

"Father said he's definitely improving, on the mend. I feel dreadful never having got over, but he is better, you say? Well, good. Psychologically of course the success of the Bellstar must have helped, wouldn't you say? Poor Phoebe, this will set her back. I talked to her on the phone and she said Tony'll be there for another week, is that what you heard?" The hands poised, waiting.

"At least that long," Scott said.

"Hasn't it been a really mad and exciting time? I must say it certainly stirs one up." A pause. "Tell me, how did you think Ann looked?" Seizing Scott's hesitation, she went on: "Oh now you don't have to be *that* tactful, Scott. Really though, knowing Annie, would you say she looked like the bride the sun shines on?"

"Well, it was a lousy Bon Voyage for her," he said. But as the image of Ann asserted itself, Ann in that surprised and buoyant instant of her father's tardy arrival in the stateroom, her glittering smile just before it was crushed by Cod Smith's first utterance—this image of her, more than her sister's veiled envy or malice, caused Scott to add: "But even so, Ann has a way of always looking pretty wonderful no matter how rough it might be."

"Now that's an interesting reaction." Myra peered at him. "Of course I'm her sister and I suppose I'm just too close to her. I did think she looked lovely, but terribly tired, you could almost feel the strain, the way she kept hoping right up to the end that Father would relent. An awful mess. It *is* a mess, and I just hope she doesn't get hurt."

A silence, into which Chester Ormond stepped like an experienced host who had been waiting unobtrusively for the right moment to break up a tête-à-tête between two of his guests.

"Please go right ahead, Scott." Myra Stratler patted, squeezed Scott's hand in a hasty maternal gesture, except that it seemed a bit too maternal to go unnoticed.

"Excuse me." He rose.

A faint flush touched her handsome features. "I've never flown anywhere with Dean or my father but that there isn't always at least one high-altitude conference—"

There was a shifting of places now as Ralph Alsop moved over to the window and Scott took his seat, settling between the two men.

"To get right with it," Ormond began quietly, "I got that memo from the hospital. Tony must have sent it right after you talked with

[334

him. He wants us to follow through on the Gifford situation, along with Ralph here, and—"

"It's not in my basket, Chet," Scott said. "I told that to Tony. I also told him I thought it was pretty late in the day for Bellgard to start showing all that largess to Negroes. I mean, getting their good-will is one thing, buying it is something else again."

"Agreed," Chester Ormond said. "But the company wants to go ahead. It'll fall into the Dealer Assistance plan."

"If Scott can give me a complete playback on the whole Negro bit —" Ralph Alsop leaned forward.

"Listen, Ralph," Scott began, "I only happened to fall into this. . . ."

"For the records," Ormond said, "you didn't fall into it, you walked into it, eyes and mouth wide open. And I'm the first to admit I was wrong for jumping you for it at the time But you did open up the situation." Ormond's face, like Alsop's, betrayed the evidence of his Manhattan nights: dark, downward grooves were carved into his otherwise round, bland features.

"All right," Scott said. "I opened it up. But—"

"I always told you, Chet," Alsop taunted amiably, "what this company needed was a few old-fashioned eggheads like Quinnley." He laughed and punched Scott's shoulder lightly. "He asks the guy are there any Negro dealers in the area. Now who but a real swinging kook would stick his neck out like that?"

"And I got a real swinging answer," Scott said. It had been after the luncheon, and they were convoying the newspapermen out to the fair grounds for the demonstration of new models, when Scott had asked one of the editors, Merrill Johnson, the question.

"Mr. Quinnley," Johnson had said, "you must be kidding."

"No," Scott had said and seen Johnson's dark-fleshed jaw stiffen.

"Come on, Mr. Quinnley," his tone was a fraction milder then, "since when is Detroit handing out dealer franchises to Negroes?"

"I believe Chrysler has—or is."

"Not around here, not in my brother's case, and my brother tried," Johnson said.

"Oh."

"And my brother is a carman from way back. Was in the used-car business and had a garage too. He had the financial backing also. But when he tried to get a franchise to open a dealership in Gifford here, they turned him down."

335]

"May I ask who turned him down?"

"Bellgard."

"I see." The reserved or unresponsive attitude Scott had noticed during the luncheon was accounted for. "Do you happen to know whom he talked to at Bellgard?"

"No," Johnson said. "But that's past history now."

"He's no longer interested?"

"To tell you the truth, Mr. Quinnley, and no offense meant"—hostility seeped into Johnson's tone—"my brother may not even have the time anymore, he's pretty busy these days, he's on the Regional Planning Board, and he's assistant chairman of the local committee on National Traffic Safety, and he's treasurer of the Gifford Community House. To tell you the truth, I think my brother feels maybe he was lucky Bellgard turned him down."

This barbed reference to the languishing business of the nearest Bellgard dealer had been neatly taken.

"Great," Alsop muttered when Scott finished his account.

"Very."

"No, I mean it, it's great. Scott, I thank you from the bottom of what used to be my heart." Alsop was growing exuberant. "Yesterday I'd got the impression from what I'd heard on the Gifford bit that we'd fallen into a barrel of shit, whereas what we've landed in is Chanel Number 5." Alsop already seemed to be losing that jowly, drooping aspect of his junket fatigue, showing now something of his customary ebullience. "Listen, Chet, I'm going to have to borrow Scott from Quality Control, just as soon as we get back, just for a while until I lay this out. For, gentlemen, I am shocked," he took on an elaborately mocking tone, "shocked to think that in the midst of another national crisis on Civil Rights, Bellgard lost—or almost lost this glorious chance to get its image enlarged and sweetened. We're going to see that Mr. Johnson's brother gets himself a franchised shop. And try as I might I'm afraid we won't be able to keep this a secret from the public at large, the colored population, that is."

"For chrissakes, Ralph, your mouth is getting wet as a hungry dog's," Scott said.

"True," he said.

"It's too obvious," Scott said. "Bellgard with all this religion all of a sudden."

"Obvious?" Alsop said. "Of course it's obvious. So? As long as we get it made. And you say his credit rating is good. So what's to lose?"

Nothing's to lose. If Scott believed the ploy was too transparent, how much did that really matter? Motives were unimportant in Cartown; results were all that had to be rung up. Did Alsop's attitude matter if in the end Negro dealerships would be established, and if this led to franchises for other nameplates of other companies?

Did the angels care who was on their side?

Yes, Scott thought privately. Yes.

But he said: "What can I do to start this moving, Ralph?"

"Ah," he said at once. "You can get through to Johnson's brother, ease open the door so my team can move in."

Scott said he would try.

Fasten Safety Belts.

He was back in his seat beside Myra Stratler when the plane began its descent.

"How it looks!" she said as the distant city, rising by the river, spoking out to its suburbs and its many-fingered factory areas, became visible below.

"How it looks! When you think how it's changed in such a short time," she said. "But you know, even today, people still have this antiquated idea that all there is here is the automobile—" She spoke almost primly, and her hands, as if in rebuke to their previous contact with Scott's, were now locked sedately. "People simply have no idea, have they?"

No, they haven't. He had heard her rhapsodies often since he'd come back, the hymns to the burgeoning "cultural life," to the architecture of a Yamasaki or a Saarinen, to the flowering in mean streets of "little avant-garde galleries," to the music groups, to the universities, the symphony—"culture" in Cartown was bumper-to-bumper.

All quite true, remarkable even, when you compared it to what had existed when Scott was a kid.

And what pride it gave Myra Stratler, Myra who worked hard to make glory for Kent Hills (and herself). Yet Scott had never been able to buy her lofty pursuits. He had seen enough of her to wonder if she was so excessively vain as to try for admiration at every turn, or if she was merely a conventional tease out for kicks, or if possibly she was a sizzling piece available if the circumstances were right.

Once, though only for a flash, he recalled now, he had glimpsed her at the Kent Hills Country Club dancing with Tony Kerwin in a

337]

way he could still remember. And there'd been more than one occasion when her shadowed eyes had reached Scott in tentative interest,
and once, today, when her hand was more than tentative.

They were still talking when the plane touched down, and when
they began to file into the air terminal, she was saying: "But of
course, Ann could never see living here, could she? And now I suppose we'll be deluged with letters about the glories of Greece."

The autumn sun was more brilliant now, bringing to the vast glass
foyer a dazzling unreal light. "It just occurred to me," Scott said,
"that I haven't even got her address."

"It's simply the Grande Bretagne Hotel, Athens, until they know
where they're going to settle. How long do you give her, truthfully
now? I can ask you, you're more or less part of the family. How
long?"

"In Greece?"

"No. With Ben. You're not as iffy about it as some of us are, are
you?" She pressed the question.

"I think it'll stick, Myra." Spoken like a loyal well-wisher (but one
who, on the bed with Fay-Faith, had found himself imagining and
resenting sex between Ann and Ben).

"You do? Really?"

And suddenly Scott felt isolated, stranded.

"Dean is sending a driver down for me, can I drop you anywhere?"

Scott was going straight to the plant with Alsop.

But looking around now, from his island, looking around for what?
There wouldn't be anyone waiting in the waiting crowd.

So much, so exactly, like another time.

"Thanks for keeping me good company, Scott. We'll see you soon,
of course—" Myra Stratler's voice.

Yes.

Exactly like that other time: that first arrival, coming through these
same lines, looking around for Phil Rothe and discovering it was Ann
Smith who'd come.

Ann.

No sneakers, no stringy ponytail as in Paris. But the blond hair soft
and curved, the slanting bangs, the Parisian suit—deliberate, an arti-
fact, a private joke like Scott's firehouse red belt, she'd come to meet
him not as a dutiful gesture on behalf of Phil, but more as a gesture,
the kind she couldn't quite resist.

Good-bye, Myra.

Ann saying: *Same old Smith body, except with a phony new grille.*
Wanting to see her now.

Why now?

"Meeting in my office, Scott. You and Ralph." Chester Ormond's voice brisk, eager, closeby.

Why now? Out of all reason, sanity. He had only just left her, only a snap of time since he'd been raising martinis with her and Ben at the Carlyle, and only a snippet of time since he'd been at the boat.

And at Le Chanteclair afterward, his mood touchy and unloving, sparked by Phil Rothe calling the score. And what had Scott said? He couldn't be that square, is what he'd said. Not Scott Quinnley.

But he was. He was the prince, the king of Squareville.

"Scott, let's move." Ralph Alsop calling.

Dimly now, seeing a dark-suited driver holding open the car for Myra Stratler, the sight sliding into view like a panel of memory: seeing Ann on that raw morning waiting for him by that wire-wheeled, chauffeur-driven black Bellgard limousine.

I know it's too big, but at least it's pretentious, Ann had said.

"See you at the plant, boys." Chester Ormond's eagerness.

Ann.

Moving along with Ralph Alsop to the parking area, waiting now as the porter tucked their gear into the boot of the Bellgard "sports" convertible. Soon crawling out of the terminal grounds, soon onto the expressway.

Ann.

"It's no Porsche." Alsop blasting forth, taking the outside lane. "No Bellstar for that matter. But you'll get yourself a ride out of it."

Cartown leaning in toward them, so soon, and she wasn't around any longer, Ann no longer on hand.

"Listen," Alsop is saying, "I'm not even out of second yet." The throaty roar of the pipes. "You can say what you want, but no one does a modification job like that cat up in Lime Rock."

Happy to be getting back. Scott had thought that. Not knowing why. But here he was, back, and wishing he wasn't.

And now this unwanted, stinging, belated sense of loss, even though he should have known that it was the very belatedness of his realization that made the loss, the absence of her, so achingly real for him now.

"Torque pays off here." Alsop demonstrating. "Scott—hey Quinnley, where are you?"

So achingly real for him now. But why? Why, when she was this far away, did he think he wanted her and needed her?

Mrs. Ben Nodina. And Scott Quinnley acting how? Like one of those poor desperate homosexuals, those lithe, aging fags who fuss over some charming woman, fondle, flatter, yearn for her, need her—when? When she's safely married to someone else and there's not a prayer their pretense will be taken seriously.

But worse. For what had been partially clear to Philip Rothe was now, belatedly, wholly vivid to Scott, clear and inescapable as a sunrise.

What he could not fathom, though, was how or why this sensation, unaccountable as nature, striking with the indiscriminate hand of death, should have struck him down now? When Ann was a thousand miles away, half an ocean away.

Leaving him revved up with resentment and rage like a lover, like —Phil had said it—her father.

Never feeling anything akin to this, not when Ellen was away, not when Jemmy went to California, not any other time before or after.

There was too much he didn't know.

It was not enough for him to know that the farther away Ann was, the more everything about her grew closer, more intense, over-magnified, and hence distorted and untrustworthy.

The eyes, wonderful, mischievous, sad, glittering; that worldly, innocent glance sudden as lightning; Ann, outrageous and rebellious and conforming, Daddy-devoted and Ben-bedding; Ann flinging aside the cardigans and pearls of Kent Hills; Ann, unhappy amalgam of Smith College and the Sorbonne and Cartown; Ann, a hybrid, souped-up with too many component parts, irreconcilable as the fusing of Jo, Meg, Beth and Amy.

I wonder what would have happened if you'd seduced me? she'd said during that evening hike to the Automobile Show.

He could torment himself with that one, too.

What had she meant? Quixotic speculation? Or a betrayal of the fear she felt before leaving?

Or was it something else? And what had Scott answered?

Whatever he'd said, it was the answer of a nut, a nignog, a wiggy, a royal schmuck with goggles for eyes, who read his insides with a tachometer.

Ann.

He could say it all, couldn't he?

[340

But like a rosy landscape painting it offered little truth of nature. His tenderest visions gave him nothing but a torment he did not deserve. Or did he? Possibly. Probably. Undoubtedly. That torment could have had his name on it.

He had to admit it now: a presence, a spirit, whose special essence and being had never existed for him until it was no longer here. And here was suddenly a wilderness.

26: Tony Kerwin

To signal Tony's triumph, the other officers at the table, led by Codman Smith, raised their water goblets in salute to him—a rather grim salute it was, though he was still the bearer or maker of the first good tidings since production woes on the Bellstar had struck down the company in early March. Two months ago. He had hastened to the trouble spot in Ohio a fortnight ago, flying back today, returning to the plant, reaching the oval luncheon table in the private dining room, that is, making it a point to time his arrival explicitly for the luncheon period when his audience would be maximum.

Even Vince Eames, who had appeared unexpectedly to meet him at the airport that morning, and who had given him a thoroughly disagreeable time—even this had been tolerable because it had kept him away from the plant, so that it was one-fifteen when he entered the white room. The sheer drama of it was enough to make him forget for a while what had transpired at the airport bar.

"Well now—" Codman Smith addressed the executives who sat around the long polished table, their faces in the cruel sun of May showing the gray ravages of night meetings and anxiety which had again enveloped them. "Let's let the man eat his lunch."

Tony smiled like a kind of gay martyr, bent his head to the boiled rice and pale slivers of chicken before him, this colorless array to be washed down with a glass of skimmed milk. (Seven months ago in New York, before the eruption of his ulcerous stomach, he would never have dreamed he'd be on a diet like this, the very sort of food which, like a bland woman, bored him.)

Fortunately many of the men began asking him questions about the Ohio junket, and he could ignore the dullness of the cuisine while now he amplified his account. He had flown to the special (sub-contracting) body plant where the new shells for the Bellstar were made —or rather where they *would* have been made except for the strike and the series of technical griefs which had developed. The chief grief had turned up because of a new process of bonding body sections with adhesives, a method designed to create greater strength and cut down weight and labor time. But in the rush to rectify the troubles, there had been a serious infraction of union laws, and this, coupled with earlier union grievances, had brought on the prolonged strike. Until Tony, along with the company's labor-relations counsel, had finally negotiated the successful compromise so that production was now scheduled to commence tomorrow morning: almost three months after the Bellstar had been promised to dealers, to the public.

Ten weeks too late.

The small triumph for Tony was valid, but it could not undo the serious damage which the long delay had cost the company: the price of anticlimax, of embarrassing failure to meet commitments, the sharp decline of consumer interest, marked by cancellations of advance orders dating back to the Automobile Show in New York last fall. Frantic concern was rampant among dealers everywhere in the United States and Canada.

In addition, the outlay in advertising billings for newspaper, magazine and television was now almost a total waste, since the already overpublicized sports car could not be delivered. News of production troubles had spawned loss in public confidence: the Bellstar must be riddled with bugs.

A vast sum had also gone into the Young Citizens' program, a new departure for Bellgard which had belatedly decided to concentrate on American youth (aged fifteen to twenty-two) who were forming their buying habits and who could best be captured by the lure of sports car performance. A hootenanny show had been organized and had been traveling across the nation; a comic book had been printed which presented the Bellstar in story and fact; thousands of records of Bellstar sounds were given away free at Hot Rod rallies; and, taking yet another leaf from Ford, a kit, the Bell-Flight Kit, had been put out to appeal to the hot-rodders, an audience of about three hundred thousand, who might like to modify old Bellgard engines for higher performance.

All this, a loud and costly explosion, had produced a whimper instead of a roar when on the long-heralded March 19, the Bellstar had failed to appear.

Bitterest of ironies was that until the twin disasters in Ohio, the fortunes of the company had begun to spiral upward, pushed by the

343]

thermal of optimism and excitement in New York, and plans for re-tooling for next season were underway.

Even the fireworks Cod Smith, Tony and the others had expected at last month's annual stockholders' meeting had not come to pass. Nor had Cod Smith's retirement. As for the Holtsbridge group, they had withdrawn rather mysteriously, a holding action of some kind, a wait-and-see policy. Nobody really knew what they were up to now. Their failure to act at the meeting could have been a special strategy or it could simply have been that they did not control enough proxies to vote in a new board, new management.

But now, as a result of one of those unpredictable catastrophes which had so often befallen other companies in the industry, Bellgard was once more looking at treacherous times.

"The ball game is still on, we're only just warming up for the biggest season of all," Cod Smith had been quoted by the press. But neither Cod, nor anyone else at the luncheon table, four of whom were directors, could believe this.

Yet the success of Tony's action, coming as it did at so cheerless a time, took on a dimension of hope, desperate as it might have been. (By three o'clock this afternoon the value of the common stock would jump one and three-eighths, reacting thus after the news release announcing resumption of production at the Ohio plant.)

"Well, gentlemen," Cod said after the coffee, "I think we can say Tony's brought back—if not the whole bacon, at least a welcome chunk of it."

There was a Finance Policy Committee meeting in less than an hour, and the group dispersed. As Tony went into the larger dining room where the rest of the executive personnel lunched, he was joined by Chester Ormond. "You know, Tony, you haven't looked this good since they sprung you from the hospital last fall."

"I still had to cancel some choice duck shooting this weekend," Tony said. "I'm opting for the quiet domestic life for the most part, Chet."

For the most part. Quite true.

Up to a point. For he'd passed that necessary period of self-chastisement, the serene, good, conjugal life, a model husband (abetted by the doctor's warnings). He and Phoebe had shared the same dreary diet, and for so many evenings he would look at her loving face, the blond hair so carefully coiffed to celebrate her happiness, he would see her framed by the silver candelabra, see the discreet spar-

[344

kle of the new antique brooch, shell-shaped and encrusted with tiny diamonds and sapphires. On the day after his release from the hospital in New York he'd gone, in a caprice of joy and guilt, to the bank downtown and taken out the necessary cash, deciding then to make a clean sweep and remove all the money, bring it back to Kent Hills where it would be handier in his safe.

During this domestic therapy, as his health was restored, Phoebe grew more resilient. As his activity at the plant grew greater and as the fortunes of the company seemed again to be rising, she had stopped fretting about the rumors she'd heard before the Automobile Show, and she almost never asked him questions which might have been uncomfortable for him to answer. He never gave her the chance: after that one unfortunate time when he'd attempted (prematurely) to warn her of the possibility of scandal touching him, after that one time in which he'd seen the whole structure of Phoebe's nature collapse, he vowed never to confide in her again.

But recently Phoebe had begun to lose ground again, as if the calamities in Ohio and the subsequent repercussions had begun to undermine her. Not of course out of fears for financial reasons, that would have been absurd; but because of that sensitive, fierce pride, not only in Tony, but in her father's name and life.

So that Tony no longer felt as sheltered in their English cottage as he had during his virtuous period of convalescence.

He had decided, months ago, that the exemplary life he'd been leading had gone too far.

Enough.

A total bore.

He'd recovered from his ulcers, and from the terror that had caused them: the threat of exposure, the miserable knowledge that Myra, with a single glance, a single question in her hotel suite in New York, had pinned him down, had cast her deadly suspicion directly upon him, had sent him fleeing from her, loathing her.

He had scarcely spoken to her since. (The old charade they'd played so long was no longer a game, for now their performances of mutual enmity had become authentic.)

By betraying her suspicions, Myra had killed off what was between them, and he hated, detested her now with the same passion that he had once craved her.

In fact if it hadn't been for his bitter hatred of Myra, he might not have started seeing so much of Blanche Bennett.

Blanche at least had brought a sensually novel and luxurious element to his life: what he needed, what he always had to have, to function at peak performance.

Blanche Bennett had come here less than six months ago, accompanying her lawyer husband Cornelius (Neil), who was general counsel of Jefferson Motors of Canada (years ago he'd been on the legal staff of Bellgard), and who now had been transferred to the home base. He was an older man; he had a judicious calm and a conservative manner which gave balance to Blanche's vivacious personality. It was her third marriage. Her second husband had been a member of the British Embassy in Ottawa; he'd died several years ago. The new pair had made a remarkable rise on the social graph of Kent Hills. And already Blanche was penetrating the small clan of culture bees of whom Myra was still the tenacious queen.

Blanche was well-traveled, a superb hostess of embassy experience, a delightful guest; she could dance or ride a streak; her tennis, as he discovered on the club's indoor court, was first-rate. She also shared his zest for stylish and luxurious living. Yet, at first he hadn't responded to her—he often distrusted women who had that athletic zeal, for more often than not they were cold, slow to start, with a sluggish acceleration. But one night last December he had seen Blanche in a different way. It was the night he and Phoebe had gone to a dinner-dance at the Pine Royal Sports Car Club at which Scott Quinnley had been invited to speak—a very good but unsettling talk on the influence in engineering, safety and styling that racing cars could make on modern passenger vehicles. It was that night that Phoebe had observed "how nervous Myra seems whenever she's around Blanche Bennett." And later when he danced with Blanche he happened to glimpse Myra watching them, the look in the mauve-ringed eyes unmistakable: almost at once Tony found himself altering his hold on Blanche, discovering just as quickly that she welcomed this change in his attention.

Toward the end of the evening, while he was standing near the dance floor talking with Scott and Virginia Colter, the club's secretary whom Scott had been taking out lately, he could not rid himself of his preoccupation with Blanche; he kept looking around until, finding her across the floor beside her husband, his eyes drew her immediate response, the exchange between them was implicit with their new awareness of each other.

The affair began a week later.

And no one the wiser. And if Myra perceived what was going on, that only made his pleasure with Blanche more erotic.

Now as he and Chester Ormond parted in the corridor, he strode on to his office. He'd have time for a ten-minute rest; he no longer needed the minimum half hour Dr. Krayler in New York had urged. As he neared his door he saw Scott Quinnley, who was just hurrying out, and he called to him. They shook hands.

"When'd you get back?" Scott said. He looked harassed, his cheeks seemed a bit hollow. Overwork. Around his eyes there showed the crevices of strain, and weren't there, now that you looked closely, a few more snips of gray in that black thatch? Tony had never troubled to notice.

"Got back less than an hour ago. Come on in. I read your entire report on the way back in the plane. Like to talk to you, Scott."

"I wanted to talk to you also." Scott's lanky frame, as he walked, seemed rather rigid, tense. "Your friend Vincent Eames—"

"Ah, Vince. Now what kind of welcome greeting is that?" Tony joked. The figure of Vince at the airport that morning rose before him once more. "He was at the terminal to meet me." It was better to play it openly. "And I've already had my ear bent and battered."

They passed through the reception room and the anteroom with the three secretaries, and on into Tony's spacious office with its paneled wainscoting. (He'd bought it for thirteen hundred dollars in England six years ago.) Above the wainscoting the walls were white, sparingly decorated with framed automotive prints of classic cars, and a few photos of outstanding Bellgard models dating back to the first one of 1907.

In passing he glanced with affection at his desk which, unlike those of other executives, was surfaced in fine olive leather and featured, in addition to the photograph of Phoebe, a seventeenth-century pewter inkwell with quill. All modern equipment was concealed beneath the lip of the desk top. He moved on to the olive leather couch and stretched out, nudging the pillow into position beneath his head. "Sit down, Scott." Then: "I gather you've been an out-and-out bastard while I was away. You know, Scott, all that hard work is going to get you nothing but fame and fortune."

"Mostly it's got me a hell of a lot of enemies." Scott lit a cigarette; he was still standing.

"I trust I am not among them," Tony said. "You made the mistake of virtually saving my life and you can do no wrong as far as this office is concerned."

"What I meant, Tony—"

"Your report. Yes, I know," Tony said. "Vince Eames and a few other lads who are afraid of getting cut out of your Last Will and Testament."

Which was one way of referring to the result of Scott's work. Seven months' work, heading the team on Quality Control and Analysis. Scott had been a tiger from the start. He had explored all corners of his open-end assignment: finding ways of reducing the incidence of component failure in the Bellgard product, pushing, pressing his team of specialists. Each day these men would examine and test parts, all parts classified and tagged and laid out on wooden platforms in the block-long length of one of the machine shops; each Monday, Scott and his men would study the weekly quality-trend analysis fresh from the test track which charted the defects or malfunction observed in engine, chassis, transmission, body. A defect could be anything, a few drops of oil on the floor, even the pressure needed to press down the heat lever or open the glove compartment.

What they were pushing for was to be able to extend the warranty or guarantee to thirty-six months. When quality was conscientiously built into a car, such a warranty was possible. Scott's work had already shown this.

The results of the report? What Tony had anticipated last fall when he'd proposed Scott for the job. He'd proposed Scott for several reasons, not the least of which was that if the program failed it would be Scott's skin, not his—though he regretted this, now that he'd become quite fond of him. Nevertheless, if certain people were offended, they would have to deal with Scott, not him. Chiefly, it would get Vince Eames off his back.

Again the image of Eames at the airport this morning. . . .

"It's not about my report that I wanted to talk, Tony," Scott was saying. "It's about something else, a hell of a lot more crucial to me. . . ."

But Tony's attention had become focused elsewhere; he was again caught up in the disagreeable encounter at the airport, by the importunate way Vince had ambushed him, demanding action against Quinnley's report.

"Listen, Vincent," Tony had had to say as soon as they sat down in a booth in the terminal's cocktail lounge, "you didn't have to come all the way here this morning just to tell me that. You've known about this program for months. Why don't you recognize the situation? The family is growing, the procedures are changing. This has been lifted out of my hands. The Old Man put in Scott Quinnley, and Scott just can't be reached."

"He can be reached," Vince had said.

"It didn't quite work in New York, did it?" Tony reminded him.

"He can still be reached. I got to better men than he is, he's no tougher than some of those boys in Kamber's department. He's no different than a lot of friends of mine, even like—"

"Like Tony Kerwin?" Wearily Tony said it first. "Come now, Vincent, I can't show dirty hands because *your* hands are smudged too, aren't they? No, we have to let it go, call it a nice pot, and walk away while we're still ahead. Not very sporting, but how much choice do we have?"

"I'm not talking sporting." Vince leaned forward, his thick neck swelling, straining against the tightness of shirt collar. "I'm talking Eames Muffler and Accessory Parts Supply Company. I'm also talking something else. Which is that if I lose Bellgard next season, I lose other accounts. Losing is like an epidemic, spreads like an epidemic. That's what I'm talking."

"You're talking prematurely," Tony said. "No recommendations have been acted on yet."

"That's why I wanted to see you now, today." He sat back and with his puffy palm pressed down the gleaming pomaded strands of his few remaining hairs.

More sternly, Tony said: "Either way, contract or no contract, we have to quit, Vince. There comes a time, and you have to know when it's the time. I'm afraid you've been spoiled, that's your trouble, you can't accept what's happening. If you do lose out for next season I'll see if I can shift interest in you elsewhere. But right now, if I can get this point through your greedy skull, right now every move has to be clean."

Vince wrinkled his nose, watching him, like a plump and petulant little boy. "This prick Quinnley, I know he's downgrading my product. This I know. The prick."

"Vince, if it wasn't for you, I'd forget how much vulgarity there is in the world." Then Tony said: "No one is singling you out. If it happens, you won't be alone. I have an idea there are going to be quite a few suppliers who are going to be unhappy. But you're in business, you've been grossing around three, three and a half million a year, all told. You're a smart man, you can build up again if you lose. You're a smart man, and you ought to be able to see that Quinnley is only doing the job he was given to do. A smart man sees exactly how things are and acts accordingly, he doesn't go around acting as if money was everything."

"Since when *isn't* it?" Vince answered at once, his liquid eyes protesting indignantly. "And since when have *you* stopped liking to spend it? Where are you getting your surplus cash from these days? Not from your Bellgard stock or even bonuses, not anymore. So where? What are you using to nurse that fancy taste? The last time you were on the French Riviera, and in Paris, I have to laugh when I think about it, the way you liked to throw it around, like that summer with you and that hot-pants baroness or countess or whatever the hell she was, you were practically living at Cartier's, running between there and that hundred-foot boat. And sending Phoebe to Vichy for the three-week cure."

Tony had to admonish him to keep his voice subdued. Then: "I am not interested in travelogues."

"Sorry," Vince mocked. "I keep forgetting you're a wealthy man. When you check out you'll leave Phoebe a rich widow, even richer than she is already, huh?"

"All right, Vince. I think we'd better take off." Tony rose abruptly, his tongue sour with the acids of the past. How macabre Vince Eames could be at times, he thought. Why speak of Phoebe as a widow? Or was this merely his clumsy attempt at sardonic humor? Of course, what was really in Vince was a twinge of envy, suspecting that if Phoebe died she would leave Tony a rich widower, which, God knows, was true, though Tony never thought of it, he almost never thought of death at all; despite his ulcers, he was much too healthy, too alive with the ways of winning his kind of life to yield precious sensations to death, his own or Phoebe's.

Then as he saw Vince rise from the booth, he hastily told him to sit down again. "We can't leave," Tony said. "We haven't given our order." He motioned for the waiter.

"I can't drink, you know that," Vince said.

"I can't either, not more than one a day." He ordered two whiskeys, and when the waiter brought the drinks, Tony paid for them, left a generous tip, and said to Vince: "Come on. Let's go." The men rose again.

[350

"Sir," the young waiter said, "your drinks, you're leaving the drinks."

"Yes. I know." Tony moved out of the lounge. The wall clock showed five after twelve. That would get him to the private dining room just about the time Cod Smith was carving his lamb chop. "Vince, we'll be in touch."

"When?"

"When? Whenever this business gets unfrozen, after the committee meets."

"Committee? I thought you could get better action than that. Kamber is the man you talk to, he speaks for Engineering."

"More or less," Tony said. "But of course now it's Scott Quinnley who kicks it off, and the committee takes it from there."

Tony felt the man's hand hard on his arm. "Listen, Tony, I don't buy this, I don't care what the new program is, I don't buy it. I count on one person. Tony Kerwin."

"Good-bye, Vince." Tony looked out to see the company car, the limousine, nearing the entrance where he waited. "Nice of you to meet me." He turned. There was a fluttering sensation in his stomach.

"Give my love to your wife," Vince said, adding almost carelessly, "To Blanche Bennett too, huh?"

"What were you saying, Scott?" Tony stirred on the olive leather couch and, as if to ease the taut span of pain in his middle, brought his knees up. How could Vince have known anything about him and Blanche? In the case of Myra he'd found out by sheer accident, a fluke; but with Blanche—how? What a contemptible little swine he was. "You were saying, Scott?" He looked up sharply then: "Resign? You what—?" In clumsy surprise Tony stared at him, not sure if he'd heard correctly, yet knowing he had and not wanting to admit it: like a veteran sportsman who, plumping down on a faulty shooting stick which promptly collapses beneath him, still can't believe this trusty prop has failed him. "You couldn't be serious, Scott."

"I am," Scott said in that succinct way which, Tony observed, often marked his way of holding back a torrent of feeling.

"Resign? Why? I can't believe you'd do this—" To Tony who needed him now, who'd put him at the helm of the Quality Control program so that the world might see that Kerwin's office was taking serious measures to improve the product, extend the warranty—and, more personally, to clean house, slice down rumors, shift shadows

351]

falling too close to him—to Tony this statement of Scott's came like a below-the-belt blow; his first reaction was that of a benefactor who has been betrayed. "I can't believe you'd do this—certainly not now of all times, at least not to me. I had the impression, Scott, that I'd tried to be a friend to you when you came with us last fall." He hoped he would not have to be more explicit or remind Scott in so many words that the banking credit extended to Quinnley Corners had been largely inspired by his, Tony's, word and position, and that he'd arranged the substantial sum in advance salaries without which Scott would not have been able to seal his good faith with the banks.

"You were very helpful, Tony. But I'm up against a situation here, a personal situation that I can't buck anymore, at least I refuse to, it's—"

"Yes, of course. Natural. I know that." Tony hastened to acknowledge what was on Scott's mind: it was what he had feared. And knowing Scott, he had reason to fear it. Yet he had to placate him, get to him in another way. "I know it's tough, but these are tough times for all of us now. That disaster at the Ohio body plant could have killed us. Almost did. We're on the move again and I expect you to stick through this, all the way. You've done a superb job, everyone concedes that, and even granting that it's never been quite your dish of tea—"

"It's not that. I've liked the work—I don't know how much good it'll do in the end—but I've liked it and I've learned a hell of a lot." Scott paused, but the flash of excitement that had touched his eyes passed. "I have to get out, Tony."

"Do you happen to have an offer elsewhere?"

Scott, obviously regarding this question for what it was, a purely diversionary tactic, did not answer it. He said: "For one thing, there's the Kamber situation. I've never mentioned anything about it. But—"

"Kamber situation? What's that? Less negative on the rear again?" Tony's smile fell stiffly into place as he attempted the familiar joke. It helped him, however, to keep his face inert, for Scott seemed to be watching him with such attentiveness.

"I mean"—the force of Scott's gaze did not diminish—"I mean that Kamber is in agreement with my report, he wants to endorse the recommendations, and he's afraid to."

"Afraid? Now listen, Scott—"

"He's terrified."

"Scott, why don't you sit down?" Tony temporized.

[352

Yes, it was this, all right, the subject of Quinnley's resignation had already opened the one gate he hoped would remain locked. To handle Scott was sometimes ticklish. It was a mistake to go along with some of his associates in their patent opinion of him; it was a mistake, he'd learned, merely to regard Scott as one of those assembly-line eggheads who still can't shake his campus where with all that collegiate pizazz he fought the good fight against the injustices of the world. No. He wasn't quite like that. Unfortunately. His drive was generated by another spark. He saw almost everything in terms of the product, the automobile, and when something stood between him and what he wanted or believed in, he could get overexercised, overheated, and he'd be worked up and go crashing in where he didn't belong. (You only had to remember what he'd done when he first joined his father, that wild, crazy stunt when he slammed down the door on factory deliveries.) The trouble with guys like Scott was not only that they might end up doing harm to themselves, but, alas, to others.

Scott was still standing, an awkward monument to the silence in the office.

"I don't get you at all, Scott." Tony had to get into the thick of the play now, there being no alternative. "Why would Kamber be afraid, for God sakes?" Then: "I mean was it a specific thing?" When Scott shook his head, Tony tried again: "He was afraid to recommend what? Hard Parts?"

Scott nodded: "Also Fast-Moving Parts."

"But why?" Tony bent forward, clasping his knees. Hard Parts. Yes. Understood. Generators, condensers, distributor points, etc. But *Fast-Moving Parts.* Closer to where it hurt. Batteries, piston rings, fan belts and, of course, mufflers and all accessories or units of the exhaust system. . . .

So Kamber had finally spun out, his conscience had cracked. Why? Why? Tony asked himself in a fever of calculation. Kamber had cracked before, but not to this extent. This time obviously it connected with Scott, Scott had been the catalyst, wittingly or not.

Out of habit, forgetting he no longer smoked, Tony reached into his pocket for the comforting weight and feel of his gold cigarette case.

As, like a whip, Scott's words lashed the air: victimized, Kamber victimized. Blackmail.

"Blackmail?" Tony sat up, as if in spite of himself the melodrama of the word had jolted him forward, though what shocked him more was discovering how much information Scott possessed, and that he was, in effect, defending Kamber. He said: "Scott, are you sure you haven't been had?"

"Kamber's been had. By Vince Eames. Bellgard's been had." But not stopping there, moving back and forth now, Scott kept talking, absently he unloosened the collar of his shirt, he lit another cigarette, all the while talking, telling him about the encounter with the engineer in New York, at the party, telling him the whole sordid saga of the call girl Eames had hired to set up Kamber, the photos, the recurring threats. The more Scott related, the more indignant he became. And when at last he stopped, Tony was almost relieved, for there was much more that Scott could have told, had he known.

"If this is true," Tony spoke carefully, "it seems to me you're not the one who should think of resigning. I'd say that was up to Ernie Kamber."

"Why? Why the hell should he?" Scott retorted at once. "I'm not saying I admire him. I don't. I'm not saying he's innocent. He isn't. But he didn't go looking for any deals, and he's never taken a nickel from anyone, as far as I know. He's been victimized in the cheapest most brutal way, and all he asks now is to be left alone. I guaranteed him that. I'm seeing that it sticks. He's a bore and a whiner, but he's a very good engineer."

"Yes. Of course." Tony lay back, his hands clasped behind his head. He closed his eyes as if to muster calm in the face of this disturbing news, though what he felt was something else. For the name of Kerwin had not been mentioned; his method had been efficacious. Despite Myra, despite rumor, his hands were still clean. On the surface. His office had merely green-lighted final contracts, based on the endorsement of Engineering, while Eames had forced the engineer's allegiance, and paid for the allegiance of the two key men under Kamber—a fact which Kamber did not know, still did not know.

Now Tony slowly opened his eyes, sat up again, and shook his head as if to dispel the sordidness which Scott had brought into the office. (And how sordid it really sounded when you heard it run down by an outsider.) "All right, Scott. I'm with you. We'll ride this one together. In the meantime"—he consulted his watch—"my time is up, but I want your word you won't go ahead with this ridiculous idea of resigning."

[354

"I'm sorry. This is how I feel."

"You can't quit on us now. You're doing too good a job."

Scott said: "I'm not quitting until the job is done, there's another month of work to clean up. After that my resignation is—"

"It won't be accepted. I won't hear of it, Scott. I won't let you get hooked on this. You mustn't. It has nothing to do with you and you must keep yourself beyond it. At least hold off for the time being. Until I get back."

"Get back?"

"I've got to go east tomorrow. That ceremony in Gifford." He had resisted this junket, but now he felt thankful that he'd taken it on. Though Merrill Johnson's brother had finally refused Bellgard's belated offer last fall, the company had gone ahead and found another Negro businessman whom they were partially financing, making of this Negro dealership a splash of news and publicity. The fact that Bellgard was sending an executive vice-president to Gifford was in itself an index of the occasion. Tony found himself anticipating the event; he was secretly titillated to think that he, who had always been a good-time, blue-chip Republican, indifferent to the woes of minorities, was stirring up news with his personal blessing of a Negro dealership. However, what pleased him now was that he would be absent from the plant. "As soon as I get back, Scott, I'll get onto this myself and give—"

"I already have," Scott said.

"What do you mean?"

"I mean I've begun. I called Vince Eames' office before lunch. He wasn't in. But I'll be hearing from him," Scott stated.

Tony said: "I'm afraid you might."

"In fact, I think I'll be seeing him before the day is out. If I know Eames."

"Well—in that case, since you're that determined—" Tony shrugged. This was even better than he could have hoped for. Scott was taking on the total burden, he was really going to sit on this one. And he was welcome to it. Let Scott be champion. But keep him here; no resigning. "All right, Scott, you're free to do what you think needs doing. You're free to do anything but quit." Tony leaned forward, his gaze was grave: "This isn't only a personal thing, Scott. There's more to it. I know you know we are trying to keep our house in order. We've still got a few stockholder groups—Ed Holtsbridge's for one—who are not friendly. They haven't come out in the open, not yet, but of course they're watching us and we have to produce results without in any way giving these people one stick of ammunition. Not one. Any major resignation, even any sort of executive reshuffle, goes down, or can go down, as evidence of mismanagement or trouble in the house. We've tried, I've tried to be considerate of you, as you know, Scott—" The fraction of a pause, so that this second reminder might not go unheeded. Then: "So for now, Scott, I ask you to stay with it. I know you aren't happy with this end, this kind of activity—"

"I never have been. I told that to you and to Cod Smith when I started here." Scott still seemed unyielding. He stood there, hands in pockets, not moving.

"Yes, I know." Tony's smile was warm, fraternal. "The trouble is you made the mistake of doing too good a job. Let's put it down like this, Scott. You stick with Quality Control until we get squared away for the next model changeover, and then we'll try to let you write your own ticket. I know Product Planning is what you're hot for, and I'm sure there'll be a spot for you by next fall, if not before." Hastily he began to tack into a softer wind: "And if you don't mind my saying so, I'd say as matters stand now—that is, with your present work and your growing reputation here—that it would be very foolish, career-wise, to break your rhythm. I'm not thinking simply about your status with the banks," Tony added, unable to resist this time, "or how it beefs up credit for Quinnley Corners. What I'm thinking of is that it just seems a little arbitrary for you at this point to do anything as rash as resigning—"

"It isn't a question of being rash," Scott interjected, "it's the kind of stigma, the atmosphere of this job that I—"

"What you've been doing . . ." Tony paused. He decided not to depend on the wind; to insure his direction he used the outboard motor. "What you've been doing happens to be the kind of job that was once done at Ford by a fellow named Dykstra. Now I'd say that John Dykstra is certainly a gent with an eminent standing in this industry, wouldn't you?"

"This is Bellgard, not Ford."

"Yes," Tony said. "And you're not Dykstra. But you're only— what is it? Thirty-three. And you're on the move. Too young? Hardly. Let's look at Ford again, at Lee Iacocca. Would you say he was too young?"

"Look, Tony, I'm not talking about this from that point of view.

This is not Tom Swift and His Mechanical Success Machine. What is bugging me is getting this involved in other people's lives—and worse"—Scott jabbed the butt of cigarette into the ashtray—"worse is the way people start looking at you as if you're some character working for J. Edgar Hoover or the Treasury Department, trying to snoop around, ferreting out people's mistakes or questioning their intelligence or their honesty! That's what I can't take. Every damn day I get to the plant I find myself sitting in the car in the parking lot, sitting there and not having the will to get out—as if I'm locked, strapped in by some goddam invisible safety belt!"

Tony rose from the olive leather couch, impatient with Scott, resentful of this outburst, knowing how truthful it must be. But he could not permit himself the release of anger. "Scott—I understand what you feel, I admire you all the more for it." He reached out and pressed Scott's forearm. "I hope I've shown you that my admiration doesn't stop with easy compliments. So for now, let's keep it business as usual, let's keep the griefs among ourselves. I'm trusting you to handle our friend Vince Eames and any other suppliers who might well come screaming around. You have the authority and the power, and I expect you to use it. Otherwise the whole point of all your work, your whole program, is apt to be canceled out. When you wrap it up, I promise you we'll put your future down on the board and design it right. Right after retooling, we'll wrap it up. Your father ought to be back strong in the picture by then, and you'll be free of that responsibility, free to take advantage of the kind of future you deserve here. Fair enough?" He put his arm across Scott's shoulder. They started from the office. He sighed and said: "There are times when I, when a lot of us, feel just like you for one reason or another. When I was in Ohio this week, I thought more than once I'd like nothing better than to take off for some beautiful Greek isle. Maybe Ann is smarter than any of us." Then as if he hoped to restore a more friendly or intimate atmosphere: "Her mother brought back what news we've had, but it was news, wasn't it? As far as Cod was concerned. Though he would have preferred a boy to start the new model series. But the clan *is* being perpetuated now." Always a delicate point, since Phoebe could not have a child, and Myra never wanted one. Delicate, too, had been the fact that the baby had been born only seven months after the marriage. "When's the last time you heard from her, Scott?"

"It's been weeks."

They were out in the wide corridor now. As they parted, Tony saw that despite all his effort, Scott's eyes still held that implacable glint, though he did offer a decent enough smile.

Decent. Or polite. Or melancholy. No matter. Tony carried Quinnley's smile along now like a Christmas gift which was appropriately wrapped but whose contents remained unknown.

Of course, he thought, moving more rapidly, on his way to Conference Room 3-M, of course there was still Vince, still not disposed of; he still had Vince on his hands, and there was still the ugly prospect that he'd come loping back to Tony.

Even so, he mused, conscious of the thrust of his old optimism, even so, he had successfully maneuvered to put the power package in Scott's hands. If Vince cried for redress, it would be Scott he'd have to confront. Yes. Nominally the power formula had changed. The company was trying a new mix.

27: Scott Quinnley

HE overslept the next morning, and it was Suzy who awakened him, tugging him to consciousness, and holding the envelope, the letter: could she have the stamps? They were Greek stamps, weren't they? That meant the letter was from Ann, didn't it? He reached out; drowsily he lifted her into bed, but almost at once from the hall came Mrs. Coombs' scratchy voice: "Suzy, we're waiting. If you want to get to play school on time—" She was out of his arms then, and as soon as she had the envelope, ran out, her footsteps receding down the stairs.

He put Ann's letter aside as indifferently as if he'd heard from her yesterday. He would slowly shower, shave and dress, and thus prolong the anticipation. But he hurried. At the top of the stairs he paused to listen: the stillness told him that Red had already left for the Corners; his morning energy was remarkable, though by early afternoon he would doze off, tilted back in his chair, unable to fight sleep. (If you happened to wake him up, he'd say, regardless of his long snoring slumber: "Just a little catnap.") Scott sat down on the steps then and opened Ann's letter:

VILLA ANATOLAS,
OLD PHALERON, GREECE

SCOTT, *mon cher copain:*

Long time, too long. Please forgive. We have a new nurse; she is much older than the first one, and she works like a demon and speaks French, unlike the young generation here who prefer English as their second language. Oh what a godsend she is. Am rushing this letter off to you this afternoon for Ben is due back from Levkas and Corfu, after nine endless days, and we'll be celebrating the baby's first month in the world. Mainly I write to thank you, to say I absolutely love you for sending that charming Staffordshire mug for Caroline, with that delightful (automotive) inscription. To think you found a mug with her name on it. It arrived day before yesterday, delayed in the mails, but not a chip or a crack. Where on earth did you dig it up? (Now there, with all the excavations always going on here, is a question that can mean something quite different in Greece.) Mother flew back last week after her visit which was longer than either of us expected. She was so relieved that Caroline did not look as "Latin" as she feared, that she was almost nice to Ben and she never once referred to the baby's somewhat untimely (I mean ill-timed) birth. How did you like that press release Bellgard sent out about my "premature" darling? If it's car sales they were worried about, maybe it might have been better if they'd said something simple, like: "The former Ann Smith, in a moment of unladylike passion, forgot to take her contraceptive pill, and she is now the happy mother of a daughter of six pounds, two ounces."

Since that last hasty note to you, have been feeling much better. I have had a few too many weeps, but I understand that's normal. Now I'm absolutely wild to see more of this country, and I hope shortly to intrude my new svelte self on Ben's busy life, and end his frustrating bachelor days. Naturally he's been biting his nails a lot, but as I said, biting his nails was infinitely better than nibbling the whatnots of his Script Girl, a trilingual lass (University of Chicago) who chickened out of the Peace Corps last year, and who ended up in Athens where my good husband dug her up— ooops, there I go again. Anyway, I must admit Ben took a beating when we first got here, before I got big as a Bellgard truck—the Greek men, though they don't go clutching after you on the streets like the gents in Rome, do make their admiration felt for any Anglo-Saxon blonde. But if the men are reticent, the Swedish girls touring here aren't. After hibernating in the Scandinavian winter, they can't thaw out until, as Ben says, they've had a hundred Greek men under their belts, or rather vice versa. Ben's film goes well, though what I wrote you months ago about the costs, doesn't seem to apply anymore. This "low budget" picture simply ain't.

The weather is getting lovely, though still too much wind. To this villa the sea breeze comes all the time, and if you go inland, the air is delicious with pine and herbs. You become so conscious of the purity of light and air here that when you're in Athens, the smell of car fumes is overwhelming, as bad as back home or New York or Paris. I know it's *vieux chapeau* of me to protest the way automobiles are polluting the atmosphere everywhere, but if you're in Greece you are shocked into realizing how ghastly (pun?) the situation has become.

Which reminds me of that talk you gave at the Pine Royal

Sports Car Club. Yes, I know about it. Jemmy sent me the magazine piece which you wrote, or I should say which was a transcript of your talk. Funny: Your ex-gal Jemmy marrying Jack Winters who was the one who taped your speech and got it published, etc. Incestuous. To get back to your talk and what you said about the poisoned air, I noticed that you departed from the good old safe-and-sound racing track long enough to get in a few licks about the need for a different kind of city and commuting transportation. Like electric cars. That was my old buddy. (You must have been tanked up on martinis.) I hear much of the local brass took a dim view of this part of your talk, and I loved the asterisk footnote in the magazine about how the sentiments expressed were yours and did not reflect in any way the policies or viewpoints of Bellgard Motors. Hmm. I've decided I have to be four thousand miles away from Cartown to follow its doings with enthusiasm.

Was happy to know your father is getting much better, though of course I can see how difficult it must be for you to live with him. How is Suzy? God, how clumsy I used to be when I saw her. Now that I'm a mother, am I less clumsy with Caroline? No. Whoever said motherhood came as naturally as breathing? Not in my case. For me it's an art that has got to be learned, though with the new nurse, I'm learning fast.

In your last letter (isn't it interesting that you and I can swap feelings at last? I mean writing letters we seem to be able to say what we can't say to other people, without, as you put it last time, having to get a mental hernia at the psychoanalyst's)—but in your previous letter you merely mentioned Virginia Colter. Are you holding out on me? How come? Is she attractive? High intelligence? Low carnal threshold? I get much of my poop from Jemmy Winters now, but all she said was that V.C. is executive secretary of the Pine Royal Sports Car Club, and the widow of a racing driver. And don't tell me it's none of my business. Now that I'm a mother I feel some kind of dull maternal worry for you —mixed in, I'm happy to say, with a little jealousy. Why jealous? After all, I had my chance in Paris, didn't I? The trouble I suppose was, as you admitted in one of your letters, you were trying to protect my base nature instead of exploiting it. That'll learn you. And me, for that matter.

I must tell you about our Easter morning. That was less than twenty-four hours before Caroline was born. We were invited to the ceremony at the King's barracks, and we sat at the King's table, stuffing ourselves with goat cheese and roasted mutton. Ben

361]

shot pictures of the Greek honor guards—many in their white skirts (very sexy) dancing in the open court, folk-dancing in a marvelously delicate yet sturdy masculine way. Ben is convinced that it was all my gorging that brought on the labor pains. Have to end this now, fingers getting numb, and I've got to dress and see that we have a fine dinner with which to greet my absentee husband. Incidentally our cook fixes an hors d'oeuvre—it's a fish paste called *tamarasalata,* and you've never had such a taste sensation, though it leaves you thirsty enough to drink up the Aegean Sea and the entire Bay of Phaleron. I'll finish this tomorrow.

A.

Scott—sorry. Never made it. Six days since I wrote the above. I boasted too soon. Had the weeps again. Also, Ben never got home. He telephoned from Corfu, hung up with more tech problems. And when he did get back, there was Mr. Arnsworth, one of the family lawyers (have you ever met him? Don't.) who had turned up with a bonnet full of papers for me to look over and discuss and sign. All sorts of legal tangles since the birth of Caroline. New will and all the rest of it, very crafty stuff, so that no one including me or the Internal Revenue gets their hands on the gold. Anyway, the legalities did put a damper on Ben's homecoming, though it shouldn't have. Ben was in a real swivet, and of course Arnsworth couldn't miss it, so he's probably passed it on to the family. In fact everyone who comes to see us goes back to Cartown and reports (the last one was the European Sales Director). All of which is a dreadful drag since they're all just waiting for my marriage to collapse. Ben has left for Crete and Rhodes, but this time I'm damn well going to join him, at least on Rhodes. From there you can get to the island of Kos where there is a tree forty-six feet thick, and where according to legend, Hippocrates wrote prescriptions and examined patients. Think of it. Ben, however, reverts to his Italian forebears and doesn't want me to leave house and cradle until I'm absolutely okay again, and with the American doctor's blessings. Maybe he's right.

Love, and tell me all, *mon vieux.*

ANN

P.S. Was leaving to mail this when Ben telephoned. He's changed his mind, and now he begs me to join him soon as possible. So I've decided to hire us a private plane for Caroline and nurse and equipment and have us zoomed over. If I need a doctor I'll consult the ghost of Hippocrates.

Scott sat there at the top of the stairs and reread Ann's letter, looking, this time, for what she had implied, rather than written. So many of her feelings were in conflict; the sureness of direction which dominated her other letters seemed absent or at least wavering. He kept going over the six gray sheets with a kind of criminal pleasure, though each round left him staring at her P.S., which left him heavy with disappointment, for he knew he would have preferred to read something else. He felt a pinch of guilt, as if he too had joined the ranks of her ill-wishers.

He took the letter downstairs. He was just finishing his second cup of coffee when the front doorbell rang, and he heard Mrs. Coombs talking in the hall. He recognized the other voice: Vincent Eames was here.

Scott went out to greet him. "What took you so long?"

"Long?"

"I expected you yesterday."

"Oh. You did? Got your messages, but you know where I was, Scott?" The chunky supplier hesitated. He was wearing one of his customary Italian silk suits, this one the color of gunmetal, and the hue seemed to have touched his cheeks. "Yesterday," he was saying, "you know where I was all afternoon?"

"No." Yesterday Ann was probably en route to Rhodes. Her letter insinuated itself. Scott let himself imagine her opening the small crated box he'd sent, and seeing her as she saw the old Staffordshire mug with its eggshell tint, it's umber-dark design beneath which was the inscription: A NEW CARRIAGE FOR CAROLINE. (It was Tony Kerwin who had put Scott on to the antique shop in Bloomfield Hills where he'd found it.)

"All afternoon, let me tell you—" Vince Eames reclaimed his attention. "Where was I? At the Midtown Athletic Club. I never go there, but I had to work off the way I felt, wanted to go around pasting everybody I ever knew. Ever feel like that?" He sat back in the chair and smiled, but his smile was rigid, like an invalid's. "I was just telling your father about it—"

"When did you see Red?"

"Outside here. When I drove up."

Scott must have betrayed surprise, for Eames said: "We had a talk. See him rarely. But I said, 'Red, you and I have a date. How about like Friday? Lunch. London House. Old times.' "

"Why?"

"I love Red."

Scott let that pass though it left him vaguely uncomfortable. "Vince," he began, determined to say what had to be said, "let me explain something right off. This job I'm doing has nothing to do with personalities, friends or otherwise." Scott halted as he saw his instinctive movement, the edging forward and the swollen eyelids blinking. He felt—and it was not the first time—like the Surgeon General of the United States might feel confronting a cigarette manufacturer. "This report of mine is very extensive, as you know. It covers all parts and components. Some recommendations call for further study. Others urge outright veto. In the case of Eames Mufflers, it is veto. I wanted to tell you this. I didn't have to, but because of what else is involved—unfortunately—it was too serious to wait." Before Eames could charge in, Scott hurried on:

"The Eames exhaust system is not all that bad, but it can't stand up in this kind of analysis, not in today's auto market. Maybe once it didn't matter. Now it does—not that the industry has suddenly got religion, it hasn't. It's just that they've been *forced* into quality in order to sell more cars, create more confidence; the same way that they were forced or shamed into simplifying, restyling, those rolling jukeboxes back in 1960—though I think we're slipping right back into old errors again. The point I'm trying to make, Vince, is that nothing can be done about Eames Mufflers. Not from my end. In tests, real and simulated, in comparative analysis with other systems, it just can't stand up. That's how it is. From my end. And—and from Kamber's end."

"Kamber?" Vince had been about to spring up, but Scott's mention of the engineer's name acted to repulse him.

"Yes." Inwardly Scott winced as he watched Eames, detesting his involvement, his participation, and knowing this would not be the last of it. "Is there anything else you'd like to know, Vince?"

He did not answer at once. Then: "In other words, you been hearing from Kamber, huh? Anybody else? Because let's cover this right now. Maybe what you don't understand is anybody who takes a deal it's because they get something they want. Fairest exchange there is. Now you've heard from that saint of saints Mr. Kamber. Anybody else in the pew?"

"I'm concerned with Kamber."

"And you have to take the action so big?" Eames said.

[364

"You know me, Vince. I'm pretty square sometimes, I even pay for my own girls."

"That's for sure." But Eames did not smile, nor alter the aggressive slant of his balding head. "Okay. Now what? Do I have to get an appointment and see Tony Kerwin?"

"Tony knows what I know. I told him yesterday."

"You did? Now think of that. Must have rocked him, huh?" The sardonic response surprised Scott. Abruptly then Eames shot his finger outward, stabbing it straight at Scott: "Listen, before you start a scramble, before you go bombing in where you don't belong, remember something—Bellgard can't take any more blasts. Remember that. There are certain parties just waiting for a kill, waiting to take over the whole show. Now if that happens and you're part of the team that loses, do I have to spell out how it makes you look? Do you have to guess what happens to your name? In this industry when you're on the hot end of a losing team, you get popular like a leper. And you are part of Kerwin's team, aren't you? You are Kerwin's boy."

"I'm nobody's boy." But the denial—the fact of having to make it to Vincent Eames or anyone else—left Scott squeamish. He drew back for another view of Kerwin, Tony who would be in Gifford today nobly officiating at the opening of Bellgard's first Negro dealership. His judgment had changed drastically. Once Scott had disliked and distrusted him, and for good reason. But since that time he had altered his opinion. Of course he still saw all his flaws and conceits, but he also saw the way Tony had rallied to his position the day of the crisis at Quinnley Corners. The wildest of rumors about him had subsided, and though the automotive press might often speculate about Bellgard just as certain analysts had speculated about, and even predicted, the demise of Studebaker's South Bend operation, no speculations were centered on Kerwin.

What struck Scott as curious, however, was that Vince Eames, always a cloying guardian of Kerwin's name, should suddenly use it so carelessly or mockingly.

"Vince, I doubt if Tony is ever going to let himself be anywhere near a losing team. He has much too high a regard for the life and times of Tony Kerwin."

"You can say that again. And do you know how I know? Because he's smart enough to distribute his . . ." But Vince did not finish. He

365]

flagged his hand, as if to deprecate what he'd been saying, going on instead: "Forget it. Forget it, Scott. Maybe you been working too hard, huh? Maybe you better knock off and take a breather, look around—"

Puzzled, Scott said: "Around what?"

"Let's just say around, let it go." He paused, leaned forward as if waiting for a second wind. Then he said: "All right, kid. Let's you and me stop trying to snow each other."

"Vince, this is not a snow job. What I—"

"Sure. I know. Now let's talk for your own good. And mine. Naturally. I'm going to move in where— How does it go? Where fools won't tread? Because I want to save you grief all the way down the line. The first thing I'm going to do is get Kamber out of your hair. After that I'll—"

"Haven't you been listening to anything I've said?"

"Every word. But—"

"I told you when you got here that I—"

"I understand. I got you, Scott. But that isn't enough, that doesn't do it. I admire you. You don't have to believe that. But I do. I know where you stand, I know exactly how you're made and I know you'll howl because I say all the wrong things. Too bad. What you're heading for, kid, is Suicideville. But I want you to listen to me, so that you can at least get yourself back off that limb—"

"For chrissakes, don't you ever give up? Don't you ever know when your time is up? You can't be as much of a—"

"As much of a what?" Without warning he leaped to his feet. "You think I can't be that much of a pest? A nuisance? A bore? You think I'll never know enough to stop pushing my product, my company? People spit in my face and I think it's raining—is that what you think I'm like? Well, I am. You're right. One hundred percent right. That's me! I'm a pest, sure. And a nuisance and a bore. I'll tell you something else: I cut corners and I don't care how sharp I cut 'em and I don't care who gets cut down. I'll tell you something else, too: I was always like that. Not just because I was born close enough to the sink end of Hamtramck to smell it, and not just because I can never forget such a smell. I don't buy that crap. What I am, I always was! And I never changed, and I'm never going to stop pushing anybody for anything. I'm saying all this like a warning. To you. So you can forget about the saints like Kamber and any other saints you hear about in his neighborhood. You know why? Because all these boys are the happy owners of all kinds of gifties they got from Santa Claus.

Why? Because they all believe in Santa Claus. And the first sonofabitch tries anything stupid—you hear me?—anything stupid, gets hurt. I don't care who, to me everyone is lumped together with the Kambers, and that goes even right up to the executive vice-presidents and even their white-haired boys!"

By now a certain horror possessed Scott as he watched the man, listened to him. For until now he had never deeply appreciated the cold shape of his purpose. His own plan to resign seemed, in contrast to Eames' almost barbaric and honest assertions, like the tepidly civilized action it was.

"All right, Vince, if you're through, I have to leave now." Unceremoniously Scott led him out of the house. "But let me say this. I wanted to level with you all the way. I hoped that would be enough. I never was interested in you in a personal way, I never even had enough interest in you to want to harm you. I felt if I made clear what I knew, how it was, you'd take it from there. Obviously I was wrong!" Scott paused, his voice taking on that coarse texture that accompanies deepening rage: "From here on I'm going flat out. If anyone comes near Kamber, if anyone tries to molest or threaten him —directly or via the mails—I'm going to be the first one to know it and I'm going to be the first one to do something about it! And if it's you who tries it, I'm going to get my hands on you and when I'm through, I promise you—"

"I'll be goddammed! Kerwin swung it!" Vince Eames' voice cut harshly into the soft morning air.

Scott stared at him.

"He worked it, he swung it, didn't he?"

Not comprehending, Scott still stared at him. "Worked what?"

"Yep." Eames mused aloud. "Took me some time to get it, but I got it now. I want to thank you, Scott. Just forget everything I said. Forget it. Unimportant. You think I'm a shit, go right ahead." He looked down at the grass and shook his head. "How about that? He worked it. Or almost. Scott, I want to thank you for this nice talk we had. I learned something. A lesson. I thought I was too old to learn any lessons. I apologize to you, Scott." He drew a breath, glanced off toward his vermilion Bellgard convertible with its hundred and one glittering extras. "I think I'll take myself over to Kent Hills, have a cup of coffee with Myra Stratler, she might even be more hospitable than you. Tell Red, count on me. Tomorrow lunch. See you, friend."

Driving out to the plant, Scott kept pondering what he'd heard: Kerwin swung it. Swung what? And learning a lesson. What lesson? And why would Eames want to push the lunch with Red? Inexplicable, too, the sudden announcement of his going to see Myra Stratler.

However, Scott discovered later that he couldn't have seen her. He encountered Dean Stratler in the lounge of the Executive Dining Room. The designer had understandably been in a despondent and often testy mood since the production delays of the Bellstar, but today there was more shine to his personality. They talked for a few moments, and Scott was just about to ask how his wife was, when Myra walked into the lounge.

She kissed Dean, and then shook Scott's hand, and Dean said: "You know, during all this mess in Ohio I've been a monster to live with, haven't I, Myra?"

She removed her gloves. "But a rather nice monster."

"Well," he said, "we'll have something to cheer about soon. Let us hope."

Myra said: "Couldn't we all have a wee drink? I'm exhausted." She went on to tell of the long morning's labors; since breakfast she'd been out at the Kent Hills Art Association. And now for a drink and some lunch and wouldn't Scott join them? He did, though only for a hasty sandwich, and shortly before twelve-thirty he left the plant.

He was well on his way when he decided to stop off and see Red. He also had business with Mr. Waterman. The Proving Grounds was only a few miles out of the way. He turned off the freeway and drove directly to the dealership.

As it developed, this was to be his last visit to Quinnley Corners.

There, rising from the roof deck, were the mighty signs, the high sharp calligraphy in neon, promising that you would WIN WITH QUINNLEY if you bought your BELLGARD at QUINNLEY CORNERS.

But absent from the glass exterior of the showroom were the gaudy banners proclaiming mythical bargains—those dubious come-ons which Red often used to lure people in off the street. This restraint of his had no noble purpose but was part of the program of changes made to appease Scott, and it was also Red's way of recognizing what his son had done to help keep the dealership alive.

The atmosphere within the great showroom was no longer the same. And though Scott had been responsible for altering the style and personnel of the sales force, there were times like today when, for some reason, he rather missed the flavor, even the drama, of former times when Marty Calhoon, Bernstein and others had flourished.

Gone now. Except for the ever-corpulent presence of Al Fogarty, the last of the old-line crew.

Scott saw him sitting in a far corner holding before him the current copy of the *Bellgard Bulletin,* behind which Scott noticed he concealed another periodical—one of a stockpile of new American magazines, gamy with breasts, navels and buttocks, girls in concupiscent attitude, pose or position sure to titillate the collector of Pop Erotica or Masturbania.

This was a recent kind of literature for Fogarty. His eyes, he said, were getting bad, giving him severe headaches. But the close-ups of nude girls had "aspirin beat a mile," he claimed. What it really was, however, was that he'd become lonely, isolated, being now the last of the old guard, and it was one of the ways in which he fortified himself against the young new salesmen Scott had recruited. He had done the recruiting simply because the old team at the Corners had become so discontented or so chronically corrupt that they had no place in a modern operation. The veteran of the Lowball or the Highball or other questionable sales tactics was becoming at best an anachronism, at worst a danger.

As he was turning, Scott saw that Fogarty had put aside his pickapack magazines. He was tensed forward like a bird dog, watching the young new salesman Les Travers in the midst of hard negotiation with a lean-cheeked middle-aged man. The man broke off the talk and stooped down beneath the tail of the four-door Compact Family Cruiser sedan, and then he lay flat on his back peering up to examine the underbelly of the car.

"He's going to give us trouble—" It was Red's voice just behind Scott. Then: "What're you doing here, son? Been almost two weeks since we had the pleasure."

"I'm on my way to the Proving Grounds, Red. I wanted to discuss something with you, and I also wanted to see Waterman."

"Anything wrong?" Red asked at once.

"Not too."

Red started to say something but gave way to a yawn. "Look at him!" He nodded toward the showroom to the man who was spread-eagled beneath the car. "He's playing big car buff. He's going to show us he's no fool, he knows his way around a car. A phony. Or maybe not. I don't care if he wants to impersonate Abe Lincoln, long as he signs some paper before he leaves the tent." Red watched for another moment. "I hope Les can handle him."

"Fogarty's covering it," Scott said, and they walked back into the big office.

Before Scott could ask him about Vincent Eames, Red said: "What's the word, son?" He settled into his swivel chair, pushing it back closer to the open windows. "Christ Almighty, the way the season started out last fall, Ward's registration shooting up, even for Bellgards, I thought it was going to be a bonanza year—" Instinctively he glanced over to the wall, to the black-framed document now tinted by time:

CERTIFICATE OF HONOR
J. R. (RED) QUINNLEY
BELLGARD DEALER OF THE YEAR
Highest Sales Volume   Zone C-2
1955

He stirred, and thumped his hand down on a sheaf of papers. "As of yesterday, nineteen cancellations on the Bellstar. And now that they're finally coming off the line again, I called each and every one of these people personally. Only two out of the nineteen are still hot. The others, got a frozen gas line, scared to touch the Bellstar. What's happening? You boys out there, how could you miss the boat? Never understand it. See that spread in *Automotive News* today? Ford, Chrysler, all out with sports cars, but models for the family, four seats, not just two goddam buckets. Just enough time lost to let the competition slip in for the midyear push. I know you're going to say it's only merchandizing, but I've got nineteen cancellations here on my desk. If two come through, I'm sitting on a shamrock. Where are the other seventeen going?"

Since they both knew the answer to that, Scott said: "Red, what I wanted to ask you about was this morning. With Vince Eames. What happened?"

"Nothing happened. Why? He was outside the house waiting for you. We shot the bull. He wants to have lunch with me tomorrow."

"I'd appreciate it if you canceled it, Red."

[370

"Hmm?" He squinted at Scott out of tired eyes, the lids leaden. "You starting to reorganize my *social* life, too?"

"Not at all. You know me better than that."

"Okay."

"But I'd rather you stayed away from him. At least now. The London House is like eating in the middle of South Main Boulevard. And Eames is—"

"Is that what you came by for?"

"Look, Red, there's quite a bit going on at the plant, and I'm not far from the center of it. I haven't bothered you about all this because what's the point? But so far as Eames is concerned, it might not look good for you to mix in that kind of traffic."

"Christ"—he yawned—"Christ, what the hell is everybody getting so pisspants scared and nervous for? Vince Eames is what? A crook? So? No more than a few other citizens I know around here. You scrap him and another one comes along and takes his place." He rose and walked out of the office, returning almost at once, the barrel-bodied Fogarty behind him. "Sit down, Al, and don't break the goddam chair." He switched on the sound system, then pressed another lever. "I want to hear how your boy Lester is doing," he said to Scott. "He's got that great car expert in the box."

". . . and I think, sir," came the young salesman's voice, "that a deal like this couldn't be fairer."

"Well," the prospect said, "on the trade-in, Max Wilkerson put a lot more fat on it, a hundred dollars more."

"Wilkerson!" my father cried out as if mortally stabbed.

"And frankly," the customer's voice went on, "the Dodge agency is willing to match it. Practically. So I've got two deals, both of them with enough fat to make it hard for me to refuse. I don't really need another car, after all my wife's V. W. is still doing nicely, but I want this new job for a birthday present, and since I moved in the neighborhood here, I thought I ought to give my business to Quinnley Corners —if Quinnley Corners doesn't start giving *me* the business."

"The Volkswagen," the salesman said soberly, not even conceding a tactful chuckle to the prospect's remark, "the Volkswagen is an excellent little machine, I happen to like it very much. But you see, the current trade-in value, according to the book—"

"Book. Book! That's all he knows," Red protested. "I told him use the book at first, then throw it away!"

371]

"To tell you the truth," the prospect confided laconically, "the nice advantage of the V. W. is that it makes so much noise I can't hear what the wife is saying half the time." Then: "So there we are. I'm ready to buy that Family Cruiser out there—it doesn't have the greatest suspension system, but for our purposes it ought to be all right. I thought, after all, the Bellgard is not the most popular car in the USA these days, so the deal ought to carry a lot of fat on it. Wilkerson is no fool and he offered me nine hundred dollars on the V. W. It's in mint condition, the wife drove it to church and for shopping and that's about all except for a few trips to see her mother."

"Who lives in California," Fogarty muttered. "Listen, Red, this kid isn't going to make it, better I should step in for the T.O."

"Give him more time, Al," Scott said.

Red's palms were up for silence.

"According to the book," the salesman was saying, "the current value of your V. W. is six hundred and twenty-five dollars. But I'm willing to go to Mr. Quinnley and try to set it for eight hundred. You see, sir, it is economically impossible, if not insane, to allow more than seven, at the very most eight hundred. If anyone offers you more than that, you have good reason to think something is wrong, seriously wrong, and I'd advise you to check very carefully into a deal of that sort. Mr. Quinnley doesn't like to lose deals and he's one of the most generous appraisers in this area, that's a fact, sir. But I wouldn't go to him with a request for nine hundred. I just wouldn't."

"Hopping Jesus!" Red groaned.

"That kid is losing his cotton-picking mind!" Fogarty hoisted his bulk from the chair.

"You mean," the man was saying, "you are shutting the door on me for a mere hundred dollars?"

"Yes, sir. Because it's really a lot more than a hundred. When a dealer gives you a figure like that he takes a complete washout on the little profit margin the factory allows him to play with. In other words, if you get a deal like that you can expect a tricky slide-up in price for the new car, or you can expect all kinds of little surprises, nonexistent taxes or transport charges or handling charges, or you can find yourself having to take the optional powerplant, you can even sign a contract and discover later that you didn't sign what you thought you had."

"Go on. Tell me more," the man said. "I'm fascinated."

[372

"Red, I can't stand it, it's killing me!" Fogarty pleaded.

"I'm fascinated too," Red said. "I'm so fascinated I'm going to throw that Boy Scout to hell out of here. Almighty Christ, Scott, where did you find this specimen? You run over him on the highway? I thought you told me he had a lot of car experience selling for Stan The Courtesy Man—"

"He got burned there, Red. That's why he was willing to work here for a minimum of—" Scott began.

"Minimum is what he sells, too," Red said.

"I'll grab the T.O." Fogarty started out of the office.

"Shh!" Red detained him.

". . . all right," came the prospect's voice, "you don't have to break my heart, I mean what I said. We've got a deal. This is crazy. But I respect your guts."

"Thank you, sir," Lester Travers said.

"I admire your way of doing business," the man said. "Nine hundred for the V.W."

"I'm sorry, sir. I'm very anxious to see you satisfied. But I know we can't go a cent higher than eight hundred."

"That's what I said. Eight hundred." The man laughed. "Which brings the final tab for the Family Cruiser to two thousand flat and even."

"Twenty-one hundred," the salesman corrected.

Silence: the scratch of a match as Red lit a cigar.

Fogarty still had his eager hand on the doorknob, waiting, like a runner, for the pistol shot.

But Red waved him back, bent forward, pressed another lever. There was the muted buzz of the telephone in the salesman's booth.

"Travers speaking."

"Lester," Red said exhaling a pungent cone of smoke, "make him a member of the Silver Key Klub. If that doesn't work, bring him in here."

"That was Mr. Quinnley," the salesman said after the conversation had ended. "He suggested that if we set the contract now, it will make you eligible for the Silver Key Klub. He said he would like to present it to you personally. Or to your wife on her birthday."

"Silver Key Klub?"

"It's a new arrangement for special deals. It entitles you or your wife to a twenty percent discount on all service, labor, parts and all

373]

lube jobs, wheel alignment—after the guarantee expires, of course."

"Tell me something," the man said, "why didn't you tell me about this before?"

"Well"—the young salesman hesitated—"I just don't like to present a deal with anything except the plain facts and figures. I think it's bad business and bad public relations. I don't think a customer should let himself be swayed by fake allowances or even special prizes."

Red and Fogarty were regarding each other.

Red said: "Looks like maybe we've got us a new kind of pitch— the *straight ball*. Who knows, maybe it'll work once in a while. If all else fails."

"I don't know." Fogarty shook his head. "Sometimes I just don't know. It's like Marty Calhoon used to say when he was cracking up: something's happening in this business, nobody knows what the hell is going on anymore."

"Al—" Red brandished his cigar. "You better check over the contract before we let the guy out of the tent. That kid is apt to throw in an extra set of tires and a free trip to the Virgin Islands."

After Fogarty had gone, Red put his cigar down on the edge of the desk. Rapidly he jotted figures on his yellow pad. When he looked up at Scott, his smile was still incredulous: "Reminds me of that first flukey deal you made here, Scott. Enough daylight on this one to give us two-point-three percent—not counting the ice cream from the finance company. Do you know how often this happens?"

Yes. Scott knew.

As he was leaving, Red said, "How about that sonofabitch!"

Scott paused and looked back at him. "Who?"

"Wilkerson."

"Oh."

"Nine hundred dollars for that German helmet on wheels," Red said. He still refused to give up his prejudices of foreign cars. To him a Volkswagen or a Rolls, a Peugeot or an M. G.—it mattered not— they were all enemies, personal enemies like Max Wilkerson.

But Scott made no comment. He never had told his father that as recently as the last state dealers meeting, Max Wilkerson had cornered him and, unlike that previous occasion at the *Concours d'Élégance* when he'd made his oblique bid to buy Quinnley Corners, had said openly that he was willing to listen to Red Quinnley's price dreams.

[374

Scott left his father's office and went to see Mr. Waterman. Less than half an hour later, when he'd finished with the accountant, he paused to say good-bye to the elderly secretary: "I'll see you soon, Mrs. Bowsley, I expect to be back the end of next week."

But she had turned slightly, the white eyebrows arched as if she had heard a disturbing sound somewhere.

"Excuse me, Mr. Quinnley." With a squirrel-like alertness she raised her head and sniffed. "Is—is that something burning? Do you smell anything?"

"No, I don't."

But Mrs. Bowsley, like many elderly women, had a sensitive nose for disaster: "It's in there—"

The odor reached Scott then. He ran past her and pushed open the door to Red's office. At first he didn't see anything, though the smell, a familiar one, was like rubbish smoking in an incinerator some distance off.

Red, he saw, was tilted around in his swivel chair, asleep, his feet propped up on the sill of the open windows.

"Red!" Cigar ashes, like small gray sausages, lay on his blue suit front. "Red!"

Scott stepped on the cigar which was smoldering on the floor. There were charred papers on the floor and others on the windowsill, and the cords of the Venetian blinds had caught fire. Scott ripped them down from their pulleys, but as he did so his attention was drawn to the outside, to the rear wall, one wing of the service garage. From an old oil drum which contained refuse, flames leaped high like giant wildflowers.

Scott had Red out of his chair. He was sluggish until he saw what was happening. "Oh Christ!"

They were halfway out of the office when Red ran back, and Scott saw him at the rear wall snatching down several of the framed pictures and documents from their hooks. Scott scooped the batch from him and as they hurried out he saw that the window curtains had caught fire and that the blaze was forking out along the acoustical tile ceiling.

"It's automatic, the system is—where the hell is that goddam—" Red's voice was thick, almost incoherent.

Scott transferred the pictures to Mrs. Bowsley and told her and Miss Mergenfreed to get outdoors. He grasped his father's arm then and led him, balking and reluctant, down through the showroom.

375]

"Get these units out of here!" He shouted to one of the salesmen. "Get these cars out of here. Somebody tell Kellog!"

After Scott had Red safely across the street, he hurried back in. Fogarty and the others were clotting the showroom, all of them clumsily trying to slide open the heavy side exit door. In the alley, however, there was a Bellgard truck which had been delivering parts. The driver was nowhere to be found. Scott climbed into the cab and drove the vehicle out of the way, and then he joined the other men and began pushing out the display cars. But they were halted. From somewhere in the service area an explosion, sharp as the crack of thunder, shook the floor beneath them. The glass partition between the showroom and the reception room split and a whole section of it crashed. Everyone went running. Through the chaos Scott heard the intermittent ring of the fire alarm gongs, the warning of the Fire Detector System. The alarm was automatically sent to central headquarters which in turn notified the nearest fire company. Detectors were located throughout the premises; they were a combination rate-of-rise with a 190 degree fixed temperature setting. What they didn't realize at the time, though, was that the detector in Red's office was in the middle of the ceiling and that the fire or heat which should have set off the first alarm did not reach it until it was too late. For the real blaze had developed outside by the rear wing wall of the Service Wing and had shot into a ventilator duct to reach into the suspended gas-heating installation hanging from the steel-framed roof of the Service Wing; it was from here that the first explosion had come.

Along with the others, Scott cleared out of the showroom. Smoke had already begun to swirl in, and there were bright spikes of flames piercing into the Reception Room. Outside, the First-in-Fire company had arrived along with what seemed like hundreds of spectators, most of whom were clustering on the opposite corner. Scott could not see his father. He hurried to the front entrance of the garage. Kellog, the Service Manager, and all the mechanics and helpers were frenziedly trying to evacuate the cars: the new units, the cars at lube pits and in the repair bays, the cars awaiting pickup, some thirty-five or forty vehicles.

Scott saw Red then. He was in the adjacent Used-Car lot, enlisting anyone he could to help him wheel cars away from the right end of the lot which was closest to the building. This time Scott held on to him, and he didn't let go until he had him back across the street. His breathing was harsh, his forehead and neck were pearled with sweat. Scott told Mr. Waterman to stay with him, and ran back to the front entrance of the service garage. But now no one could get through.

For now the entire façade of the building was blocked by firemen and police. Hose lines were being connected and run into the burning interior. Only eleven cars were saved. For another unpredictable accident had occurred. The blaze had evidently reached the electric controls of the motorized garage doors, causing them to malfunction: they kept going up and coming down and no one seemed able to arrest the freaklike movement of the two huge doors. As a result a powerful suctioning of air began pulling through the entire service garage. The fire went completely out of control.

A second and third alarm had gone in, and more equipment kept arriving. The street was scarlet with engines and ladder trucks. Auxiliary policemen were pushing back people into the now densely crowded sidewalks. And Red had escaped once more. This time he was in the middle of the block shouting directions to the Battalion Chief, standing beside the man directly in front of his red patrol coupe.

When the Chief left, Scott started over. But Red refused to go. Or he seemed unable to. He stood beside the red car watching mutely the chaos and devastation before him.

He was aware of Scott's closeness, maybe even grateful for it, but he seemed unable to acknowledge it. Fortunately he was oblivious to the arrival of new spectators; news of the fire had drawn many people they both knew. Scott saw Marty Calhoon near the corner and Mr. Max Wilkerson in the company of Halister McGregor, who was striding about in his familiar white suit; even Sophie, the profane proprietress of Sophie's Tavern, had driven up in her newest coral-hued Cadillac convertible, top down, her fleshy shoulders and arms protected from the sunshine by a platinum mink stole.

"Red . . ." Scott tried again.

No response. Above the showroom and offices, smoke and low flames were licking along the flat "insulated" roof, which was comprised of layers of asphalt and felt and which was afire, the smell acrid as burning rubber. And the pitched roof of the large service garage was now hidden in darkness. Sooty smoke rose, thrusting upward, opening like great amorphous black umbrellas. And now the flat deck above the showroom and offices suddenly erupted in terrible bursts of golds and yellows and greens, and then the skeletal frame of the neon signs, like a sandwich man faltering on high stilts, began to buckle.

For all the fire fighters, the rasping orders, the equipment, the maze of serpantine hoses spewing their pressured silver jets, the effort seemed almost toylike against the now arrogant rage of the conflagration. The spectacle of black billowing smoke and brilliant flames appeared as a cruel joke being played to taunt the mild blueness of the May sky.

Unreal—the closest Scott had ever been to a fire was seeing a racing car spin out and crash upended in flames—unreal and terrifying came the rapid artillery of smaller explosions and the smell of kerosene, motor oil and tires burning, and the cremation of the automobiles, and the sounds of glass shattering and the mighty roar, ceaseless and cacophonous upon the serene afternoon.

The Battalion Chief, an old friend of Red's, returned and ordered them to get back across the street. But Red only looked at him and remained inert.

Scott touched his arm. "Red, there's nothing we can do. We've got to get out of the way. Come on."

But hatless, his blue suit hanging open, Red kept staring at the holocaust, this monument of almost four decades of his love and pride, his ego and his prime years, a charred ruins, a pyre leaving little except its radial heat and its evil smell.

Red was so motionless Scott could not stop watching him. His mane of russet hair was like dead flames. Only very slowly now did the first trace of movement become visible as, from his unblinking eyes, tears swelled and ran searing down his cheeks.

28: *Tony Kerwin*

HE was with Blanche Bennett in the apartment in New York that evening of the day of the fire. He was coming awake, feeling now the tip of Blanche's tongue curve delicately along his cheek to rest on the dark bud of his mole. He rolled over to meet her face and in that sensual aftermath of sleep tasted her mouth and breathed in the fragrance of her body. Like other times with her, yet altogether unlike the other times. Since the night before, what had been between them had changed, and he was still surprised by the tide of his new feelings, and hers.

"You wanted to make that call. It's seven o'clock," Blanche said.

"Hmm?" Drowsily.

"Do you want to?"

"Want to what?" he teased. He raised his hand and brought it down to trail lightly between her thighs. "The answer is yes."

"Make the call, I meant," she said.

"I know that's what you meant," he said.

"And I know you know that's what I meant," she responded.

He squinted toward the telephone on the bedtable: that call to Scott Quinnley. "What time did you say it was? Seven?"

"Yes."

"Morning or night?" he said.

Blanche left the bed and went to the windows and drew open the lined, crewelwork curtains, so that suddenly the lowering sun flushed the bedroom crimson. The room was still unfamiliar to him; not until now could he appreciate its space and handsomeness. This Fifth Avenue apartment comprised eighteen rooms, one self-contained wing of which was reserved for guests; the apartment was owned by a good friend of Blanche's who let her use it when she was in New York.

From the bed he could see the glass shafts of Midtown rising against the blood-streaked sky. He did not want to move. But there were two calls that had to be made. Scott. Phoebe. He glanced toward the telephone again. "I suppose I ought to," he said.

"You're supposed to be at the Berwyn in case you've forgotten." Blanche returned to the bed.

"Yes." He had gone to his apartment at the Berwyn yesterday, immediately after the opening ceremonies of the new Negro dealership on Long Island, and he had attended a meeting of Distribution at the Manhattan offices of Bellgard. Since then he had been with Blanche, who had come east several days before "to visit her oldest friend." Tony said: "I've forgotten where I'm supposed to be tonight and where I'm supposed to be tomorrow. I don't want to remember."

"I'd rather not remember, too," she said.

"I can't get it through my head that, after tonight, we go right back to where we were," he said.

"There was a time"—Blanche spoke contemplatively, drawing her light chestnut hair to one side of her face—"when I thought Neil would never balk at a divorce, he's so very set in his ways, so completely the bachelor he was when we got married. He loves to go out with me, but at home he wants to be left alone. I've told you that before, I know, but now it means something quite different. Kent Hills is a pattern, a habit, and I suppose he's never been happier. In his own rigid way." She paused and a tart smile touched her features. "It's fantastic, isn't it? Talking like this, the way we have?"

"It's being this far from home base. Maybe that's part of it. A taste of honey. It took time for it to catch up with us." He regarded her with absolute possessiveness—a novel sensation for him—as she sat there on the edge of the bed. Her torso, her upper arms, her thighs, showed the supple slimness of a sportswoman as well as the care and skill of her masseur. (Not unlike Sylvie, that Contessa he'd had the summer with on the Riviera. That first day he'd met her at Cap d'Antibes he'd said something about the way she looked in the white bikini, and she'd said: "Why shouldn't I? I give the entire winter in Rome or Paris to my masseur, and in between times it is sport or exercises always.") Now, still contemplating Blanche, he said: "What I can't understand is the way it hit me without warning, without the slightest warning. The way it hit you. It isn't as if we *had* to decide what we did. And it isn't as if we didn't have it quite perfect back home. Considering. It's taken all this time to know it wasn't perfect at all."

She nodded.

"The idea of having to face Phoebe tears me up," he said then. "What're you thinking?"

"I was thinking," Blanche said, "what can happen if you tell her. And if Cod Smith knows about it, which he will."

"Cod doesn't worry me as much. I think he'll take it."

"I doubt it, Tony. How could he?"

"You didn't see him when Ann got married or when she sailed for Europe. I saw how he was, I got to know what he was really like then. For the first time," he said. "I'm not at all convinced that my divorcing Phoebe would change my business relationship with him. I used to think it would, for years I've thought just that. But I'm not positive anymore. I think I'd rather handle Cod than Phoebe."

"You look—you sound as if you had to do it tomorrow," Blanche observed.

"I wish to God I could." He paused in dismal reflection. "It'll be a year. Maybe less. I know that much. I can't make any moves until the company gets out of the bind it's in now."

Blanche said: "Why don't you make love to me?"

"I have to make those calls."

She reached for the telephone. But he took it from her and placed it back on the bedtable. He could not think of yielding the momentous sensation of this kind of love. She was the only woman who had ever spoken to all his needs. Unlike Phoebe, obviously. Unlike all the others, and a distance beyond Myra for whom he would never have made any serious sacrifice, and for whom he felt only hatred. Yet his knowledge of Blanche Bennett had taken a long time to develop: what had started out as a crash program had become a permanent project. With her the discovery and the decision had happened at the same time. Last night. After they'd made love. And after he had answered the compulsion to tell her what she didn't know; for he told her precisely what had transpired in his dealings with Vince Eames, and he had not omitted a single truth. The catharsis had been overwhelming for him. And he had not had to see in her eyes the dread suspicion or contempt he'd seen in Myra's. Blanche had accepted his admissions almost as if she had been partner to his complicities. There was a pure hard unsentimental core of understanding or knowledge in her acceptance that redeemed the sordidness of all he'd had to confide. None of it, or course, had been easy for him. But it was over; he knew he would never have had the courage for it if he hadn't wanted her on those terms; he knew he had never wanted any woman

381]

at a price like that. (Once or twice while he was telling it to her, he was faintly conscious of the old Tony Kerwin peering at the new one with disappointment.)

Much later—it must have been near dawn—when he asked her why she was willing to give up a very secure and agreeable marriage for the prospect of uncertainty, she'd said: "Darling, part of it is that I've reached the age when I'm suddenly sick and tired of kidding myself or the rest of the world. For once, I'd like to get what I want. That's you. Both my marriages were disasters because I compromised. I'm entitled now to say to hell with it all."

Now, with the telephone back on the table, he pulled her down across his chest. The calls to Scott, to Phoebe, were postponed, lost in the sharp rise of lust between them. But perversely, sweetly, he whispered to her—it was the byplay of a game they had fallen into months ago—"Not now. Impossible. I'm dead. No more, baby."

"Oh please." And Blanche's tongue slithered like a lizard between his lips, and she kissed him a long slow time, and soon he felt her as she slid downward, and he let her pretend to revive him with her mouth.

For a few seconds. No more. And he reached for her, drew her back up against him again; he held her, not moving, not breaking the embrace until he could no longer wait. Neither of them saw—or cared—that the rose light which had suffused the room had darkened to mauve.

It was past nine o'clock when he dialed Scott Quinnley's number. He sat, still unclothed, on the side of the bed. He could hear Blanche in the guest kitchen. They had decided it would be the better part of valor to stay in, have some supper here, despite the fine night and the kind of restaurant which they felt this occasion called for.

"Hello? Scott?—Yes. I'm in New York. I heard the news but I haven't had a chance to call until now. Yes. Horrible. How is your father?"

"Not too great, of course," Scott said. "I was scared as hell he'd never make it home today. He's holding up, but don't ask me how. I'm taking him to the doctor's tomorrow for a checkup."

"Is there anything I can do?"

"Thank you, not a thing, Tony. We've got insurance adjusters in hot contention all over the place."

[382

"What was the car loss?" Tony asked. "I understand something like twenty units—"

"Twenty-seven," Scott said. "Oh yes, there is one thing. I'm going to have to take off a few days, I can't let Red carry this kind of weight."

"Of course." Then: "I meant to ask you, did you get that call from Vince Eames you expected?"

"At breakfast. Today," Scott said.

"Breakfast?" An air of consternation was in the room. Breakfast. That was how Vince Eames would operate; always the wrong, rude, inconsiderate time, his way of striking to catch you off balance, just as he had arrived to meet Tony at the airport without invitation, to press upon him his questions and threats. Tony said calmly: "I trust you gave him coffee, Scott."

"I gave him everything, including a bad time," Scott answered. "I made it very clear that if he tries anything with Kamber or anyone else, I'm going to be right on his neck. I think I made my points."

"Yes. I would say so." Tony breathed deeply. Life was beginning to take such a generous and beautiful form. He felt outright affection for Scott now, Scott having more than fulfilled the role Tony had cast him in, Scott now the hammer man with Vince Eames. Perfect and beautiful, all of it. "What?"

Scott was asking him about the opening of the Negro dealership. "Went perfectly, beautifully," Tony said. "Damn near a civic event. Ralph Alsop was ecstatic. *Automotive Monthly* gave it thorough coverage. The news conference went off with plenty of torque. I'm afraid we'll be seeing my haggard profile, alongside our new dealer's, in all the weeklies. Quite a day. By the way," he continued, needing to make the gesture, "I gave something of the history of the dealership and I tied a few laurels around your head, though you never know what they'll print or what they won't."

That wrapped it up. And as soon as he'd finished, he telephoned Phoebe in Kent Hills. "Good evening, madame, I'm calling to say I'm still alive, no collapse with ulcers in any strange Men's Rooms this time."

"Oh Tony." Her pale, tremulously happy voice. "Where are you? I've been waiting and waiting. I got home early from that meeting because—"

"What meeting?" He yawned.

383]

"You know. The Camp Fund. Reverend Cass sends you his regards."

Reverend Cass: great boy. Phoebe, like the other women, bought what the good Reverend had to sell; it would be Phoebe who organized the fund-raising to get underprivileged kids to summer camp.

"Are you coming back tomorrow? Father said he thought you were due back tomorrow," Phoebe was saying, not naggingly, but with that sweet anxious concern.

"It'll be late in the day, if I can make it," he said.

"Are you at the apartment now? I called twice and there was no answer," she said.

"It so happens I'm at a wicked orgy with six nude dancing girls," he said.

"Seriously, Tony."

"All right," he said. "Unfortunately I'm merely working for the company, I'm being talked at by an advertising wheel who is pitching for the chance to make a new presentation for the Bellstar campaign."

"You're not overdoing it, Tony? Please don't drink and watch what you eat."

"Listen, Phoebe, it's silly for you to stay alone, why don't you go over to your mother's or to—"

"Mother and Father went to Cobo Hall."

"Wasn't there a bridge game with the Piersons this week?"

"I asked them to put it off until you got back, Tony."

"I see." He could see her vividly now: Phoebe in sweater and pants, her figure superb in clothes, and so bony and unexciting without clothes; Phoebe dining alone tonight, reaching over to that conveyer belt of vitamins, drugs and the thousand products of the food and health faddist's delight; Phoebe at this moment sitting in his library, at his desk by the green student's lamp, nervously playing with the string of pearls around her throat; Phoebe retiring later, a net over her blond hair, ointments and creams glistening on her face, sitting up in the bed with a cup of herb tea and some new book whose title invariably promised *Health, Beauty, Joy.*

". . . and did you hear about the awful fire today at—"

"Yes," he said.

"Simply terrible. They say it's gutted entirely. The evening papers were full of it. It must be terrible for Scott."

"Yes," he said. "Well—I'll be in touch. All right?"

"Myra called before."

"Oh?"

"She said Blanche Bennett was in New York. Did you know that?"

"I didn't," he said at once. "That is, not until five this afternoon. Ran smack into her in front of the Plaza. I think she said she was here shopping. I didn't have much time to talk. If she tells you I was rude to her, I trust you to get me off the hook as you usually do. Well —all right, darling."

"Love me?"

"Umm."

"Please be careful, darling. And you will call so I'll know when to expect you?"

"Yes." And now he saw Blanche coming in from the kitchen in a floor-length robe, and carrying the tray on which there were the plates, glasses, the bottle of unopened white wine. "Well, sleep well, darling," he offered gently.

"I will. Don't worry," Phoebe said. "Remember how it used to be when you went away? I never knew how I'd get through the nights. My eyes would never close. Goodness, when I think of what those vile hours must have done to my system!" A jaunty, even seductive tone then: "If you were here now, darling, I know what would be best of all for my system, don't you?"

"Certainly do." And a sudden dryness dusted his throat.

29: Scott Quinnley

HE wrote the letter twice. But despite his effort to keep it simple and, now and then, lively or cheerful, it still seemed a fraction rigid. It was almost impossible, feeling as he did, to express himself in a consistently natural way:

DEAR ANN AND BEN—

I've been meaning to answer your last letter and the one before that, but alas I've been bogged down by a few too many woes, namely of course, Red, and the tedious and titanic hassle with the insurance people.

But tonight a breather. At any rate, I want to thank you for the thoughtful messages. Red is holding up remarkably; there was a while during the fire when I was sure he'd never last out the day, and how he did I'll never know. However, he did rally and except for an occasional black Monday, he's been rolling ever since.

If it will make you feel any better, I can't help thinking sometimes that in a monstrous way the disaster might have been the best thing that could have happened to him. At least he was able to walk away with his pride more or less intact; that is, he's been spared the inevitable humiliation (and destruction) of bankruptcy. Quinnley Corners would never have held out without our resorting to measures that, I know, would have broken Red's heart. There are times when he seems dazed or lost by the unbelievable fact that Quinnley Corners no longer exists or that he can no longer go there, but these spells pass. Today he had his best day. When I came home from the plant I told him the news about Max Wilkerson, who has jettisoned his Bellgard franchise. Red was jubilant. I did not tell him that Wilkerson is arranging to lease the land where Q.C. stood; he is going into a new operation. Leasing and Renting; all makes. For this the property's location is very good. As matters stand now it looks as though the insurance money will be forthcoming shortly. It's a complicated mess but after all debts and losses have been repaid, Red will see enough daylight to retire. On this the doctor insists. I am making plans accordingly.

In the meantime I've been spending much more time with him, that is, what spare time there is. Played golf, which as you know is my idea of nothing to do; and two ball games (he's an avid Tiger fan from way back); a picnic last Sunday with Suzy and the Rothes. We went to a picture that was playing near us, a rerun, something called *Under the Yum-Yum Tree,* which I blithely assumed would be a Japanese avant-garde film. But as the doctor says, the best thing would be to get Red away from here, away from the weather, and down to the Caribbean. Tony Kerwin has put me on to a friend of his, a V.P. of Vanguard who has a small house, plus housekeeper in Jamaica, and I am hoping to rent the place beginning this fall. Suzy and I could fly down to see him on occasional weekends or holidays.

What other news from Cartown? I'm sure you are as *au courant* as I. By the way, yesterday I sent you a book, *God's Own Junk-yard,* by Peter Blake, which ought to make you feel very smug living in Greece. One nugget Ann will appreciate: "America, in short, is no longer landscape, or townscape, but simply carscape." The trouble is, after reading it you will never want to return to these misbegotten shores.

You keep asking about Virginia Colter. What can I say? She's making a life for herself after some tough times. Her husband, Sandy Colter, was killed in the 1962 Beachside Trophy race. You would think her interest in cars would now be justifiably negative. Not so. What else? She's attractive. She's also bright, as evidenced by her preference for the likes of me. She runs the Pine Royal Sports Car Club with a driving glove of iron. I'm sure Jemmy must have told you much of this by now.

We all miss you and Ben to an immoderate degree. We talked about you a lot the other night—Phil and Lorie, Jack and Jemmy Winters, and the Steve Sturgeses. (I am planning to write a long piece about Sturges' new company for my magazine—that is, for what used to be my magazine—if I can ever find enough time away from the plant.)

Always yrs.

Scott

Before going out to mail the letter, he read it over once more, searching carefully for anything that might convey a suspicion of what had happened to him since last October.

30: Vincent Eames

HE dressed that morning with love but with more haste than on an average day. He relished this ritual, just as he liked his penthouse high in the apartment-hotel near the river. "One of the most important views in town, you get from here," he liked to say. For on a clear day you could see Grosse Pointe and Grosse Pointe Shores.

Today, however, he was too absorbed with the tricky mission before him to notice the view or even bother making conversation with the girl who sat sleepily smoking a cigarette in his "fabulous King of King's" bed. "Try throwing the old canister on that workbench," he liked to say to friends, as he showed them around the apartment. Girls were here a lot of the time because, as he would say, "they make the best kind of interior decoration." But you had to have pussy around just in case, never knew when you'd run into some wheel who appreciated a special favor. Not that the place was jumping all the time. It wasn't. You couldn't carry a business like his—automotive parts and accessories was the most competitive side of the industry— and be boffing broads every night. But people who got around knew that at Vince Eames' place was where the action was, or could be had.

Now Vince, having shaved, was ready for the final run. He had copied the idea from Dean Stratler—this neat and efficient assembly-line method of dressing.

From the bathroom you stepped into the long dressing room where all your clothes were quickly accessible in the proper succession of stages. From the built-in drawers you picked out the monogrammed shirt, going on then to the tie hinge, then to the pants line, and on to the sloped shelves of shoes, and then on to the wardrobe display of his two dozen suits, finishing off at the wall chest of accessories, handkerchiefs, tie pins, cuff links. . . .

Of course he'd never seen Dean Stratler's bedroom suite, but he'd heard it described often enough, and he'd had two of the carpenters from his plant build the dressing room in their free time.

Resplendent now in his summer suit of Continental cut and Italian fabric, he stepped into the bedroom. "You can check out at noon, doll," he told the girl. He deposited a few bills on the bureau. "Unless you hear to the contrary."

But he knew he wouldn't be calling in. Not today. He'd be in Cleveland seeing Mr. E. Holtsbridge. The only thing Holtsbridge wanted to screw was the present management of Bellgard.

Vince telephoned the garage in his building and ordered his car. He drove to the factory, and after his business was completed he set out for Cleveland, driving sedately in his scarlet Bellgard (his last one, that was for sure!). He tuned in some music, settled back in the bucket-type seat and began to review the entire situation: his car was his Think Machine.

Today's mission was one he hadn't planned until three days ago; he supposed, however, it had been in the making ever since the morning when he'd called on Scott Quinnley at breakfast time, that morning when he'd tried once more to get Quinnley over to his side.

Only to find Quinnley was having none of it. Worse than that was hearing Quinnley threaten him if he put any more pressure on Ernst Kamber. Nothing had worked that morning.

He should have known Quinnley couldn't be had, that had been made clear to him once before in New York, hadn't it? Well, that's how it was with guys like that—they were nothing but employees, and that's what they'd always be, weren't interested in anything except doing their job, and Vince could drop dead.

Yes, but then in the middle of the whole shebang, as Scott was kissing him off, Vince had suddenly seen the other side of the picture.

It wasn't Quinnley who was kissing him off—it was Mr. Tony Kerwin. Sure. Tony the Kerwin, who'd maneuvered Scott into his present slot, nicely transferring the hatchet to Scott, and Scott thinking all the time he was the Action Boy.

Nice footwork for Tony. This was Tony the Kerwin, none other than Vince's chum and one-time partner.

And here was Vince all this time keeping to himself what he knew about Tony and Myra, hoarding it, a bundle to be used if he had to. But hoarding it too long maybe.

Why?

Because the situation at Bellgard had changed. It would be pointless now to go to Myra Stratler and say: look Myra, I know how you've been laying Tony, I know the whole story, I've known it since the day I saw you spinning out of the driveway at his farm, and since I know it, why don't you go see our mutual friend and tell him unless he continues doing business at the same stand, for example, Eames Muffler and Exhaust Supply Company, that I'll pass the word along to your husband or to Tony's wife.

But that hadn't been the play after all. The bundle he'd been hoarding was worth exactly nothing.

The situation had changed. Wild. Vince no longer wanted Bellgard's business because he knew he was dead there. Scott Quinnley was performing the Last Rites.

Since he couldn't get the next contract from Bellgard (from Tony), he'd do the next best thing: Make a deal with Holtsbridge who, if Vince's info was correct, was the man who'd be in the Bellgard saddle sooner or later.

Go to Holtsbridge, tell the story, blast Bellgard open. Vince, the injured party, Tony Kerwin bleeding him all these years.

With ammunition like this, Holtsbridge could have the stockholders in an uproar and blast out the present management. After that, of course, it would be that prick Sam Kyssin who would probably be manufacturing the mufflers for Bellgard. Let him. Vince might be out, but he wouldn't be out all the way. The thing was to get to Holtsbridge, not pushing his way in, but like a gentleman. Suede gloves. Who could fix it? Simple. Sam Kyssin.

All this came to him just three nights ago, right in the midst of a little party he was having at his apartment.

He'd sat himself down on the side of his King of Kings bed, picked up the telephone (it was the same color as his bedroom—*Pompeii Red*, as that fancy-hatted bandit of a decorator had called it), and got through to the residence of Mr. Sam Kyssin, that brilliant young man of the new generation, his fine competitor who manufactured such a "superior product." But Mr. Kyssin was out, his wife said, half-asleep. He was at a meeting at Mr. Steven Sturges' house.

(Sturges. Sure. Another of those smart kids like Scott Quinnley who had all the answers.)

In fifteen minutes Kyssin had called back, suspicious and brisk. But Vince soon had him listening hard: "So how would you like to get yourself a break over at Bellgard?"

[390

"Why all this magnanimity?" Kyssin the snothead asked.

"How's that?"

"You're being very generous, aren't you? What can you gain, Mr. Eames? I can assure you if Holtsbridge ever does get control, your product might not make it. Are you on to that?"

"Sure I'm on to it. I know I won't be in the Bellgard camp anymore if the picture changes. But maybe you will, if you arrange a little matter for me in the right way. I don't know Holtsbridge. You do. Of course if you are too busy to arrange a meeting—"

Twenty-four hours later Vince was on the highway. Mr. Sam Kyssin, that King of Kreeps, had not been too busy to arrange the meeting.

The Holtsbridge Construction Company occupied the 33rd, 34th and 35th floors of the Holtsbridge Building in Downtown Cleveland. And never had Vince been more beautifully received.

Holtsbridge was, for Vince's money, not much of a dresser, no dash, that tan suit looked like it came off the cheapest pipe rack in town, and as for that tie? Funeralville. But he was built. And tough. Eyes like ball bearings. Big chunk of nose, lips thin, bloodless. A Good Joe though. Reminded you of Cod Smith, except he wasn't as snotty as Smith. Yes, Vince judged in a few minutes, Holtsbridge was Okay People.

The proposition? They got around to it now after all the gentlemanly double-talk.

In return for a given percentage—Vince called it a "royalty"—on all future muffler contracts from Bellgard, regardless of who the supplier was, Vince would give to Holtsbridge and his Group the ammunition needed to blast open the next stockholders' meeting.

"What would that be?" Holtsbridge fingered a sterling-silver replica in miniature of the Ableson Tower, a skyscraper which his company had built, one of the big architectural prizes in Ohio.

"Well," Vince lit his second cigarette, "there are two ways of telling you about it, Mr. Holtsbridge. The long way and the short way. The long way, that's like a history of the United States or a labor union contract. The—"

"The shorter way might be all we have time for today," Holtsbridge said quietly.

"All right." Vince drew deeply on his cigarette, then put on the blasteroo: "I'm getting tired of having to pay out. I've been kicking

391]

back to Bellgard for over ten years now. I decided I didn't want to be bled anymore."

"I see." The man's big face wrinkled, cracked to produce a hundred more lines. "In other words Sam Kyssin's guess was right, though it was more than a guess."

"Kyssin was right."

"Too bad," Holtsbridge said.

"Too bad?" Vince frowned.

"I don't like to play like that, don't like it at all. Too bad." Holtsbridge was shaking his head. Then: "But tell me something, what evidence do you have?"

"Enough," Vince said. "But I don't have to show my hand. That's up to the other end."

"That being who?"

"Mr. Tony Kerwin."

The man put aside the silver skyscraper. "Kerwin. I see. What makes you think he'll admit this if you don't show a hand of evidence?"

"I think," Vince said, "if Cod Smith questions him about it, that will be all that's necessary."

"What makes you so sure?"

"I know the people." (And wouldn't that be something, Vince rejoiced now in this anticipatory moment: Tony the Kerwin hadn't wanted any part of him anymore, had he? Tony the Kerwin had put the load on Scott Quinnley's back, hadn't he? Tony the elegant Kerwin was cleaning house at Bellgard and had swept him outside, hadn't he? Thinking he would never be called on it. But that's just where he'd been wrong. For now Tony the great cocksman Kerwin, that great mastermind for the third floor, was going to get it. From where? From his chum and one-time partner Vincent Eames. That was for sure. Remember how Tony the Kerwin always assumed Vince would never dare open his mouth? Remember how Tony the great sport Kerwin would say: "Vince, there's no point threatening me. You can't bring out my dirty linen without exposing your own, can you?" Well, friend, the answer to that was not going to be what Tony the Kerwin had always assumed. Why? Because the entire deal with Holtsbridge was based, in addition to money, on the one-sided indictment. Vince merely gave the information and the big brass would carry it from there. Why? Because they weren't interested in

Vince's manipulations, they were interested in Kerwin's. Right? Right.)

Holtsbridge was peering at him: "I'd like to see the figures and dates, if you have them."

"I have them. But they won't be necessary."

"I'd like to see them."

"They are yours, Mr. H., as soon as I see an agreement in black and white, plus a binder in cash to show good faith. We can arrange terms as long as there is a meeting of happy minds."

"I'm sure we can. Let me sit on it for a while."

"How long?" Vince said.

"Oh—thirty days, possibly less," Holtsbridge said.

It was less. Two weeks later Vince was back in Cleveland. He went into the office with the figures, dates, all the information demanded and he left the office with the agreement and the cash binder.

Such a small part of the day, such a small package, but Vince was convinced that the fifty-five minutes just passed was the beginning of the end for Mr. Anthony James Kerwin and many other upstanding officers, as well as that fine upstanding member of the team, Mr. Scott Quinnley.

Driving back from Cleveland in his ruby-hued Think Machine, Vincent Eames said to himself: Tonight calls for a party. Why not? And in one of those philosophic strokes that rarely fell upon him, he thought: Yes, Automation, Electronic Computers, along with Call Girls, have made a real contribution to American Business.

31: Codman Smith

ONE autumn noon, an elegiac day, amber-hazed and raw, he received a call from Cleveland, Ohio. It came a few minutes after he'd returned from the Board of Directors' meeting, a not very happy conclave.

His palm was moist on the telephone, as he heard the quiet voice from Cleveland. He did not know why Holtsbridge was calling, but he did know the reason would not be worth celebrating. (Just as at breakfast this morning, when his wife had said: "Think of it, Cod, it's a year since Ann's been gone—" he'd answered bitterly: "Well, that scarcely calls for a celebration, does it?")

"Yes, Mr. Holtsbridge? What's on your mind?"

"Quite a lot, Mr. Smith. I find I'll be around your bivouac tomorrow, and I'd like to have a talk with you if it wouldn't be too inconvenient. Short notice, I realize."

Codman Smith said: "Anything special?"

"Yes. I'd say it was special."

Cod did not consult his calendar, his agenda; he knew all his commitments. And he was not canceling them. The only free time he had was at half-past eight: ". . . if that isn't too early for you."

"Not at all," Holtsbridge agreed. He was flying in in the company helicopter, and he could touch down on Bellgard's strip.

A canny moment. Holtsbridge choosing this time for a talk. Of course Holtsbridge's group had been quiet, too dormant too long. He might have known they'd work up some noise one day: the day was here.

A time, Cod knew, when he would need all the coolness for which he was renowned.

With the precision timing of a rocket-firing, Holtsbridge was shaking hands with him in the office the next morning as the clock showed eight-thirty, not a half minute less nor a minute more. Which Cod appreciated. He had to admit, also, that his initial reaction to the man was positive. For what that was worth.

Would he care for some coffee?

No. Never drank it.

"Well"—Codman Smith leaned back in the black leather chair, taking the position, if not the attitude, of ease—"I'd like to think you're going to surprise me and talk about something that won't be connected with the next stockholders' meeting."

"No, I'm afraid there won't be any surprises, Mr. Smith. Except in the wrong places." From his vest pocket Holtsbridge brought out a silver pencil, one of those gadgets which, when pulled full out, become an eighteen-inch rule. He tugged at the pencil's tip and drew forth the long rod of silver. "I'll get right to it. Our group is in possession of material that's going to look very unattractive in the proxy statements."

"What material?"

"This concerns what is obviously a conflict-of-interest situation. One of your officers and directors has been on the taking end for quite some time—"

"Just a moment, Mr. Holtsbridge," Cod stopped him. Irritably he said: "Exactly what is this? Where does it come from?"

"From Mr. Vincent Eames."

"Eames?"

"Yes."

Cod's immediate reaction was one of relief. "I can't take that seriously. Eames happens to be—"

"I understand what you mean," Holtsbridge said, while at the same time handing him the papers. "But in relation to Mr. Kerwin, it's all here. All of it is in this deposition."

He might not have heard him correctly. Had he said Kerwin?

"Yes."

Kerwin.

As Cod read the document, something close to nausea seized him.

Kerwin.

He reached for the carafe of water, poured a glassful, drank it.

Tony.

Except that now he thought not only of Tony. But of Phoebe. And of the family, and of Codman Smith. And the name of Bellgard. (And of yesterday's Board of Directors' meeting when he'd had to read a single figure, the dollar tally of Bellgard's automotive losses for this year.)

Kerwin.

He could not believe or accept it. He put aside the document. A year ago in New York he had ignored the rumors—a shoddy tactic to stir up stockholders.

He peered at Holtsbridge. A man like that. No. But a man like Eames, a source as devious as Eames . . .

"I'm sorry," Holtsbridge was saying. "However, here it is. The story goes out on all proxy statements, and to the S.E.C. If a director fails to answer the charges truthfully—"

"Yes, I know." Criminal offense.

Tony.

"We aren't anxious to get a proxy fight started—not one that could get as dirty as this," Holtsbridge said.

"You haven't got the necessary votes to lick us." Cod's defiance betrayed a loss of control.

"I'll concede that. We haven't now." Holtsbridge snapped the silver rule back into its sheath. "However, we will have them if we use this material. The point is I'd prefer not to. Do the company too much damage. I have no intention of using any of this if we can come to a decision among ourselves."

"As to what?" But Cod had an intimation of what was coming.

"Kerwin is your son-in-law. Your daughter's husband. Naturally I understand what this means. But you'll have to be prepared to get rid of him. I'm sorry."

Cod tried not to swallow. He said: "Anything else?"

"You'll have to lose Kerwin and three others, and give us four of our men on the Board. In that way we can drop the charge."

"I see." A measured bitterness spaced his words now. "Who would you have in mind for the four?"

"I was thinking of Carl Ritter of Martex Missile Systems, Fred Burke of Bur-Fair Machine Foundry, Harvey Logan of Amo-State Appliance. And," Holtsbridge added wryly, "just possibly myself."

Cod was familiar with the names, and their significance tolled heavily within him. He recognized the theme of the proposed Board: diversification—defense contracts and all the other revenue potential (and risk) of wide-spectrum subsidiaries—all nonautomotive. And hence, as far as the new group was concerned, non-Codman Smith.

[396

"Naturally," Holtsbridge said, "it would be our hope—our privilege—to have you with us on the Board."

"Thank you." With coolest courtesy Cod acknowledged this tribute which he knew merely represented good manners on Holtsbridge's part, as well as a modicum of respect.

At best Cod would be voted in for another year, after which a testimonial banquet rich in calories and sentimentality for the outgoing President or Chairman. He said: "Is there any particular hurry about this?"

"We ought to settle it within twenty-four hours," Holtsbridge said.

Cod was unprepared. He said: "The next stockholders' meeting doesn't come up until April."

"Mr. Smith, you must know I own enough stock to demand a special meeting within forty days. Though I hope that won't be necessary."

Abruptly Cod tilted forward. Without talking to Tony, any further discussion with Holtsbridge was a waste. They agreed to convene again tomorrow at five o'clock. He was grateful that the Clevelander had at least kept his mission mercifully short. As soon as the man had gone, he telephoned Kerwin's office and asked him to come over at once.

Waiting then.

Rising, going to the glass wall. He looked out to the Esplanade, to the architectural dignity of the buildings flanking it, to the distant overpass and the underpass and the railhead, to the sprawling units of production—so much of what he saw had been built or expanded during his tenure.

Tony.

Somehow he still could not accept what he'd heard, what, in fact, he had read. More time. How he needed it. Time. So that his bones and flesh would stop resisting what his intellect told him must be true.

His affection for Tony had been lodged deeper than he'd suspected. Even now.

He heard the sound of the door opening. How he dreaded this confrontation. He turned.

"Sit down, Tony." As he moved to his desk, Cod's gaze remained fixed on him with a force so powerful that it might have extracted from his son-in-law's face an avowal of total innocence.

There was only a quizzical glance in return, and that same charming half-smile which he knew so well.

"You sounded a bit exercised on the phone, Cod," Tony said, as he might often have said.

"I was. I am," Cod said, as he seldom would have said.

"Oh?"

As much as Cod wanted to be rid of the painful process before him, he could not bring himself to speak at once.

"Cod, you do seem a bit—"

"Tony—" He broke the seal of his helpless silence. "Tony, before I say much, let me just say I've taken no action, I've made no commitments or decisions on any of this—"

"Any of what, Cod?" Alertness was suddenly in the room. Or was it that? Goddammit, the way Tony looked at him now, it was more like concern for him, as if it was *Cod's* well-being he feared for.

Cod seized the hope. (He wanted to.) He saw in Tony's face, the now steadfast eyes, no trace whatever of those signals which mark the guilty.

It could not be true. (It must not.)

A man of Tony's position. Why? It wasn't as if he were desperate for money. His private life was serene enough. His marriage to Phoebe was certainly as good as any marriage he knew. Phoebe worshiped him. She was a sensitive woman, almost pitifully honest; her needs were never extravagant, she was scarcely the kind of wife who would drive her husband to this extreme. . . .

No.

Certainly Tony, for his part, was often unduly extravagant, but that was part of his charm, part of what sparked his personality, illuminated the Bellgard roster. . . .

No. This could only have originated from Eames this time, a devious and detestable maneuver of Eames'.

Cod said: "Holtsbridge was just here. From Cleveland. He thinks he's on to something that looks pretty scandalous. He claims . . ." And here Cod hesitated, reluctant, unwilling to say what he was about to say, deciding instead not to level the charge directly at Tony. He rephrased it so that it would be like an open indictment inviting the guilty one—if guilt there was—to identify himself. "He claims," Cod said now, "that one of our people, our directors, is involved in a conflict-of-interest situation."

"Conflict-of-interest?" Tony repeated it. Sunlight on his face, and Cod believed he saw a tensing in the muscles of his jaw. Unless that could only have been the play of light.

[398

Unless Cod did not want to see anything.

"Yes." Cod had to keep watching him. "I'll have to call the Board together. But I wanted to discuss it with you first."

Hurriedly Tony said: "Are you sure this isn't the same sort of muck Holtsbridge's group tried to throw at us last year?" A pause, but Tony seemed steadier, less hurried now. "I mean—it's possible—that is, after that mess at Chrysler a few years back, this gang thinks maybe they can scare us, and—"

"I wish it were that."

"Is that all he told you?" Tony leaned forward. "Who is supposed to be involved? Conflict-of-interest between who—whom?"

"Between," Cod said evenly, "one of our people and Vince Eames."

"Oh." Tony's hand lifted, the finger rising to touch the mole on his cheek. Familiar habit of nervousness. He brought his hand down hastily. More rapidly he said: "Vince." And stopped. "Matter of fact, now that I think of it, Scott told me ever since he had it out with him, Vince has been going around town like a—"

"You haven't seen anything of him, Tony?"

"No."

"You used to, of course," Cod said.

"Yes." Tony folded his arms, unfolded them. "Vince has changed a lot since the old days. He's a sick guy. I wouldn't put any of this past him." A silence. "Would you?"

But Cod did not answer this time, so that the silence grew, and into it came the sound of Tony getting to his feet. "If it's Vince, then I suppose it could be me he's trying to get. God knows, from his point of view he'd have reason enough. Wouldn't he?"

Again Cod did not answer. Not yet. Only watching him, making himself examine or interpret what Tony had just said. Yet thinking it was not improbable in the sense that Tony could, conceivably, have felt that as Cod's son-in-law he would have been free of suspicion, he would have the immunity of a family member. With this kind of protection, he could have run a sideshow of his own.

Not improbable. But surely not probable.

"I wouldn't know, Tony," he finally answered.

Tony said: "Cod, it might be premature to call the Board. We—I don't think we can rush into this—"

"It isn't up to us."

"I mean we ought to give ourselves a handicap on getting the Board in too soon," Tony said.

"Why?"

"I've got to chase this down." The level of Tony's voice seemed unwavering. "I've got to go to Vince and see for myself just how in hell he expects this to stand up."

"Yes—" Cod heard himself temporizing, looking at Tony, still hoping, needing to hope it could be done, Tony producing a bill of health. Yes. Even though Vince Eames' deposition stood up, high, confronting him, vivid as a signboard.

Yet taking hope as he saw Tony move purposefully to the door. However, he said: "Tony—"

"Yes?"

"Holtsbridge is pressing us on this. We'll have to call—at least notify the Board to stand by today."

"Today?"

"Yes," Cod said. Fortunately (or unfortunately) after yesterday's meeting, the members were still around and could be summoned.

Tony hesitated: "I'll be running into half of them before the day's out. If anyone asks questions—"

"If anyone asks questions there's nothing to say. None of this can get out of the office. It won't remain secret—it's bound to leak—but until the meeting, nothing, not a word." Then Cod said slowly: "This is what I'm going to do with the Board. I'm going to read the charge as written by Holtsbridge's counsel. And I'm going to ask that if anyone present is in any way connected with the charge, that he turn in his resignation within an hour after the meeting is adjourned."

Cod saw his son-in-law turn, stir, stare toward the corner window-wall. Was there a lingering, almost wistful glaze coming over Tony's eyes—as if he could not quite bring himself to leave, or as if he were lingering, clinging to something from which he could not bear to be parted? A cruelty of life seemed to imprison him, for he failed to move; though the moment passed and there was the quick, familiar flash of his smile as he turned to open the door.

Alone now, Cod sat stone-still.

He refused to project his fears beyond the moment. He refused to allow himself to think of Phoebe or the others or himself.

Yet shortly after four o'clock that afternoon, when the envelope was delivered to him, and he opened it and saw that the resignation was signed by Tony—even then, or perhaps not *until* then, did the

impact reach, stab through his mind to the flesh that had been resisting it all this time.

All he'd held back, contained, during the past hour, the past day,
burst to flood through him, a blood river of rage.

He was beyond his desk now, he strode across his astringently
plain office, unable for a long time to quell his feelings which were
so fierce because they were so new and so close and so alien.

Not only the depth of his disenchantment; not that alone. But the
sudden, unwieldy contempt he felt for his son-in-law. Which was not
much greater than the contempt he felt for his own fallible judgment.

This degrading of Bellgard's name, of Cod's name, even of the
marriage to Phoebe.

Ah, Phoebe, how could she be told? Phoebe, who, like Ann, deserved so much more of life.

Of all his daughters, only Myra seemed to have found or developed
a way of unbroken unhappiness. . . .

Cod moved back to his desk. His legs felt weak, and it was true
that he was unused to passion and it drained his strength.

Now by force of will and the return of discipline, he turned away
from his torment to get on with the work of the day.

By company law a resignation had to be endorsed, acted upon, to
be confirmed, denied or accepted. He endorsed the acceptance even
before it was to be presented to the Board at tomorrow's emergency
meeting.

And that night, carrying the still-secret knowledge of dishonor, he
and his wife, Dean and Myra, and Phoebe (Tony had had to beg off,
"crucial business at the plant") attended the charity benefit concert at
Ford Auditorium.

32: *Tony Kerwin*

ALL he had to do was turn back. Thirty steps. Go upstairs. Phoebe was awake. Go upstairs and tell her. It was a mistake not to have told her yesterday or last night. Now no deferring it. The news release would be issued tomorrow.

Still he sat there, only the faintest appetite for breakfast. Seven-thirty. Sitting at the head of the long dark table with his unfinished bacon and eggs and English muffin. And milk, that dreary, chalky, mouth-puckering milk. And his stomach.

Dear Lord, why couldn't he have had a wife like Blanche? Resilent, comprehending, ride it out with him. . . .

"Tony?"

Phoebe's voice, soft, tentative, but causing him to swing around, startled, as if she'd fired off one of his hunting guns.

Yes, right behind his chair, an apparition; he turned slightly, saw the hem of the lemon-colored robe, the slender feet in mules— He liked slender feet, and Phoebe's were that. And now her hand on the back of his neck, stroking it.

To close his eyes now, all woes stroked away. If only. "Phoebe," he said. "You're not having your breakfast upstairs?"

"I wanted to ask you something before you left." Still kneading the back of his neck with her thin fingers. A scent of night cream. "There's a problem, darling." Her statement soft and wifely. She came around and he drew over a walnut Chippendale chair for her.

"What's *your* problem?" He didn't even try to subdue the irony in his voice. But how pleasant it might have been, this pleasant, ordinary morning with all the pleasant ordinary sounds. No more. "I was just coming up to see you." He noticed she was still wearing her white lace hairnet.

"Oh?" She sat down beside him. Then: "What I wanted to ask you was about that donation for the Kent Hills Hospital Fund. Do we want it on my check or yours? Or the joint account? I mean, I recalled your saying something about it last year—"

"Joint. Mr. and Mrs. Kerwin." Wistfully thinking: Such a pleasant problem, such a pleasant solution. He lifted his glass of milk, doggedly downing its lactic whiteness as if it were some elixir that would fortify him for what he had to tell her now. "Phoebe—"

"Yes?" And the way she leaned forward, interest and anticipation all bright and cozy on her face.

"Phoebe," he began as if he were talking to a child, "you remember that time when I told you—or tried to—how rough it can get in this business when they start taking potshots at you, and—"

"Do I remember? You half scared me to death! Why?" Then: "Tony—what is it? Is something wrong?"

"Everything's wrong." And there at once, like a child, the quick fear in her eyes. He wished there was some way to spare her, some way to protect her from it. "But bad as it is, it could be worse. It will all be done quietly, privately. Behind closed doors. And we've got to be grateful for that."

"For what?" And already her hand fluttered to the lace edge of the hairnet.

He pushed his glass to one side. "I've resigned."

"Resigned? From what?" she said. Then: "From the company? You don't mean the company?"

"Yes."

"Tony, if this is your idea of some kind of joke—"

"It's no joke." Having to see her face now was more punishment than he'd asked for. And hurriedly, for her sake (for his), going on with it, having to tell her all of it, and all the while the way she sat there, so still, so tense, a hunter hiding in the bush. And now finishing it: ". . . this leaves Holtsbridge the next move, to pack the Board with his boys. Cod had no choice, and I had no choice. It's one of—"

"I—Tony, I can't, I just can't believe it." Phoebe still had not moved, but her face, devoid of makeup, was losing color.

"I can't either," he said all too truthfully.

"Oh Tony—if you, I mean if you actually didn't take any money from Vince, if—"

"Listen, this was a long time ago, that is . . . ." Here he had to pause before airing for the first time the defense he (not his attorney) had decided on, a half-truth which could no longer be proved or disproved. "What Vince didn't say was that I never asked for any

403]

money. It would never have occurred to me. I was given it. And even that, in the beginning, was due me. He gave it to me after I went with Bellgard, he said it was earnings due me retroactively."

"Didn't you tell that to Father?" Phoebe protested indignantly. As he knew she would.

"No."

"I'll tell him then!" she asserted.

"Too late, too late for that," he said. (Just as, for all his battles for the Bellstar, for all its initial success at the Auto Show, that three-month calamity in Ohio had destroyed it. Too late. And now there was the Mustang, the new Corvair, and others, which already had left the Bellstar trailing in defeat.) "It's very complex, Phoebe. But what it is, is the timing of it, a time when the company's losses are over nine million at the third quarter, and Vince is making it possible for the big grab, and everyone wants to be on the right side. That's Holtsbridge's side. He's got Vince's claim, even though no actual proof exists, figures and dates can't prove the movement of cash. Vince knew that. I know it. And—"

"But Father would never force you to resign if you—"

"Phoebe, from Cod's point of view—and this is what you have to understand—from Cod's point of view, even if I got one dollar too much—and I probably did—to Cod it might just as well have been a hundred thousand." Alas, the God's truth.

"How do you know?"

"I know Cod. Don't you?"

A dreadful moment. "Yes," she said.

"He made that very clear to me when he presented it," Tony said. "It was a question of resigning, for a deal of privacy, no scandal, or my fighting it. I would have lost, Phoebe. Technically. This way at least Cod and the company—and even I—have been spared what could have been a—"

"Oh, Tony—Tony!" But no more then, and staring at him now in that despairing bewilderment, her mouth stiff, locked, her hands working on her lap.

Until, in a burst of tenderness—or pity—he reached out and drew her against him, holding her fragile body for the comfort he could give, just as, he saw now, all the years they'd been together had grown a comfort he'd needed, just as he'd needed her unpretentious dedication to him, this guileless devotion which was a rare commodity in anyone's world, and certainly in his. Certainly on this day.

[404

Though there was now no woman for him except Blanche, it could not alter what at heart he would always feel for Phoebe.

But now, without warning, Phoebe drew away from him, rose. "Oh Tony"—tears blurred in her eyes—"Tony, how could you have let it happen?" She moved aimlessly around the dark, wax-scented table, and now and then absently her fingers would tap nervously along the table's edge. "What are you . . . we . . . going to do? How could you have let this—I mean we can't just let it happen, how could . . ."

Oh dear God. Tony turned away. This was unbearable, the way she fell apart. Understandable, but he couldn't endure it, this whining, sobbing reproach.

How in hell did she think *he* felt?

Did she think he welcomed this vicious act of Vince's? Did she have any idea what he'd been living through? Had she known what it had been for him to write out that resignation? Had she seen him the night before last, when she'd been at the concert, waiting in his car near Vince Eames' apartment, waiting for him to come home, pain spiking into his stomach, but heedless, waiting wildly to get at Vince, not with words, with bare hands? No. No one knew this. Not even Vince, who never returned home. Mr. Eames is on vacation in Canada. . . .

"Phoebe, will you please sit down. I can't stand this. Will you try to be calm—"

"I can't! How can I?" she cried.

"Phoebe, don't go shouting all over the place." Firing a warning glance toward the pantry door.

"Tony, I—"

"Will you stop it. Stop it!" He went to her, grasped her, held her hard.

Again: "What are you—we—going to do?" Still sobbing.

"Will you sit down!" But softening his tone. He knew she was close to hysteria. He pressed his arm around her, walked her back to the high-backed chair. "I'd like to finish this."

As she now blotted the wetness in her eyes, he said: "I've had to live with this alone, this is the third day now. I've had enough time to know what I should have done or what I shouldn't have done. You don't have to tell me. I know how you mean it, but . . ." a pause. "Listen to me, Phoebe—are you listening to me?"

Nodding her head, the handkerchief still at her eyes.

405]

"I haven't been happy at the plant for a long time. Not really. I've never gone along with Cod and the others on policy. As you know. But I had to. Now there's this. At least I'm free. I'm not going to waste myself on another move unless I—"

"Tony, how can you talk like this? Free. What move? Where could you go?"

"Phoebe, will you try to be calm?"

"I'm sorry—I don't, I just can't understand it, I can't, Tony. Can you tell me, not so quickly, exactly how it happened? I'm confused."

"Oh for God sakes, Phoebe, I can't go through the whole damn mess again! I'm not built like a saint. What do you think this is doing to me?" The familiar, dreaded fire was jabbing in his stomach.

"I'm sorry—Tony, where are those pills of yours? Oh yes—" For the first time she seemed to have pulled herself together; she was leaving the dining room. He heard her start upstairs, turn back to answer the telephone in the hallway: "No—no, I was going to call you, Marion. I feel perfectly awful—no, I think I must have had too much to eat the night we went to the concert. Yes, well thank you. Yes, I'll call you." Marion Bassman, whose husband was group vice-president, manufacturing, Jefferson Motors.

When she returned with his medication, he said: "I wish you wouldn't cancel any engagements. I'd rather you wouldn't do that now."

"I couldn't possibly see Marion Bassman today. I couldn't face anyone." She waited as he downed the two capsules. "Tony, who else knows about this?"

"I told you it's not public. It's only among a few people, all of whom are interested in *not* letting this blow up. Holtsbridge and Cod have agreed on this. No lawsuits, no countersuits. There'll be a new Board voted in next stockholders' meeting—"

"I don't care about that, I care about now. Right now, Tony!" Her eyes and hands again showed rising agitation. "Tony, if you had a right to that money how could Vince Eames have dared to start this?"

"Phoebe, I've told you, why do you keep—"

"I only want to know."

"I told you."

"You didn't tell me how Vince could start anything as serious as this, unless he—oh Tony—if you did, I mean, if there is something you—"

[406

"Dear God, will you please try to keep straight what I've been trying to tell you! Will you, Phoebe? I've been viciously maligned. I've been made a victim. For a reason. And there's nothing any of us can do about it. At least not now. The main thing right now is to go on doing everything as normally as you can. Don't make any changes. Do you understand, Phoebe?" No answer. In a final burst: "There's only this. This town can have a short memory sometimes. And I've still got a long time ahead of me."

She looked up at him, saying yes, though not making any sound, and he bent down then hastily, almost lovingly, to kiss her moist cheek. Leaving the room.

Tony.

What?

Where are you going?

The office.

Office?

Yes.

And out. For the office—it would be his last day—could not be as stultifying, or as painful, as it was here. At his house, this Kent Hills prison.

33: Scott Quinnley

"JESUS Almighty Bleeding Christ!" Came Red's cry on the telephone. "Been trying to get you. Did you know anything about this, Scott?"

"Not until today." He put down the notebooks on his desk. He had just returned from a meeting on the third floor.

"Scott, what's the inside?"

"I don't honestly know, Red." But from Kent Hills to Bloomfield Hills, from Grosse Pointe to Dearborn, from Detroit to Flint, the talk must have been of little else. At Bellgard what he'd witnessed since the news release had appeared in today's papers was a normal surface of activity beneath which was a bedlam of shock and speculation.

"Goddamdest thing," Red was saying. Then: "This going to affect you in any way?"

"I don't know." He did know, however, that a subtle or indefinable difference had come to exist today in the way some people talked to him or looked at him.

"How'd you find out, Scott? The papers?"

"Tony told me. This morning before he left the plant."

"*He* told you?" Red seized the item. A retired man now, a Senior Citizen, an idle time for the idle tongue. Tomorrow on the golf course, or at the football stadium watching the Lions, he'd say to cronies: *According to my son—Kerwin told him this personally before it hit the newspapers* . . . "Well, it sure is something I never expected to happen," he said.

"No one did," Scott said. "By the way, Red, I received that lease for the Jamaica house. I'll bring it home with me."

"Oh, yes. Yes. Thanks, son."

"We couldn't swing it for the first. The place won't be ready until the fifteenth."

"Sure. All right, Scott." Then: "Virginia Colter coming to Sunday dinner? Mrs. Coombs asked me to check."

"Yes."

[408

"All right. I'm going out now for nine holes."

"Easy on the booze, Red."

"My word on it. Okay. Very anxious to talk to you, son."

That was Thursday afternoon, and there was little Scott could have told him.

But by noon Sunday when he drove out to call for Virginia Colter, who was working at her office at the Pine Royal Sports Car Club, he had learned quite a bit more. In Cartown, money was easier to keep than secrets. What he'd heard was not necessarily reliable, but it was surely depressing.

"Hi, *commendatore*," Virginia greeted him. One of the nicest things about her, and there were many, was that she didn't remind him of Ann. Being a very tall girl, she had to stoop low to get into his car. Scott now owned a black Bellstar, that ill-starred sports roadster —a test model which had seen rough days but which was still a finer piece of iron than that *hausfrau* of a Bellgard Red had given him almost two years ago. Virginia leaned back in the bucket, opened her leopard coat. "You know what I heard today?"

"What?" Scott circled around and back to the highway.

"And believe me, I'm not trying to pry into company secrets, Scott. I'm just telling you what I heard. Which was that Kerwin was *forced* to resign. I was talking to this gal at Chrysler, and she said it was all over the place. She'd heard it from—"

"An unimpeachable source?"

"*Overheard* it from an unimpeachable source," Virginia said. "I wasn't even sure you'd get out here today. Sunday or not. I suppose all hell has broken loose at Bellgard."

"It has. But you can't see it unless you're looking for it."

"Isn't that the worst kind?" She lit a cigarette and handed it to him, then lit one for herself. "Anyway"—she crossed her legs—"what I heard was that he was forced to resign. A woman."

Scott didn't answer.

"I see," Virginia said. "Well, I figured that was much too interesting to be true." She waited, watching him. And then she said: "But it's not impossible—I remember when you introduced him to me at the club, the night you gave your talk, and I've seen him a few times since. I wouldn't discount the idea. Kerwin definitely has an eye." And then, undaunted, came the facetiously rich and rolling Irish accent: "Sure, and it's the eye he has for a passing wench. Wouldn't you say that now?"

Scott shrugged. He tapped his cigarette ash into the console tray. She said: "I gather you don't want to talk about it."

After that, a long while driving and no conversation until Scott nosed into a hard curve. Virginia said: "This corner's like a pork barrel."

"You're used to stiffer suspension," he said. Virginia owned a secondhand Ferrari. "Do you want to drive this cannon for a while?"

"I wouldn't mind at all. I never have, you know," she said. "You sure you can entrust it to a nice lady driver like me?"

"I'll risk it." Scott drew over to the shoulder and changed places.

As soon as she had the wheel she made for the first exit and after an exploratory period of trial and error she found a lovely band of back road. She stopped and put on her driving gloves. When she was ready she said: "Okay, if for fun, we come out of the hole hard?"

"Okay."

And out she came with rear wheels kicking, the engine in throaty roar, gunning through from zero to 140 mph in what must have been just under record acceleration performance. She had a sure instinct and touch for the feel of a fast car. She slowed down then, keeping the needle at sixty-five as they sped past the autumn foliage bright as flags in the crystal day.

Scott appreciating her skill, knowing this kind of excursion would soon be a thing of the past. ("Forget the damned motorcars," Lewis Mumford once said, "design the cities for friends and lovers.")

Alas: the back roads and the side roads were disappearing fast, while cars were spawning by the millions. And the air was death.

"You know," Virginia had said one night last week when in the course of some martini rhetoric Scott had got on to air pollution and the need for an electrically powered public transportation system, "you know, I think you've got a kind of Love-Hate thing about automobiles. Don't you think so?"

Yes. He thought so.

"I mean," she'd said, "for a guy whose life has been hot gasoline machinery, you turn around and spend half your time pitching for an electric jukebox that goes forty-five miles an hour. Now you know that's pretty inconsistent."

"Middle age," he'd said airily.

But thinking now: middle age, here I come; the good old days are passing, nothing's like it used to be, and when I was a boy . . . Now

[410

you take today, what's left? What we need is a safe, odorless and silent automobile. Let's go back to the old-fashioned ways. . . .

Except that a project like that of Steve Sturges' was still so far out that many respectable conservative automotive moneymen wouldn't go near it.

Now as they neared the environs of Greenwood Park, Virginia thumped her hand on the stick shift. "You're right about this pony. They probably couldn't have done much better. Except for the transmission. You really have to watch it, don't you? Loses a lot of rpm's between shifts."

"Yes." And they talked some more about the Bellstar and what a bad shake the company took in that Ohio production disaster last year. Had the car rolled off when scheduled, it would surely have come in a winner. Instead, the time lag put in the competition with sports models of beefier powerplants of four-place seating packages, rendering the Bellstar a virtual museum piece in today's sales sweepstakes.

"Do you think that had something to do with Kerwin's resigning?" Virginia asked.

"Not directly," Scott said. "Except that if he'd brought it in as the barn-burner of the year, it's possible we wouldn't have this situation now. If you've got a winner, nobody asks questions and—" Scott stopped; he'd said enough. But he kept it running in his mind. Clearly he saw the ancient ratio which still produced the same results. For the success of the Bellstar would have meant high profits—money; when you put money against immorality— "What do you say we give it a rest for a while, Virginia?"

"I say all right. But reluctantly."

Soon Virginia turned the car into the driveway of the house. "Well." She took off her driving gloves. "I must say that was a luxurious ride. It'll spoil me." She glanced into the rearview mirror and fussed with her hair. Then: "I meant to tell you, when I talked to Suzy on the phone last week she said she was the one who wanted me for dinner today."

"A slight exaggeration, Virginia," Scott said. He was no longer quite as anxious about Suzy as he had been in the past; at least he was reconciled to the fact that no matter what woman he might be interested in, seriously or not seriously, Suzy would become part of it. It was inevitable, and he'd come to accept the pattern.

411]

"Why an exaggeration?"

"Suzy's just desperate for a mother figure," he said.

"I guess that lets me out." Virginia smiled. "I'm just too tall to make a nice little mother figure." She shook her head. "And I remember everybody warning me at boarding school, don't smoke, it'll stunt your growth."

Virginia was, in fact, scarcely less than two inches shorter than Scott. Graceful, slender, yes. But a long girl. With very fine legs and fine dark hair, with all major points of interest in between of equally tasty proportion.

Red stood in the doorway to greet them, Suzy appearing behind him then, coming out in Sunday finery, finger-smudged but trying with all the wiles of a five-year-old siren to look chic and beguiling.

They were having drinks in the living room, and Scott had no sooner started on that second chilled martini when Mrs. Coombs called him to the telephone.

"Scott?"

"Yes."

"Tony." A sharp thrust to the voice. "I'm out here at the farm."

"Oh?"

"I'm sure you're busy with a full Sunday schedule. . . ."

"Yes," Scott said. "It is a kind of full day. Why, Tony?"

"Well, I wanted to ask a hell of a favor of you, Scott. But if . . ."

"What is it?"

"I need a batch of stuff I left at the office, and there aren't many people I'd care to trust with it," Tony said. "And for obvious reasons there aren't many people I'd care to see anyway. Phoebe is home flat on her back with one of those ghastly migraines. I can't leave here. I'm expecting a lawyer who's flying in from New York . . ."

"When do you need it? I mean, how soon?"

"This afternoon. As I said, there's really no one I want to trust with this material. I just found out I didn't have it with me."

Scott merely had to say no, and normally, of course, he would have. But normally Tony would never have asked this of him.

He could not decline. It was impossible. Regardless of what he'd heard about him or what he thought about him, he couldn't very well join the popular movement of freezing him out. In fact, he found himself wanting to overcompensate, wanting to help Tony just for the reason that he *was* in this shabby and unpopular predicament.

Scott said he'd start right after dinner. Tony told him exactly where to find the black leather briefcase, and he gave the directions to the farm. And as soon as dinner was over, Scott drove Virginia back to her place and went on to the plant.

By four-thirty he had battled his way through the insanity rampant on the Sunday roads and reached quieter country, bombing ahead then until he saw Kerwin's farm, set in the property of flat woodlands.

More like a manor house. The gross Victorian origin had been refined, altered, cut down, refaced with stone. Flanking the central unit were two low wings with high end chimneys of the kind that were more proper in Williamsburg, Virginia, than in southern Michigan.

Tony was out in front when Scott drove up. "Damn nice of you, Scott." Greeting him and taking the leather case. "Come in, you'll need a drink, though I'm afraid I won't be able to join you, much as I'd like to." He was very country in his tweed trousers and the mustard Shetland sweater.

The telephone was ringing inside and he said: "Damn thing's been going like that for the last twenty minutes. Just ignore it. I'm in no mood to talk to a soul." They were in the living hall, as Tony called this wing, a raftered room with mighty fireplace and a collection of antique and modern guns. He fixed a Scotch. "Sit down." And leading the way to the leather couch by the fireplace: "I hope you understand, Scott, that during this—hiatus—I'm not quite my hospitable self. Prefer to hole up out here, no newspaper people, no social obligations." He moved over to the windows at the back. "There were a few points of business I wanted to clean up with you. I'm afraid I was a bit rushed last Thursday. That drink all right?"

The drink was fine. And welcome.

He was peering at Scott. "You're—I hope you're not uneasy about this, are you? Being compromised out here with such an 'infamous character'—that's one of the latest epithets they've hung on me." He touched his cheek. "I suppose it shouldn't come as a shock to me that when I'm in a bind like this, a lot of old friends turn out to be kind of scarce."

"Hell, Tony—"

"What I mean to say"—he tugged at the mustard pullover—"is people get scared off even if they know damn well one couldn't be *that* infamous. But that's because basically a lot of people are chicken. Which, at least, you're not." He came back, sat on the arm of the couch, perched there unrelaxed, alert, like a bird poised on one

413]

branch before taking off for another. Too cheerily he said: "What's the grapevine around your way, Scott? You can tell me."

"Nothing I'm sure you haven't heard, Tony. It's all—well, more or less the same." He had to improvise—what could he possibly say? He certainly couldn't repeat what he'd heard the other night from Phil Rothe, via Steve Sturges by way of Sam Kyssin, that the industry's backroom gossip about conflict-of-interest involving Kerwin was true, that it might never have come to light if Vincent Eames, for reasons no one knew, had not defected to Holtsbridge's group.

"You know, Tony," Scott said then, for this was something he had never talked about and which during the present crisis he had had to keep to himself, "and this concerns me. It's been bugging me quite a bit." Then: "It didn't occur to me until this mess started. But if I hadn't put Vince Eames down the way I did, I mean if I hadn't jumped him that morning he came to see me, I don't think he'd have pulled this on you." He recalled again how in the midst of his blast, Vince had suddenly ignored him, murmuring to himself: "Kerwin swung it. He swung it!" And Scott had had no idea what he'd meant. Now he did. Vince had come to protest Scott's veto report of his product and to see what possible means he could use to win Scott's co-operation, but he'd seen that it was futile, and more importantly, that his friend Tony Kerwin had transferred control to him. This disloyalty or deception so enraged him he'd turned in revenge to Holtsbridge. "If I had known more, Tony, I probably would never have sounded off the way I did."

"Why, Scott"—Tony was regarding him now with a sudden and curious affection—"I didn't know you were really that much on my side! You see—let me just say this quickly—this thing has snow-balled to such an extent that people have got me down one notch above a criminal. I can tell you this: very few of my friends have come over to my side the way you have. I appreciate this more than I can ever say, Scott!"

In a horror of embarrassment Scott saw Tony had misinterpreted what he had said. "Tony . . . I . . . you must have misunderstood me. I didn't say I've been out there cheering for you—I mean, I'm afraid I take the same dim view of this as a lot of other people. It's just that I regretted my own position in it, and that I'm damn sorry it had to be you who's in this mess."

"I see. Yes." On Kerwin's ruddy cheeks was the deeper stain of a blush. But then swiftly summoning control: "About this so-called 'mess.' You've got to understand it's basically political. I don't deny it was foolish or careless of me letting Vince get too generous. I'm the first to admit it. But it was small potatoes. I happen to know better than most people that Vince Eames would never have parted with that kind of money. No. The real crime here is a political one. That's what Vince committed. And the company, unfortunately is too vulnerable now to fight it. That's why it all worked out. Otherwise a swine like Vince would have gotten no place—" He turned irritably as the telephone began ringing again. "I should have ripped the damn thing out!"

The ringing continued.

"Scott, would you do me a favor and answer it, for God sakes tell them I'm not here, tell them whatever you want."

Scott crossed the room to the Governor Winthrop desk. "Hello?"

"Tony? Is this—hello? Who is this?"

He recognized the voice then. He pressed his palm to the mouthpiece. "Tony—it's Dean Stratler."

"Dean? I'm not here." Tony glared furiously at the telephone. "Tell him I'm gone, tell him you just dropped off some papers we—"

Scott nodded. "Hello, Dean. This is Scott. Yes. No, I came out a short while ago, there was some material Tony had to have. But he's —he's not here at the— What?" Scott said. "What?" Repeating it, and trapped there in helpless silence. Then: "Just a minute." And looking over at him: "Tony, you'll have to talk to him."

"Tell him—" But Tony stopped. It must have been all over Scott's face, for at once he strode to the telephone.

Scott opened the Dutch door and stepped out onto the brick terrace, and there was the damp fragrance of woodland plant life. He would have given anything to leave. But that was not possible for him now. He'd heard, before Tony had, of Phoebe's suicide.

415]

34: Scott Quinnley

ANN flew from Athens for the funeral. The ceremony was private, attended only by family and those few friends of oldest standing. Scott saw her late the next day at the house in Kent Hills when he called on Codman and Mrs. Smith. Dean and Myra Stratler were present, along with several other officials of the company. As for Tony Kerwin, he'd gone to New York that morning, back to the hospital for extensive examination. Jack and Jemmy Winters arrived just as Scott was preparing to leave, so that they only exchanged a few words. Jemmy's pregnancy was beginning to thicken her once-slender middle. When Scott reached the entrance hall with its high curve of white stairway, Ann had overtaken him and asked if they could talk. And they started out of the house to the great circular driveway. (How long ago had it been since that Sunday noontime when Scott had first come there, when he'd accidentally seen disguised beneath the hood of a standard passenger sedan that test-engine which was later to power the ill-fated Bellstar? How long since Ann had waved, beckoned to him from the threshold of the Smith house?)

Now as they got into Scott's car, Ann said she wanted to talk about Phoebe and about Tony. She wanted to hear from Scott what perhaps she hadn't heard from the others. He told her what he could, though he did not tell her—it still disturbed him too much—of how he'd thundered down the law at Vince Eames the morning he'd come to Scott's house, and how thinking later that had he delayed him or tactfully placated him, Eames might not have turned to expose Tony, and Phoebe Kerwin might not have taken her life. This was emotional reasoning, Scott knew. It would have occurred anyway; it had to. Except that the circumstances being what they were, it had happened sooner. Or more unexpectedly. Even so, Scott still felt too uncomfortably close to it—just as you might feel if a friend is killed in an auto accident, having taken a particular route that you recommended.

Understandably, their talk was cheerless. Ann herself seemed extremely remote, and when Scott left her, her remote and melancholy presence was still in the car, riding all the way home with him.

He waited three days before telephoning to ask her out to dinner. He insisted she needed the diversion.

"Oh yes, yes I could use it, Scott," she said. "But I'm cutting my stay short. I just can't take— Well, I'm going back."

"You are?" Disappointment dulled his tone. "When?"

"Tonight. The ten-fifteen flight to New York. There are a lot of things I want to buy there to take back."

"I have to see you."

"I'm afraid it's—"

"Look," he said then, "you've got to get out of that house."

"I know. But—"

"Why can't I take you to the airport?" he said. "Better than that, I'll come by early, say seven, so we can have time for a drink and some dinner. I insist on this, Ann."

"Can I call you back?"

He was out of his office when she returned the call, but Scott's secretary took the message: Seven o'clock. *Chez* Smith.

The restaurant of the Skywatch Motor Inn was a glass-walled room on the second floor. Below, fanning out on either side of a long motor court, were the motel units with carports. Ann had suggested they come here, for the Inn was close enough to the air terminal so that they wouldn't have to make one of those frantic getaways; also it was a place where you wouldn't run into friends from the industry.

As soon as they were seated—from here, diners could see the blinking play of the lights of aircraft as they circled for landing or rose to assigned altitudes—Ann brought from her handbag two color photos of Caroline. Age: six months. "I suppose"—it was her first lighthearted utterance since Scott had called for her an hour ago—"it won't be too long before Suzy can baby-sit for me."

"Yes."

After their second round of drinks she said: "Am I ever glad you got me out here! God, what a wicked business this has been." Then: "I don't want to talk about it. Don't let me. We've done that too much already." Scott knew that though she had never felt very close to Phoebe, or interested in her, this in no way lessened the impact, the sorrow she'd felt at her sister's death.

"How's Ben?" He made it sound as natural as he could, but the effort showed.

417]

"Ben?" She didn't answer; she looked out to the night sky. Her profile—the faintly Roman nose, her cheek partially hidden by the long topaz hair—seemed somehow changed; that is, some delicate quality of youth seemed to have ineffably blunted its contour. "Oh" —she turned back to Scott—"not too great, Scott." Then: "Lousy, if you must know. Just lousy."

"Since when? Your letters were . . ."

"Oh, my letters."

"Is it serious?" All concern. But a spasm of purest joy trembled disloyally and treasonably through him.

"I don't know. I suppose it's serious enough for me." She drank more of her martini. "Nothing's been said about it here. I refused. I couldn't. Not only because of poor Phoebe, but—well, not even pride —but how could I?"

"Yes." Down went the rest of his drink. He called the waitress: two more, very dry.

"I don't know, Scott. Thank God, I can talk to you. But—oh, it's so damn scary, I mean he's just nothing at all like I thought he was and I thought I knew him. Maybe it's been this picture—he hasn't been the same since he started shooting it. He's simply never home. He's been to New York twice. There seems to be a lot of interest in it."

"New York?" Nothing of this had even been hinted at in her letters.

"Yes. And—well, you might just as well hear the whole pukey thing—he's been sleeping with this gal, this awful bitch, the one who's been working on the picture with him. I don't know, maybe she's not a bitch, but—"

"Christ, Ann!" And seeing how the life left her eyes, "Are you sure he's . . ."

She didn't seem to hear. She said: "You know how I am, Scott, how I've always felt about money. I had an awful time with Ben at first, the way he kept saying if there was one thing he wanted no part of, it was my money. I finally gave up. I thought he was just hopelessly neurotic about it. One day, at breakfast, he said he needed to get a loan to finish the picture. He needed forty thousand, and he said he thought he could get it in New York with this much of the film finished. Naturally I said for God sakes don't go to New York. If you have to have more money let's at least—borrow it from the house, is the way I put it." A pause. "Anyway—and this is the point—he took

[418

it. Without a murmur. I couldn't figure it at all. But I did know he was changing the entire concept of the film, shooting much of it all over, bucking for a full-length, or almost full-length, kind of documentary feature, and he was starting to use actors instead of local people. Then it turned out, he needed money again. That was two months ago. And—this is even crazier, Scott—I just wouldn't give it to him. I just couldn't. God, he exploded, he was so furious. I suppose you can't blame him. All this time my begging him to forget all this silly jazz about a man not touching his wife's funds, and then on the second time around I refuse him. Naturally he went into a spin, but in a way you wouldn't believe. I scarcely recognized him." Ann hesitated. "What it really was, of course, was that I'd found out about this girl. And I called him on it—a really dreadful, sordid, awful battle. It was that degrading. And he said yes he was sleeping with her. It started during the last month of my pregnancy. But it didn't end there. He's got this idea, this *idée fixe* about her—a noble figure, very poor, scholarship all the way through college, Peace Corps—he's absolutely gone. But he has no real idea what she's really like, anymore than I know what *he's* really like." Ann lifted her glass and drank. "That's how it is, and I don't know what to do. If—if poor Phoebe—if this hadn't happened here, I think I'd have come back. To stay. But I can't. Not now. And with Father in this . . ."

"Yes."

"I can pick them, can't I?"

The waitress was asking about their order now. But Ann said she didn't want to eat yet, and could she have another drink?

"You'll get yourself swacked," Scott said.

"I'm on the way and it's wonderful." She lost the smile, saying then: "I'm sorry, that was dirty pool, my loading you down like this. I'm sorry, Scott."

He took her hand, and it felt cold in his. "I wish to hell you'd come back. I've wanted you back ever since—"

"Since when?"

"Since that day I stepped off the ship."

She didn't seem to understand.

"The day you sailed from New York," he said.

"Oh." Then: "Why?"

"Because I suddenly did." It was as close as he could come to telling her.

"But why? I'm so flattered. Really. I should have had that to think

419]

about all this time in Greece. I suppose we ought to order dinner—" she glanced up to the globular clock suspended from the glass-domed ceiling. "The time is getting away, isn't it?"

The moment had passed. They started in on the third set of martinis, and by the time they'd finished them, the lobster cocktails were served.

Ann said: "I haven't caught up with you at all, have I? Your letters were marvelous, you'll never know how I looked forward to them. How is Suzy now? And your friend—Virginia? I'd like to have seen your father. How is he?"

"I got him a house in Jamaica, a small place."

"Oh, that'll be wonderful for him. Does he look forward to it?"

"I think so. Most of the time anyway. Sometimes he seems at loose ends and depressed, and then he drinks too much." Scott nodded toward his glass. "Like his son." Then: "What are you going to do?"

"Hmm?"

"When you get back."

"I don't know. I dread it. Isn't that awful? I mean going all the way back there and feeling I'd rather go anywhere else in the world. Oh God, it's going to be such an ignoble mess before it's over— Everything's such an ignoble mess, isn't it? Poor Phoebe. And Father now. And me." The waitress set down the lamb curry and when she'd gone, Ann said: "When did you see her last? Phoebe, I mean?"

"I saw her about three weeks ago. They had a dinner party. She seemed fine, certainly much better than that night we crashed Tony's birthday party."

"Yes."

"Are you all right, Ann?"

"Yes." She looked up. "Why?"

"Must be the light in here." But there was that growing pallor.

"She never kept sleeping pills, she never used them," Ann said. "She always said she was scared of them."

"These were about two years old. That's what Tony told me when we drove back from the farm." Then: "Look, Ann—you've been through enough—"

"Oh, I don't know, you get to the point, I suppose, when it doesn't matter that much—" She widened her eyes as if warding off drowsiness; with some purposefulness then, she dipped her fork into the curry.

The uneasy sensation grew in Scott that he had somehow let the occasion fall apart. He should have diverted her more. And even though she'd wanted to tell him about Ben, even though it had given her some measure of relief, he could see now how much this outburst had taken from her.

"Scott—"

"Yes?"

"I—" She swallowed. "If I could get some air—" An opaque grayness deadened her cheeks and her forehead was suddenly moist with sweat.

"Come on, Ann." Holding her arm, he led her outside to the motor court. "Do you want to sit down here?"

"I don't know, I feel too awful to know what I want. I'm sorry, Scott." She stopped, leaned against his arm. "I don't see how I can face it, I can't get on that plane—" She turned away, faint with nausea.

"I'll get you home after you are—"

"No. I just couldn't, Scott. I can't take any more. I feel too—"

"Sit down here." He held her, lowering her to one of the stone benches which stood like flat-slabbed tombstones around the long court. "I'll be right back."

"Where are you going?"

"See if I can get a room for you. Unless you'd—"

"Oh, yes. Yes."

At the desk inside, he paid the check and arranged for the room. He signed in for her—Mrs. B. Nodina—and a maid went with him to the court, and led them to the "Motor Cottage"—an independent unit which provided carport, veranda, spacious bedroom, television, air conditioning, room service. As soon as Scott closed the door, Ann ran into the bathroom, and it must have been almost ten minutes before she came out. She looked sallow and ill.

"Sorry, Scott, I . . ." She reached the twin bed, flung herself down, pressed her face into her arms. Once she looked up: "God, I'm glad you thought of this!" And shut her eyes again.

He asked her if she wanted coffee or tea, and she said no. Then she said: "I think it must have been those tranquilizers—the doctor kept giving them to us. I've had three since this noon. And the martinis . . ."

He sat down by her, and for a while he rubbed the back of her neck, and she murmured: "Oh, that feels so good."

But then she was out, on her side, her mouth open and looking

421]

sick even in sleep. She was still sleeping at ten o'clock. Scott telephoned the airport and canceled her reservation.

He went outside and brought the car back, and took Ann's two suitcases into the room, and then he waited on the narrow veranda, but moving nervously to and fro, and undoubtedly looking like the original comic strip expectant father. A jet zoomed above and he watched its lights, and he thought again of the airport and that time so long ago when he'd arrived, and Ann meeting him and extending herself to make him feel welcome and cheerful.

Restively he went inside. She was still sleeping, she had not moved, not stirred all this time.

The sight of her was irreconcilable with that vision of her at the airport, greeting him, lifting his jacket to look for the red belt, leading the way out of the limousine.

He looked down at her and he could not put the past together with this, with now.

Her voice: "Scott . . . could I have some water please? My mouth tastes awful. What time is it?" Sitting up then, blinking her eyes.

"Almost twelve."

"Oh God."

He said he'd canceled her flight. He brought her the glass of water. "How do you feel?"

"I don't know. Better." She drank all the water. Then: "What an awful thing to do to you, Scott."

"It was better than putting you on that plane."

From somewhere she drew a small mischievous smile. "Putting me on this bed, you mean?"

"Yes."

Slowly she got up. "I think I do feel better." She moved to the bathroom, and when she returned the change in her was more noticeable. She'd washed her face again, she said. And lipstick. And combed her hair. "I wonder when the next plane leaves—"

"Tomorrow morning."

"How do you know?"

"I don't. I just think you'd better not try flying tonight," he said. "And you'd get into New York in the middle of—"

"Yes." She sat down on the bed and lit a cigarette. A rueful look. "Well, this has been a jolly little evening, hasn't it?" A pause. "Look at this suit. Do you suppose I could get it pressed here? I'll have to do that." She studied the cigarette for a moment. "I was thinking, Scott—I was a walking case history in Paris when I met you. And here we are, and I'm right back on your hands again. Except worse."

Scott had dropped down beside her, and now he put his arm around her shoulders in a show of camaraderie that was less honest than when he'd sat with her at cafés along the Boulevard St. Michel. "You still don't know what you're going to do? About Ben?"

"No." A shiver passed through her body. "I mean, I'm not sure . . ."

"You still love him?"

"That's the worst of it. Yes—love. Or what's left of it. I don't know. I don't know, Scott. Maybe I can't judge anymore. Ever since that last awful row—that's two months ago—he doesn't even bother to come home half the time. I don't know anymore if it's love or if it's hating to live with my failure, or if it's—" Thickness came into her voice, and she stirred, half turning. Scott felt her breast against his arm. But she got up at once, moving with taut, nervous steps, stopping to take a cigarette from the table but not lighting it.

Moving all that time, and stopping short in front of him. "Look, Scott—I certainly don't expect to keep you here any longer. I'm all right. I'm . . ." The cigarette fell from her fingers, and she bent down to pick it up. "Oh, Scott—"

"Ann." He said it too loud, and immediately he was on his feet, his hands shaking, his body cold and trembling, reaching for her so stiffly now, having her to hold in this stiff embrace, awkward, clumsy, wild, crushing her to him.

He was dimly conscious of her resistance or the way she held back or how her lips barred his—dimly aware of it at first, but as his awareness grew sharper, as the reluctance of her body began to reach him, there was the change, her mouth parting, her arms around him with a strength of despair, and saying something he couldn't fathom.

Then she freed herself, a flash of time, to draw away, her eyes in startled gaze, and then again she threw her arms around him and called his name.

He unbuttoned the jacket of the black wool suit and her white shirtwaist, looking, waiting numbly as the skirt dropped to the floor, not until then fumbling out of his own clothes, then at last naked with her and in a fever of kissing. She was breathless, her eyelids shuttering sight, and her hands never releasing him, wanting him as much, more—if that was possible—than he wanted her, and saying it then, asking him to have her, crying out and a soft gasping when he went into her.

But in a delirium it was over, and they were inert, their breath in the acoustically walled room breaking loud as ocean waves. So it seemed.

But strange, mostly the strangeness now, the inert, silent nakedness beside him, Ann beside him. The current of his feeling must have reached her for she suddenly drew the battered bed sheet up over her slim body.

A silence upon them so sudden and unbroken. The totality of that silence. Scott knew how to end it, almost feared to end it, and all that time something insinuated itself upon him. What? Unknowing, he tried to look for it, and then realized how there seemed no air of celebration in the still room.

This he resisted. There had to be joy. Joy could be silent, it could clamor silently inside you and there would be no outward sound.

"Scott—" Her head turned slightly, her body still inert. "How did it happen?"

"You know how it happened," he said.

"I do?" she said.

"Maybe not, maybe you don't." He shifted onto his side. "I know exactly when it happened. For me. The day you sailed. Only I didn't know it then, and all the time I wrote those letters to you I—"

"Oh." She said nothing. Then abruptly: "Yes—all this time I've been wanting to ask you."

"What?"

"All those letters were addressed to me always," she said. "For no reason one day they started 'Dear Ann and Ben.' I wondered about it then. It was so odd—"

"Guilt. I was trying to be proper." He reached out for her and in a rush of some new need he couldn't explain, he drew her hard against him.

"Scott—" She freed herself. "All this time, you—"

"Yes."

"Oh Scott."

"You look"—he floundered—"startled."

"Well—I guess I am. I'm absolutely dumbfounded."

"How?" In black dismay he waited.

"I—well, I just am. I mean—" Ann sat up abruptly. "Oh, Scott, you aren't. Not really!"

[424

He nodded as if in protest.

But surprise was still dominant in her eyes. "Oh, Scott. I didn't know." Fingering her long hair. "If I'd had any idea of this. But it just never occurred to me. Fantastic, how we . . ." She paused as if in surprise to see her own nakedness. "I mean I don't regret this—I'm glad it happened. I *did* want it to happen."

"Why?"

"Why?" she said. "Why did *you?*"

"I told you that, Ann."

"Do you believe it, really? I mean do you still believe it? Now?"

"Why shouldn't I?" His resistance was almost hostile. "But obviously you don't."

"Well—nothing is obvious for me, I'm not sure of anything anymore." She stopped. Slowly she began to fold the corner of the bed sheet slowly, in frowning throught. "No, maybe I am sure, I mean, I can see how it's been. With us. I think I can see how it's been. For each of us." She dropped the corner of the sheet; she looked up. "I must have had some kind of tick in me for a long time. Like you. Some hidden or mysterious little tick. I think if we'd been in love in Paris, if at least we'd been lovers—you see"—she was still jabbing for the words—"I mean, whatever it was, must have been working in us all this time. Can you see that?"

Yes. He could see it. Yet: "That has nothing to do with the way I felt after you'd gone."

She said: "Maybe—I mean, isn't it possible that my going is the very thing that made you feel like that?"

He didn't answer.

"Like losing a chance you thought you'd waited too long to take?" Ann pondered, rather than asked the question. "Could it have been anything like that?"

Yes. But even so, the sensation had been too powerful.

"What is it, Scott?"

He said: "Do you think what happened to us tonight would have happened even if you hadn't gone?"

She nodded. "I'm sure of it."

"You are?" But resistance in him had already collapsed, and he could admit it to her: something had grown between them, a tick, as she put it, or some other quirk of life. Except that it had grown, erupted in him first. He'd been the first to experience it, the first to see and succumb to it. Like finally giving way to something that has

425]

been forbidden for so long that it begins to obsess you with some secret and glorious promise. . . .

"Yes, I'm sure of it." Ann's voice was low, her smile near sorrow.

And, as if in quick mutual need, they held each other for a time, until he could ask her and she could tell him how, though love had eluded them, though Ben's love had died (or hadn't even existed), though her sister had been buried only four days ago, she could give herself to passion or lust, and receive "merciful release, though I think, Scott—I know, it couldn't have been with anyone except you."

But love was not in the room.

It had never been there. What had taken its place Scott couldn't define. Not yet. Even though he felt its presence, as surely as he saw now, crumpled on the floor by the bed, her black suit of mourning.

[426

35: Scott Quinnley

"SCOTT." Red hastened into his bedroom. "Telephone. It's Codman Smith." His father's announcement was eloquent with drama.

"All right." Buttoning his shirt collar, Scott crossed to the closet for his jacket.

Only seven-thirty in the morning.

Spring now. And the long months over since last autumn, since Ann's plane soared eastward, and all this time for the slow sealing of old lesions.

While now the new season was underway, and with it a critical period of decision for him. For in Cartown, spring is the second most crucial time.

Foremost among the rites of spring is the annual stockholders' meeting; and the one Bellgard was to have next month was already being heralded as an event in automotive history. Shareholders had already received proxy statements, they had already seen, among other things, the proposed changes for the Board of Directors. Notable was the name of E. W. Holtsbridge and three other men new to the Bellgard roster.

To all it sounded the overture for the new theme, the new directions the company would take in the near future.

Even more meaningful than next month's annual conclave was the special Board of Directors' meeting which was to convene later that week and for which maneuvers and decisions were being made in covert sessions on the third-floor offices of Administration, in the barroom of the Kent Hills Country Club, in living rooms at Grosse Pointe and Bloomfield Hills, in the locker room of the Detroit Athletic Club.

"Hurry up," Red urged. He retied the sash of his Paisley dressing gown and waited for Scott by the door. Red had postponed the trip to the Caribbean; he'd decided he preferred to stay on a while longer; he just wasn't ready to go down there, he'd said. And would Scott mind?

427]

No. Of course he wouldn't mind. The fact was that he would have missed him. And he had told him so. The plan now was that he would definitely go next year. "Hurry up, son."

And now, as Red followed him downstairs, speculating on Smith's early morning call, he said: "For my money, I'll still take Cod Smith! How about that sonofabitch, up and at 'em at this hour of the day!"

Scott picked up the hall telephone.

"Good morning, Scott. I assume I didn't awaken you," Smith said. Nothing in his casual tone suggested that this call represented anything unique or urgent. "Like to pick you up, about fifteen minutes. Ride in with me, if you would?"

"Yes."

"A few items on my mind, and this'll save time all around—"

The black limousine drew up to the curb at seven forty-five. Scott said good-bye to Red and Suzy, and joined Cod Smith in the car (sitting now where he had sat on that first morning of his arrival, when the car's interior had been warm with Ann's presence, the perfumed air alien amidst telephone, dictaphone and the other appurtenances of business).

"Dandy morning," Cod Smith said, and Scott waited, knowing his offhand manner was the prelude to something more serious.

Time, he noticed more accurately today in the pure morning light, as he glanced at Cod Smith's features, had not touched him benignly. The flesh of the familiar face was more deeply grooved, and those fine winter-blue eyes no longer reflected quite the steady, supreme confidence that had once so impressed him.

Yet how could it have been otherwise? He'd had to demand the resignation of his own son-in-law; he'd had to suffer the shock and scandal of Phoebe's suicide; he'd had to see his favorite child leave for Europe; he'd had to see his fears realized when she divorced her husband; and now still being deprived of her, for Ann had gone with the baby to live in Rome. And he'd had to witness the swift decline of the company whose rise he had captained.

Codman Smith said: "It's going to be a pinched day and I wanted to fit you in."

A pause. It was coming now. Scott glimpsed by his side the copy of his magazine (what had been his magazine), the latest issue of which had come out yesterday. Was that going to be the blast for the day? He doubted it. Despite his piece on Sturges. No. The magazine

[428

lay there with others, and with a sheaf of papers. Morning work in the car.

"Scott—" Cod Smith turned to face him. "I happened to hear something last night, and I wanted to ask you about it."

"Oh?" Immediately Scott knew what it was, or could be; though it was inconceivable that Smith could know this soon.

"I happened to hear you were going to leave the company," he said then. "Is this true?"

Scott hesitated, not because he didn't wish to answer, but because he was disarmed by the suddenness of the statement, by the fact that Smith could have heard something which he himself had only decided on only two days before. It should not have tipped his balance, though. Cartown.

"It's true, I take it," Smith said.

"Yes." A dismal admission, for Scott had planned to see him, discuss it with him this week. He'd deferred it only because he knew this week would be a bad one, a black one for Cod.

"Is it definite? That is, have you made any legal commitments with these people?"

"Not yet. But—"

"Good. Scott, I don't want to see you rushing into this. I'm sorry, in fact, that you didn't consult me on it."

"I was going to," Scott said. "But I knew this week was not the best time for you. . . ." He saw at once his unwitting error.

Cod Smith peered at him sharply, then looked away. Then he said: "I've been talking about your situation with Holtsbridge and some of the others. Your record, as you know, has been more than excellent, you've done a creative lot of work. And I want to see it recognized. I know it's Product Planning where your interest lies." He paused. "The board meets day after tomorrow and you are being put up for a vice-presidency in Product Planning. Of course when we decided this, we didn't know you had other plans. That's why I wouldn't want to see you rush into this Sturges project." He waited. "Holtsbridge and the others definitely want you on the team. It's going to be a new team. You know that, of course."

"Yes," Scott said. "I don't know, Mr. Smith. I'm really flattened out by this one. . . ."

"Think about it. It's a new team, it'll be a tough team. But you'll fit." In a gesture rare as it was personal, he thumped his fist against Scott's arm. "I think you'll kill 'em, Scott."

429]

"Thank you." Awkwardly Scott felt the corner he was in. He was touched and pleased and gratified and surprised. A vice-presidency in Product Planning was rewarding, and not only financially. He knew too, theoretically, that it was not too late to accept it. He also knew he would not accept it.

"It'll be a different team, no doubt about that," Cod Smith was saying. "There won't be too many familiar faces around the third floor. And now that I'm leaving—"

"Leaving?" Out of courtesy Scott offered as much astonishment as he could.

"I've stayed a year longer than I planned. My resignation goes to the Board day after tomorrow. You don't have to be all that polite, Scott. I'm quite aware it's no secret."

"I *did* hear something, but—"

"Of course you did." His smile was less reserved, but somehow more vulnerable.

And Scott could see, with the clarity of hindsight, what had happened to this man he admired. His leadership of the company had been long and able, yet he had not moved with the times. He thought he had, but somewhere he had been slowed, upshifting too late to gain a hill's crest while the others had already made it. Cod Smith was an automobile man, a true one, but he'd been forced to take on, to manipulate, more and more machinery of administration and politics. He'd done this very well, but his heart had not been the real force of this effort. The other auto companies were now being run by men brilliantly gifted in matters of business, finance, organization, men whose first instincts were directed to the stockholder and the profit per share and who seldom involved themselves emotionally (as had Cod) with the processes of styling, engineering and production. Bellgard seemed to have turned inward upon itself. And Cod Smith had entrusted Tony Kerwin with too much, likewise Dean Stratler and many other officers. Yet he'd always imposed his own concepts. For too long he'd insisted racing was a dangerous or meretricious way of stimulating car sales; for too long he had held on to the successful product he'd produced earlier. And when at last he had given up his long-held concepts, it was once more too late. He'd pushed the Bellgard dealers too long, too hard, and he'd attempted to reorganize them when they were beyond help. He'd undertaken the program of market surveys when it was too late to benefit by them. He had refused during the past decade to splinter the company's capital or resources

[430

to acquire subsidiaries which might have forestalled the financial debacle that often came when all the corporate eggs were put in one basket.

"Of course you knew I was leaving," Smith said again, "just as I knew what your plans were. But I do wish you'd think this over carefully, Scott. All of us have been known to change our minds—though sometimes some of us wait a bit too long." Rueful regret charged his tone. More briskly then: "I don't believe it's necessary to point out that the difference between your income as a vice-president here and what you'll be getting with the Sturges company will be considerable."

Considerable. The loot was large and it was here.

And it is never too late to change your mind.

You are free to act. Except that what you want to act on, do, is what really lessens that freedom. What you want most costs the most; what you want most to give yourself to, takes the most giving.

Cod Smith was saying: "My interest in this is not altogether unselfish or impersonal, Scott. I'd like to see as many of our good people in the right places as I can before I go. We're losing Dean. You knew that."

"Yes." Dean Stratler was going to start his own firm: Design Consultants. Negotiations (also "secret") were underway to raid Jefferson Motors of their chief stylist.

"When I'm in Florida," Cod Smith said, "I'd like to think I encouraged or developed a few good people along the way. I'd like to see you stay on, Scott."

"Thank you," Scott said.

The car was crossing the intersection of West Main Boulevard and Timber Trail Road. Cod Smith looked out: "He's moving fast, isn't he?"

On the site where Quinnley Corners had stood, construction was rising, near completion. A vast black and white billboard proclaimed:

GRAND OPENING SOON
Max—why buy? why worry?—Wilkerson
DRIVE A CAR WITHOUT CARE
Renting—Leasing
All Makes

The last time Scott had driven past with his father—last Sunday—Red had looked at the new building and his eyes had glazed with indignation, and he'd lowered the window and with a contemptuous shot of spittle consecrated the earth which would soon hold Max Wilkerson's automotive temple.

"Can I ask you this?" Codman Smith said now. "Are you getting satisfactory terms if you join Sturges?"

"Mostly my salary will be in the form of stock in the company. To begin with."

"I see." Then: "I'm very sorry we couldn't have talked about this sooner."

Here this man was, Scott thought in renewed admiration, about to leave the company, to go to Florida, yet concerning himself with another man's future, urging him to stay on at Bellgard, wanting him, getting the advance endorsement of Holtsbridge and the others who would be running the show. Cod Smith, not unlike Scott's father, was unable to quit altogether, was holding on, and now with this dead-serious concern, was still worrying, still trying to staff Bellgard with the people he felt would be best for the new life of the company. This inflexible passion of his, regardless of all that had happened, was slow to die. It was still "his" company, still a formidable part of automobile history, still something he had shaped, and its form, even after his presence would no longer be needed, still held all his energies and all his heart.

"Scott"—he hadn't stopped—"you're too bright not to know you're going to have a long haul ahead of you. You must know this town isn't ready to jettison its immense investment in piston engines."

"I used to think so," Scott said, though he needn't have. "I'm not so sure anymore. By that I mean if there's not enough interest here, I'm going to try to go out and see if I can't bring it here."

Cod said: "The electrochemical situation is not exactly being ignored by Bellgard's research, you know."

"I know that." But Scott also knew that it was a minor phase and had no priority whatever. He could not say this, any more than he could have said to him that the gasoline piston engine had to pass on, that it would end a long and important era. It would pass on just as architecture and concepts of building construction had passed on with the advent of Frank Lloyd Wright and others. It would pass on just as production methods had given way to automation, just as the unwieldy gropings of scientists, mathematicians, economists, teachers, were giving way to the universe of computers.

"Yes, you know it, Scott. But you won't believe me when I say it's

[432

too damn soon for you to give up here and—" Abruptly he turned and picked up the car magazine. "I read this article of yours on Sturges, read it early this morning. I had insomnia. But this piece of yours only made me mad and kept me awake. Not mad. I was somewhat shocked, though. I mean, it's one thing to talk about the future. I like that. I love the dream stuff. But it's something else when you try to kick the entire industry in the—" He tapped the magazine. "Well, one just doesn't go condemning the gasoline piston engine in such a high-handed, arbitrary—"

"I didn't," Scott said. "That is, I do happen to feel this way, but I was quoting somebody else. Dr. Jacobs. In fact *The New Yorker* published some of this first. Jacobs is at my alma mater, and—"

"Who is he?"

"He's an associate professor at Columbia's School of Public Health. He specializes in industrial toxicology."

Cod Smith rustled the magazine in his hand, stiffened it out before him and began to read aloud, his forehead furrowed by the creases of disapproval as he came upon the first of Dr. Jacobs' statements on air pollution and the automobile: " 'The automobile has a lousy engine. It's been lousy for sixty years. Each year, the auto manufacturers spend millions on the design of a fender but next to nothing on means of eliminating air pollution. And, of course, the oil companies don't want more efficient cars, because they would use less oil and gas.' "

Cod Smith lowered the magazine. He resumed then, going on with Dr. Jacobs' comment about the antipollution "blow-by-device" which some car manufacturers were now installing in engines: " 'It's a device that takes unburned gases from the crankcase and runs them back through the engine again, and the manufacturers say it will eliminate forty percent of all pollution by automobiles. But such gadgets require maintenance, like anything else. Unless they're cleaned every five thousand miles, they clog up and there's more pollution than ever.' "

He shut the magazine, dropped it to the seat. He seemed relieved for having read it again. He said: "Fortunately, Scott, the company isn't going to pay much attention to this article of yours. At least I hope not. Though it could make me look a little foolish, since I've done a certain amount of tooting on your behalf."

"I'm sorry—naturally—but—"

"I understand," he said. Then: "I only wish *you* did." A sigh. He looked out. Ahead of them was the first underpass, and soon they were driving through the plant area. Codman Smith was silent now; his gaze had become concentrated, rapt, as if he were touching, absorbing, remembering each unit, each building that comprised the sprawling plant.

Reaching the Esplanade now, the striped bars raised for their entry. Now slowing down and stopping before the granite edifice of Administration. Cod Smith, however, did not get out of the car.

"You heard anything from Ann lately?" he said.

"I got a letter from Rome about two weeks ago," Scott said.

"Yes. That's when I heard from her last. I was hoping she'd get out of there. No place for her." Then: "She say anything about coming home?"

"No." And again Scott did not say what he suspected: that Ann would not come home for a long time. He imagined her leaving Rome after a while, perhaps going on to Venice or Florence, and after that to Paris, possibly London, but drifting on like some of the American women he'd seen in Europe, moving from one paradise to another and looking for what was lost.

The vision always left Scott in gloom. And he hoped he was wrong.

Many times he thought how easily she might have deceived herself and tried, with him, to make a love, a future. It would have been so easy for her. And for him. But she'd perceived the truth quickly, quicker than he, and she'd spared them.

"I'll tell you something that might surprise you, Scott." Cod Smith coughed, a nervous, artificial sound. "There was a time after you first got here, when I had the notion that you and Ann might get to be something more than friends—it's one of my foolish, fatherly disappointments that this never happened." A pause. "Of course, this is between us only."

"Ann knew it, more or less," Scott said. "She mentioned it to me one time."

"She did?"

"Yes."

"I wonder how—where she could have come by an idea like that," he mused aloud. "Except for my objection to Ben, I thought I always kept my feelings to myself." He was staring ahead. A wistfulness seemed to pervade him.

"Well—" Cod Smith roused himself from this undisciplined indulgence. "Another day." Swiftly then, as the chauffeur held open the door, he stepped out. Scott followed him. Just as they reached the glass doors he stopped. "Scott, before you make this move to Sturges,

[434

I want you to think it over very carefully. Understand, I'm not opposed to a man taking risks. I know that without risk, nothing new gets accomplished. But I also know that for every man who lives to see a long shot pay off, a hundred die on the losing end. The graveyard of this industry is overcrowded with those who tried to buck the shape of things too soon."

Or those, Scott thought in sudden commiseration as he watched him, who bucked the shape of things not soon enough.

Codman Smith's hand was on the polished bronze door disk. "I'd like to hear from you before three tomorrow, Scott." His face firm, the smile brusque now, no longer for Scott Quinnley but for the world.

36: Scott Quinnley

MANY times during the year that followed, Scott thought of that last drive he'd had with Codman Smith and the warning the man had given him. Scott thought of their talk again on this night, the eve of the trip to Washington. For after all the vicissitudes he'd suffered trying to help get Sturges' new company on a first footing, he'd learned how right Smith had been—or could have been. But it did seem, at this stage, that there was a close chance that tomorrow's conference in Washington would mark the serious beginning of business for the young organization.

Tonight, in Downtown Detroit, as he turned off the Lodge Expressway, on to the helical ramp corkscrewing up to the parking roof atop Cobo Hall—he was meeting Virginia Colter, the Rothes and the Sturgeses for the opening of a traveling exhibition of antique and classic American automobiles—he had occasion once again to think of Cod Smith. For he'd just parked his car on the vast roof deck when a lustrous new Vanguard V-8 sports car drew into the adjacent space, and Tony Kerwin and his wife Blanche stepped out.

"Scott—hello! This is wonderful. How are you?"

It had been almost a year since that time at Kerwin's farm, the afternoon of Phoebe's suicide. Shaking hands with the man now, the demons of the past kept jabbing at Scott's poise, though Tony showed no sign of discomfort: the warm voice, the winning half-smile, seemed inviolate; in fact he and Blanche looked nothing less than superb, their faces still coppery from the sun of Honolulu where they'd been on their honeymoon.

"I think," Tony was saying, "I'd still be in Hawaii if Vanguard hadn't reached out that well-baited line to reel me back."

"Vanguard?" Scott said.

"Yes." It had just happened, Tony reported; he had been offered the post of executive vice-president of Vanguard's European operation. He and Blanche would be going abroad the end of the month.

"Congratulations." Scott spoke as brightly as he could, still stunned by the irony of Kerwin's good fortune, Kerwin whose own father-in-law had had to ease him out of Bellgard, Kerwin who had been professionally and socially ostracized, but who evidently had landed right back on his feet again, flourishing once again in the sweet sun of high-echelon management and respectability.

Scott recalled that oft-repeated aphorism of Tony's: *In Cartown memories can be very short.*

"Well," Tony said, "this is really nifty, we've got to rendezvous before we leave, Scott. You knew Ann was back, of course."

"Ann? No. No, I didn't." Scott reached for his cigarettes.

"Yes. She's down in Palm Beach with the family." Codman Smith had retired to Florida last year.

"When did—"

"Oh, two or three weeks ago. I bumped into Ralph Alsop yesterday and he told me. He said they'll be up for the annual stockholders' meeting. Well, we'd better get ourselves to the show." He took his wife's arm. "I hear exciting stuff is going on over at your shop."

"Yes," Scott said. "What made her come back, do you suppose?"

"Hmm? Oh, you mean Ann?" Tony said. "I've no idea." The Kerwins went on their way.

Scott waited by the car, and presently Virginia Colter, followed by the Rothes and the Sturgeses, arrived, and they went downstairs and started on the exhibition rounds of the vintage cars. The evening at Cobo Hall, however, had to be a short one for Scott and Sturges: their flight to Washington was scheduled for very early the next morning, and they were both desperate for sleep. Overwork and overtension had been the way of life of the new company.

He had made many previous trips to Washington. There had been those interminable and tedious conferences with Army officials. But this trip, as it turned out, netted what they'd been working for all these months: the commitment from Army Ordnance (three hundred and fifty thousand dollars) to produce the prototype for an electric M-46, 2.5-ton vehicle.

By the yardstick of Cartown, this was a modest, if not minuscule, order. Except that it could lead them closer to the objective Scott had chartered: electric vehicles for public transportation systems.

Twenty-four hours after their return from the capital there was a meeting in Sturges' office—they had rented adequate-sized plant facilities situated off Route 23, not far north of the General Motors Proving Grounds—and Scott, addressing the other officers and many of the investors of the firm, outlined for them the final program for the Washington project, and he went on to say that now with government money they had a voice of confidence behind them. More importantly, he said, he could now return to San Escudo, California, an industrial town plagued by air pollution and traffic paralysis. He believed that with the federal contract already in hand, the city's Board of Public Transport might be pushed into a pilot order for the small (fifty-passenger) electrically powered public buses, the designs for which were already on the company's drafting boards.

Scott's mood must have been infectious, for the meeting soon took on all the enthusiasm and zest which he'd brought to it. And later as he was leaving the office with Phil Rothe, he said there ought to be a celebration of some kind, this was a landmark time. "At the very least," he said, "I don't know why I shouldn't throw a party, a real bash."

Phil said: "You owe it to yourself, if no one else. The way you've been working."

Scott had never thought of it quite in those terms. For he was coming to see, feel, some sense or direction shaping his life. At last. It was three years now since he'd arrived, and he'd done many things he'd liked, but mostly he'd had to do too many things he didn't believe in. So that now, all he could feel was how good it was to be free of all of it, to participate in something for which energy and passion were not wasted.

It was this that he wanted to celebrate.

"Maybe around the end of the month—" he speculated. "No, Red'll be south by then, and I don't think he ought to miss it."

Phil nodded. "When's he leaving?"

"Sunday after next."

Rain silvered the April night of the party. But from the chill, starless street the house looked its best, for you couldn't see the errors of its architecture: a stalwart Midwest colonial, circa 1940, with windows too wide in the whitewashed brick façade, and a slate roof pitched too steeply. The entryway, with its heavy portal flanked by pilasters, falsely endowed the house with the solemnity of a bank or library.

What it lacked aesthetically, however, it compensated for in space and high ceilings. And two years ago Scott had had the downstairs painted white, and this helped bring a certain grace to the many ill-proportioned rooms. Happily, as the party progressed, he realized that this house was almost as ideal for a bash as Mount Parnassus was for Apollo and all the Muses.

At this point, about half an hour before midnight, with two white-vested barmen making their ceaseless rounds, the party was moving with an easy and lubricated freedom. Some of the people invited had been unable to come. Dean Stratler was down with a chest cold, and his wife Myra had to preside over a committee meeting of the Kent Hills Art Association. Virginia Colter was away on another of her frequent junkets, this time to New York on business with the National Sports Car Club.

It was mainly a company party, though Scott had asked a few of Red's friends in, and Ann was there. With two escorts.

"I hope you won't mind, Scott," she'd said last week when he'd invited her. "I made the date with Bob, and then Howard turned up from Florida, and I couldn't really say no. He'd come all that way. If I could bring them both, then I—"

"Certainly," Scott had said. There was still a veil of constraint between them, which time—it was a year and a half since that night at the Skywatch Inn—had not yet lifted completely. Ann looked well. Thinner perhaps, but very suntanned. The natural blondness of her hair had been streaked lighter by the Florida sun.

"They're interesting characters, I think," she'd said. "Neither of them are in the good old automobile industry, thank God."

Tonight when she arrived in a white Italian dress and green evening cape and green shoes, the two men with her looked conspicuously out of place in their sport clothes. But of course Ann minded that not at all. When she introduced them, she said, "Scott, this is Bob Burns—same as in the cigar. And this is Howard Lynch—same as in the South."

Howard Lynch laughed good-naturedly. He was a wheel in Florida politics. Lean and nearly bald, but attractive in a vigorous, nervous kind of way. He wore a Madras plaid jacket of tropical hues.

Bob Burns, more conservative in gray tweed and slower of move-ment, was a young professor of Romance languages from Ohio who'd come to Detroit recently to take a new post. He had a snub nose and a mouth that turned up crisply at the corners, giving his somewhat sullen face a cherubic aspect.

In the library—now set up as a barroom—Scott got them drinks. The Florida politician immediately asked Ann to dance, and while they were in the other room Scott talked, or tried to, to Burns. From what little he said, and it was very little, he seemed quite bright, though doctrinaire. (Scott thought incongruously of Fay-Faith, that wonderful and cantankerous and honest call girl of a long-ago New York night, and he thought yes, this was what the good professor needed: a Fay-Faith.)

He heard the music stop and another record fall into place, and Ann was back with Lynch, and took the professor off to dance. Lynch smiled all the while, and as they talked he kept looking around the library. He talked a great deal. He said he was curious to know something about Scott's product, but he didn't pursue the point, going on instead with an anecdote about Florida's early history. He might have been entertaining but he seemed to grow slightly irritated by the noise around him: for now Steve Sturges, Phil Rothe and Sam Kyssin had moved to the bar table, and their voices rose in a swell of shop-talk.

As soon as Ann returned with the professor Scott guided him and the Florida man over to Jemmy Winters and Betty Sturges, who were now seated on the floor, and retreated quickly, taking Ann to the living room to dance. The carpet had been cleared from the floor, and the stereo was emitting its explicitly defined jazz. There were six or seven couples dancing.

And holding Ann. The sensation was curious: it was warm, distant, friendly, formal, awkward, intimate—all at once. She might have experienced something similar, for she was improvising conversation rapidly, asking what Scott thought of Burns and what he thought of Lynch, and saying, after all, his opinion was as valuable, if not more so, than her own.

And talking now about everything except what had happened between them and what had not happened between them, and nothing was said about Ben or about why she'd left Rome to return to live in the United States.

It should have been more difficult, a backbreaker, yet somehow it wasn't. If there'd been more time—but Scott saw Red breaking away from one of his friends in the dining room, making his way now across the floor toward them. He'd had more than his allotted two drinks, but he was enjoying himself immensely and Scott could not put him down. He touched Ann's bare arm. Would they mind if he cut in?

For a while Scott toured the house. A host. As he stopped to talk to another friend of Red's by the buffet table in the dining room, he could not help overhearing the conversation of the two men behind him. They were repeating more or less what Sam Kyssin had been saying earlier:

". . . three thousand people Bellgard's letting out."

"Thirty -two hundred. Next Friday."

"Think of that. Too bad."

"New comptroller. Slashing the overhead on all levels."

"But thirty-two hundred workers. That's going to be a lot of men out of jobs. Can't blame that on automation."

"Just the beginning. They're already starting to diversify. Just a question of time, two years, three—they'll be going the way of Packard and Studebaker—"

"Too bad."

Scott moved away from the obituaries. He snatched Scotch from the tray of a passing barman. He thought of Cod Smith.

Red and Ann were back in the library, and when Scott walked in, Steve Sturges saw him and unsteadily raised his glass in high salute, and, wrinkling that thin and freckled nose, and speaking with the magisterial, alcoholic tone of one who seldom boozes, he toasted Scott's health. For the second time that night. "And what do you have to say, Quinnley?"

"Me?" Scott swallowed the rest of his drink. "I say farewell."

"To what?" Steve Sturges demanded, and someone laughed.

"The fumes and furies of the gasoline monsters we all loved and grew up with. That's what." Scott paused. "Eight million going to be sold this year, eight million of them on the road—with their three-foot proboscii and four-foot assendii all over the place! Farewell to that, Steve."

Vociferous applause.

"To your good health, Scott," Steve Sturges declared again.

"I remember a night," Jemmy Winters turned to Scott, "when a guy I used to know knocked Steve Sturges' Scotch glass smack out of his hand." She leaned forward and kissed his ear. This was her first public appearance since she'd had the baby, a boy, last month. Jemmy looked very good, and her elegant black dress was a far cry from the

Ann Arbor days. Though Jack Winters was still as parsimonious as only the rich can be, and though he still kept a hawk's eye on the household budget, he stinted not a penny on Jemmy's wardrobe.

"You'd better sit down, darling." Betty Sturges motioned to Steve. He squinted at her for a moment, then lowered himself to the floor. From the living room now, you could hear the piano of Thelonious Monk.

"Say, Scott—" Red stirred restively on the couch. He'd been very quiet. He rose then and stepped to the bar table and poured himself a jigger, and Ann said would he mind getting her a brandy? "Scott," he said after he'd given Ann the drink, "I've been thinking. About that trip."

"Oh?" There was a familiar air to his words.

"And you know what I think?" Red said, looking now like some carrot-headed colossus as he stood splay-legged in the center of the room above the group sitting on the floor. "I'll tell you what. Why should I go? Who needs it? What's wrong with Greenwood Park? Unless maybe you're going to object—"

"No. No, not at all, Red," Scott said as he'd said the year before. Again, even though he feared it might be a disservice to Red's health, he was pleased, he found himself very pleased to know his father didn't want to leave.

"I mean," Red said then, "what am I going to do with myself down there?" He glanced around at the others as if seeking some answer.

"The baseball's better up here, Red," Philip Rothe said.

"That's right, Phil," Red said. "And when I think of all that god"—he checked himself, withholding the always ready expletive in deference to the ladies—"all that swankeroo, and everyone drinking Bloody Marys all day, boozing up—"

"Oh, you wouldn't like those Bloody Marys, I can tell you that, Mr. Quinnley," Ann said, and the Floridian smiled in a puzzled way.

"Exactly," Red said. "That's it exactly. And down there I'll feel shut off, I have to know what's going on here in town. You sit me down on that hot beach and all that goddam calypso music . . ." Belatedly he stopped.

"Mr. Quinnley," Ann said, "please watch your language. There are men present."

"Yes." Red's laughter was loud. Then to his son: "What do you think, Scott?"

[442

"If you're sure that's what you want . . ." Scott began.

Red swept his arm in an arc. "Here are my witnesses."

"I think he's absolutely right," Ann said. "I couldn't agree with him more."

"Well," Red said to her, "it's kind of a dirty trick on Scott. He's gone to a lot of trouble to get me set down there."

"Look, Red, I'd much rather you stayed here," Scott said. "If—"

"We got a deal?" Red said at once.

"Certainly."

Relief, bright as diamonds, shone in the now tired, pallid blue eyes. "Great. I'll tell you something, it's great to know I'm staying—when everything seems to be going. You hear about Bellgard?"

"Yes."

He shook his head. "I don't know," he muttered morosely. Then: "Well, Red Quinnley's not going. I'm staying. Scott, I feel like a new man. Great." He eyed his drink. "Goddammit, this calls for something!" He hoisted his highball. "A drink of the Lord's blessed waters!"

Ten minutes later Scott could see he'd had enough, if not too much; he got him out of the library, and like a stern, joy-killing parent, insisted he call it a night. It was half-past one. Upstairs to Scott's room, for it would have been impossible for Red to sleep in his own bedroom downstairs, the party traffic being what it was.

"All right, you don't have to put me to bed," Red said. "Better get back down there—"

"Yes." Scott noticed then the letter on his bedtable, and as Red began to remove his clothes, he quickly picked it up. It was from his mother. If Red had seen it there would have been a mighty outcry. It was not an ordinary letter, since it contained further information about Harry Mitfield, whom she was marrying. Out in the hall he put it in his breast pocket.

He wished he could have felt more joy for his mother, but he knew her too well. Her marrying Harry Mitfield and his money was no great second blooming, but rather the fulfillment of a goal. An achievement. A way of life.

"Hey, tiger!" Phil Rothe was calling from the hallway below. Scott started downstairs.

"Lorie and I have to pull out," Phil said.

By three o'clock the celebration was over. Except for Howard Lynch and Ann, all had gone and the house was a wasteland. Lynch excused himself to go to the john, and Scott got Ann's long green cape for her.

"Really, Scott"—her back was to him as he helped her on with the wrap—"I can't tell you how wonderful it was."

"Was it?" Scott said, but when she turned around, a stain of color, vivid and ebullient, showed on her face.

"I mean really. I didn't expect to have a time anywhere near so good." A pause, she looked down as she drew on her gloves. "But do you want to know something terrible? About tonight I mean?" Another hesitation. "I started out having quite a ball with my two characters. But—and this is the terrible part—halfway through the party when I was talking with them—and it was damn interesting—I found myself not paying attention, what I was really doing all that time was listening with one ear to everything else around me, mostly to you, Steve and Phil—all that shoptalk. Is that wild?"

"For you, yes."

"It's just not diggable, is it?"

"I don't know—"

Howard Lynch, still bright-eyed and pulsing with energy, was back. "Say Scott—that's quite a collection you've got in that john, how long have you been at it? Never did see so many old license plates. Go back, some of them, to 1906."

"There's a 1903 one there too, it's a leather one."

"How long have you been collecting them?"

"Oh, on and off, half my life."

"How about that!" He buttoned the Madras jacket. "Too bad you haven't got any old Florida plates. Tell you what. Next time I'm in Tallahassee, I'll see if I can't rustle one up for you."

"Thanks, Howard."

"Well—" He took Ann's arm.

Scott said: "Whatever happened to the professor?"

"Ill. Had to leave," Lynch announced with candid satisfaction.

"He's not used to drinking. Like Steve Sturges," Ann said. "I mustn't forget to call him tomorrow."

"Well—I guess we better hit the road, Ann," Howard said. "We're the last dogs hung."

Scott accompanied them to the door. "The rain's stopped."

"You'll have to remember, Scott, when this precipitation gets too much for you up here, there's only one place to go. Need I say where? Forgive me if I sound like a loyal son of the Fountain of Youth state."

"Howard," Ann explained, "expects to be governor in 1968." She bent forward and Scott kissed her cheek. "Good night, Scott."

He watched them leave. Ann had another car now, a Bellstar. Lynch held the door open for her, but then he saw her speak to him and turn back to the house. And Lynch settled himself in the driver's seat.

"Scott—" She approached along the walk.

"Did you forget something?"

"No. I—I just wanted you to know what a marvelous time it was for me—" Stopping then, and an extensive silence. "I guess I said that before, didn't I? What I mean is, that somehow it was, well, it was more like it used to be."

From the still and vaporous street you could hear the music. Lynch had turned on the car radio. "Is what you're trying to say, Ann, that you're finally getting yourself back on the track again?"

"No—well, in a way yes. I don't know. What I meant was, with you and me—it's just that this evening made me feel how much I hated to lose it. After all—how many people does anyone have in his life who—" She stopped once more. Then: "Do you really think, Scott, that that night had to make such a difference?"

"I don't know."

"I don't either," Ann said. "Except that now that I'm back, I just can't imagine myself being cut off—never seeing you again because of what happened. I mean, having to give up all our old—" Not finishing, glancing out to the car nervously. "I picked a stupid time to try to say this, didn't I? But I couldn't leave until I at least tried to tell you how I feel about it."

"We're never going to make the old days again, if that's what you mean, Ann."

She looked up at him. "Does it have to be that cut and dried?"

What he'd said, he realized, had come out as a renunciation. Cut and dried. That was how she'd read it. And he needn't have said anything more. He hesitated. He lit a last bitter cigarette.

Carefully, even reluctantly, he reexamined his feelings. What he had to see, remember, was that because something could not be resumed did not mean it couldn't take another form. To deny that a genuine bond or link had existed between them, still existed, to say,

445]

in their case, that you had to forego the future because of a single emotional error in the past—to say this would be as arbitrary as it was dishonest.

And yes, nothing was truer than what she'd said a moment ago: how many people *did* one have in one's life?

"Does it have to be that way?" Ann's voice.

"What?"

"Does it, Scott?"

"Not necessarily."

In the extended stillness came the night music from the car. She stirred, absently she began to tug off one of her white gloves. "Look," she said, "if you're not doing anything, why don't you come to the house for lunch Sunday?"

"That's tomorrow," he said. "That's practically now."

"Oh. That's right." She waited. "But can you?"

"Yes, I think so . . ." he began, and added: "Junior."

But he did not get to the Smith house that Sunday.

That was the morning he woke up in the downstairs room, in the unfamiliar bed, and listening for the familiar Sunday sounds which failed to come. The house was quiet. But it was a special kind of quiet, like the sudden ceasing of rain after a thunderous summer storm.

Eleven o'clock almost. Late. Even so, nothing seemed right or familiar about the morning. Immediately then he hurried upstairs, and in a chaos of alarm he knew, even before he opened the door, that his father was dead.

It must have happened during the night, in his sleep. His face already discolored, livid, plum-dark. And Scott stood there—how many times he'd prepared himself for this—not knowing what to do now, and feeling sick and incapable of moving.

Until he heard the sounds from downstairs, the front door opening, Suzy running in. He had to act then. And he turned away from his father, left the room, shut the door. As soon as he got Mrs. Coombs alone in the kitchen, he told her to take Suzy to the Rothes' for the day. Red, he said, was very sick. He knew that the housekeeper did not believe him, he knew she recognized the truth, for she moved in such flustered haste to take the child away. As soon as they'd gone, he telephoned the doctor. Then he called Phil Rothe and asked him to notify Steve Sturges and also to tell Ann or the Smiths.

[446

Stranded then, Scott was unsure of what to do. So he went outside. The street held the familiar Sunday quiet and he turned his back to it. He faced the doorway of the house. Red upstairs. He could not yet yield to what had happened. All the preparation for this moment, but of course it hadn't helped, nothing he felt was in any way lessened. What was new, unexpected, what he found surprising, was the abrupt sense of loneliness. He was moving now, senselessly, to and fro, waiting for the doctor, and he began to wonder if the love he'd finally come to feel for Red was something he'd truly communicated to him.

On the day of the funeral the sky was cloudless but pale, and there was a breeze which seemed to carry with it winter's parting sting. The funeral made Red's death seem unreal somehow: he was the kind of clamorous man, Scott thought, whose final silence was hard to believe or accept.

The ceremony was brief and when it came time to leave the chapel, Scott, as if for the first time, became aware of how many people had come. Many more than he would have imagined, though perhaps his father would not have been surprised by the tribute of this turnout: *A real show,* Red often said, *will always bring 'em into the tent.*

It was almost a month before Scott got out to Kent Hills for that luncheon at the Smiths'. (He had only just returned two days before from a second trip to San Escudo, California.) A vernal day, and as he drove along the serpentine roads and lanes with their fine houses of many styles, like an architectural smörgåsbord he thought how different this Sunday was from that initial excursion he'd made three years ago.

Soon he was passing the former residence of Tony and Phoebe Kerwin. The sturdy neo-English house had been sold, and you could tell by the preponderance of Jefferson cars where the new owner worked.

Forking rightward onto another road he soon passed the low-roofed Japanese-modern house of Dean and Myra Stratler. A white Bellstar there.

More houses set on turfed acreage. Glittering glimpses of Fords, of Cadillacs, of Chryslers, of Continentals, of Pontiacs, of Buicks, of Corvairs, of Corvettes, of Oldsmobiles, of Mustangs; of limousines, of jeeps, of station wagons—the cars like splendid, chrome-engraved calling cards explicit with the rank and automotive affiliation of each proprietor's house.

Scott found himself wondering, as he neared the Smith estate, how much he had come to understand of this society: he knew he was less patronizing toward it, but now that he was a part of it, had he become less critical?

If he knew that Cartown was still in the greedy grip of the status quo, wouldn't he also have to admit that one day, however belatedly, they would meet the challenge of the nation's ever-strangulating streets and highways? They'd be forced into it, of course. But once pushed, they'd probably make the attack with speed and ingenuity (and vast fiscal profits).

Maybe, he thought, he could take this view because he and his group were now in the vanguard, and they knew what could be accomplished in the industry, even though the beginnings were still small.

He braked the car, making the turn into the Smith property, parking on the circular drive in front of the quasi-Virginia manor house. And as soon as he stepped down onto the crushed gravel, the feel of the stones beneath his feet precipitated the recollection, specific and intense, of that noontime three years ago when he'd come here for the first time. But almost at once the present possessed him again: he glanced up to the house; there would be no ball game on this Sunday, and this time he would not get himself all revved up about what people might or might not think of Red Quinnley.

He moved toward the entryway. A tremor of anticipation brushed him. So much had happened, not only to him, but to Codman Smith and to Ann, that in a sense all of them might well be like a family whose members have been dispersed and who are coming together today as if to reclaim warmth and identity in the resumption of a fond ritual.

Scott rang the bell now, and waited on the threshold.